RED PHOENIX

ANDREW WARREN

Boldwood

First published in 2017. This edition published in Great Britain in 2025 by Boldwood Books Ltd.

Cover Design by Head Design Ltd.

Cover Images: Silas Manhood Photography, Alamy and iStock

The moral right of Andrew Warren to be identified as the author of this work has been asserted in accordance with the Copyright, Designs and Patents Act 1988.

Every effort has been made to obtain the necessary permissions with reference to copyright material, both illustrative and quoted. We apologise for any omissions in this respect and will be pleased to make the appropriate acknowledgements in any future edition.

A CIP catalogue record for this book is available from the British Library.

Paperback ISBN 978-1-83703-857-2

Large Print ISBN 978-1-83703-856-5

Hardback ISBN 978-1-83703-855-8

Ebook ISBN 978-1-83703-858-9

Kindle ISBN 978-1-83703-859-6

Audio CD ISBN 978-1-83703-850-3

MP3 CD ISBN 978-1-83703-851-0

Digital audio download ISBN 978-1-83703-852-7

This book is printed on certified sustainable paper. Boldwood Books is dedicated to putting sustainability at the heart of our business. For more information please visit https://www.boldwoodbooks.com/about-us/sustainability/

Boldwood Books Ltd, 23 Bowerdean Street, London, SW6 3TN

www.boldwoodbooks.com

1

A cool breeze cut through the night and sent ripples across Hong Kong's Victoria Harbor. Han Sui-Yen shoved his hands in the pockets of his leather jacket. He hunched his shoulders as he walked along the waterfront. He was a young man, in his late twenties. His face was round and soft, and his eyes glinted with a sharp, intelligent glow.

In the distance, the jeweled spires of Hong Kong Island East thrust up into the dark night sky. The buildings' lights twinkled in the evening mist like a second set of stars. Flashing neon reflected in the dark, rippling waters of the harbor.

Han paid no attention to the stunning city panorama that played out before him. Instead, he scanned the waterfront for any sign that he had been followed. He saw no one. For all its glamour and modern innovation, Hong Kong was China now. And the People's Republic of China would take a dim view of his activities this evening.

Satisfied that he was alone, he continued his lazy walk along the promenade. A lone cargo freighter cruised between him and the city lights, blotting out the horizon like an enormous dark shadow. Its horn sounded a deep, mournful tone into the darkness.

Up ahead, Han saw the famous Kwun Tong Promenade sculpture. Pulsing neon lights lit the erratic stack of glass cubes from within. The cubes symbolized bundles of paper, a testament to the area's history as a shipping yard. Now that the city council had built an upscale planned community in the area, the land had been repurposed as a park.

Han watched as the cubes pulsed and changed color. They shifted from a soft purple glow to a deep, almost hellish red. To the left of the promenade, a freeway overpass rose up, towering over the sculpture. A few cars streaked back and forth, but the hour was late, and traffic was light.

Han moved towards the glowing sculpture. His footsteps echoed through the cool night air. Another figure rounded the sculpture in front of him, a Chinese man, in his early fifties. He was wearing a charcoal business suit and a black wool topcoat. His face was half-lit by the pulsing red light. The rest of him was hidden in shadow.

Han fished in his pocket and removed a crumpled pack of Furongwang cigarettes. He walked over to the older man. '*Hei, you guang ma?*' Han asked, as he slipped a cigarette in his mouth.

The man reached into the inner pocket of his coat. He held out a cheap plastic lighter. He lit Han's cigarette, cupping his hands around the flame to block it from the breeze.

'You're not the usual guy,' Han said in a low voice.

'We rotate,' the man said in a flat, bored voice. 'Keeps our exposure low. Safer. You've been busy.'

Han looked around, but the area still seemed deserted. The sculpture's lights pulsed again, bathing them in an icy blue glow. 'Yeah. Saving up for an apartment, island-side. Gonna move my girl in with me next month.'

The older man smiled. 'Moving up in the world. You have what I want?'

Han slipped his hand in his pocket and removed a small plastic case that contained a memory card. 'Here. The project folder is called "Yu Jian," but its specs are basically an updated CX-1 missile. Based on the same Russian tech, but its targeting margin of error has been reduced by 7 percent.'

The older man reached out for the card. Han handed it to him but didn't let go. '*Deng yi xia*, hold on. The file's encrypted. You get the decrypt key when I get paid.' He let go of the drive.

The older man nodded. 'Of course.' He slid a smartphone from his coat pocket and tapped a code on the glowing screen.

Han pulled his own phone from the rear pocket of his jeans. He opened his banking app and watched as his Bitcoin value ticked up. The virtual currency was anonymous, private, and untraceable. He would transfer them later into a hidden account on the dark web. There, they would be laundered into hard currency, for a small fee.

Han sent a text message to the other man's phone. A string of letters and numbers filled the small screen.

'There you go. Decrypt key. The files prove China Aerospace Corporation based the new guidance system on United States designs. Pleasure doing business with you.'

Han turned and began to walk away. In the distance, he saw another figure walking towards him, along the promenade. He frowned. Something felt off. He hadn't seen anyone else in the area a few minutes ago.

'Han Sui-Yen,' the man behind him called out.

Han spun around. The older man was holding a gun, a QSZ-92 pistol. Han heard footsteps echoing behind him, moving closer.

'Ministry of State Security,' the older man sneered. 'Afraid you're gonna have to change your real estate plans. You'll be moving to a different location.'

Han barely heard the man's words. His brain flooded with panic-induced adrenaline. He darted left and ran as fast as he could.

'Han,' the man shouted behind him. '*Tihing dai*, stop! Don't make this worse!'

Han sprinted towards the overpass, overcome by fear.

Maybe I can get to the freeway, he thought. *Get a car. Maybe I can get away.*

As he raced beneath the overpass, he saw dark forms moving ahead of him. A group of three police officers in Hong Kong SWAT gear emerged from a black van parked on the other side of the promenade. They charged towards him, wielding Benelli M1 shotguns and batons.

Han tried to run around them, but one of the SWAT team members tackled him. The two men tumbled to the ground. Han moaned as his head struck the polished concrete with a loud crack. His vision went blurry, and he felt the warm sting of blood trickling down his face.

The SWAT officer spun Han's body over and zip-tied his hands behind his back. He lifted Han to his feet and dragged him back out from under the freeway.

The older man was waiting for them. Another man had joined him. He wore dress pants and a black windbreaker that said HONG KONG CIB in large white letters on the back. He approached Han.

'I'm Detective Yen, and this is Special Agent Chan. We have you on tape selling state secrets.' Detective Yen, a lean, fit man in his forties, looked Han up and down with disgust. '*Mo ming qi miao,*' he muttered, shaking his head. 'Jesus, kid, how old are you, twenty-four? You traded your whole future for a fucking apartment?'

Special Agent Chan shrugged. 'Kids are the same everywhere these days. Money is all they care about.'

Han glared at the detective and spit blood on the ground. 'I want my lawyer.'

The SWAT officers clustered behind him. Special Agent Chan slipped his gun into a shoulder holster and grinned.

'Lawyer? Who said you were under arrest? No, Han, first we're going to go somewhere nice and quiet. You can tell us all about your American friends and the money they gave you.'

Chan looked over Han's shoulder at the SWAT team officers. He nodded. 'Take him away.'

Han felt heavy gloved fingers dig into his shoulder. They pulled him away from Chan and Yen. The detective glared at him for a moment, then looked away.

Suddenly, a high-pitched whine echoed through the air. Han saw a burst of blood spray from the detective's forehead. It glowed pink in the pulsing light of the Kwun Tong sculpture.

As the detective collapsed, Special Agent Chan spun around. 'What the hell!' he shouted. He drew his pistol and aimed at the dark stretch of freeway looming over the park.

Again Han heard the strange, whining sound. A dark circle opened in the center of Chan's head. Blood and brains sprayed behind the special agent as he fell to the ground.

One of the SWAT team raced over to Chan's body. As he futilely checked for a pulse, Han felt something soft brush against his arm. He looked up and saw a black rope dangling from the freeway overhead. With a loud hiss, a dark figure slid down the rope, descending towards them at rapid speed.

The SWAT team swung their weapons up towards the sound,

but it was too late. The figure crashed into the middle of the tight group, knocking Han down in the process.

As soon as he hit the ground, Han rolled away as far as he could from the SWAT team. He could hear shouting, men struggling. He stopped rolling and looked back. The dark figure wore black tactical gear. A hood and pair of night-vision goggles covered their face. Knives, pistols, and other equipment hung from clips and pouches on their harness.

The black-clad figure exploded into action. Han could barely follow the blur of motion. The attacker lassoed the rappel line around one of the SWAT team members' necks and yanked it tight. Another SWAT officer moved in behind the assassin and looped their shotgun around the dark figure, going for a chokehold.

Without letting go of the rope, the assassin drove an elbow backwards. The SWAT officer stumbled, loosening the grip on the shotgun.

The third heavily armored policeman raised a pistol and aimed at the shadowy figure. He fired, but his shots streaked through empty air. The figure flipped up and over the shoulder of the SWAT team officer, landing behind them. Reaching forward under the man's arm, the assassin grabbed the shotgun. The weapon's barrel swung towards the pistol-wielding officer.

The shotgun fired. The semi-automatic weapon chugged as it sent a hail of AP-20 armor-piercing shells into the air. The arrow-shaped projectiles slammed into the SWAT team officer. He stumbled back, blood seeping from multiple punctures in his body armor.

The officer trapped in the cord reached down to his belt and unsheathed a knife. As the cord bit deeper into his neck, he raised the blade and slit the line. The noose went slack and he dropped to the ground, gasping for breath.

The assassin kicked the shotgun-wielding officer forward. He recovered his balance and spun around, swinging the shotgun in front of him like a club. The assassin ducked under the blow and exploded forward, just inside the officer's reach. The man grunted and stumbled back as the black-clad figure's head crashed up into his chin, followed by a flurry of punches into his chest and abdomen and a knee to his groin.

The gasping officer, now free from the rope, rose to his feet. He fired his shotgun, but the assassin was already moving, dropping to the ground and rolling. The shots sparked off the concrete a few inches away from their target. The dark figure popped up and grabbed the barrel of the shotgun, yanking it forward over their shoulder. Before the officer could pull the trigger again, he felt a white-hot pain in his chest. He looked down and saw the glint of a blade protruding from his ribs. His face went white, and he collapsed.

The assassin tore the shotgun from the falling officer's hands and whirled around. The remaining officer had just recovered from the savage flurry of blows. He staggered forward and raised his weapon.

He was too late. The killer fired.

The semi-automatic shotgun barked three times. The last officer fell to his knees, then collapsed face forward to the ground. For a moment, there was silence. The boat in the harbor once again sounded its mournful wail.

Han's eyes were wide with fear. He looked up at the assassin. The ground around them both was littered with the bloody corpses of the SWAT team, along with Yen and Chan.

The black-clad figure turned to face him. Han found himself staring into the twin green lenses of their night-vision goggles. He felt like he was looking at a robot, some kind of unfeeling killing machine.

Han scrambled backwards, but his back slammed into something solid. He saw lights flashing over his shoulder. He realized he had backed into the towering sculpture. A harsh green glow illuminated the figure as it stalked towards him.

Han saw his reflection in the electronic eyes of the goggles.

'Who... who are you?' he gasped.

The figure said nothing.

* * *

Ted Lapinski leaned back in his chair. He swirled his vodka tonic, listening to the ice clink against the glass. Then he sipped the clear, fizzing alcohol as he stared at the images on the computer screen in front of him. The vodka was a cheap, store brand. Not top shelf, but it got the job done.

The image on the computer's screen panned over to look at the kid, his asset. Han Sui-Yen. It was the assassin's point of view. A digital camera built into their night-vision goggles transmitted the image to Ted's monitor. The rig also sent back encrypted GPS coordinates, so Ted knew they were in Hong Kong. The signal placed them on the Kowloon side of the city, on the Kwun Tong promenade. The display on the top-left of the screen showed local time as 2:00 a.m. Hong Kong was twelve hours ahead of Virginia time. The screen showed a dark, grainy image, even though it was a sunny afternoon outside the window of Ted's home office.

The assassin spoke. 'Red Phoenix reporting. Resistance neutralized. Proceeding on mission.' The communication system scrambled their vocal tones as a security precaution. The killer's voice sounded cold, electronic, and artificial.

Ted leaned forward and spoke into a microphone connected to his computer. 'Nice work. Do you have the package?'

The assassin held up the memory card to the camera. 'Package is secure.'

'Good. Leave it at the usual drop point.' Ted checked his watch. 'You have twelve hours to get to Beijing. I have a matter that requires your attention there.'

The image on the screen did not move. The assassin was still staring down at Han.

'I want to speak to her. That was the deal,' the killer said. The strange electronic voice echoed from the speakers of Ted's computer.

'You'll speak to her in Beijing,' Ted answered. 'Don't push me on this.'

The POV on the camera stared at Han. 'Fine. What about your asset?'

Ted took another sip of his drink. He sighed and looked up at the ceiling. He could see cobwebs forming on the white blades of the fan that hung over his desk.

Han had been a stellar asset. His position at China Aerospace granted him access to detailed information regarding the PRC's aerospace and cyber-warfare capabilities. Once Ted's operation had whetted Han's appetite for the finer things in life, he had supplied them with a steady stream of valuable intel.

But now the Chinese authorities were on to him. Tonight's operation proved that. Ted doubted the kid could evade the Ministry of State Security for long. And even if he could, there was no way he would be able to provide any more information.

For Ted, intelligence was a business. Like all businesses, it came down to a simple equation of risk versus reward. After tonight, Han was a variable that leaned towards the risk side of the equation.

He spoke into the microphone. 'He's compromised. You know what to do.'

He watched as the silenced barrel of a pistol rose into the frame. Han screamed. The gun fired twice.

Ted closed the video monitoring program. Then he opened a secure chat app and typed a message into the small black window on the screen.

SECURE CONNECTION REQUEST. RF-90038. STATUS: DIAMOND

He waited, watching the text blink as the person on the other end of the connection typed their response.

SECURE CONNECTION INITIATED. DR-22441. STATUS: PICASSO

Ted began typing his reply.

HONG KONG OPERATION CLEAN. RED PHOENIX EN ROUTE TO BEIJING. PLEASE CONFIRM DEPLOYMENT STATUS.

There was a pause, then:

BRIEFING TOMORROW WILL DETERMINE RED PHOENIX DEPLOYMENT. STAND BY.

He was about to type a response when a knock at the office door interrupted him. The door swung open, and a pretty blonde woman in a yellow sweater leaned into the dim room.

'Ted! Your son has been moping around in the front yard for the last twenty minutes. Stop chatting on the computer and help him set up that stupid remote control helicopter thing. Hell, you bought it for him!'

Ted looked up and smiled. 'Julie, I told you I had some work today. Almost done, I promise. And it's not a helicopter, honey. It's a mini drone.'

Julie smiled and pointed her finger at him. 'Five minutes, Mister. The clock is ticking.' She shut the door.

Ted closed the chat window and disconnected from the secure network.

Risk versus reward, he thought. If things didn't go well in the briefing tomorrow, he was about to take a very large risk indeed.

He stood up, drank the bitter last dregs of his cheap vodka, and left the office.

2

It was well past dawn in Riga, Latvia, but the sun struggled to carve a path through the heavy clouds that hung in the sky. The city's clustered rows of quaint buildings and gothic cathedrals stood bright and beautiful as always. They defied the gray skies above but cast long shadows over the winding canyon of streets below.

A lone figure limped across the cobblestone expanse of the ancient city's town square. The clicking of his footsteps echoed off the surrounding buildings. The man looked up as the clock on the oxidized green spire of the town hall struck the half hour. A lonely bell chimed.

Although it was warm for Latvia, there was a damp chill in the air. The man wore a thick, hooded wool sweater under a black peacoat. As he glanced up at the clock, the hood fell away. The dim morning light revealed a mosaic of scars and burns on the right side of his craggy, weathered face. Thick black-framed glasses magnified his dark brown eyes. His withered lips pursed as he stared up at the magnificent tower. He looked out of place in the peaceful surroundings.

He pulled the hood back over his head, turned away from the tower, and continued on his way across the square. Rounding the corner, he turned down a narrow street flanked with tiny cafes and coffee shops. A few scattered people sat at tables outside the shops. They were sipping coffee and munching on pastries, enjoying the quiet morning.

The burned man hunched his shoulders to hide his face and walked past the cafes. The street continued to wind through the colorful tiny shops until it passed a small park. Perched at the edge of the park was a tiny white brick tower with a gray roof. It looked like something out of a fairy tale. A minute, secret dwelling. A place where dwarves or elves might hide, spinning straw into gold.

It was, in fact, a small coffee shop called the Coffee Tower. There were several such towers scattered throughout the city. The man in the dark hood, however, had chosen this location for a specific reason. Its park location gave him an unobstructed view of the opposite street. He walked up to the window, ordered his coffee, and scanned the park with his dark, intense eyes.

There were a few early morning joggers, a couple walking their dog... nothing that aroused suspicion. But nevertheless, he knew with absolute certainty that someone was following him.

His meandering path through the city had begun when he left his normal drop point, at a cafe near his apartment. Something had felt wrong. He had noticed a man in a black leather jacket standing across the street. The man was reading a newspaper, standing at the corner. There were no buses or taxis running at such an early hour. The man with the newspaper had no good reason to be standing at that corner in the cold gray dawn.

So he had continued on his peculiar route. He walked the long way through the town square. He doubled back down several narrow winding streets. And now he was cutting through the park. The path he took was known as an SDR. A surveillance detection route. It was designed to force anyone following him to reveal their presence.

Some might have dismissed such thoughts as paranoia, but the burned man in the dark hood knew better. He knew he had enemies. He was a wanted man.

His name was Allan Bernatto.

The girl behind the service window handed him his steaming cup of coffee. He watched as her eyes darted across his shriveled, burned skin, then looked away.

He set off across the park, hoping that the open space would flush out anyone else that might be following him. He stopped and turned, looking for any sign that someone was watching him. People stopping abruptly, or making sudden movements to keep up. But he saw nothing.

He crossed the park, turned left, and headed away from the town center. Above him, the clouds grew thicker, darker. The shadows of the buildings grew longer and seemed to follow in his wake.

It took about twenty minutes to reach his neighborhood. The SDR detour through Old Town slowed his normal pace. His legs were throbbing, and his limp became more pronounced after the long walk.

But now, he left the colorful buildings and fairy-tale beauty behind him. Ahead, the streets were cracked, chipped concrete rather than cobblestone. Crumbling tenement buildings and Russian dive bars replaced the pink and blue pastel cafes. This was the 'Quiet Center,' a dismal, run-down suburb that lay on the outskirts of the beautiful city. For the last few months, it was where Bernatto had made his home.

As he walked past a graffiti-covered bar, Bernatto tensed. He noticed movement from the corner of his eye. He turned and saw it was just a passed-out drunk rolling over on the sidewalk outside the bar.

A few Ukrainian and Russian men stepped past him on the sidewalk. They eyed him with surly glances as they made their way down the street to the bus stop. Bernatto paid them no mind.

But then... *There, across the street*, he thought. It was him, the man from before. The one with the newspaper. He'd changed out of his leather jacket and replaced it with a blue windbreaker. But Bernatto recognized his face. There was no doubt about it now... He had a tail.

Bernatto stepped past the snoring drunk and turned right. He limped down a narrow alley that ran alongside the bar. The alley stank of beer, piss, and vomit, but Bernatto pushed forward as fast as he could. The alley made a right turn and ran behind a series of crumbling Soviet-era apartment buildings.

Bernatto approached one of the buildings. He took one last look. The alley was still empty; no one had followed him. He pushed open a cracked, chipped old door and ducked inside.

After limping up three flights of stairs, he finally made it to his apartment. The keys jingled in his hand as he unlocked the door. There was a dusty, cracked window in the stairwell. Bernatto could see the alley outside was still empty. Whoever the man was, he appeared to have lost him.

He swung open the door and stumbled into the tiny, dark room. He slammed the door behind him, turned the deadbolt, and slipped the chain in the lock.

He took a deep breath.

The apartment stank of mold and paprika, remnants of the previous tenant's cooking. The shades in the sitting room were drawn closed. Only a thin crack of light illuminated the torn furniture and peeling wallpaper. The rest of the hovel lay hidden in shadow.

Bernatto made his way to the tiny kitchen and opened the refrigerator. He removed a pitcher of water and poured the cold liquid into a cracked glass tumbler.

He shut the refrigerator and brought the glass to his lips.

A calm, quiet voice called out from the darkness. It was a man's voice.

'Hello, Allan.'

Bernatto whirled around, dropping the glass. It shattered on the tile floor, dousing his worn leather shoes with water.

He knew the owner of that voice.

One of the shades in the living room was raised just enough to let in more light. A dark figure was sitting on the torn, sagging sofa.

The figure leaned forward. A beam of sunlight cut across his chiseled, tan features. His cold, emerald-green eyes sparkled in the light. He held a Beretta PX4 compact pistol balanced on his knee, aimed at Bernatto.

It was Thomas Caine.

Allan raised his hands and backed up into the narrow kitchen.

'Tom, I—'

Caine snarled and leapt to his feet.

3

Rebecca Freeling pressed a button on a small remote. There was a click, and the next slide was projected onto the white screen. It was a map of southern Afghanistan. The room was dark for the briefing, but she could make out the silhouettes of the men sitting around the table.

Some sat ramrod straight, eying the information on the screen. They took notes, in case their superiors required a summary of the bi-weekly intelligence briefing. Others ignored her and looked down at their phones. The briefing had run long and, as usual, her presentation was not exactly the most popular of topics.

'Let's move on to the next slide,' she in a strong, clear voice. 'In the provinces of Kunar, Nangarhar, and Paktika, once again we see the same pattern repeat.' She pressed a button on her remote. Glowing dots appeared in the three provinces. A graph of statistics appeared to the right of the map.

'In each case, extremist group recruitment surges after every drone strike. My sources on the ground confirm this data. What's more, there is a direct correlation between recruitment success rates and civilian casualties.'

A man at the head of the table sighed. 'Thank you, Director Freeling, I think we see your point. Lights, please?'

'Sir, there's one more slide I'd like to—'

'We've seen enough. Lights.'

Rebecca pressed another button on the remote, and the briefing room's lights came up. Her wheelchair emitted a soft hum as she took her place next to one of her colleagues at the table.

John Blayne, the man who had interrupted her presentation, removed his wireframe glasses and sprayed cleaner on them. He did not look up at her as he wiped the lenses with a soft cloth. He was dressed in a slim, tailored charcoal suit. The gray fabric matched the thin fringe of salt and pepper hair that ran around the sides of his head.

Blayne was the Director of National Intelligence. It was his duty to assess and advise the president on all intelligence matters pertaining to national security.

Rebecca looked around the table. The other men nodded and mumbled amongst themselves. Across from her she saw Ted Lapinski, the NSA's head of Section S32, also known as TAO. His 'Tailored Access Operations' group was tasked with hacking into foreign computer networks for espionage purposes.

The man's ruddy, cherubic face twisted into a sympathetic smile; his aqua-blue eyes sparkled, and he gave her a tiny shrug. His cheap suits and practiced joviality reminded her more of a used car salesman than a high-level intelligence official. Still, Blayne seemed to value his council. She had to admit, his unit had pulled off some spectacular intelligence coups in China and Korea.

She turned back to Blayne. The man slipped his clean glasses onto his face and stared at her with small, beady eyes.

'Let's cut to the chase, Director Freeling.'

'Director Blayne, the data is clear. Our current drone strategy is ineffective. It's like Hercules fighting the Hydra. For every head you chop off, two more grow to take its place.'

Blayne scratched a patch of flaking skin on his bald, wrinkled head and smiled. 'Hyperbole aside, you do make some good points. I'll pass your report along to the president. Now, unless anyone has any more questions for Director Freeling?'

The other men at the oval-shaped table were silent. A few coughs filled the room.

'I have a question,' Rebecca said. 'Where are we on the prisoner exchange with the People's Republic of China?'

Ted coughed and shifted in his chair. 'Rebecca, with all due respect, Sun Wai Tong is an NSA asset. And let's be clear, we're talking about a state-sponsored hacker. A digital terrorist, who has already provided us with critical intel on China's cyberwarfare capabilities. And you want to give him back, in exchange for some snot-nosed journalist?'

'That journalist is the son of a CIA officer, Ted,' Rebecca replied. 'It may not be politically expedient, but I try to take care of my own. And my understanding is the president feels the same way.'

'That's correct,' Blayne added. 'The president has made it clear to China that he's willing to deal with them on this. He's rolling out his new climate change initiative, the Global Environmental Accord. He wants the Chinese on board, and this is part of his diplomatic push. It's up to them to make the next move, but it's going to happen. Ted, your people need to prepare for that. You'd better get as much information as you can out of Mr. Tong while we still have him in custody.'

Ted gave another one of his shrugs, this time more exaggerated. 'Whatever you say, Boss.'

Blayne shuffled the papers in front of him and slipped them into a manila folder. 'Very well. Gentlemen, ladies, thank you. That will be all. I'll see you in two weeks. Ted, could you stay a few minutes? I want to go over those international restrictions on the PRISM program one more time.'

'No problem, John,' Ted said with a chuckle. 'But I'm telling you, I still think the president's throwing the baby out with the bathwater on this one.'

Rebecca joined the other members of the committee as they filed out of the room. To her right, warm sunlight beamed through a long row of floor-to-ceiling windows. She stopped and turned, moving closer to one of the towering panes of glass.

She stared at the trees in the park across the street. The sun cast a dappled pattern of light and shadows on the ground as it filtered through the canopy of foliage. A narrow dirt trail wound around the park. Rebecca watched as a young, slim girl ran down the trail. Her blonde hair trailed behind her, catching the sunlight like fine strands of gold. Her pink and white sneakers kicked tiny puffs of dirt into the air as they drove her forward.

Rebecca felt a hand on her shoulder. 'Director Freeling, you okay?'

She looked up and found herself staring into the warm brown eyes of Josh Galloway. Josh was a couple years younger than she was. Crow's feet around his eyes, and worry lines that ran across his tan forehead, made him look older.

She had balked when the CIA had insisted on supplying her with a security detail. It had made her feel weak. Would they have assigned men to protect her if she was a man sitting in the chair? But over the last few weeks, Josh had proven that he was a capable operative, and an asset to her team. He was able to balance protecting her life with staying out of her way.

Plus, she had to admit, the former marine was easy on the eyes.

She noticed two other men, beefy military types, walking up behind Josh and flanking him. She frowned.

'Josh, I told you to keep the babysitters downstairs.'

Josh looked at his watch. 'And I said I would. Until the meeting ended. You're five minutes late. May I?' He gestured to the handles on the rear of her chair. Rebecca shook her head.

'No thank you, I'm fine.' She pushed the tiny joystick mounted to her armrest and spun the chair around. 'Let's go. I'm going to be late for the meeting with the SIGINT team.'

'No worries, Director. I called your assistant, told him you were running late. He rescheduled the meeting. We should just have time to stop for coffee.'

Josh walked alongside her as she guided her chair towards the elevator. 'Josh, you know me too well.'

The man smiled. 'Well, if your Intelligence Community meetings are anything like my old recon briefings, you're gonna need a pick-me-up. But I recommend we stop at a different coffee shop. You've been to Dean & DeLuca three times this week.'

'So? It's called a preference.'

'No, ma'am, it's called a pattern, and it can be dangerous.'

The elevator door opened. 'You know what else is dangerous? Getting between me and my favorite latte. See you downstairs.'

The elevator doors shut behind her. Josh smiled. He turned to his men. 'You heard the lady. Bring the car around. Dean & DeLuca it is.'

* * *

John Blayne slid his cell phone from his pocket, turned it off, and placed it on the table.

'Recording equipment is off. Cell phone?'

Ted smiled, rummaged in his pocket for a few minutes, then pulled out his cell phone and put it down next to Blayne's.

'All right, this is about as private as it gets in the Office of the Director of National Intelligence,' Blayne sighed. 'Give it to me straight. How bad is it? What does this kid know?'

Ted sighed. 'Sun Wai Tong is one of China's most talented state-sponsored hackers. I mean, this kid is good. Scary good. I tell you this so you understand that what I tell you next... John, it's just the tip of the iceberg.'

Blayne peered at Ted through his glasses for a second. 'Christ, do I even want to hear this?'

Ted shrugged. 'Someone should.'

Blayne took a sip of water, then nodded. 'Fine. Go on.'

'This kid found his way into servers I didn't even know existed. Deep Black, off-books stuff. He downloaded evidence of at least two sanctioned assassinations. You know, that thing we say is illegal and don't do, but everyone knows we really do? Well, this kid has the files that prove it, buried on some hacker's hard drive, God knows where.'

Blayne folded his hands beneath his chin. 'That's manageable. As long as there's nothing that ties those files to the president, we can pass it off as a rogue operation. Hell, maybe we can pin it on Bernatto now that he's gone underground.'

'There's more, sir. Much more. Guantanamo videos. Records that should have been destroyed. Enhanced interrogation. And I'm not talking the embarrassing stuff, like stress positions or forced rectal feeding. I mean real, hardcore torture. You ever see those videos?'

Ted looked Blayne in the eye. Blayne looked away.

'Jesus Christ, this is a disaster,' he muttered.

Ted nodded. 'Yes sir, it is. And more importantly, it could derail the president's new deal with China.'

Blayne looked up and squinted his eyes. 'What do you mean?'

'I'm telling you, this kid dug up shit as far back as 1989. Personnel records, CIA-planted agitators that were part of the Tiananmen Square protest. Operation Canary ring any bells?'

Blayne shook his head. 'That's all ancient history. That's—'

Ted cut him off. 'John, this kid has intel, somewhere, that links a United States intelligence agency to the goddamn Tiananmen Square massacre! You think the Chinese will sign the president's bullshit environmental deal if that leaks out?'

Blayne ran his hand over his bald scalp. 'Fuck. Look, Ted, the president is adamant, he wants to give them back this hacker for the journalist they're holding in Beijing. I've tried to talk him out of it, but he's not budging. It's not just the trade deal, he's got an election coming up. He's afraid the Chinese will execute this kid on some trumped-up espionage charges. Something like that, with national news coverage... there's no way his approval ratings don't take a hit.'

Ted stood up and slid his phone in his pocket. 'Then he's going to have to deal with the worst intelligence blowback this country has ever seen. We're talking thirty-plus years of dirty laundry, hand delivered to the PRC.'

Blayne grimaced. 'We can't allow that to happen, but we must maintain deniability for the president. What if this hacker... What if he had an accident?'

'That could still leave us exposed. What if the information is on a dead man's switch somewhere? Or with a hacker who was instructed to release it in case of Sun Wai's death? Until we can get our hands on everything he downloaded, we can't afford to lose him. But there is another way.'

'Such as?'

'We approach this from the other end. What if something happened to the journalist, in China? No journalist, no trade. Less exposure for us, and it buys us time to put some real pressure on this guy.'

'Can you make that happen?'

Ted smiled. 'Well, as you know, John, the NSA is not chartered to operate on foreign soil. But if you give the word, I may know someone who has an asset in place.'

Blayne sucked in a breath of air, then nodded. 'Do it.'

'Yes, sir. See you in two weeks.'

Ted waved and strode out of the room. He stopped in the hall outside and turned his phone back on. As he walked, he began to tap out a text message.

> DNI on board. Permission to deploy?

He waited for a few minutes. Then his phone chirped with an incoming message.

> Go for Red Phoenix deployment.

Ted slid the phone into his pocket, whistling a tune to himself as he walked down the stairs.

4

HELMAND, AFGHANISTAN. 0600 HOURS.
YEARS AGO…

Caine coughs as his eyes flutter open. A dusty haze fills the air, pierced by an occasional sliver of light. He looks up. The stone well has collapsed above them. Crumbled rocks and wood beams block the shaft's opening.

They are trapped.

Operation Big Blind, he thinks. *Bernatto. The bastard sold us out.*

A soft, wheezing gasp echoes in the darkness. Caine blinks and sees the outline of Jack Tyler's body in the shadows, lying on the ground. His partner is half-buried in rock and debris. Caine forces himself to sit up, then brushes the rocks and dust from Jack's chest.

'Jack, you okay?'

'Yeah, I'm just peachy. What the—' The rest of Tyler's words are drowned in a fit of coughing. His breathing is rapid and shallow. Caine removes more rocks from his chest. Warm blood soaks through the man's clothes.

'Try not to move. You're hurt.'

'Not moving anytime soon,' Tyler gasps.

Caine feels along Tyler's side until he locates a series of

pouches. He opens them and rummages around, wrapping his fingers around a plastic cylinder. He snaps the plastic and the stick lights up with a green phosphorescent glow. The light casts looming shadows across the walls of the dark well.

Caine holds the light in one hand and examines Tyler's wound. The man's skin is cold and clammy. Caine tears off a section of his shirt.

'This is gonna hurt,' Caine says.

Tyler nods and looks away. Caine presses the cloth down on the gaping hole in Tyler's abdomen. The bleeding man sucks in a deep breath. Within seconds, the cloth is saturated with blood. It looks black in the green light of the glow stick.

'Tom,' Tyler says, his voice weak but calm. 'It's no good, kid. Forget it.'

'You're about five minutes older than me, Jack.' Caine grimaces as he examines the blood-soaked cloth. 'Stop calling me kid.'

Jack chuckles, then coughs. 'Five minutes? Hell, that's enough time for your whole life to flash before your eyes. Kinda like right now.' Tyler grabs Caine's hand and presses a scrap of paper into his palm. 'You need to do something for me. You have to promise me.'

Caine tries to speak, but no words come out.

Tyler looks Caine in the eye. His pupils are dilated, tiny pinpricks of black in a sea of blue. 'Just promise me... Tell Sean... Tell him I did it for him. All of it. The good, and the bad.'

Caine narrows his eyes. 'Who the hell is Sean?'

Tyler closes his eyes. He does not answer. His wet ragged breath echoes through the dusty darkness.

* * *

The Present

Caine charged across the dim apartment towards the withered form of Allan Bernatto. His green eyes seemed to glow from within with rage and hate. Bernatto stepped back and grabbed a frying pan off the tiny stove.

As Bernatto swung the pan like a club, Caine raised his left arm and blocked the feeble blow. He slammed the butt of the pistol into the older man's forehead as he drove his knee up into his abdomen. Bernatto gasped in pain and bent forward. Caine grabbed his wrist and twisted. The frying pan clattered to the floor.

Keeping his hold on Bernatto's wrist, Caine yanked backwards. Bernatto flew towards him. Caine slid aside and lashed out with a savage kick. The blow sent Bernatto flying into the sitting room. He fell to the ground and sprawled across the dusty, faded Turkish rug.

Gasping for breath, Bernatto rolled towards the couch. He reached into the dark space under the dilapidated furniture.

As Caine charged towards him, Bernatto drew a small pistol from a concealed mount under the sofa. He raised it with a shaking hand and pointed it at Caine. But he was too late. With a swift kick, Caine knocked the gun from Bernatto's grasp.

Caine grabbed the older man by the collar of his shirt and dragged him to his feet. He spun and hurled Bernatto into the wall. The man's glasses flew from his face as the drywall behind him buckled and collapsed.

Bernatto struggled to pull himself from the hole in the wall. Before he could get free, Caine's forearm slammed into the older man's throat.

'Do you know how long I've been waiting for this? How long

I've dreamed of killing you?' Caine hissed, his eyes glowing with fury.

Bernatto struggled to speak, but Caine pressed his arm down harder. The older man clawed at Caine's arm as it crushed into his larynx and windpipe.

'After I crawled out of that well, the White Leopard clan captured me. They tortured me, Allan. For days. Weeks. I don't even know how long. I lost track of time. You burned us, set us up. And then you framed me for the whole thing.'

Bernatto struggled to form words. 'Not... supposed... to torture. You... were supposed... to die.'

Caine grabbed the old man again and pulled him from the wall. Chunks of plaster and drywall exploded from the hole as Bernatto flew through the air again.

He slammed to the ground and immediately rolled over. His fingers clawed the carpet, searching for the gun Caine had knocked from his hand.

'Don't,' he hissed. He cocked the hammer of his Beretta PX4.

Bernatto froze.

'Hands where I can see them,' Caine said. His voice was cold and emotionless. He kept his distance from Bernatto, making sure the older man could not reach him with his feet or hands.

Bernatto raised his hands and slowly turned around. He sat up on the floor, facing Caine. His chest heaved as he gasped for breath.

'The man outside, the one with the newspaper... he was with you?'

'Just a local I hired. I wanted you to see him.'

Bernatto nodded. 'Made me waste time with a surveillance detection routine. Gave you a chance to get into position. Smart. Are you here on your own? Or did someone send you?'

'Your friends at the CIA finally realized what a snake in the grass you were. Rebecca saw to that. She's shining a light on all your unsanctioned ops. Assassinations, bribes, drugs, arms deals... Christ, Allan, you tried to provoke a war between China and Japan. You're an embarrassment now. A mess that needs to be cleaned up.'

Bernatto's chest heaved as he struggled to breathe on the dusty floor. 'So Rebecca survived? Good for her.'

'You put her in a chair, Allan. You took her legs.' Caine took a step forward. His cold, green eyes glinted in a shaft of sunlight. 'The CIA wants you dead or alive. But because of that, more than anything else... because of what you did to her, I'm thinking we go with dead.'

Caine leveled the pistol at Bernatto's head.

'Wait, there's something you need to know—'

'Goodbye, Allan,' Caine said. His finger wrapped around the trigger.

'Jack Tyler's son is in danger!' Bernatto shouted.

Caine stopped.

'What are you talking about?'

Bernatto lowered his hands. Caine didn't move the pistol.

'Jack Tyler, your old partner. He had a son, Sean. He's in danger. He's going to be killed. And I know where he is.'

'Bullshit.'

Bernatto picked his mangled glasses up off the floor. He twisted them into position and put them back on his face. One of the lenses was cracked. He squinted up at Caine with his dark, scowling eyes.

'You promised Jack you would look out for him. But you never checked up on him, did you?'

'You son of a bitch. You sold us out, buried us with that missile strike. Then you listened to Jack die for your own fucking amusement?'

Bernatto shook his head. 'I took no pleasure in it. You were wearing a mic, so I listened. That's all.'

'Operation Big Blind, the job in Afghanistan,' Caine snarled. 'It was all just a setup, so you could line your pockets with deniable assets. Guns. Drug money. I was a fool to trust you. But I won't make the same mistake twice.'

'I betrayed you. That's the past. It's over. But killing me isn't going to erase the blood on your hands. And it's not going to save Tyler's son.'

Caine started to speak, then stopped. He glared at Bernatto.

'Sean. Where is he?'

'He's in China. And that's all you get until you let me go.'

Caine's eyes glinted in the harsh light. His lips twisted into a grim smile. 'I can make you tell me, Allan.'

Bernatto looked up. 'Yes, I'm sure you could. But Sean doesn't have much time. I know exactly how long I have to hold out for. And you don't. That gives me leverage.'

'So I'm supposed just let you go? And trust that you'll tell me? That this isn't a setup?'

'That is exactly what you're going to do.'

'And why on earth would I do that?'

Bernatto peered up at Caine over the rims of his bent glasses.

'You risked your life in Japan, twice. First to save a gangster's son. Then to save that girl, Hitomi. You barely knew those people. This is Jack Tyler's son we're talking about. And I swear to you, Sean Tyler is a dead man unless you do as I say.'

Caine's face was still, unmoving. His features looked as if they were carved from stone.

'You're a killer, Tom, but you're not the operative you once were,' Bernatto said. A trace of his old arrogance crept back into his voice. 'Maybe it was Rebecca that made you soft. Maybe it was the torture, after the White Leopards captured you. Or maybe you just burned out. Lord knows this life can do it to a man. But we both know you're not going to stand here and let Tyler's son die. Not when there's a chance, no matter how small, that you can do something about it.'

Caine gritted his teeth. His mouth twisted into a snarl.

He pulled the trigger.

The gunfire was deafening in the tiny apartment.

Then there was silence. Smoke danced in the narrow beams of sunlight that cut through the room. The bitter smell of gunpowder filled the musty air.

Bernatto shook his head to clear the ringing in his ears. He turned to his right and saw a smoking bullet hole in the dusty carpet, just inches away.

He turned back to Caine. His lips curled into a sneer. 'I take it we have a deal?'

Caine kept the pistol trained on Bernatto. 'If you're lying to me, there's no place you can hide that I won't find you.'

Bernatto lowered his arms.

'I know that.'

Caine lowered the pistol.

'Get your things. We're leaving.'

5

The old hospital's cafeteria smelled of body odor and animal dung. A thin layer of dust and caked grease covered the old steel furnishings. Flickering fluorescent lights overhead bathed the large room in a sickly green glow. The building had not been used to treat patients for some time. Its new owners seemed unconcerned about hygiene and cleanliness.

A row of detainees shuffled in line, each holding a dented metal tray. The detainees were all men, and they wore rumpled, unwashed street clothes. The black jail did not provide uniforms or laundry services. According to official records, the facility did not exist. And as far as the outside world was concerned, the tired, shuffling men locked within no longer existed either. For now, they were just memories. Phantoms who lived on in the thoughts and minds of their loved ones.

As each man reached the end of the line, a bowl of thin, gray porridge was deposited on their tray. A greasy, foil-wrapped bundle was placed next to the bowl. One of the guards wore a stained white apron over his uniform. He spooned broth into chipped plastic bowls. Another handed the bowls out to the detainees as they traipsed past the counter.

The guard deposited a bowl onto the tray of an elderly man with thinning gray hair. The man gave him a shallow bow.

'*Xie xie*,' he muttered.

'*Xia yi ge!*' the guard barked. 'Next!'

A young Caucasian man stood next in line. He was tall and muscular, maybe early twenties. Khaki cargo pants and a concert T-shirt hung from his athletic frame. A thick fringe of straw-colored hair swept across his forehead. His eyes were a bright, piercing blue.

The guard turned to his partner and mumbled, 'Who the hell is this *lao wai*?'

The other man dropped a steaming foil bundle on the Caucasian's plate and shrugged. 'Transfer from Shanghai, Tilan-qiao. I don't know who he is, but he must have pissed someone off to wind up here.'

The guard shook his head and set a bowl of soup on the tray. '*Ni zui hao zai zhe li, xiao xin yi dian!* You better watch yourself, kid!' the guard exclaimed in a loud voice.

The young man shook his head. 'Uh, I have no idea what you're saying to me. Thanks for the soup. I mean, *xie xie*.'

He took his tray and headed to a small, empty table near the corner of the room. Guards in camouflaged jumpsuits flanked the metal doors leading into the dining area. They glared at him and followed his movements. He gave them a wary glance as he passed their post.

He took a seat at the table and began to slurp the gruel-like soup into his mouth. The broth tasted of old rice, with a harsh, vinegar aftertaste. He grimaced, then unwrapped the foil bundle, revealing a stale white bao. Breaking the circular bun open, he examined the questionable brown filling inside. It was supposed to be pork. He gave it a sniff. Its odor reminded him of wet cardboard.

Before he could ingest the rancid food, a pair of guards pushed through the swinging doors. The uniformed men forced their way through the crowd and stalked towards one of the long tables that ran down the center of the room.

'Lung!' a guard barked. 'Alton Lung!'

A short, wiry Chinese man looked up from his soup. A pair of rectangular glasses perched in front of his mouse-like eyes. His hair was black and mussed, and his skin was tan. He looked to be in his early thirties. As the guards approached him, he hunched his shoulders. A series of mottled red bruises ran up his arm. The marks continued under the rolled-up cuff of his stained, tattered dress shirt.

'*Qing, qing!* Please,' the man pleaded. 'I can't take any more!'

'You should have thought of that before you made so much trouble,' one of the guards barked. 'The governor of Jiangsu Province sends his regards!'

The detainees eating next to Alton slid away, giving the guards a wide berth. The small man darted under the table and grabbed the bench with his slim fingers. 'I have done nothing wrong! You have no right to hold me here!'

'You're just making it worse, Lung,' one of the guards grunted. He slid a security baton from his belt and rapped the club on the table.

The other guard grabbed Alton's bruised arm and tried to yank him out from under the bench. 'Let's go, little man.' Alton lashed out with his leg, kicking the guard in the shin.

'Stay back! *Bang wo*, someone help me!'

The young man grabbed his tray and stood up. He ambled towards the commotion, a wide grin plastered on his face.

The guard Alton had kicked slammed his baton down on the bench, crushing Alton's fingers. The small man yelped in pain.

'That's for kicking me! *Ni zhe ge xiao huai dan!*'

Alton released his hold, and the guard dragged him kicking and screaming from under the table. He shoved him back, and Alton tripped and crashed to the ground. His glasses skittered across the cement floor. They came to a stop in front of the young white man. He bent down and picked them up, then looked up at the guards.

'Hey, come on,' the young man said. 'How about we do this after lunch?'

The guards cocked their heads and looked at him with surprise. 'Sit your ass down, *lao wai!* This doesn't concern you,' one of them snapped.

The young man slipped Alton's glasses into the pocket of his cargo pants. 'Sorry, my Chinese isn't that good. You speak English?'

'*Ta ma de ni you ma fan!*' the guard shouted, his voice rising in volume with each syllable. He lunged towards the young man, swinging his baton at the man's skull.

The white man swung his tray up. The bowl of slop flew through the air, striking the guard in the face. The metal tray deflected the baton blow with a loud clang.

The guard wiped the porridge from his eyes. Before he could react, the young man locked his weapon arm in the crook of his elbow. Then he drove his knee upwards. The guard's face turned bright red and he bent forward. He gasped as the blow drove the air from his lungs. The young man reached over with his right hand and grabbed the tip of the baton. With a quick yank, he freed it from the guard's grasp. Then he snapped it down, striking the side of the man's head.

The guard crumpled to the ground. Alton looked up at the

foreigner, his face twisted in fear. 'You *feng zi*? Who the hell are you?'

'You're welcome. My name's Sean. Sean Ty—' Before he could finish, two more guards broke through the crowd and tackled him. 'Hey, wait,' he shouted. 'They were beating that guy!'

More guards poured into the room. The rest of Sean's words were lost in a series of grunts and screams, as the guards pummeled him with their batons.

* * *

Sean winced as he pressed the icepack against his blackened right eye. His face was flushed from exertion and adrenaline, but his injuries were minor. Only a few cuts and bruises marred his chiseled, brooding features.

A stoic Chinese man wearing a white doctor's coat muttered to himself as he dabbed at Sean's wounds. Using a long cotton swab, he spread a clear antibiotic gel into one of the gashes on the side of Sean's forehead.

'That stings,' Sean muttered.

The doctor hissed and shook his head but said nothing. He applied a sterile white gauze over the cut, then began to pack up his tools into a black leather satchel.

The doctor turned to another Chinese man sitting across the table from Sean. The man wore a lustrous navy pinstripe suit. His hair was flawless and well-groomed, but his skin had a pale, wax-like appearance. Something about his handsome face seemed plastic, almost artificial. He seemed absorbed in several files and dossiers that were spread out on the table.

'*Ta hui hou xia lai*,' the doctor said. 'He'll be fine.'

The other man did not look up. '*Xie xie*. Leave us now, please.'

The doctor grabbed his bag, and hurried out of the small, sterile room.

The man in the suit continued to focus on his files. 'The doctor says you'll be fine. You seem to have trouble making friends, Mr. Tyler.'

Sean tossed the icepack down on the table and looked around the small room. Featureless gray concrete walls, stainless steel furniture.

'What the hell is this place?' he asked. 'Some kind of secret prison? One of those black jails your government swears don't really exist?'

The man finally looked up and smiled. The smile did not touch his eyes.

'For you, this place is a safe haven. The men you crossed back in Tilanqiao Prison belonged to the Luen Ying She gang,' he said. 'They're Triad-connected,' he added. 'Do you know what that means?'

Sean stared him in the eye. 'Yeah, it means they're bullies. Just like your guards.'

The man cocked his head. 'If we left you in that cesspool, you'd be a dead man. You're an American. You're far from home, in quite a bit of trouble. And you picked a fight with Triad gangsters in a foreign prison.'

Sean sighed. 'Well, when you put it like that... Look, what's your name, anyway?'

'My name is not important, Mr. Tyler. What is important is that I work for the Ministry of State Security, and my job is to keep you safe. That's why I transferred you here. I've arranged for you to have your own room, away from the other detainees. And from now on you will take your meals in your room, separate from the others.'

'Hey, look man, it's been what, a month of this shit? I haven't talked to a lawyer, I haven't been given my phone call, I—'

'Enough!' The man's voice rose in pitch and cut through the air like a knife. Sean was silent, and for a moment, a worried look flickered over his face. 'There will be no lawyer, do you understand?'

The man gathered his papers and slid the thick bundle into a leather briefcase. He stood up from the table.

'This is not America. You are not a cowboy, or a superhero. You know nothing of the matters you involve yourself in. You are an outsider, and a criminal!'

'I'm a journalist! I write for—'

'I've seen your pathetic little website. It means nothing. The offices you broke into belong to a prominent businessman with important government contracts. The Ministry has declared you a threat to public security. If they wish it, they could have you executed!'

Sean leaned back in his chair and exhaled.

The man smiled again, and a facetious tone crept into his voice. 'Luckily for you, as of right now, they do not wish that. They wish to resolve this matter and send you home. So, I would think the least you could do to show your gratitude would be to shut your mouth, keep your head down, and stay out of trouble!'

Sean nodded. 'Okay, okay. You win.'

The man breathed an exasperated sigh. 'Thank you. With any luck, you'll be home soon, and we can both put all this behind us.'

The man in the suit turned to leave.

'One favor. Lung, the little guy.'

The man turned back to him. 'Alton Lung. He's a lawyer. A public nuisance. The governor of his province ordered him detained here for inciting violence.'

'Give me a break. Just look at the guy. Does he look like a violent offender to you? You know as well as I do the governor just doesn't want him petitioning the higher-ups here in Beijing.'

'So? What of him?'

'Transfer him to my room. The guards out there have a hard-on for him now. They'll really do some damage next time.'

The man narrowed his eyes and leaned against the wall. He crossed his arms in front of his chest. 'You need to stop worrying about the less fortunate, Mr. Tyler. And start worrying about yourself.'

'Story of my life. Look, just transfer him to my room, and I swear, I'll do whatever you want.'

'You can't protect him forever, you know.'

Sean shrugged. 'I know. But if I can help him now, why not?'

The man nodded. 'Very well. I'll put in the request. But I have a question for you in return.'

'Shoot.'

'I watched the security tapes. That move you pulled on the guard... that took skill. Training. Where did you learn to fight like that?'

Sean looked down at the table. He did not meet the man's piercing gaze. 'Something my dad taught me. Only thing he taught me, in fact. When I was a little kid, there were bullies in my neighborhood. They used to go around with baseball bats. So he taught me that move to defend myself.'

The man nodded. 'I see. Your father taught you well, then.'

Sean barked a short, bitter laugh. 'I was twelve years old when he taught me that. I remember, because it was the last time I saw him in person. So, yeah. Father of the year, huh?'

6

HELMAND, AFGHANISTAN. 0600 HOURS.
YEARS AGO…

Tyler explodes in another fit of coughing, spraying flecks of blood across his torn shirt.

Caine looks down at the paper Tyler had thrust into his hand. It is a small picture, a crumpled, faded photograph of a young boy. Caine turns the picture over. On the back, in Tyler's handwriting, there is a single word.

Sean.

Tyler's breath is a soft, wet rasp. 'Why do you do it, Tom?'

'What are you talking about?'

'This job. There's only a few reasons guys like us do what we do. You do it for money. You do it for your country. Or you do it for someone else. You look at the world, and you see bad things in it. And you just want to make it better for that person. Because that person is more important than everything else.'

'Jack, I—'

'Tom, promise me… You find Sean. Look after him. And you tell him. Tell him I did it for him.'

Caine nods. He has seen men die, countless times. He knows Tyler is slipping. There isn't much time left.

'I will,' he says. 'I'll tell him.'

Tyler's lips settle into a peaceful smile. His eyes remain closed. 'Good. That's good. Thank you.'

The wounded man's hands fall to the ground. His breathing slows to a heavy pant. His chest rises and falls. Then it stops.

Caine sits down and leans against the wall of the well. He wipes the dirt and sweat from his face. His fingers leave a crimson streak of blood on his cheek.

Jack's blood.

He looks down again at the photo Tyler gave him, staring at the boy in the picture. He didn't know that Tyler had a son. In their years working together, the man had never mentioned it. After a few minutes, he folds the picture and slips it into his pocket.

In the deathly silence, he hears the faint sound of running water. Using the glow stick, he searches the floor of the well. A trickle of water flows from the pile of rocks.

Caine tears into the rocks, digging and scraping with his fingernails. Heaving piles of sand and debris over his shoulder, he uncovers a small hole in the side of the well. Beyond the hole is pitch-black darkness. He continues digging until the hole is large enough to fit through. An underground stream flows through the bottom of the well.

Caine knows the airfield isn't far from the Helmand River. If this underground stream connects with the river, it must come up to the surface somewhere.

He pushes himself through the hole and craws forward. Shards of rock scrape against his head and shoulders. A sharp stone slices though his knee as he pulls himself forward. The glow stick's soft green light reveals the tunnel grows even narrower up ahead. Caine wedges himself deeper into the tight space.

He will either make it out. Or he will die trapped in a tiny, dark hole in the ground. A silent vow echoes in the dark recesses of his mind.

If I survive, I'll find Bernatto, and whoever else betrayed us. And I'll keep my promise to Jack.

The glow stick flickers and dies. Caine drags himself deeper and deeper into the darkness ahead.

* * *

The Present

It was a twelve-hour flight from Latvia to Beijing, with a three-hour layover in Moscow. Caine spent the layover in a small airport bar. There, he used the time to memorize the maps and guides to Beijing he had purchased before leaving. As he flipped through the pages of the guide books, he sipped a cold Ochakovo beer from a tall, frosted glass.

The alcohol helped calm his nerves. He still felt flashes of anger, white-hot bolts of rage, running up and down his body. He realized his hand was shaking, and he clenched his fist. Memories raced through his mind... thoughts of his dark, hot cell, his imprisonment after his capture in Afghanistan. The torture that had been inflicted upon him. The pain...

Rebecca.

He took another sip of beer and returned his focus to the map.

That's the past. It's over. Now you have a job to do, he thought. *Focus!*

He checked his watch. It was time.

He pulled out his cell phone and dialed the number he had arranged with Bernatto.

The phone rang.

Nobody picked up.

It's a trick. Caine thought. *It was all bullshit. He played me!*

The phone rang three more times. Caine moved his finger to the lock button. Before he could press it, he heard a long beep, then a click.

'Hello, Tom.' It was Bernatto's voice.

'Scrambler?' Caine asked.

'Of course. Just in case you routed this call through to Rebecca. You won't be able to get a fix on my location, so don't bother trying.'

'I don't need to trace your phone to find you, Allan.'

'Do you want to make threats, or do you want to help Sean?'

'Start talking.'

Bernatto cleared his throat. 'Sean Tyler is a journalist. Writes for an activist website called Human Rights Now. You know the type. Young, idealistic, and utterly ignorant of how the world really works.'

'Not interested in your politics, Allan,' Caine said. 'Get on with it.'

'Sean was in China, working with a local chapter of the group. He was investigating a story about a man named David Fang. Made a fortune in chemicals and pharmaceuticals, has factories all over China. Sean and some members of his group were caught breaking into an office building of his in Shanghai.'

'So why the hell am I going to Beijing?'

'Shut up and listen. About a year ago, I headed up an extraordinary rendition operation. The target was a state-sponsored hacker named Sun Wai Tong. The NSA has him now, under lock and key.'

'What's so special about this hacker?'

'This is no ordinary hacker. Tong cracked the mother lode.

He found his way into an NSA server that was so black, it's practically non-existent. The data he accessed... I can only assume someone in the NSA was keeping it to cover their ass. There's no sane reason not to have erased these files years ago. Some of the classified information he accessed goes back decades. It absolutely cannot be disclosed, both for political and security reasons.'

'This information he stole... is it out in the wild?'

'Somewhere, yes. We... I mean, the NSA, just doesn't know where. According to their intelligence, we were able to grab him before he reported to his handlers at the Ministry. But not before he was able to offload the information from his servers.'

'I still don't see what this has to do with Sean.'

'The Ministry has moved Sean to a secret black site in Beijing. They've made an offer to the president, behind closed doors. A trade.'

'Sean for the hacker?'

'Precisely. The president has approved the trade. The NSA can't, or won't, reveal the extent of the information Sun Wai has. And the president is looking at a public relations nightmare if he refuses the trade and the Chinese execute Sean. He's in the middle of negotiating a massive environmental deal with China. Something like this could derail the whole thing and give China an excuse to walk away from the table.'

'I don't give a crap about trade deals or public relations. You said Sean didn't have much time. What did you mean by that?'

'What do you think, Tom? The NSA can't let this trade happen. It would be a disaster for their organization, and for the entire nation. They're looking for an out, anything that will scuttle the deal and let the president off the hook.'

Caine clenched the phone tightly in his hand.

'They're going to kill him, aren't they?'

'If Sean dies in Chinese custody, it insulates the president from taking responsibility for the fallout. And they already have an asset in place. A double agent within the Chinese government.'

'Who is it?'

Bernatto paused. 'I don't know.'

'Dammit, Bernatto!'

'It's the truth. I don't have that intel; I wasn't directly involved in that operation. The only info I have is the asset's code name. Red Phoenix.'

Caine scanned the other faces in the bar. He confirmed no one was paying attention to their conversation.

'How exactly do you know all this?' he asked in a low voice.

'A little while back, a director from the NSA, Ted Lapinski, came to me for help. He needed some good freelancers, someone to help him gain leverage over an asset. I provided him with some men, contractors I had worked with. That's all.'

'If I find out you're lying to me, if you're holding anything back...'

'That's all I know, Tom. I've kept my end of the bargain.'

'Just so we're clear, you bought yourself some time. That's all. I'm still coming for you.'

Bernatto coughed. 'I have no doubt. That's why I'm helping you. Every minute you spend looking for Sean is a minute you're not looking for me. I'll take all the head start I can get.'

There was a click and the call disconnected.

A text message came through. It was the address in Beijing. If Bernatto was telling the truth, it was where the Ministry of State Security would be holding Sean. A deniable, off-books site. Easier to cover up, if something went wrong...

The feelings of rage returned, even stronger. Caine clenched his fist tighter, digging his nails into his palm.

Had he done the right thing? Was this all just another setup? Had Bernatto played him yet again?

He remembered the picture of Sean. A tiny, crumpled piece of paper Jack had clutched in his trembling hands. Caine no longer had the photo. But the image of the young boy, that faded, torn scrap of a photo, was burned into his mind.

Jack's words from the collapsed well echoed in his head. He could hear the man's voice, as clear as if it were next to him.

'You have to promise me. Tell him... tell him I did it for him.'

'All right, Jack,' Caine muttered to himself. 'Let's go tell him.' His fist stopped shaking. A Russian voice announced his flight over the loudspeaker. Caine stood up, slung his backpack over his shoulder, and made his way towards the gate.

He had found Bernatto once. He could do so again. And the sooner he was back on his trail, the better.

But first, he would keep his promise to Jack.

After that, the hunt would resume. The next time he and Bernatto met, there would be no deals. He would not pull his aim.

He would shoot true.

As he disappeared into the airport crowd, more of Jack's words came to mind.

This job... why do you do it, Tom?

Caine had no answer. The thoughts in his head were as cold and silent as death.

7

David Fang scrutinized the small ivory tile in his hand. The white rectangle was engraved with a serpentine green dragon design. A small number adorned the upper-left corner. It was a mahjong tile, and Fang had a decision to make.

Discarding the tile was risky. He suspected Lewis, the player to his right, held a dragon in his stack of tiles. On the other hand, he had noted the tiles Lewis had discarded. He doubted the man had enough dragon tiles left to make a pong, or three of a kind. Lewis was one of Fang's most trusted lieutenants in his chapter of the powerful *Lu Long* Triad. He was fierce, loyal, and determined.

But he was also predictable.

Fang was tall, lean, and handsome. His skin was a deep tan, and his eyes were dark, lively, and intelligent. His hair was jet black, without a trace of gray. Fang was in his fifties, but he looked younger than men ten years his junior. He wore a white suit and a black silk knit tie. The crisp fabric barely moved as he shrugged and set his tile down on the lustrous green felt of the gaming table.

'Pong,' Lewis cheered, flipping over his three dragon tiles to show the other players.

Fang smiled. 'Well done, Lewis. Fortune favors you tonight.'

Wei Laiwai, a short, rotund man who sat opposite Fang, chuckled. His eyes rotated from Lewis to Fang. He ran a hand through the fringe of gray hair that surrounded his speckled scalp.

'Perhaps,' he rumbled in a deep voice. 'But I suspect that will be the last dragon tile he sees for the evening. He played his hand too soon.'

The fourth man at the table, one of Laiwai's bodyguards, exploded in laughter. His high-pitched giggle echoed off the vaulted gold ceilings and red-lacquered walls. The mahjong table sat in the center of the chamber. The lights above the table were the only source of illumination. A pair of massive, ornate gold doors were the only exit from the cavernous chamber.

A towering bank of windows dominated the far end of the room. They overlooked the neon spires of the Shanghai skyline. The famous Oriental Pearl Tower was just off to the east. Its upper sphere lit up the night sky with purple light. The brilliant, colorful glow reflected through the glass and onto the faces of the men sitting at the table.

Statues and display cases loomed in the shadows surrounding the table. The room's walls were solid red and decorated with Chinese scrolls. The ancient slivers of parchment depicted famous proverbs and legends. Fang had played here many times before. He often looked to the scrolls for inspiration as his luck in the game ebbed and flowed.

He repeated one of the mantras from memory. 'Silence is a true friend, who never betrays.'

Lewis grinned. 'Quoting Confucius, eh? Ah, you're right, Boss. I got excited. Revealed my hand too early.'

Fang looked down at his tiles. He arranged them in a new order and spoke in a soft but commanding voice. 'At the risk of making the same mistake, Mr. Laiwai and I have a private matter to discuss. I'm afraid we must pause the game. You and his associate may wait outside.'

Lewis eyed Laiwai's bodyguard with disdain. He stood up and turned to Fang. After a short, brief bow, he cupped his fist in his other hand and held both hands centered in front of his chest. '*Shi de lao ban!* It is my honor to obey.'

The guard stood and returned the gesture. 'I'll be outside, sir.' He gave Fang an uneasy look from the corner of his eye as he followed Lewis out of the room.

There was a burst of wind and light from outside as the men stepped through the massive golden doors. The lobby was a skeletal framework of girders and beams; construction was not yet finished. The lights of Shanghai blazed in the distance, and a cool breeze whipped through the building. It rustled the plastic sheets that hung between the girders. Then the doors slammed shut, and the cavernous room was once again dim and silent.

Wei Laiwai leaned back in his chair and sighed. 'Now we see why you really invited me here tonight. I'm sure it wasn't to watch me beat you at mahjong again!' Once again, the rotund man chuckled, but this time he stared Fang straight in the eye.

Fang continued arranging his tiles. He took a sip from a glass of clear liquid that sat on the table. *Mi jiu*, a rice-based wine. Fang licked his lips as the bittersweet liquid struck his taste buds.

'I wish to speak carefully, Wei,' he said. 'We have known each other for many years. We fought each other as rival Red Poles, rising up in the *Lu Long*. But we have grown strong through peace. We have watched as others weakened themselves through stupidity and infighting. Squabbling over scraps, like packs of wild dogs.'

Wei raised his hand. 'You have my respect, David. But I have no patience for careful speech. Say what you came to say.'

Fang looked up and smiled. His face was pale in the dim light. 'Direct as always, Wei. A courageous foe is better than a cowardly friend, as the saying goes. Very well, I'll come to the point.'

Fang slid three tiles across the table and turned them face-up. They were all dragon tiles, and the digits in each corner formed the number 489.

Laiwai smiled and nodded. 'I thought as much.'

In the hierarchy of the Triad gangs, each rank within the organization was assigned a code number. The complex system was designed to confuse outsiders. Over time, the various numbers and their meanings had acquired almost mythical significance. The number 489 was well-known to both men. It referred to the most important position of all.

Dragon Father... the patron of the Triad. Ruler of all organized crime undertaken by the *Lu Long*, and the other organizations they controlled.

'I will be Dragon Father,' Fang said. 'This is a fact. I have no wish to spill more blood if it can be avoided. But do not mistake my rationality for weakness. I will not fail in my destiny.'

Laiwai took a sip of his own wine, a darker vintage made from fermented red rice. It left a crimson stain on his cracked lips. He quickly wiped his mouth with a cloth napkin, but the stain remained.

'The election will come soon enough,' he said. 'We'll see what destiny has in store for us then.'

Fang slammed his fist onto the table. The mahjong tiles bounced and tumbled across the felt surface. 'I will hold the dragon rod in my hands. I will lead the *Lu Long* Triad into the future. No other outcome is possible. No action by you or any other man in this world can stop it.'

'This is crazy talk,' Laiwai said, his voice rising in intensity. 'What do you want me to do? Remove my application? Step aside and allow you to rise above me? I have waited as long as you!'

'I am asking you to wait a bit longer, yes. But not forever. Stand by me. Work with me, as my deputy. You will be my number 438, a Triad Mountain Master. With my legitimate business interests, I can take the organization's funds public. You'll make more money under me than you ever would alone.'

Laiwai shook his head. 'Listen to yourself, David. What would you say if I made you the same offer?'

'In three years' time, I give you my word I will step down,' Fang continued. 'I will throw the full weight of my organization behind your candidacy then. No one will be able to stand in your way. Your time will come.'

'I asked you to speak frankly,' Laiwai said, his voice low and calm. 'So now I'll do the same. The current Dragon Father favors me. He has thrown his support behind me, and the other families will vote accordingly. They don't trust you, David. The *Lu Long* has thrived for years because it works in secrecy. It lives in the shadows, it is the Triad behind the other Triads. But your businesses are out in the open. Government contracts, regulations, lawsuits, news stories... You attract too much attention, David. You may be the future of the *Lu Long*, but they are not ready for things to change just yet.'

'I will make them see wisdom. Don't fight me on this, Wei.'

The rotund man shook his head. 'Not my style. I don't roll over for anyone, not friend or foe. And here's another cold, hard fact. You can't afford it. Your money is tied up in your factories and business ventures, and the economy is not what it once was. You can't liquidate fast enough to pay the tithe. And your... other expenses... have burned through your cash. The current Dragon Father knows this. That's why he set the price so high.'

'I'll have the money. My new factory—'

'What new factory?' Laiwai interrupted. 'I happen to know the government denied your land sale, didn't they? All because of this Global Environmental Accord... A foolish trade deal with the United States, I'll grant you. But your factories don't pass the new emissions standards. Now, your investors' money is sitting in an offshore escrow account. Without the land, you can't touch a single yuan in the account.'

For a moment, the two men stared at each other across the table. They said nothing. The air between them seemed to crackle with electric tension.

Suddenly, the two golden doors crashed open. The men turned and gazed upon the view of the Shanghai Skyline, sparkling in all its vivid glory.

Spears of red, green, and purple thrust into the sky, surrounding the iridescent Pearl Tower. The famous tower consisted of three bulbous spheres, separated by a support beams and pylons. The upper sphere changed colors, flashing from purple to bright red. Rings of dancing lights shimmered around the base of the tower.

But the spectacular view outside paled compared to the woman who stepped through the golden doorway. The host shut the doors behind her, blocking out all distractions.

She was tall for a Chinese woman, nearly two meters in her shimmering black heels. She wore a long cheongsam dress, slit to the thigh. The traditional garment was cut from a rich blue embroidered silk. It flowed up her body and rose to a choker collar around her neck. The tight sheath of shimmering fabric hugged her figure, accentuating every line and curve.

Fang stood up, but Laiwai remained seated. He peered up at the woman with an intense stare.

'There you are,' Fang said. 'I'm sorry, we had Lewis play in your seat.'

'*Yuan liang wo*,' she said. 'Forgive me. My last appointment ran late. I hope I didn't miss too much.'

'Not at all. I was just discussing your specialty with Mr. Laiwai here.'

He pushed in the woman's chair as she lowered herself into Lewis's former seat, then he sat next to her. 'Wei Laiwai, allow me to introduce—'

'Iris Yip. I know of her. Everyone in the *Lu Long* knows about your I-Ching witch.'

Fang stiffened, but the woman placed a slim hand on his forearm. 'It's fine,' she said. 'I'm sure Mr. Laiwai meant no offense.'

Laiwai sipped more of his dark red wine. His eyes shifted over her body with a cold, clammy leer. 'I would think a woman who took up with the man that murdered her husband might be called much worse.'

Iris reached into the black clutch that sat on her lap. She withdrew a set of bamboo dowels. Each stick was long, narrow, and square-cut. A series of lines and dots decorated the four sides of each rod.

'Fate calls to us all, Mr. Laiwai,' she replied. Her voice was quiet, but deep and husky for a woman. 'My late husband could not escape its song any more than Mr. Fang could. Nor can you or I, for that matter.'

The older man broke eye contact as she met his leer with her own inscrutable stare. Her eyes were set just far enough apart that it seemed difficult to look into both at the same time. Her sharp, wide cheekbones accentuated the effect.

Her skin was a dark, creamy tan. She wore her hair long and straight and parted in the center. It was a simple style. Two dark slashes of black that framed her face and flowed down past her shoulders.

She rolled the sticks back and forth in her hand. The gentle clicking sound they made filled the air. She began to chant in quiet, half-formed whispers. Her words seemed to drift just out of comprehension in the dim, cavernous room.

'Let's make a wager,' Fang said, his lips curling into a smile. 'Give me a chance to convince you. If I can change your mind, you will offer me a toast. If not, I will do the same for you.'

Iris ceased her chanting. The sticks were still and silent in her hands. She looked up, her wide, dark eyes shining in the reflected light like onyx flame.

'In divination, as in life,' she said, 'answers come only to those who understand the nature of what they seek. The I-Ching is like mahjong. It is based on numbers. It is fate's equation. It reveals the patterns of energy that lie beneath what men perceive as chaos. Touch the sticks and ask your question. For one who truly understands their desire, knowledge shall be granted.'

'Fine. I'll play along,' Laiwai grumbled. 'But you best begin polishing your words, David. You're going to owe me one hell of toast.'

Laiwai reached out with a gnarled, stubby hand and caressed Iris's slim, tan fingers. 'Will I win the election and become Dragon Father of the *Lu Long*?' he asked in a booming, melodramatic voice.

Iris cocked her head, but her eyes did not shift from Laiwai's gaze. She counted six sticks from the pile and set them onto the felt table. She closed her eyes and shuffled them over each other, rolling them back and forth.

'What is the likely outcome of Mr. Laiwai's desire for power?' she said in her low, husky voice. Her eyes fluttered open.

The patterns on the sticks lined up to form two hexagrams,

each one a set of six horizontal lines. Some of the lines were solid, while others broke into two dashes. Iris ran her fingers over the engraved ridges of the lines.

'On the left, a solid line above five broken. The Still Mountain above Receptive Earth. A house with a shattered roof must soon collapse. In such times of adversity, the superior man knows it is not cowardice, but wisdom, to submit and avoid conflict.'

Her finger drifted right, over a small red dot that stood between the two hexagrams.

'A change line... action on your part may alter the patterns of energy. On the right, the likely result of such a change.'

Laiwai leaned back in his chair. 'What kind of change?'

Her fingers brushed over the patterns as she looked up at Laiwai's round face.

'The hexagrams shift. They become Still Mountain over Arousing Fire. The leg of your bed is split. This signifies a severe threat to one's well-being. There is no protection here. Those who forge ahead... will be destroyed.'

Laiwai downed the rest of his wine. 'Luckily for me, I don't believe in fortune tellers, Miss Yip.' He stood up and tossed a coin on the table. 'Here... a tip for a fine performance. David, I'll see you in Hong Kong. The election will decide our fates. If you want me to stand aside, you'll need more than a pile of sticks and a pretty face. You'll need an army.'

Fang stood up as Iris collected her I-Ching sticks and placed them back in her bag. 'You're not convinced?' he called after Laiwai. 'Then I owe you a toast, old friend.'

'You can toast my victory when I am crowned Dragon Father,' the man said as he threw open the doors. 'But don't worry. Your time will come.'

Laiwai stepped out into the unfinished lobby. He paused. He

sensed something was wrong before he could even process the grisly details of the sight before him.

His eyes were drawn up to the ceiling. Hanging from one of the support beams that crossed overhead were four bodies. Laiwai gasped as he recognized the pale, battered faces of his bodyguards. The corpses swayed in the breeze that swept through the open construction. Below, the Shanghai lights continued to twinkle through the hazy air.

Each body hung from the end of a silk cord looped around their necks like a noose. Their heads lolled forward; their mouths gaped open. Their wide eyes were unblinking and still.

Lewis stepped out from behind one of the massive golden doors. With a vicious snarl, he kicked Laiwai. The man stumbled forward and fell into the center of the room. He landed beneath the swaying corpses.

Twin elevators chimed from across the unfinished room. The doors slid open, and a man stepped out. His footsteps echoed across the rough concrete floor as he walked towards Laiwai.

He was slim, of average height. Although he was Chinese, his skin was stark white, and his eyes were a pale, pinkish red. His hair was a fierce tuft of blonde, perfectly coifed and styled above the strange, albino face. He was dressed in a tailored black suit.

As he marched forward, Laiwai saw more men filing in behind him from the elevators. Within seconds, about a dozen filled the room. They were all young, in their twenties, and wearing street clothes. Laiwai had seen enough Blue Lanterns in his time to recognize these men as foot soldiers. Their torn sleeves and open shirts revealed an intricate tapestry of Triad tattoos... dragons, koi, and numbers that represented good fortune. The wind whipped through their clothes and hair as they stared down at him.

The color drained from Laiwai's face as he realized they were all wielding swords and knives.

The albino stood over him. He clasped a short, curved sword with an ornate hilt in his right hand. The man smiled and raised the blade into the air. Laiwai blinked as he noticed a strange detail... only eight fingers wrapped around the hilt of the sword. Each of the man's stark white hands had only three fingers and a thumb. Four... *si*... a number associated with death.

The albino's smile widened. He swung the sword down.

'Stop!' Fang's voice cut through the air, and the throng of men ceased all chatter. The albino halted his killing blow. Fang strode into the room, with Iris following a few steps behind.

Laiwai scurried away from the albino and turned to face Fang. 'Are you crazy? What are you doing? This is forbidden!'

'You did say I would need an army,' Fang replied. 'The blades these men wield are known as Dai Dao. They're a favorite of the Vietnamese drug cartels that have been causing so much trouble on the border lately. Tonight, witnesses I have paid will say they saw a gang of Vietnamese men enter one of your warehouses. A shipment of their methamphetamine was stolen. It will be located at your building. The Dragon Father will accept the police report. He may favor you, but he will not go to war against me without more proof.'

He snapped his fingers, and Lewis handed him a fresh glass of *mi jiu* wine. He took a sip, then knelt before the panting figure of Wei Laiwai.

'I still owe you a toast. I gave you a chance, old friend. I allowed Iris to show you the hand of fate. I would have accepted a different result. I believe in destiny, in the I-Ching. But your reading confirmed what I already know. You could have risen with me. Now, you must fall before me.'

Fang took a long drink of his wine, then spat it in Laiwai's panicked face.

'Fate leads those who are willing but must push those who are not.'

He stood and watched as Laiwai scrambled to his knees. 'David, don't do this... You win, I will withdraw. I withdraw!'

Iris slinked over to Fang and draped her arm around his shoulder. Her long, dark hair trailed behind her in the breeze. The lights from the Pearl Tower cast an eerie red glow across her face. 'Fate is calling, Mr. Laiwai,' she cooed. 'Your time has come.'

Fang nodded. The albino raised his sword.

The blade sliced down. This time, nothing halted its descent. A spray of crimson spattered through the air. Laiwai collapsed to the ground.

The albino surveyed his handwork, then removed a white handkerchief from his pocket. He wiped his blade clean.

Lewis hurried over to Fang. 'You should go, sir.'

Fang gripped Lewis's shoulder. 'Clean this up when they're done. Did you call the hospital?'

Lewis nodded. 'Yes. The doctors say she is still refusing to take her medicine.'

Fang gritted his teeth. 'Then you tell the doctors I pay them to administer treatment, not to cower from an elderly woman! If they can't do their jobs, I'll fire them all and find someone who can!'

'Yes, sir.' Lewis paused, frowning. 'But there is another problem...'

'What is it?' Fang snapped.

'The American. The journalist that police arrested at your Shanghai building,' Lewis said.

'You said he would be taken care of in Tilanqiao Prison.'

'Yes sir, arrangements were made, but I just received a call. He is no longer in Shanghai. The Ministry of State Security moved him to Beijing. He is being held in a black jail, run by a government security contractor.'

'Why would they move him there?' Fang muttered.

Lewis stared back at him but said nothing.

Fang sighed. 'Never mind. Send Lucky Si to take care of him. We must move quickly. Laiwai was right about one thing. The Ministry of Land has refused my proposal. We will move forward with Operation Dynasty. Tell Tan to be ready.'

'Yes sir. *Shi pei le*. I will make the arrangements.'

Fang nodded. 'Call me when you've dealt with the American.'

He took Iris's hand and led her to the exit. Behind him, the men descended on Laiwai's corpse. They hacked and cleaved at the body like a pack of wild dogs. Within minutes, the concrete floor surrounding them was awash in blood.

Laiwai, the American, the Ministry of Land... They are nothing, Fang thought. *I know my destiny.*

And I know what happens to those who stand against it.

8

A blast of warm air struck Caine as he walked through the glass doors of Beijing Capital International Airport. He was wearing a khaki Harrington jacket, white oxford shirt, and jeans. He slipped a pair of tortoiseshell sunglasses over his eyes and scanned the crowd as he waited in the taxi line. A single small roller case stood next to him on the sidewalk.

The atmosphere outside was thick and hazy, and each breath left an acidic tang in his mouth. China's explosion of growth and industry had not come without a cost. Millions of motor vehicles, heavy use of coal, dust storms from the north... They all contributed to the blanket of smog that enveloped the sprawling city.

After a short wait, he slid into the back of a green taxi cab and handed the driver a small card with the address of a hotel. It was late morning, and the traffic was light. As they drove, Caine kept an eye on the cars around them. He looked for any that followed too closely, or that made unusual maneuvers to keep up with them. He instructed the cab driver to make random stops at gas stations, restaurants, and convenience stores. Each time they pulled off the freeway, Caine would watch to see if any cars followed their movements.

The cab driver muttered in frustration after each request. But Caine knew that Bernatto had directed him here. This could all be an elaborate trap. He would take every precaution.

After several stops, Caine was satisfied that no one was watching him. As they cruised towards the city center, he looked out the windows through the dense, hazy air. Gray apartment buildings and rusting factories soon gave way to gleaming modern architecture. The cab ride took him past the silver arch of the China Central Television building. Then, they drove by the stunning Beijing National Stadium. The thin, winding strands of metal that circled the glowing, oval stadium gave the structure its nickname, 'The Bird's Nest.'

Caine booked a room at a Crowne Plaza near the financial district of the city. Then, after a scalding hot shower and a change of clothes, he walked to the nearest subway stop.

The streets around the hotel teemed with pedestrians, motor vehicles, and bicycles. Street lights and warning signs were taken as mere suggestions by the throng of traffic. More than once, Caine heard the squeal of brakes as he crossed an intersection. Motorists swerved to avoid bicycles and pedestrians as they careened through the busy streets.

Caine could not read Chinese, but the subway system was modern and well laid out. He was able to decipher the complex web of train lines using a map mounted to the wall in the underground station. After a quick ride, he walked up a flight of metal stairs to the street. He found himself a couple blocks from the address Bernatto had given him.

Now, he stood on the roof of an office building across the street. Using a small pair of binoculars he had purchased at the airport, he scanned the building where Bernatto claimed Sean was being held. It wasn't difficult to spot.

The building was a three-story slab of gray brick, with chipped red lettering hanging over the entrance. The basic shape of the building made Caine think it may have been a state-owned hospital at one point. A ten-foot-tall chain-link fence ran around the grounds. Coils of razor wire topped each section of the barrier. Guards dressed in camouflage jumpsuits patrolled along the interior of the fence.

Caine's attention turned to a crowd gathered outside the fence. A large group of protesters filled the street in front of the building. They were chanting and shouting. Their voices carried through the air up to Caine's elevated perch. He watched as they thrust picket signs up and down and marched in tight circles. Some of the signs featured large, grainy black and white photos of elderly Chinese men and women. Caine assumed they were inmates held within the bleak gray building.

A few of the protestors leapt onto the fence and shook the wire mesh back and forth with their swinging bodies. He estimated that at least a hundred people had gathered below.

Bernatto had called this place a 'black jail.' The bleak facilities were used to hold Chinese petitioners. This kept them from complaining about their local governments in the larger city courts. In the Chinese legal system, local officials could be penalized if they accumulated too many complaints from their districts. Thus, they were incentivized to jail as many petitioners as possible. The black jails served as secret detention centers. They were a gray area, a quasi-legal institution. They kept the overwhelmed city courts from drowning in petition requests.

But the building before him was larger and better-guarded than most black jails. The guards inside the fence looked alert and moved with precise, well-coordinated motions. Their uniforms marked them as private security, most likely ex-military. Caine suspected this was a higher security facility, meant for political prisoners and dissidents as well as petitioners.

If Sean was being held here, there would be no prison records, no transfer orders. Nothing to tie the Chinese government to him if anything went wrong. If the trade deal failed to go through, they could do whatever they wanted with the young man.

A sudden commotion caught Caine's eye. One of the guards had opened the front gate and grabbed a woman near the entrance. The woman appeared young, perhaps in her early thirties. She was wearing a red hooded sweatshirt, with white lettering on the back. Caine zoomed in on the lettering. It read 'HRN – HUMAN RIGHTS NOW.' That was the organization Bernatto said Sean was working for. Did this woman know him?

Several protestors grabbed at the woman's clothes. They struggled to pull her from the guard's grasp. Others rushed towards the open gate. They hurled glass bottles and rotten fruit at the guards inside.

This is going to be a problem, Caine thought. He knew it was only a matter of time before the protest turned violent.

Zooming out, Caine saw a group of six men leaving the compound through a side entrance. They wore civilian clothes, but they moved with the same military precision as the guards. They were armed with security batons, clubs, and other makeshift weapons. They were moving around the outside of the building, making their way towards the crowd.

Caine lowered the binoculars and ran a hand through his short brown hair. He knew he should stay away. If he got involved, he could find himself arrested, or worse. He was a foreign operative on Chinese soil. He had no legal authority to operate in this part of the world. As far as Rebecca knew, he was still chasing Bernatto in Eastern Europe.

But if the woman below knew Sean, perhaps she could confirm if he was in the building. And she might have information about the facility itself. He was operating completely in the dark, going only on Bernatto's word. Any intelligence he could glean was critical at this point.

He bit his lip, then turned and strode back towards the roof's access doors.

He had made up his mind. The time for doubt was over. It was time to act. Things were about to get violent below.

And Caine was no stranger to violence.

9

By the time Caine made it to the street, the scene had devolved into a small riot. Two more armed guards had exited the front gate. They were helping their comrade subdue the woman in the red hoodie. The angry voices of the protesters filled the air. Their shouting was a wall of noise, drowning out all other sound as Caine pushed his way through the crowd.

Two of the protesters tugged at the woman's shoulders and tried to drag her away from the gate. One of the guards managed to grab hold of her ankle. He raised a security baton to strike, but as his arm lowered, the woman lashed out again with another kick. The heel of her suede boot slashed across the man's wrist. He cried out and jerked back his arm.

Caine was more worried about the group of men he had seen approaching from the other side of the building. The men at the gate wore uniforms. They were security guards: corporate employees with personnel files, military history, payroll records. They would limit their liability and operate within the confines of the law. The other men, the ones dressed in civilian clothes... They were the so-called 'black guards.'

They were the men who snatched protesters from their homes. Recruited from the ranks of ex-cops, criminal muscle, and street hoods, they were nameless thugs looking to make a quick buck. Paid in cash, they appeared on no official employment records. And once they got their hands on you, you disappeared. Sometimes their victims were released after a short stay in the black jail. Other times, they were never seen again.

The black guards moved closer to the crowd. Caine knew they would use whatever tactics were necessary to disperse the protesters.

Caine pushed through the crowd towards the woman. Sweat dripped down his forehead. The sea of bodies pressed together, engulfing him. Their rage seemed to ignite the air like a crackling wildfire.

He heard a scream. He shouldered through another layer of angry bodies. He saw the woman up ahead, struggling to stand up as the guard swung at her with the baton. Another guard clubbed one of the men trying to help her, driving him back into the crowd.

Caine jogged to the woman's side and extended a hand, as if to help her up. He turned his back to her attacker but tilted his head to keep the man in his peripheral vision.

The guard shouted at him in Chinese and swung the baton down again. Caine twisted his body and raised his right arm, allowing his shoulder to deflect the force of the blow. The forceful swing left the guard off balance. Before he could recover, Caine took a step backwards. He drove his right elbow into the guard's abdomen. Even over the noise of the crowd he could still hear the man grunt in pain and surprise.

Before anyone could even see what was happening, the guard stumbled backwards. As he stepped away, Caine grabbed a small pouch at the man's belt and yanked as hard as he could. The thin leather straps tore free. Caine unsnapped the pouch, revealing a can of mace. He aimed the can towards the battered guard and covered his mouth and nose with his free arm. Then he depressed the nozzle.

A stream of gray vapor hissed towards the guard and his compatriots. They dropped to the ground the instant the cloud surrounded them. Tears streamed down their faces. The burning mist stung at the mucus membranes in their eyes, nose, and mouth.

A few protestors were also hit by the gas. One fell to the ground in front of Caine. He grabbed the man and dragged him backwards. He choked as he began to feel the effects of the gas, but he forced himself to push through it. Squinting, he saw the woman in the red hoodie stagger to her feet. She was coughing and gagging as the gas drifted towards her.

Caine reached out and grabbed her arm. He started to pull her away from the crowd, but she resisted.

'Let go of me! Who the hell are you?' she demanded. She spoke English with a high-pitched, lilting voice. A slight British accent tinted her words.

'I'm here to help, but we have to move. Trust me, this is going to get worse any minute.'

She looked up at him and blinked. Her eyes were unusually large. Their deep brown irises looked warm and serene, even in the middle of the chaotic riot.

After a moment, she nodded. 'All right, let's go.'

Caine took her hand and pulled her through the crowd. He heard more screams up ahead. The sound of men shouting carried above the general noise of the crowd.

'*Hui jia!* Go home! Leave the street, or you get hurt! *Yi dong!*'

Caine clenched his jaw. The black guards had entered the fray. The crowd ahead parted, and Caine saw the group of men surging through the protestors.

They had tied bandannas over their mouths to hide their features. One was swinging into the crowd with his security baton, randomly striking protestors. Another wielded a hand-held stun gun. Caine saw a burst of blue sparks flash from the silver diodes at its tip. The black guard prodded one of the protestors with the weapon, and the man collapsed to the ground. His body shook in a violent spasm as fifty thousand volts of electricity arced through his muscles.

The black guard turned towards Caine. The corners of the man's narrow eyes crinkled as he smiled. He held up the stun gun and depressed the switch. Another arc of white-hot electricity crackled from the weapon.

Caine cursed and pushed the girl away from him. She yelped in surprise as she stumbled backwards. The guard stalked towards Caine. He held the crackling weapon in front of him like a knife. Sparks danced and popped from the device as he closed in.

A group of protestors marched on Caine's left side, towards the gates of the prison. Caine reached out and grabbed one of their signs, yanking it from an elderly man's grasp as the group surged past him.

The guard lunged forward, shoving the stun gun toward Caine's chest. Caine spun the sign in front of him like a club, knocking the man's weapon arm aside. The cardboard sign tore free, leaving a beam of wood in Caine's hands.

With a quick snap of his wrist, Caine clubbed the man's face with the stick. Using his free hand, he grabbed the wrist of the guard's weapon arm, twisting backwards. He drove his knee up, slamming it into the man's gut with all his strength.

The guard dropped to his knees. Caine twisted the arm wielding the stun gun, forcing the weapon into the man's chest. The guard gasped for breath. His eyes opened wide as he realized what was happening.

Caine took a step back. His fingers found the weapon's trigger.

He pushed the button.

A gurgling snarl escaped the guard's lips as his body began to shake. He fell backwards and his head cracked against the pavement. His body was still trembling from the massive shock to his nervous system as Caine quickly pocketed the stun gun.

Caine took a deep breath and scanned the crowd. One of the other black guards was battering a helpless protestor with a billy club. Blood gushed from his target's face as the weapon slammed down over and over. He shouted a series of curses as the dazed man fell to the ground. The guard looked up and eyed Caine. He had a shaved head and a hairy black mole growing above his sneering lips.

Caine turned to his right and saw the girl in the red hoodie standing a few feet away. She was staring back at him, her eyes wide with shock and fear.

He grabbed her wrist. 'Come on, let's go!'

The two of them burst out of the crowd. Caine heard sirens wailing in the distance. He looked back, over his shoulder. Mole Face, the black guard with the club, was pushing through the crowd. He struggled to follow after them.

The girl gestured down the street. 'This way, I have a car!'

Caine shook his head. 'Leave it! The plates will lead them right to you. This way.'

He pulled her across the street. They darted through a narrow alleyway between two buildings. The sirens grew louder behind them. The police finally arrived to break up the riot.

Caine was sure any protestors left behind would be arrested. Those who were lucky enough to escape would have to keep a watchful eye over their shoulder. The black guards might choose to pay them a visit.

They came to an intersection in the alley, where it split left and right. 'We need a taxi,' Caine panted.

'This way,' the girl said.

He followed her to the left. The smell of roasting meat and ginseng filled the narrow passageway. They ran past a row of merchant stalls selling fresh vegetables, herbs, and dried noodles. Past the stalls, she stopped in front of a battered metal door. She threw the door open, and Caine followed her inside.

They entered the kitchen of a small restaurant. A heavyset cook wearing a white apron was lopping the head off a roasted duck with a cleaver. Sweat streamed down his face as he looked up in surprise. They charged past him and ran through the tiny kitchen.

'*Gao shen me gui?*' he shouted, waving the cleaver at them. 'What the hell is this!'

'Sorry,' she called back. '*Qi wei da!*'

They burst through a plastic curtain into the dining room. An elderly man looked up at them, then shrugged and took a sip of tea from a small cup. Caine followed the girl as she darted between the tables. The front of the restaurant was open, and they stumbled out onto the sidewalk of a busy city street.

Caine grabbed the girl and pulled her backwards. A group of men on bicycles just missed them, as they pedaled past the restaurant at high speed.

The girl raised her hand and whistled. '*Chu zu che!*' she cried. 'Taxi!'

A battered yellow and blue sedan darted from the rows of

cars. It screeched to a halt in front of them. The sides of the vehicle were painted with red Chinese characters. Caine opened the rear door, and the girl slid in. He leapt in after her and slammed the door shut. The vehicle lurched forward.

Caine looked back through the rear window. Behind them, the sun was beginning to set. Streaks of pink, red, and orange painted the sky. The stunning colors were a beautiful side effect of the smog-filled air.

The cab driver, an older man wearing glasses and a hot pink T-shirt, looked back at them with a wide smile. 'Happy evening! My name Zhang Wei! Most common Chinese name! Everyone in China named Zhang Wei! *Qu na er?*'

Caine looked over at the girl.

'He wants to know where we're going,' she said.

'First things first. What's your name?'

The girl tilted her head and examined him. She hesitated for a second, then said 'Jia. Jia Zhao. And you?'

'Call me Tom. I'm a friend.'

He held out his hand. As she shook it, he felt a tremble run through her arm.

'You're shaking,' he said. 'You might be in shock.' He looked out the rear window again. 'When's the last time you ate something?'

Jia spoke in rapid Chinese to the driver. Then she turned back to Caine. 'You're right, I'm starving. I told him to take us somewhere. We'll get some food, and you can tell me exactly what kind of friend you are.'

Caine kept his eyes out the rear window, scanning the cars behind them. 'I'm the kind who saves your life. Isn't that good enough?'

'That all depends.'

'Depends on what?'

Jia's large, liquid eyes darted over his face again, drinking in the details of his features.

'It depends on what you want in return,' she said.

Then she turned and looked out the window at the explosion of colors left behind them by the setting sun.

10

It was dark when their cab jerked to a stop on Dianmen Outer Street. Zhang Wei, their driver, pointed to a narrow alleyway across the street. 'This as far as I go. Streets too narrow. You walk that way.'

They stepped out of the cab, crossed the street, and entered the alley. The narrow opening led to a larger pedestrian street. Caine looked around in surprise. A hidden little enclave of buildings, shops, and dwellings surrounded them.

It was as though they had stepped back in time. Invisible from the street, the tiny buildings and narrow passages looked like they had not changed in centuries. The streets were composed of alternating smooth tiles and patches of rough bricks. The buildings were small, built from gray stone and wood timbers. Their sloped, pagoda roofs rose up into decorative peaks and spires. They stood silhouetted against the dark, purple velvet of the evening sky.

A web of phone and power lines crisscrossed overhead. The mass of wires and antennas were a strange reminder of modern technology. They seemed crudely grafted on to the quaint streets and buildings below. Neon signs and electric lights were joined by the soft glow of rice paper lanterns hanging outside every shop and cafe.

Caine had to force himself to focus. He kept an eye on the crowd of pedestrians as Jia led him farther down the narrow street.

'Have you been to China before?' she asked.

Caine nodded. 'A long time ago, yes. I remember seeing the Great Wall, and the Forbidden City. But I didn't see anything like this.'

She smiled. 'This is called a *hutong*. My country is famous for its beautiful temples and palaces, but *hutong* are the true soul of China. Places like these are where the common people lived, on the outskirts of the larger cities.'

She waved to an old woman pushing a cart of vegetables down the street. The woman nodded and smiled at her, then continued on her way.

'Every *hutong* has its own stories, its own gossip, and local characters,' Jia continued. 'I love to come here and listen to the old timers talk. There's a real sense of community, a sense of belonging. It can be hard to find that in a city as large as Beijing.'

They turned and walked down an adjoining alley. Caine noticed the color red seemed to be everywhere. Red paper lanterns hung over the streets. Red-lacquered wood framed the doorways of the shops and homes. Red ceramic tiles lined the roofs and archways that hung above their heads.

'Is there a significance to the color red?' he asked, as they passed a row of parked rickshaws.

She laughed. 'Well, it doesn't stand for communism, if that's what you think. According to tradition, we attach great meaning to certain colors. Red is associated with the element of fire, and the vermillion bird. It is a symbol of prosperity, so red is a lucky color for us.'

'Vermillion bird?'

'It's a heavenly creature. A spirit bird, whose body is covered by fire.'

'Sounds like a phoenix.'

Jia shrugged. 'As you say.'

They continued walking, and soon the street opened up to a wide lakefront walkway. The surface of the water was dotted with floating lanterns and tiny boats. Rickshaws and bicycles zipped back and forth along the waterfront. Their carriages glowed with twinkling lights and hanging lanterns. The tiny vehicles wheeled through the crowd like nimble fireflies darting through a forest at night.

As Jia led them over an arched stone bridge, a small, wooden boat floated beneath them. It drifted forward on the lazy current. An elderly man sat in the stern, setting glowing paper lanterns afloat in the water. They left a trail of tiny flickering lights in the boat's wake.

They reached the other side of the arch. Caine followed Jia through a series of narrow alleys. The night grew darker and quieter, as the pedestrian crowds thinned out. Caine's senses were alert. These dark, narrow passages would be the perfect spot for an ambush.

Jia stopped in front of a small doorway. A battered old moped leaned against the wall, next to the door. A red sign hung over the building. Most of the writing was Chinese, but Caine could make out two words written in yellow, English letters.

'Hutong Pizza?' Caine read. 'You went all this way for pizza?'

Jia scrunched her nose and laughed. '*Ni zen me le?* You were expecting Peking duck? This is the best pizza in Beijing!'

Caine opened the tiny, chipped red door. 'Well, that I have to try.'

Jia walked past him into the restaurant. Caine turned and scanned the dark, narrow street behind them one last time. A pair of fat white chickens waddled past his feet. Aside from them, the slim stretch of pavement was empty.

He turned and shut the door behind him.

* * *

'Well?' Jia asked. 'What do you think?'

Caine sipped from a small cup of hot tea. Then he swallowed another bite of the greasy rectangular pizza that sat between them. The thin slab of crust was topped with curried chicken, chile peppers, and yoghurt. Despite her petite figure, Jia had managed to clear half the tray of the strange pizza herself.

Caine nodded and cleared his throat. 'It's not going to replace sausage or pepperoni anytime soon. But I have to admit, this is really good.'

The small table they were sitting at was perched on a raised platform. A thin wood railing ran along the edge, covered in the now familiar red paint. Beneath the platform lay a small, rectangular koi pond and a few other tables. Caine watched as several of the white and orange fish swam to one end of the pool. Their gulping mouths broke the surface of the water as they sucked down crumbs that fell from a nearby table.

'You like the koi?' Jia asked.

Caine smiled. 'They just remind of me of someone I know.' He turned back to Jia. 'Your English is perfect. Hong Kong?'

She nodded. Her face looked small and pale in the flickering light of the table's single candle. 'Yes, I grew up there, although I've lived most of my life here in Beijing.'

Caine eyed her in the candle's radiance and tried to guess her age. Her skin was smooth and flawless, and her face had a vibrant, youthful glow. But her confident manner and speaking made her seem older, more mature. He pegged her as early thirties. 'So, you work for the Human Rights Now organization?' he asked.

'Yes. How did you know that?'

'Your hoodie... I noticed it at the protest.' Caine took another bite of pizza, then set the slice down on his plate.

She took a sip of tea and rested her chin on her hands. She gazed at him with her large, luminous eyes. 'That's right, of course. I forgot I was wearing it. But now I have to ask, what were you doing there? You're not a member of HRN, are you?'

Caine shook his head. 'No, I was looking for someone. Another American.' He examined her face as he spoke. 'His name is Sean Tyler.'

Jia's eyes grew even wider, and her lips parted in surprise.

'Sean? You were there for him as well?'

'You know him?'

'I know of him. He was working with HRN, here in China. He was reporting on the conditions in Yanglinggang, Shangba, Xingtai... cancer villages.'

'What do you mean?'

Jia sighed. 'China is the fastest developing major country in history. Hundreds of thousands of people here live in cities that didn't even exist fifty years ago. But that growth comes with a cost.'

'Pollution,' Caine said.

She took another sip of tea. 'Yes. Cancer villages are small towns on the outskirts of factories, manufacturing centers, industrial areas. There are almost no regulations there, and the demand for productivity is high. The corporations have poisoned the rivers and the soil with chemicals and toxic waste. Residents in these towns suffer cancer, birth defects, and other ailments at a rate 80 percent higher than average.'

Her eyes drifted down to the koi pond in the center of the room. 'Nothing will grow in these places anymore. The farmers and field workers have to take jobs in the factories. They must work for the same companies that are slowly killing them.'

'I heard Sean was investigating an industrialist. A man named David Fang.'

A shadow seemed to pass over Jia's face. 'I've heard of him, of course. Fang owns several companies in the chemical and pharmaceutical industries. Rumors say he has ties to the Triads... organized crime.'

'Why was Sean so interested in him?'

'His factories are some of the worst polluters. He has violated what few regulations are in place, but he hides behind shell companies and lawyers. Sean and some HRN volunteers broke into Fang's offices in Shanghai. They were looking for records that would tie Fang to his polluting factories.'

'I take it Sean was caught?'

'Yes, the Ministry of State Security is holding him on espionage charges. I've been working with HRN leaders to secure Sean's release for months. He was being held in Tilanqiao Prison, just outside Shanghai. But a few weeks ago, he was transferred here. When we found out he was moved to that black jail, we organized the protest.'

Caine looked up at her over the rim of his cup as he sipped more tea. 'You almost wound up an inmate there yourself. You take a lot of risks for your work. You must be very brave.'

A shudder ran through her body. She looked away, lowering her eyes. 'I don't feel brave. I feel like I don't do enough. The black jails are an abomination. Many of the people imprisoned in them are elderly, poor. They came to Beijing to petition the capital. They just want to improve the living conditions back in their villages. But this place where Sean is being held is even worse. The people that go in there… no one ever sees them come out.'

She looked up at Caine. 'How did you know Sean was there? How did you even know that place existed? Are you a friend of his?'

Caine thought for a second. He wasn't sure how much he should tell this girl. She could be useful, if he could earn her trust. But he had learned firsthand that those who became involved in his life often ended up in harm's way. And the more they knew about him, the more danger they could be in.

'No, not really,' he answered. 'I knew his father. I promised him I would take care of Sean. I… I didn't do such a great job, I guess.'

She sipped her tea, appearing lost in thought for a minute. Then she looked up at him. 'China's laws are different from yours. You have no legal way to get him released. Until recently, the government denied that such places even existed. If they put him there, it must be for a special purpose. A lawyer cannot help you. And the police will do nothing.'

Caine finished his tea and placed some yuan notes on the table. 'Lawyers and police weren't exactly what I had in mind. Come on, we'd better get you home. Pizza's on me.'

She smiled. '*Xie xie*. Thank you for the food. It's been a long day.'

'Well, it's not over yet,' Caine muttered in a low voice as they walked towards the door.

They stepped out into the cool darkness of night. Outside, the two chickens still wandered in the narrow street. They pecked at the ground in search of scraps.

Caine felt a familiar sensation, a tingling on the back of his neck. He turned to his right and saw two men standing further down the street, tucked into a tiny alcove. One of the shadowy figures brought a lit cigarette to his lips.

Jia turned left and started walking. Caine followed her. 'We can get to a main street this way,' she said. 'We should be able to catch a taxi from there.'

They headed down another narrow, dark alley. Caine heard the faint echo of footsteps behind them. He grabbed the woman's arm. 'Jia, listen to me. When I give the word, we have to separate.' He looked to her right and saw the intersection of another tiny street. It was lined with garbage cans and rows of hanging flower-pots and herb gardens. 'Go down that street there, run as fast as you can. Don't look back.'

'What are you talking about? What about Sean? I want to help you!'

The footsteps were closer now. Caine could smell the smoke on the man's cigarette wafting towards them on the night air.

'We're being followed. In about two minutes, we're going to be attacked. I can handle it, but you need to leave.'

Jia shot a quick glance over her shoulder. 'Them? Why would they be following us?'

'They're the black guards from the protest. You're a target now.'

Jia's face went pale, and her nostrils flared. 'How do you know it's them? How did they find us here?'

'They've been following us since we left the protest. I spotted them on the way here. I've been watching them since before dinner.'

An angry scowl filled her face, and her cheeks flushed red. 'They've been after us the whole time? And you didn't say anything? You used me as bait?'

Caine shot a quick glance back, over his shoulder. 'I didn't want to scare you. And I didn't want to tip them off.'

'But what will you do?' A note of concern crept into her voice.

'I'm going to get some answers about Sean. One of them is going to give them to me.'

'Are you crazy?' she hissed. 'There's two of them!'

Caine pushed Jia to the side and spun around. The two men were about twenty feet behind them.

The one in the lead dropped his cigarette and smiled. In the dim light, Caine could just make out his features. It was Mole Face.

The man sneered and slipped a knife from his rear pocket. With a snap of his wrist, he flicked the weapon open. The long steel blade glinted in the moonlight.

He uttered a bloodthirsty scream and charged towards Caine.

11

Caine stepped back and raised his fists as the men charged him. From the corner of his eye, he saw Jia back into the shadows of the alley. Then the men were upon him.

Caine focused on the leader, the man with the knife. He twisted his body, avoiding the attacker's opening slash. He countered with a right hook. As the blow connected, he levered his right forearm into the man's windpipe. His free hand grabbed his target's outstretched knife arm and held it at bay.

The maneuver left his back to the other guard. He sensed the other man closing in behind him. Pivoting on his right foot, he used his forearm to push the knife-wielding guard around in a circle. He stacked the man's body between the other attacker and himself.

Caine released his hold on the guard and launched a powerful forward kick. The blow knocked the man into the other attacker. The two men slammed into the stone wall of the alley.

Caine slipped his hand into his jacket pocket and removed the stun gun he had taken from the protest.

The men rebounded from the wall and lurched forward in

tandem. Caine ducked, letting Mole Face's knife swing over his head. The other man leapt forward, driving his knee up towards Caine's face. Caine crossed his arms and threw his weight forward. His forearms blocked the knee strike, and the top of his head slammed into his attacker's neck. He looped his arm around the man's forward knee and yanked up.

The guard hopped backwards, struggling to regain his balance. Caine let go of the leg and thumbed the trigger of his stun gun. The crackle of electricity hummed through the air. He drove the sparking weapon into a nerve cluster on the man's inner thigh.

The guard spasmed and fell to the ground. Caine delivered a swift kick to his face. The man's head snapped sideways and he lay still.

Caine spun around as Mole Face moved to attack again. The man thrust with the knife, a quick jab at Caine's left side. Caine turned his body, but the attacker diverted the blade mid-strike... It was a feint! He slashed downwards, and Caine felt the blade graze the back of his hand. He winced, and his fingers flexed in pain. The stun gun fell to the ground. The black guard kicked it, sending it clattering across the stone alley.

Caine pressed forward, using his right arm to block the man's knife attacks. He drove a left-handed palm strike into his attacker's nose. The man's head snapped back. He stepped away and raised the knife above his head. Caine's right arm shot up as the man drove the blade down in an overhead stab.

The impact of Caine's forearm knocked the knife strike wide. Caine reached out with his left hand, grasped the man's neck, and pulled his head down. He drove his knee up, pummeling the guard with a series of strikes to the solar plexus. Then, he grabbed the man's wrist and snapped it over his knee. The knife clattered to the ground.

Caine spun his attacker around and slammed him forward into the brick wall. The man struck the hard surface with a loud crack. Caine pulled him back and saw a spatter of blood on the dark gray bricks.

Blood gushed from the black guard's crushed nose. Caine clutched the fabric of the man's shirt in his hands and slammed him forward again. This time the man groaned and fell to the ground.

Straddling his body, Caine wrapped his forearm around the man's windpipe. He jerked upwards, pulling the chokehold tighter with his other hand. The guard began to kick and spasm as the pressure of Caine's forearm cut off the supply of oxygen to his brain. Caine pulled even tighter.

Caine struggled to maintain the sleeper hold on the spasming man. He heard rapid footsteps rushing towards him. A woman's voice called out, echoing through the alley.

'Look out!'

Caine turned his head. The other attacker had regained consciousness. He loomed over Caine, wielding the discarded stun gun. With a grin, he depressed the trigger. Crackling blue sparks leapt from the diodes at the weapon's tip.

Beneath Caine, Mole Face continued to thrash and kick, but his movements grew weaker. *Just one more second*, Caine thought.

As the second man took a step towards him, Caine saw Jia charge up behind him, swinging something over her head.

It was one of the hanging flowerpots, from the gardens down the street! The pot exploded into ceramic shards as it crashed into the man's skull.

Caine watched as the man's eyes rolled back in his head. He took a step forward, then tumbled to the ground. Jia stood behind him. She clutched the frayed ropes of the shattered pot in her small, trembling fist.

The man in Caine's chokehold stopped moving. Caine released his arm and let the body slump to the ground. He staggered to his feet, cupping his wounded hand. 'I told you to leave.'

'You also said you could handle it! *Zhu weishou de sha gua!*'

'What does that mean?'

She shook her head. 'Never mind. Now what? Are they dead?'

Caine shook his head. 'If they are, this was a huge waste of time.'

He put his hand on the girl's shoulder. 'Jia, I appreciate your help. But things are only going to get worse from this point. It's better for you if you don't get involved.'

'I'm already involved. Like you said, I take risks every day. If you are going to free Sean, if I can help him, or the other people trapped in that place... I have no choice. I must do whatever I can.'

'I thought you said you didn't even know him?'

'I know he is here to help the people of China. How can I do less?'

Caine nodded. 'All right. We can't just leave a body here. Looks like we take both of them.'

'Take them where?'

'You have an apartment in the city?'

'I'm staying with a friend, but they are out of town.'

'That will have to do.' He hefted the smaller of the two men onto Jia's shoulder, draping his limp arm around her neck. The petite woman was surprisingly strong. She managed to support the man's weight as Caine handed her the stun gun.

'Here. If he moves, let go, and hit him with this. Make sure you're not touching him, or you'll get shocked too.'

She nodded as Caine lifted the other body off the ground.

'You know, this isn't what I was expecting when you asked me to dinner,' she said with a nervous laugh.

Caine examined her small, round face. He couldn't tell if she was joking or not. He shrugged and they shuffled down the alley, carrying the dead weight of the two guards.

'I didn't ask you to dinner,' he replied. 'I said you should eat. I thought you were in shock.'

'Oh, please. *Zhu weishou de sha gua!*'

'You said that before. What does it mean?'

She shot him a sideways glance, and her pink lips turned up in a smile. 'I'll tell you later.'

'I can hardly wait,' Caine grunted, as he hefted the weight of the guard on his shoulder.

12

Rebecca clenched her teeth and grunted with exertion.

Beads of sweat dripped down her face, and dark pools of perspiration stained her T-shirt. The soaking fabric clung to her body like the partially shed skin of a snake.

Her arms trembled and shook. She knew she couldn't support her weight much longer. Her fingers were wrapped around two parallel bars. The exercise equipment ran along the south wall of her sleek, modern condo. She had installed it against the wishes of her doctors. 'You need to take this slow,' they had said to her. 'You've got to be patient.'

Rebecca was *not* patient.

The room was dark, lit only by a thin sliver of morning sun that cut through the long curtains. She could hear the distant rumble of engines and honking horns outside. The muted sounds were barely audible beneath the soft electronic music that played over the speakers in the ceiling.

'Volume up,' she said. The digital assistant that controlled the lights and sound system complied. The music increased in volume, drowning out the traffic noise. She closed her eyes and let the percussive beat wash over her. She took a deep breath.

Move, damn you! her mind shouted, but her body did not even twitch. She willed her left leg to step forward. An inch... half an inch. Anything.

The quivering in her arms increased. They were shaking harder, and the wooden bars began to rattle and vibrate.

No, damn it! No, move! Move! Mo—

Rebecca cursed as she felt her muscles turn to jelly. Her left arm buckled and gave out. She tried to pivot as she fell, but her muscles throbbed with fatigue and were slow to react. The side of her face struck the polished concrete floor with a loud crack.

She lay on the ground for a few seconds, catching her breath. She willed herself not to cry, not to give up. Not to lose hope.

No one learns to walk without falling, she reminded herself. *You want to learn again? You have to fall again. As many times as it takes.*

Her anger and frustration subsided, and her panting breath slowed to a normal pace. Using her hands, she rotated her body on the smooth floor and crawled back to the other end of the bars.

Her wheelchair was waiting there for her. She stopped moving and stared up at it for a few seconds. Her eyes gleamed with rage and fire. But then the fire inside her seemed to dim, as if it had run out of fuel to burn.

She grabbed one of the bars and pulled her body up off the floor. She spun around, shifting her hands from bar to bar, until her back was to the chair. Then she lowered herself down into a sitting position.

'Open curtains,' she said in a loud, clear voice.

'Opening curtains,' the feminine electronic voice replied. The thick curtains slid open, allowing warm sunlight to flood the room. The condo's sparkling white floors and metal appliances gleamed with reflected brilliance.

Rebecca turned and looked at a clock mounted to the wall. It was just past 9:00 a.m. She was almost done with her workout.

No. You're not done, she thought. *You're just getting started. You need to get stronger.*

The chair was equipped with an electric motor, but she had turned it off for her workout. Slim cords of muscles in her arms and shoulders rippled as she wheeled herself towards her new home gym.

She maneuvered herself underneath a lat pulldown bar. She adjusted the weight stack, increasing it by ten pounds from its last position. Then she reached up, ignoring the pain in her back and shoulders. She gripped the bar and began to pull it down to her chest.

One... two... three... New trails of sweat dripped down her face as she continued to exert herself. Spasms of pain shot through her arms, but she ignored them.

Four... five... six...

She pushed herself harder. She would not stop. She would keep going as long as it took.

She was a runner. She could go the distance.

The music dipped in volume, and she heard her cell phone ring from across the room.

'Incoming call,' the electronic voice chimed over the speakers. 'Unknown number.'

Rebecca let go of the lat bar. It shot up and clanked back into position, swaying in the air above her.

She gasped for breath. She knew she was pushing herself, but she hadn't realized how far she had gone... how long she had been exerting her body. Her muscles flared with pain as she wheeled over to the nightstand to pick up her phone.

She recognized the ring tone. It was assigned to only one person, and if he was calling, it had to be important.

She gulped some water from a bottle on the nightstand, then answered the phone.

'Hello?'

'It's me,' said the voice on the other end.

Caine.

'How do you like Eastern Europe?' she asked. 'Did you visit that coffee shop I told you about?'

'The Coffee Tower? It was nice, but the line was too long. I went to Miit Coffee instead. Better espresso.'

'But not as nice a view,' she answered.

The code phrase confirmed he was not speaking under duress.

'I expected to hear from you by now.' She felt her pulse quicken. She thought about Bernatto and the last time she had seen him, at an abandoned chemical plant in Thailand. He was with his hired killer, a sociopath who had kidnapped her, who had nearly killed her. She had escaped. There was a gunfight. An explosion.

She had been injured. Her spine... her legs... They were responsible for—

She forced herself to calm down.

They could have killed you, she reminded herself. *You're still alive. And at least one of them is dead.*

'There's been a change of plans,' Caine said. 'Things are... complicated.'

'Have you made contact with the target?'

'Yes.'

'Then why haven't you delivered him to the rendition team?'

Caine was silent. A quiet hum buzzed on the line.

'Tom, what's going on? Where is Bernatto?'

'I let him go.'

'You what?' She spat the words into the phone. 'What the hell are you talking about?'

'Rebecca, something came up. New intel. I had to.'

'I... I don't even know what to say. You told me you wanted to work with me, you wanted to do this freelance, on your own. And I let you do it on your terms, despite my better judgment.'

'Rebecca—'

'I'm telling the team to move in. I'm taking this operation out of your hands.'

'He's not in Latvia anymore. I told you, I let him go.'

'Where the hell is he, Tom?' she snapped.

'I don't know,' he said. 'I found him once. I can find him again. This couldn't wait.'

'What couldn't wait? What intel was so important that it's worth letting a monster like Allan Bernatto go free? You of all people... you know what this man did! You know what he did to you, what he did to—' She paused. 'What he did to this country,' she finished.

'Sean Tyler. Jack Tyler's son.'

'Wait, what?' Rebecca's brain whirled in circles. 'What about Sean?'

'He's being held in China. He's part of a human rights organization, protestors.'

'What does that have to do with...'

'You knew, didn't you?'

Rebecca bit her lip and moved over to the window. She looked down at the verdant green trees surrounding the Logan traffic circle. She felt the need to move. To run.

'Yes, I knew. It came up in an intelligence briefing. But I don't see how—'

'Why didn't you tell me?' Caine interrupted.

'You have to ask? It's classified, Tom!'

'That's a load of crap.'

'Look, I offered to bring you in. I offered to clear your record, debrief you with the higher-ups. I offered you your life back, but you wanted to stay on the outside. I guess I can understand that after what you've been through. But just because we have a history, that doesn't mean I can break confidence and share restricted information with you whenever it's convenient.'

Caine was silent.

A thought flashed through Rebecca's mind.

'Tom, where are you?'

'I'm where I belong. On the outside.'

'You're in China, aren't you? What are you planning to do?'

'The PRC want to trade Sean for a renditioned asset in your possession. A Chinese hacker named Sun Wai Tong?'

'How do you know that?'

'So my intel is good. Well, at least I know where I stand.' His voice was terse, cold.

'Tom, let me handle it. I know how close you and Jack were, I know he was important to you. I knew you'd react to this emotionally. I've got the situation under control.'

'Not according to my intel. Sean is in danger. You know a guy named Lapinski? NSA?'

Rebecca felt her sore muscles tense. She remembered Ted's reaction during the intelligence briefing. 'Yes, I know him. He's head of S32.'

Caine's voice crackled on the other end of the phone. 'Tailored Ops. The blackest of the black hats. Tong is in their custody, isn't he?'

Rebecca thought for a moment. 'Yes. But what would TAO want with Sean?'

'It's not Sean. It's Tong. He accessed and released classified intel into the wild. The NSA can't afford to cut Tong loose until they locate and contain the data. Lapinski has an asset in China, I don't know who. Someone in their intelligence apparatus. An assassin... Code name is Red Phoenix. They're going to kill Sean to sabotage the exchange.'

'That's crazy. The president approved all of this, the exchange is going to happen. It's tied to his whole Global Environmental Accords, and the trade deal with China. Lapinski isn't going to stand in the way of that. And where is this intel coming from? Bernatto?'

Caine didn't answer.

'You don't trust me, but you trust him?' Rebecca asked in a quiet voice.

'You know I don't trust him,' Caine snapped. 'But his intel checks out so far. I've verified that Sean is in China. You just confirmed the rest. There's an exchange deal in place, and Lapinski is involved.'

'So you *are* in China,' Rebecca said.

Caine laughed, a soft chuckle. 'Very good. You're getting better at this.'

'I'm not sure that's a compliment. What are you going to do?'

She heard Caine take a deep breath. 'Jack saved my life. I watched him die, saw him bleed out right in front of me. With his dying breath, he asked me to take care of Sean. I promised him, Rebecca. And I broke that promise. I got so caught up in... everything, all the rest of this shit. I never even gave it a second thought.'

'Tom, what you went through, with Bernatto... I still don't know everything. But I know you were tortured. I know you endured things most people couldn't survive. You can't blame yourself. You did the best you could.'

'No, I didn't. But now, if there's even a chance Bernatto's intel is accurate… Look, it's better you don't know.'

'Well. You really don't trust me.'

'When this goes down, you're going to need deniability.'

Rebecca knew it was pointless to ask him again. He would never tell her. 'Let me do some digging on Lapinski. I'll see if I can verify this asset you're talking about. Can you at least sit tight until then?'

'No. I can't. But I'd appreciate the help.'

She sighed. 'How will I contact you?'

'I'll be in touch. And listen. These Tailored Ops guys, they're more dangerous than you think. Data is their lifeblood. They feed off it, and they'll do anything to protect it. You know what their motto is?'

Rebecca repeated the words from memory. 'Your data is our data. Your equipment is our equipment – anytime, anyplace, by any legal means.'

A note of concern softened Caine's voice over the phone. 'I don't think they put too much emphasis on the "legal" part. Be careful.'

'I will.'

She was about to hang up, but Caine spoke again. 'Rebecca?'

'Yes?'

'I called you because I *do* trust you. I only trust you. You're all I've got.'

'I… I'm sorry,' she stammered.

'No. I'm sorry. And I promise you, after this is over, when Sean is safe… the bastard dies.'

There was a click and he was gone.

* * *

Caine hung up the phone and brushed aside the curtain. Outside the spacious loft apartment, the night sky was dark and the air was thick with humidity. He looked down at the shadowed forms of the other buildings nearby, a cluster of gray concrete slabs. An array of neon signs and billboards topped each tower. Fourteen-foot-tall Chinese characters blinked on and off, lighting the hazy air with a soft, indistinct glow.

As he slid the phone in his pocket, he thought about Rebecca. It had been good to hear her voice, but he still felt a hollowness, an emptiness in his gut when he spoke to her. A longing.

Ever since his betrayal at the hands of Bernatto and the CIA, Caine had lived a life of detachment... On the run, always hiding, no close friends. No one who could be used against him.

Now, he found it difficult to let go of that life. Somehow, he was still adrift. He could not reattach.

He wondered if it was fear that held him back. Fear of what might happen to him. Or fear of what might happen to her?

No, said the voice in his head. The one he could never silence. *Not fear. Guilt.*

He remembered the last time he had seen her. The scars and wounds on her legs.

The chair.

He slid the curtain closed. Whatever it was he felt, fear or guilt, longing or isolation, it didn't matter. What he and Rebecca had shared, what they had given and what they had lost... That was in the past now. These days, they were both just voices on the phone. That slim, faint connection was all he had, all that kept him from sinking into the bleak shadows of memory.

Jia's rustling pulled him from his melancholy thoughts. He turned and watched as she laid out the sheets of paper beneath a soft circle of light cast over the dining table's surface. Caine walked over and stood beside her as she taped the sheets together.

'You found a map,' he said.

She turned and smiled. Her mischievous eyes twinkled in the dim light.

'Human Rights Now works with many other activist groups. We have a good relationship with a collective in Shanghai known as the Jade Enclave. They are, mmm, how should I put it? Skilled computer technicians.'

'Jade Enclave? Sound like hackers to me,' Caine replied with a sideways smile.

'They prefer the term "hacktivists,"' she said. 'They help us spread information, plan protests. And they warn us of government surveillance. They take great risks for us.'

Caine leaned over the table. 'Well, looks like your friends came through.'

He slid the map closer and began scanning the architectural details. He mentally noted the placement of doors, stairwells, emergency exits... anything that his experience told him might be useful in an extraction.

'This building was once a hospital, years ago,' Jia said. 'Then it was purchased by a private security contractor for use as a black jail facility. They may have made changes to the structure, I can't be sure—'

'This is the best we're going to get,' Caine said, snatching the map off the table and rolling it up in his hands. 'Every second we wait, Sean is in danger. I'm going to need our guests to point out his location. You should wait here.'

Caine walked out of the room and turned down a narrow hallway. Jia hurried after him. '*Deng yi xia*, wait! What are you going to do?'

Caine ignored her, opening the door to a gleaming modern

bathroom. The two black guards lay struggling in the massive white tub. They were bound and gagged. Their bruised faces and tattered clothes were a strange contrast to the pristine white tiles of the bathroom. Mole Face turned his head and glared with hatred at Caine as he entered the room.

Jia stopped at the door. Her eyes darted from the men to Caine. 'Tom, these men are monsters, I know. But I can't just stand by and watch you torture them. That's not who I am.'

Caine turned and glared at her. 'I know,' he said. His voice had a metallic echo in the small tiled room. 'That's why I told you to wait outside.'

He reached over the tub and turned on the water. The men continued to grunt and struggle. The water splashed onto their clothes and began to fill the basin. He spread the makeshift map out on the floor.

'Just stop! Think for a second,' she said, her voice tinged with concern. 'You don't even speak Chinese, how will they understand—'

'They'll get the gist of it.'

Caine slammed the door shut, blocking out Jia's words and her wide, staring eyes. The outside world no longer existed.

He allowed himself to sink, to fall into the bleak shadows.

You're not falling, the voice inside him said. *You're just letting go.*

13

Caine winced as the old white van bounced over a pothole in the crumbling city streets. He was lying in the back, under a filthy moving blanket that stank of sweat and old food. Every bounce and shudder of the van's suspension rattled through his bones. The impacts sent tremors of aching pain through his body.

He lifted a corner of the blanket. Even in the dim light of early morning he had to squint his eyes. After a second or two, they adjusted to the harsh glow outside the windows of the battered van. He prodded the flimsy upholstery of the driver's seat with the barrel of a Chinese Number 5 revolver. He felt Mole Face shift in the seat as he guided the van around a corner.

'Tell him to take it easy,' Caine muttered in a low voice.

Jia sat in the passenger seat. She angled her body to put as much distance between herself and the driver as possible. Her eyes darted between Caine's face and the gun in his hands. She gave him a pensive frown, then turned to the driver.

'*Jian su*,' she snapped in a harsh voice. 'Slow down.'

'*Hao ba*, all right,' the driver muttered. Mole Face glanced back at Caine then returned his eyes to the road. For that brief second, Caine saw a familiar expression on the man's face.

Fear.

Good, he thought. *That means he still wants to get out of this alive.*

The van slowed as they approached the grounds of the old hospital.

Ironic, Caine thought. *A building devoted to healing now serves as a black jail for the city's lost and disenfranchised.* Peering out from under the blanket, Caine looked through the front windshield. He saw the gray, desolate structure looming ahead of them.

The other black guard was still bound and gagged back at the apartment. After confirming the location where Sean was being held, Mole Face had led them to the van. He and his partner had left it parked outside the *hutong* the night before.

A quick search of the vehicle revealed the tools of the black guard's trade: some plastic zip cuffs, a mangy black hood, and the revolver, all stashed in the glove compartment. The serial numbers on the gun's frame were filed off. Caine guessed the weapon was stolen from a police officer, or confiscated from a crime scene.

A rapid-fire series of doubts began to flash through his mind. What if the other guard escaped, or was discovered back at the apartment? What if Mole Face betrayed them to the guards? What if there was a signal, some code or passphrase he didn't know about?

And Jia. What about her?

All of his instincts screamed that bringing her on this mission was foolish. A civilian, a humanitarian, a woman he barely knew... But the simple truth was, he needed her, at least for now. His Chinese wasn't good enough to monitor Mole Face. He

needed someone to alert him if the man tried to warn the guards
at the gate.

You're doing what you always do, he thought. *You're putting her
in harm's way and justifying it to yourself.*

He took a deep breath. *Enough.* There were a million things
that could go wrong, but it was too late for doubt. They were
approaching the gate. Once they were through, there was no
turning back.

'Jia,' Caine said. 'I need you to translate. Tell him you'll be
listening. If we're not through this gate in fifteen seconds, I start
shooting. Whatever happens to us, he dies first.'

'Tom, I—'

'Tell him!'

Jia hesitated, then rattled off the words to Mole Face. A shiver
ran through the man's body. He nodded and answered back.

'He understands,' Jia said.

'All right. Follow my lead. If anything goes wrong, take cover
back here as fast as you can.'

Jia looped her hands through a set of the guard's plastic cuffs
and brought the tab to her teeth. She pulled them tight but left
just enough slack to allow her to slip free if needed. Then she
slumped down in the seat and let her body go limp. She
appeared unconscious.

Caine ducked under the blanket and lay still on the floor. He
kept the barrel of the revolver pressed firmly into the back of the
driver's seat.

The van slowed to a stop. Caine was engulfed in the darkness
under the blanket. He could hear a tapping sound as the guard
rapped on the window with his baton. Mole Face rolled the
window rolled down. The men spoke to each other in rapid
Chinese.

Caine had no idea what they were saying, but his muscles

tensed. Mole Face's voice cracked. The man sounded nervous. He began to stutter. Caine pressed the pistol forward deeper into the seat.

The guard laughed. 'Crazy *lan zui*!' The man spoke a few more sentences, then Caine heard the metal clank of the gate opening. The van lurched and began to crawl forward. He remained still, his senses on fire. His fingers flexed, grasping the butt of the pistol tighter.

He heard Jia's voice. 'These men are disgusting pigs. The guard asked about his partner, then said... things about me. But we're past the gate, heading into the garage. I don't see anyone...'

Caine flipped up the blanket and sat up. Peering out the front windshield, he watched as they pulled into a dark, cavernous garage. A few other vans and service vehicles were parked in random spots throughout the space. Puddles of spilled engine oil stained the concrete floor. They shimmered a reddish-black in the dim light, like crusts of dried blood over a wound.

The van came to a stop.

'There's one guard, in uniform,' Jia whispered. 'I see him... He's walking this way.' There was a quiver of fear in her voice.

'Tell our friend to call him over,' Caine said.

'What? Are you crazy... What if he sees you?'

'He won't.'

Caine cracked open the rear door of the van and crouched. Jia whispered to the man.

Caine aimed the revolver at Mole Face and cocked the hammer back. The metal click echoed through the van. 'Do it.'

The man rolled down the driver's side window. '*Hei, guo lai*!' he shouted, waving his hand. 'Come here a sec!'

The guard ambled over. Caine could smell the faint odor of cigarette smoke drifting through the air as the man got closer.

'*Ni xiang yao shen me*?' the guard asked. 'Don't tell me the van has another leak?'

As the guard approached the window, Caine slipped out the rear door of the van and dropped to the ground. His movements were quick and silent. He scanned the garage, looking for any signs they had been noticed. If another guard entered the area, at this particular moment...

He saw nothing. There was only the lone guard.

The man looked in the window, leering at Jia. 'Well, well, *zhei shi shui de*? Who's this then?'

Caine crept up behind the guard, using his thumb to lower the hammer on his revolver. As he approached the man, he saw Mole Face's eyes track his movement. His mouth opened and his eyes hardened. Caine processed all this in less than a second, but he knew exactly what their prisoner was going to do.

He was going to try to warn the guard.

The uniformed man stiffened as he caught the strange, determined look in Mole Face's eyes. He straightened up and began to turn around. But he was too late.

Caine swung the butt of the revolver down, striking the guard's skull. As the man staggered from the impact, Caine grabbed the back of his head. He slammed the guard's face into the doorframe of the van.

The man uttered a brief, guttural snarl of pain. Before he could make any more noise, Caine looped his right forearm around the man's throat and squeezed down, choking him. He struggled at first, but his thrashing soon slowed to a lethargic pace.

Caine looked over the guard's shoulder and saw Mole Face twisting in his seat. He heard the click of the driver's side door opening.

Caine held out his left arm, still grasping the bloodied

revolver. Mole Face looked up and saw the gun's barrel aimed directly at his face.

'Don't,' Caine said, his voice a harsh rasp from exertion.

The man froze.

Keeping his gun aimed at Mole Face, Caine lowered the unconscious guard to the ground. He watched as Jia slipped a hood over Mole Face's head, then zip-tied his arm to the steering wheel.

Caine dragged the guard to the back of the van and pulled him inside. Working quickly, he unzipped the man's jumpsuit before striping off his own clothes.

Jia's eyes traveled over the hard lines of Caine's lean, muscular torso. His body was decorated with a series of lines and ridges... a dark mosaic of scars, left behind by long-forgotten wounds. One scar stood out from the others, a small circular patch of pale white skin, just below his shoulder.

'What on earth happened to you?' she asked.

'Kind of a long story,' Caine grunted as he slipped into the guard's uniform. It was a tight fit, but he managed to tug the zipper closed. He grabbed the man's cap and put it on, pulling the brim down low to cover as much of his face as possible. He glanced over at Jia. 'I'm here to help. That's all I can say. The less you know about me, the better. Do you trust me?'

Jia nodded. 'Perhaps I shouldn't. But I do.'

'Good. Now cut him loose.'

Jia removed a pair of wire cutters from the glovebox and cut the zip ties that bound Mole Face.

Caine walked over to the driver's side of the van, brandishing his revolver. He opened the door, grabbed Mole Face, and yanked him out of his seat. As the hostage stumbled to the ground, Jia slid over into the driver's position. She looked down at Caine and bit her lip.

'What if you need my help? You don't speak Chinese, what if—'

'I'm not going to be doing any talking. And no offense, but I'll be faster on my own. Wait here and keep your head down. If anyone sees you, or if someone starts checking out the van, haul ass. Just go, ram through the gate if you have to.'

Caine fastened new zip cuffs around the black guard's wrists. He turned the man around and bound his hands behind his back.

Jia brushed a long strand of hair from her face and looked down at him from the driver's seat. 'You sound like you've done this before.'

'Not exactly this, no. But I've been in similar situations.'

'What the hell is similar to this?'

Caine looked her in the eye as he pulled the zip cuffs tighter. 'If I'm not back in fifteen minutes, things didn't work out. If that happens, you have to bail. Get as far away from here as you can, ditch the van, and run. Don't go back to your friend's apartment. Leave Beijing. Got it?'

She nodded.

Caine jabbed the revolver into Mole Face's back. The man shuffled a few steps forward. Caine stopped and looked over his shoulder. Jia stared back at him, eyes wide with fear.

'And Jia... thank you.'

'You want to thank me? Be back here in fourteen minutes.'

Caine nodded and gave her a reassuring smile. 'I will.'

He turned and prodded Mole Face with the gun. 'Let's go,' he hissed. He tilted his head down, and the two men made their way across the garage into the shadows.

14

The hallways inside the black jail complex were long, narrow, and dark. Fluorescent lights flickered overhead, bathing the peeling white walls in a sickly, dim glow. Many of the bulbs were broken, and glass shards glittered among the piles of dust and refuse lining the corridors.

As Caine and Mole Face moved forward, they passed several supply rooms and medical offices. The doors were all fitted with key card locks. The cleanliness of the electronic hardware indicated the locks were a new addition to the building. Probably installed after the facility had been repurposed as a detention center, Caine assumed.

They came to a T-intersection, and Caine turned right. He had memorized the blueprints of the hospital provided by Jia's hacker friends. He couldn't read the signs on the walls, but he knew they were heading in the right direction.

As they walked down the new hall, Caine spotted a security camera. It hung in the northwest corner, and its smoked dome lens rotated towards him. He kept his head turned down and pulled Mole Face in close to block his face from view.

'Stairs,' Caine said in a low voice. 'To your left.' Caine knew Mole Face spoke just enough English to understand the simple directions. He pivoted the man left and swung open a gray metal door. His captive stumbled down the dark, narrow stairwell. Caine followed close behind. Their footsteps echoed in the darkness as they descended to the basement.

They emerged into another hall. After the pitch-black of the stairwell, the dim fluorescent lights seemed white-hot. Caine blinked as his eyes adjusted to the light. He gave Mole Face a shove, and they continued marching forward.

The passage was narrow, lined with industrial pipes and valves. Caine heard men laughing up ahead. He pushed Mole Face forward past an open doorway. Next to the door, an old, dented fire extinguisher hung lopsided from a broken bracket on the wall.

As they moved past the open door, he saw two more guards inside. They were smoking cigarettes and playing a game of cards. One of the men laughed and blew a cloud of smoke from the corner of his mouth.

'*Ma de ka!*' he shouted, throwing his cards down on the small table that sat between them. 'What a shit hand!'

The men didn't even look up as Caine marched past the room. He breathed a sigh of relief.

'Up ahead, left turn,' he muttered, tightening his grip on Mole Face's shoulder. They turned and moved down another dark, narrow corridor in the cramped basement.

They came to a large door, this one painted a shocking bright yellow. Caine couldn't read the sign, but there was no mistaking the lightning bolts and other warning symbols painted on the door.

This was the right place.

He pulled on the door's handle, but the giant yellow slab

wouldn't budge. It was locked. Caine fished in his pocket and removed Mole Face's key ring. Jingling through the keys, he tried them one by one. Finally, he heard a click as the deadbolt cleared the lock. He swung the door open and pushed his captive inside.

The door shut behind him with a loud thunk. He kicked Mole Face forward, knocking him to the concrete floor. The man grunted in pain as he struck the hard surface.

'Don't move!' Caine growled.

His eyes scanned the room. Three tall metal cabinets surrounded him, one on each wall. An array of thick wires and pipes ran into each cabinet. A symbol decorated the face of each metal door. It was a yellow triangle surrounding a black lightning bolt. The international symbol for high voltage power lines.

Caine checked his watch. Five minutes had elapsed since he had left Jia in the garage.

Ten minutes to get upstairs, get Sean, and get back to the garage, he thought.

Assuming the guard had told the truth about his location...

Caine took a deep breath. He would find out soon enough.

He slipped the stun gun he had confiscated into his hand. Stepping over the groaning body on the floor, he threw open the doors of each cabinet. Rows of industrial circuit breakers were mounted inside each metal box.

He triggered the stun gun. The weapon crackled and popped as blue sparks leapt from the tip. He ran the sparking weapon across the first set of breakers. The metal switches popped and hissed. The sudden influx of electricity fried the delicate copper wiring inside each breaker.

The lights in the room flickered and dimmed, then went dark. A harsh electronic siren squawked to life and echoed through the hallway outside.

Caine's mouth twisted into a grim smile. He triggered the

weapon again and proceeded to fry the remaining sets of breakers. A shower of glowing sparks illuminated the room for a few
brief seconds. Then darkness settled over them once again.

Caine grabbed his hostage from the floor. 'Next stop,' he
muttered as he led the man out into the hall. Outside, the halls
were dark, but not pitch-black. The power outage had triggered
the building's backup generators. Spinning red emergency lights
cast rotating pools of crimson across the walls and floor.

He pushed Mole Face back the way they had come. Up
ahead, he heard frantic shouting, just audible above the
squawking siren. They were approaching the room with the two
guards.

Caine triggered the stun gun once more, jabbing it into Mole
Face's back. The man jerked and stumbled as the voltage coursed
through his body. Caine threw him forward and he flew past the
doorway, just as the first guard was exiting. The guard turned to
look as the body fell past him. As he looked away, Caine pressed
the trigger on the weapon again.

Nothing happened.

Damn, he thought. *Battery must have discharged.*

He wanted to avoid a gunfight for as long as possible. The
sound of gunshots would carry even over the siren.

The guard rushed over and knelt down next to Mole Face. He
ripped the hood off the twitching man.

'*Gau shen me gui*? Hey, I know this guy. He works here!'

He turned and looked up, his eyes wide as Caine charged
towards him. Caine tore the fire extinguisher off the wall as he
lunged at the guard.

The uniformed man leapt to his feet. '*Rhu qin zhe!*' he yelled.
'Intruder! Who the hell are—'

Caine swung the metal cylinder in a sweeping arc. The blow
struck the guard across the chin before he could finish his warn-

ing. The force of the impact spun the man around and he dropped to the floor like a stone.

Caine whirled around to face the second guard just as he exited the room. The man saw his partner slumped on the ground and drew his revolver from its holster.

He raised the pistol towards Caine, but he was too slow. Caine slammed the bottom of the extinguisher into the advancing man's face. The blow struck with a dull, echoing thud. As his target stumbled backwards, Caine jabbed again. This time he used both hands to power the canister into the man's gut. The guard bent forward from the impact, gasping for breath.

Caine took aim and depressed the handle of the extinguisher. A burst of white chemical smoke whooshed from the nozzle, blasting the dazed guard in the face. He stumbled backwards through the door. The extinguisher filled the small room around him with an impenetrable haze. Caine could hear the man coughing and wheezing within the thick cloud.

Holding his breath, Caine stepped into the room. Grabbing the top of the extinguisher with both hands, he swung it like a baseball bat. A metallic clang rang out as it connected with the coughing guard's head. The man went silent, dropping to the floor.

Caine pivoted to his right. He slammed the extinguisher down on the knob of the open door. The heavy metal canister battered the knob clean off the lock assembly. Caine kicked it outside and left the room, slamming the door shut behind him.

He dropped the empty fire extinguisher, letting it clatter to the floor next to the unconscious bodies of Mole Face and the guard. Then he advanced towards the stairs. He checked his watch.

Six minutes to go...

* * *

Sean Tyler crouched next to the door of the small concrete room. He put his ear to the door and heard faint noises above the screeching siren that echoed through the complex. Gunfire, glass breaking, screams and shouts. The lights in the room had gone out, and there were no windows. His face was lit by flashes of red light, bursting from the crack under the door.

Alton paced back and forth on the other side of the room. 'This is bad, no good! Dangerous out there!'

Sean reached up and gripped the door lever. 'It's dangerous in here too. You know better than anyone, people don't leave here. They come in, and they disappear.'

'But not you! Some big shot from Ministry of Security comes to see you. Moves you to private room, moves me in here too... Who are you? Why you so special?'

The young man shrugged. 'I dunno, I just thought it was 'cause I was American.'

Alton Lung shook his head and ran a hand through his tuft of black hair. 'Typical. Trust me, they want you for something. Something special. Otherwise, they just leave you in Tilanqiao Prison.'

'All I know is, I have to get out of here,' Sean said. 'There's something I have to do. You can stay here if you want. Maybe that's safer.'

Sean pulled the lever. It clicked open. The door was no longer locked.

Alton stopped pacing and sighed. 'Screw that! I go with you. Maybe your luck rub off on me.'

Sean shook his head. 'I'm under arrest for industrial espionage. I'm locked up in a secret jail that no one knows exists. And I'm about to walk into a prison riot. You call that luck?'

Alton smiled. 'Could be worse.'

'Man, I hope not. Okay, we go on three. You ready?'

Alton wiped his glasses on his shirt, then set them back onto his face. He nodded.

Sean tightened his grip on the door. 'Okay, one... two... three!'

He opened the door and stepped into the hall.

The wail of the siren was even louder outside. A few other doors along the corridor hung open. Several of the older inmates shuffled back and forth in a confused daze. Sean saw a stooped, elderly man look up at the flashing emergency lights and shake his head. The man slinked back into one of the rooms and shut the door behind him.

'Kind of quiet up here,' Sean said.

'They keep most inmates on first floor,' Alton hissed behind him. 'You one of the special ones they move up here!'

A long panel of square windows ran along the right side of the corridor, overlooking the first floor. Crashing furniture and shattering glass rang out from below. The angry shouts of guards rose above the chaos. Sean jogged over to the windows and looked down. A throng of prisoners surged through the double doors of the cafeteria. They exploded into the halls of the facility, screaming in rage.

Alton hung back in the cell's doorway. He peered around the corner, sweat dripping from his brow.

'It sounds bad...' he said, his voice trailing off. He turned as heavy footsteps echoed towards them. A dark figure jogged down the corridor, heading their way.

'Sean,' he whispered. 'Look, we're busted!'

Sean turned and looked down the hall. He took a step backwards. A prison guard in a camouflaged jumpsuit emerged from the crimson glow of the lights.

'*Huilai!* Get back!' he shouted as he worked the pump of his riot-control shotgun. 'In your room, now!'

Sean froze, overwhelmed by the flashing lights and the piercing wail of the sirens. The guard aimed the gun at the ceiling and fired. Sean's face twitched as the light fixture above them exploded.

'Move it, *gui lao!*' the guard shouted.

'Sean, come on!' Alton shouted. 'It's not worth it!' He ran out into the hall and grabbed Sean's shoulder. 'Get back inside!'

As he shook Sean, the guard moved closer to them. 'Go back *ma shang*! Now! Or I—'

The guard's shouting ended with a wet, choking sound. His eyes bulged, then closed. His body fell forward, and he slammed face first into the floor.

A fire axe was buried in his back. A pool of blood spread from the twitching body.

Alton's eyes jaw dropped. 'What the—'

Another figure emerged from the shadows. As he stepped into the spinning circle of light, Sean broke from his trance.

'Who the hell is that?' he asked.

The man was slim and of average height. He was Chinese, but his skin was pale, almost stark white. His eyes glowed a strange, rat-like pink in the crimson emergency lights. His hair was blond, cut in a short, sweeping, modern style.

He marched towards them and stopped at the corpse of the guard. He reached down and wrapped his slender fingers around the handle of the axe. Grunting with exertion, he pulled the weapon from the dead man's body.

He looked up at Sean, and his mouth stretched tight into a wide grin.

Sean took a step back. 'You're right,' he said in a low voice. 'Let's get back in the room.'

The albino charged towards them, swinging the axe over his shoulder. He wailed a battle cry as Sean and Alton scrambled back into their cell. They slammed the door shut and threw their weight against it. The door buckled as the albino slammed into the other side.

'Lock it! Lock the door!' Alton screamed.

'I can't!' Sean shouted back. 'The power's out, it's an electronic lock!'

The door buckled again. They heard a heavy crash, followed by the sound of splintering wood.

'Get the bed, push it over here!'

Alton slid the metal bunk towards them. Together they pushed both their beds up against the door, then braced their shoulders against them. The crashing and splintering continued behind them as the madman pounded against the door.

'Who the hell is that guy?' Sean shouted.

'I don't know,' Alton gasped. 'I never saw him before!'

The axe blade crashed through the splintering wood door.

'You were right!' Sean grunted.

Alton panted from exertion as they both struggled to keep the door closed. 'About what?'

'Things just got worse!'

15

Caine made his way back upstairs, surprised to find the first floor almost empty. The cafeteria's double doors were smashed into jagged fragments of splintered wood. A thin, bitter-smelling haze wafted through the air. Caine recognized the smell. The guards had used tear gas to quell the surge of inmates as they rushed to escape the holding area.

He walked past the battered body of an unconscious guard. A few men in plain clothes lay on the ground as well, moaning and twitching from their injuries. Caine wasn't sure if they were detainees, or more guards like Mole Face. Either way, it appeared most of the inmates had managed to escape the building after the power went out. He could hear the muted shouts and screams of guards outside.

Jia... is she still safe in the garage? He forced the thoughts from his mind. No time for that now.

He grabbed a pair of tear gas grenades from the unconscious guard's belt. A few feet away, he spotted a discarded shotgun lying on the ground. He picked it up and examined the weapon, recognizing it as a Hawk Type 97-1 pump action. Based on the reliable and time-tested Remington 870 design, the weapon was a favorite of the Chinese police. He checked the tube under the barrel and found it still held three of its five loads.

He slipped his revolver into the inner pocket of the jumpsuit. Then he pumped the shotgun and proceeded to the next set of coordinates on his mental map. He turned the corner and moved towards the main stairs. Another domed security camera was mounted next to the stairwell. Caine assumed that China's Ministry of State Security had a file on him and his past activities. *I'm sure that operation in Macau raised a few eyebrows,* he thought, remembering an old mission.

He had not yet been debriefed by the CIA. His file still listed him as a traitor, KIA. That was the narrative Bernatto had pushed after betraying him in Afghanistan. To the rest of the world, he was dead. Killed in action while trying to sell the contraband that had disappeared after Operation Big Blind. But he doubted the Chinese government would put much stock in that. Not if they identified him on video assaulting a building in the middle of Beijing.

He ducked behind a corner wall as the camera rotated in his direction. Popping a gas grenade off his belt, he tossed it under the camera. The grenade detonated with a loud pop, and a cloud of white vapor exploded into the corridor.

Caine took a deep breath and closed his eyes. He charged forward into the cloud, covering his mouth and nose with his arm. The vapor burned at his skin, but he pushed forward. He had experienced the gas many times before. He was trained to ignore the pain and discomfort.

After he ascended two flights of stairs, he opened his eyes and exhaled, then coughed and gagged. His eyes were swollen and watery, but his vision was unimpaired. He heard a series of crashes on the floor above. Each impact echoed through the vertical shaft of the stairwell. The loud noise cut through the incessant howl of the siren.

There was no more time to waste.

Caine emerged on the third floor and took a deep breath. The dank, mildewed air was like a fresh summer breeze compared to the stinging mist below. The crashing was louder now. Whatever was making the noise was just around the corner.

Caine held out the shotgun and turned around the corner. He found himself staring down another long, dim hallway. A series of large glass windows broke up the wall on his left and looked down on the cafeteria. A row of doors stood to his right. Most of them were open now that the electronic locks had disengaged.

Caine squinted. The spinning red lights illuminated a figure at the end of the hall. It was a slim, lean man, swinging something over his shoulder.

As he walked closer, Caine realized the man was wielding an axe.

The man threw the heavy weapon forward, striking the door with another loud crash.

Caine did a quick mental check of the building's floor plans. The room up ahead was where Sean was being held. This man, whomever he might be, was trying to force his way in.

The assassin... Red Phoenix!

Caine raised the shotgun. 'Move away from the door, now!' he ordered. His voice boomed down the corridor.

The man whirled around and Caine stared in disbelief. Lit by the spinning, crimson pools of light, the figure looked like a ghost.

The pale man cursed at him in Chinese. Uttering a high-pitched scream, he raised the axe and charged towards Caine.

Caine did not hesitate. The shotgun bucked and roared in his hands.

The man uttered a short bark of pain. He jerked to a stop and looked down at his chest with a curious expression.

Caine took a few steps forward. Something was wrong. The man was still standing.

Caine pumped the shotgun, ejecting the old shell to the ground and loading the new one. He fired again.

The explosion of gunfire echoed through the corridor. The albino stumbled back as the slug struck his shoulder. His hand shot up and rubbed the point of impact, but again, he did not go down.

He looked up and stared at Caine. His eyes seemed to glow a hellish red in the overhead emergency light. His thin, pale lips twisted into a smile.

Caine looked down. In the dim light he could see the spent shell casing of his last shot rolling across the floor in front of his feet.

Normal shell casings were red. The one on the ground was blue. He couldn't read the Chinese markings on the side, but he knew exactly what they must say...

Non-lethal, he thought. *Rubber bullets. Should have checked. Stupid, careless...*

Caine debated reaching for his pistol, but there was no time. The albino charged forward, screaming. His stark white skin and shrieking cries were unnerving. They made him seem even more like some kind of malevolent ghost or spirit. He swung the axe above his head in a double-handed grip.

Caine raised the shotgun horizontally in front of his face, blocking the downward swing of the axe. The metal blade clanged against the barrel of the gun, just inches away from his skull. The pale man was stronger than he looked. The force of his attack knocked Caine back a few steps, and it took all his strength to hold the blade at bay.

Recovering from the force of the blow, Caine thrust the gun forward, knocking the axe back. He snapped the butt of the gun towards his attacker's face.

The albino ducked his head down. As he evaded the blow he pivoted his body, launching a powerful side kick into Caine's left knee.

Caine staggered backwards again and felt his leg wobble. *If I could just get clear,* he thought. *Get a shot at a vital organ.* At close range, even a rubber bullet would incapacitate his foe. But the albino didn't let up in his assault. A forward kick thrust into Caine's abdomen, sending him crashing to the ground. He gasped for air, struggling to replenish the oxygen that had been forced from his lungs.

His vision cleared. He saw the axe once again swinging towards him. He rolled to the side, and the blade clanged against the concrete floor. The blow sent a shower of sparks into the air.

Caine rolled to his feet as the albino wailed his strange battle cry and swung the axe again. Caine thrust with the shotgun, blocking the swing. His attacker pushed Caine forward. He felt his back slam into one of the plate glass windows that ran along the hall.

Dropping the axe, the albino grasped the shotgun in both hands. He pushed forward, digging the weapon into the flesh of Caine's throat. Caine threw up a knee towards the man's groin, but his attacker blocked the blow with a raised leg.

The albino grunted with exertion. Caine could see long, slim muscles in his white forearms rippling with strength. His attacker forced the gun down. The cold metal bit into Caine's throat, crushing his windpipe. He tried to shift the gun left or right, struggling to lift it even a fraction of an inch off his throat. He needed a second to catch his breath.

But his attacker was relentless. More cords of muscle burst

from the pale skin of his neck and shoulders. No matter how hard Caine struggled, he could not force the gun back. Despite his slim frame, the albino seemed inhumanly strong.

Caine's vision began to blur and fade. Looking down, he noticed something strange about his attacker's hands, wrapped around the barrel of the gun... He counted six fingers on each of the man's hands.

Must be hallucinating, he though. *Lack of oxygen...*

From the corner of his eye, he could see through the thick glass window. He could make out the shattered remains of furniture far below them on the first floor. Prison guards swept through the large room, checking for survivors amidst the debris.

A reflection shifted across the glass. Caine saw a beam of splintered wood swing through the air. It smashed across the side of his attacker's face.

The albino's head snapped sideways from the force of the blow. He did not release his grip, but Caine felt the pressure on his throat loosen. It was just enough... He sucked in a lungful of air and his vision began to clear.

Caine twisted the barrel of the shotgun, pointing it over his left shoulder.

He pulled the trigger. The gun fired. Caine clenched his teeth in pain as the deafening blast sounded a few inches from his ear.

At point-blank range, the rubber slug was powerful enough to break glass. The window exploded behind him. A barrage of glittering shards fell forty feet to the ground, shattering on the floor below.

Caine dropped to the floor and pulled his attacker forward. As his back slammed into the ground, he kicked upwards, rolling the albino up and over the window frame.

The man screamed as he summersaulted over Caine and flew through the shattered window. He plummeted down to the cafeteria and slammed into a broken table. The table had been snapped in two, and jagged shards of wood lanced upwards. As they punched through the albino's back, he coughed a fine spray of blood and his eyes fluttered closed.

The guards on the ground looked up at the window in surprise. '*Ni zai nali?* Don't move!' one of them shouted as they charged out of the room.

Caine staggered to his feet, gasping for breath. His ears were still ringing from the shotgun blast. The albino's strangulation attempt had left a savage red bruise on his neck.

Standing before him was a young Caucasian man, panting from exertion. He was clenching a broken beam of wood in his hands. His eyes were blue, wide, and frightened.

'Dude, are you okay?' he asked.

Caine recognized him at once. He had seen Sean's picture on the HRN website. But the eyes... He remembered seeing those eyes in a small, crumpled photograph, years ago.

'Sean,' he croaked. 'You're Sean Tyler.'

Sean looked him up and down. 'You know me?' he said in an uncertain voice.

'I knew Jack. Your father,' Caine said, his voice returning to normal.

'What the hell is going on? Who was that guy with the axe?'

'I don't know, but you can't stay here. People want you dead. Powerful people. Our only chance is to keep moving.'

A short, nervous-looking Chinese man ran up behind Sean. He looked back and forth between Sean and Caine. 'Who the hell are you?' he asked.

Caine nodded towards the man. 'Never mind that, who is he?'

'Alton. He's with me.'

Caine shook his head. 'No, I came for you. He'll slow us

down. The doors are all unlocked; the guards have their hands full. He can find his own way out.'

'I said, he's with me.' Sean's voice took on a stubborn, hard edge. Caine recognized the tone. He had argued with Jack many times. He didn't recall winning many of those arguments, either.

Caine looked down into the holding room below. The guards were gone. He knew they would be heading upstairs to intercept them. They could be in the corridor in seconds.

'Fine,' he said. 'Let's go.' He marched towards the shattered door of Sean's room and turned right. Sean and Alton jogged behind him.

'You know, you still haven't told us who you are.'

'That's kind of a long story,' Caine said as he opened the door to another stairwell.

'Funny... my dad used to say exactly the same thing. Whenever I asked him a question he didn't want to answer.' Sean followed Alton down into the dark stairwell. He paused and looked up at Caine. 'Before, you said you *knew* my dad... past tense.'

Caine closed the door and drew his revolver from inside his jumpsuit. He pushed past Sean and Alton, taking the point position on the stairs. 'There's no time for that now. I'll explain everything later.' He descended into the darkness of the stairwell.

Sean gave him a sullen look, then clanged down the metal stairs after him. 'Yeah, right. He used to say that a lot too,' he muttered.

* * *

Caine guided Sean and Alton through the dark, winding corridor that led to the service garage. As they scrambled behind him, Alton grabbed Sean's shoulder.

'Hey,' he whispered. 'This is bad, we could get in big trouble. Maybe we should stay? How do you know we can trust this guy?'

Sean shrugged. 'He didn't try to cut me into pieces with an axe.'

Caine glared back at them. 'You're free to stay here if you want.'

Alton shook his head. 'No, never mind, thank you.'

Caine threw the service door open, and they sprinted into the garage.

The dark, cavernous chamber was the same as he had left it. Dark slicks of oil still stained the concrete floor. Dim fluorescent lights beamed down from overhead. But one thing was different.

The white van was gone.

Caine ducked behind a metal dumpster as a trio of guards jogged into the garage from the front entrance.

'Get down,' he hissed. 'Over here!'

Sean and Alton didn't listen. They kept running, driven by fear and adrenaline. The guards saw them and immediately raised their pistols.

'*Bie dong!* Don't move!'

Sean saw the guards advancing with their guns drawn. Like a deer in headlights, he froze. Alton stopped a few feet away, turning his head left and right.

Caine popped out from behind the dumpster. 'Get back here, now!' he shouted. The men pivoted and sprinted towards the dumpster. Caine fired twice, sending two shots towards the guards. One shot missed and sparked against the concrete floor. The other struck the lead guard's leg, and he stumbled to the ground.

The other two guards opened fire. Their bullets ricocheted off the dumpster as the two men dove for cover.

'I thought you said there would be a van?' Sean shouted.

'It took longer than I thought to get out,' Caine snapped. 'I guess my friend had to leave.'

'So now what?'

Another hail of bullets slammed into the dumpster. Caine ducked around the corner and returned fire. He aimed for the ground near the fallen guard. His shots kicked up chips of concrete near the man's feet. The other two guards stopped firing. They grabbed the arms of their wounded partner and began to drag him out of the garage.

Caine ducked back behind the dumpster. He had bought them a few seconds, but the men would be back once their comrade was out of the line of fire.

Caine flipped open the cylinder of the revolver. He had one shot left.

'I don't know... Maybe we go back inside, try another way out. Or—'

The roar of an engine drowned out Caine's words. Brakes squealed as the battered white van lurched into the garage. It barreled towards the guards at full speed.

'*Kan de chulai*, look out!' The two guards standing opened fire on the van. Caine winced as the windshield shattered into a spiderweb of cracks, but the van continued charging towards them. They stopped firing and dove out of the way, leaving the wounded guard on the ground.

The van's tires squealed in protest as the lumbering vehicle swerved around the fallen guard. Then it skidded to a stop a few feet from the dumpster. Jia opened the side door and waved to them.

'Get in, move!' she shouted.

'You heard the lady, go, go!' Caine ordered. Sean and Alton charged for the van, piling in through the open rear door. Caine ran around to the passenger door and leapt in next to Jia.

She glared at him as she shifted the van into drive. 'You were late!'

'Sorry. Resistance was heavier than I thought.'

The van charged out of the garage. 'Head for the southwest corner of the fence,' he said. 'There's a rear gate, it's not as heavily—'

'I saw it,' she said, cutting him off. 'The garage was filled with guards. They were taking all the vehicles, chasing down the detainees that escaped. I had to leave in case they tried to take this van. I drove around in circles outside. I didn't know what else to do.'

Caine put his hand on her arm and smiled. 'You did great, Jia. Thank you.'

She bit her lip and gave him a nervous glance but said nothing.

Caine looked ahead through the shattered windshield. 'Gate's coming up. Punch it!'

Jia stepped on the gas. Caine rolled down his window and took aim at the lone guard standing in a small booth next to the gate. The bouncing vehicle made accuracy almost impossible. Caine fired. The shot missed but it had the desired effect. The man ducked down in the guard house, taking cover.

Caine sat back down and fastened his seatbelt.

'Brace yourselves!' he shouted back to Sean and Alton.

Jia closed her eyes and screamed. The van slammed into the gate at full speed.

Sparks shot from the metal fence as it tore free. The engine whined and groaned as a section of the wire mesh caught in the front axle.

Caine grabbed the wheel from Jia's hands and jerked it to the right. The van's tires skidded across the Beijing city streets. They heard a thud as the last chunk of metal and wire dropped from underneath the vehicle. The van shuddered, then charged ahead at full speed.

'Turn left up here,' Caine said. 'Then make a right in the first alley.'

Jia nodded. 'You remember the streets here? You have a good memory.'

Caine looked back at Sean. The young man's eyes were wide with fear, and his face was pale. But there was also a firmness in his jaw, an uncompromising determination in his stare.

He looked like his father.

'Forgetting things has never been a problem for me,' Caine said, turning back to face her. 'Just the opposite, in fact.'

16

Ted Lapinski scanned the info on the page in front of him. He flipped to the next section of the report as he paced down the hall. The dark, tinted windows of the NSA headquarters rose up on either side of him. The building was a vast canyon of black glass and chrome. Skylights overhead allowed soft pools of sunlight to pierce the shadowy corridors.

'Are these figures correct?' he asked. 'Your people can guarantee a 40 percent resolution improvement in these lighting conditions?'

Avi Kramer, a younger man wearing a rumpled, ill-fitting suit, kept pace with Ted.

'At least 40 percent,' he said. 'When you combine that with our social media algorithms, you're looking at, what? A 70, 80 percent increase in data density.'

Ted flipped the report closed. 'I've already got social media taken care of. Your algorithms are last year's model. But this image amplification software... This is the fucking Ferrari. I want it.'

'Ted! Ted, hold on a second!' a woman's voice called out

behind him. Ted looked over his shoulder and spotted Rebecca Freeling heading towards him. Sunlight from the massive skylights overhead sparkled in her fiery red hair. Her eyes seemed to hone in on him, picking him out of the crowd with laser-like intensity.

Ted shoved the report into Avi's hands. 'Avi. Can you give us a minute?'

Avi grasped the mass of papers in his twitching hands and gave Ted a nervous smile. 'Yeah, sure. But we're good right? The funding—'

'Prepare a demonstration for next week. I want to run this up the flagpole before I commit.'

Ted heard the hum of Rebecca's motorized chair as she pulled up next to him. He smiled and rested a hand on her shoulder. 'Rebecca, did we have an appointment this afternoon? Hope I didn't double-book you.'

Rebecca shook her head. Avi appeared mesmerized by the highlights of copper and auburn exploding through her hair. Ted glanced over at him and laughed.

'Rebecca, meet Avi Kramer. Avi, Rebecca Freeling. Avi's company does facial recognition algorithms, image enhancement technology, great stuff.'

Avi shook her hand. 'Pleased to meet you, Ms. Freeling. You know, if you like, I could demo our new—'

Ted scowled. 'Avi, why are you still here? Rebecca, I'm late for a briefing... Roll with me?'

Rebecca rolled her eyes and maneuvered alongside him.

'Charming as always, Ted,' she muttered, as they left Avi behind in the corridor.

'I can't stand these start-up guys,' Ted muttered. 'All they do is bitch about privacy and oversight and other bullshit. But then they come to us for money. We're an intelligence agency, not

Kickstarter. What do they think we're going to do with their tech?'

'That's your cross to bear, Ted. I work in Human Intelligence. I'm a "boots on the ground" kind of girl. Not that you'd know it from the DNI's reaction to my drone report.'

'The drone missions are a CIA program, speaking of crosses to bear. But I have to say I agree with Blayne on this one.'

'That wouldn't have anything to do with our reliance on NSA SIGINT for coordinating our strikes, would it? Or should I say, over-reliance?'

Ted smiled. 'Well, you know what they say about opinions.'

They came to a security checkpoint in the hallway. Ted held up his ID badge and then dumped his cell phone and keys into a plastic bin. He stepped through the metal detector in the center of the hall. Rebecca approached a uniformed security officer and allowed him to search her bag.

She followed Ted through the checkpoint, then stopped as they came to a silver metal door. Armed guards stood at attention on either side of the passageway. Ted typed in a series of letters and numbers into the keypad. A green light flashed over the door as it unlocked. Ted held the door open for her, and Rebecca moved forward into the vast, dark chamber that lay beyond.

Ted closed the door behind them. They were standing on a long, narrow catwalk. The walkway ran along the edge of an enormous server room, several stories below. The air was cool and dry. The hum of electronics seemed to vibrate all around them.

It took Rebecca a few seconds to adjust to the dim light. She looked down into the dark chasm of black towers and flashing blue lights. 'God, this place always gives me the creeps,' she said. 'Feels like I'm on the Death Star.'

Ted slowed his pace and moved forward along the catwalk.

'We draw more power in this room than the average small town in Maryland. The spinning servers down there actually generate enough friction to reduce our heating bill by 40 percent in the winter.' He spread his arms and smiled. 'See? Even the NSA is going green!'

'Ted, I know you have to get going, but I wanted to talk to you about the briefing yesterday. Specifically, about the prisoner exchange.'

Ted glanced down at her, but did not look her in the eye. 'What's there to talk about?' he said. 'It's the president's call, not mine.'

'You don't sound too happy about it.'

He stuffed his hands in his pockets and surveyed the galaxy of blinking lights beneath them. He rocked back and forth on his heels. 'I'm *not* happy. It's a bad deal, and you'd see that if you weren't taking it personally.'

Rebecca positioned her chair in front of Ted and spun around to face him. She tilted her head, forcing him to make eye contact. 'The transfer is a presidential order. There's nothing personal about it.'

The blinking blue lights of the server farm blazed in the darkness. They illuminated Ted's round, cherubic face with a soft, indigo glow.

'Rebecca, despite what you may think, I like you. And I respect you. After what you've been through, I'd be a fool not to. So I'm going to be honest with you.'

'Well, now we're finally getting somewhere.'

'Bernatto went off the reservation, no doubt about it. He killed Jack Tyler, hurt friends of yours. And he hurt you. So now you're throwing all your weight behind this kid. And I get it... he's a victim here, an idealist in the wrong place at the wrong time. But I think, on some level, you're still fighting Bernatto. Still trying to undo the damage he did. That's not your job. Your job is to defend the interests of the United States.'

'My job is to provide the president with accurate, objective, and actionable intelligence. Not to make policy.'

Ted shook his head. 'That's a cop-out. For all Bernatto's faults, at least he had some skin in the game. You want to do his job, you're gonna have to pick a side and start playing offense.'

He smiled and started walking towards the other end of the catwalk. 'I have to get to my briefing. Next time you want to drop by, call my assistant, she'll put you in my book. The cafe here makes the most amazing Waldorf salad. It's got candied apples in it, tastes like those Jolly Rancher candies!'

'Ted!' Rebecca's voice crackled through the dry air. Ted spun around but kept walking backwards. Rebecca moved towards him.

'Sorry girl, gotta go—'

'It's my turn to be honest. I received intel that the NSA is running black operations in China. That you have an unauthorized asset in place there.'

Ted stopped walking and laughed. 'What? Where did you hear that? WikiLeaks?'

'I have assets of my own, Ted. Is it true?'

Ted shook his head. 'Like you said, you're the "boots on the ground" girl. I'll stick to my computer geeks and web crawlers.'

'The exchange is happening, Ted. The president signed his approval.'

Ted smiled. 'I know, I know. We've both played this game long enough to know how these things work.'

He walked away from her down the catwalk. He turned and looked back over his shoulder. 'You win some, you lose some.'

* * *

Outside the shadowy confines of NSA headquarters, the sun overhead seemed almost blinding. Its rays battered the shimmering black glass building, as if struggling to expose its secrets to the light of day. But the massive obsidian cube remained a dark enigma, a vault of shadows, even in the face of the most powerful light in existence.

Rebecca was glad to see her SUV was already waiting for her outside the entrance to the building. The driver-side door opened, and Josh hopped out. 'One second, ma'am.'

He jogged around to the passenger side of the vehicle and opened her door. With the flip of a switch mounted on the doorframe, a metal platform emerged from the passenger area. It lowered to the ground with a hydraulic whine.

Josh smiled, his eyes sparkling in the bright sunlight. 'Here, I'll help you up.'

'No.' Her voice was harsher than she intended. She shook her head. 'No, thank you,' she said, softer this time. 'I can manage.'

'Okay then.' He touched the radio mic in his ear. 'Package is on the move. Repeat, package is on the move.'

He got into the car and started the engine. Rebecca glared at him as she locked her chair in place and fastened the seatbelt across her chest.

'Josh, I'm going to give you a tip if you want to keep working with me. Don't ever refer to me as "the package" again.'

Josh chuckled. 'Yes, ma'am, you got it.'

Rebecca stared out the window at the glossy, sinister black building. As they drove toward the front gate, they passed row after row of parked cars. The building now housed a staggering number of employees. The NSA's operational budget grew larger with each passing year.

'How did your meeting go?' Josh asked as he turned the wheel, taking them out of the complex and onto the main road.

'That depends on your point of view.'

'How do you mean?'

Rebecca looked in the rearview mirror and saw the second vehicle in her security detail pull up behind her. For once, she was thankful for the extra protection.

'Just about every other word out of his mouth was a lie. But that tells me something useful.'

Rebecca pulled out her phone and opened her calendar.

'What would that be, ma'am?' Josh asked as she checked her agenda for the day.

'It tells me he doesn't want me to know the truth. By the way, if there's one thing I hate being called more than "the package" it's "ma'am." Got it?'

Josh kept his eyes on the road and forced himself not to grin. 'Yes, ma'a—Yeah, got it.' He looked over at her. 'For what it's worth, I do want to keep working with you. You're the only spook in this business I trust.'

She slid the phone back into her Hermès purse. 'Why is that?'

Josh kept his eyes on the road. 'Guys like Lapinski... they sit behind desks and make life and death decisions for people like me. Soldiers, spies, men and women in the trenches. We're the ones eating sand, taking bullets, and sweating blood. But these jokers...'

He glanced at the black building's reflection in the rearview mirror. 'It's all just a game to them. They're playing poker with someone else's chips. When they win, they take the credit. But when they lose, others pay the price.'

'What makes you think I'm any different?'

Josh stared at her for a second. She found herself examining the tiny crow's feet that surrounded his eyes. They reminded her of—

'You're a fighter,' he said, cutting off her train of thought.

'What you did in Thailand. That took guts. Most people in that situation... they would have folded.'

She looked out the window, silent.

'You paid a price, ma'am,' he said, lowering his voice. 'You know what it means to fight for something you believe in, to put your life on the line.'

'Josh?'

'Yeah, sorry, I guess I'm rambling.'

'You called me *ma'am*.'

Josh's rugged, weathered face broke into a grin. The wrinkles around his eyes turned upwards, like miniature reflections of his smile. 'Yeah, sorry about that, Director Freeling.'

'Let's go with Rebecca.'

He nodded and smiled again. 'Rebecca it is.'

They continued down the winding, tree-lined road.

17

Caine walked down the center aisle of the bullet train as it streaked through the Chinese countryside. Outside the windows, the scenery was a blur of green and brown. Factories and forests, cities and suburbs... All reduced to ambiguous streaks of color rushing past.

The train shuddered, and Caine rested a hand on the seats to either side of him to maintain his balance. An elderly Chinese woman looked up at him and smiled. Caine nodded and continued down the car.

When he reached the end, he pressed the button next to a narrow door. The door slid aside. He moved through the tiny, flexible corridor connecting the two cars. For a moment, the noise outside rose to a loud, violent clatter as the train hurtled forward. Then he moved into the next car. The door slid closed behind him, and the noise died down once again to a dull roar.

He looked up at the digital display mounted over the entrance. The crimson LED lights ticked up as the train increased in speed. He watched as they hit 348 kph. Despite the occasional lurch or shudder, the train was remarkably smooth for traveling at such a high speed.

After their escape, they had abandoned the van in an empty warehouse outside the city. Caine had doused it with gasoline and set it aflame to hide any DNA evidence that might link them to the vehicle. They took two separate cabs to the train station, where Alton had purchased a ticket using money borrowed from Caine.

They boarded the high-speed rail one by one so as not to attract attention by traveling in a group. This was the second stop the train had made since leaving the city. At each station, Caine exited onto the platform and did a quick recon, keeping a close eye on the passengers boarding the train. He scanned the crowds, looking for police, or agents from the Ministry of State Security. So far, no one had caught his eye.

A petite woman in a navy-blue attendant's uniform pushed a trolley cart down the center of the aisle. She stopped next to a row of seats. '*Yin pin he xiao chi*,' she announced in a soft, gentle voice. She pushed the cart forward again and repeated the phrase a few rows down.

Caine had no idea what she was saying, but her cart was filled with drinks, snacks, and boxed meals. He pulled some yuan from his wallet and held it out to the woman. 'Lunch?' he asked, holding up four fingers.

The woman smiled and handed him four boxes, a collection of drinks, and some change. 'Braised beef,' she said in English. 'Very tasty!'

Caine looked down at the strips of gray meat and withered vegetables. The questionable meat was sealed beneath the cellophane box wrapper.

'Looks delicious,' he said. '*Xie xie*.' He gathered the stack of food and slid sideways past the attendant. She continued pushing her cart forward down the aisle. '*Yin pin he xiao chi*,' she continued to call out.

Caine made his way through another sliding door to the next carriage. It was a sleeper car. A narrow corridor ran along one edge of the car. A series of wood-paneled doors lined the other side of the passageway.

A young Chinese couple approached him from the opposite side of the car. They were laughing, holding plastic cups of what he assumed to be beer. He pressed against the outer wall and let them pass. When he was sure they were in the next car, he turned and knocked on one of the doors.

The wood panel slid aside, revealing Jia's worried face. 'What took you so long?' she said, uttering an exasperated sigh.

Alton looked up at Caine over the rims of his glasses. 'You get food? I'm starving.'

Caine stepped into the tiny sleeping chamber and slid the door shut behind him. The cabin consisted of two bunk beds facing each other. The upper bunks were folded back into the walls.

Caine sat down next to Alton on one of the bunks, and Jia sat across from him. She crossed her legs and looked out the window at the scenery rushing by. Her eyes appeared to glaze over, and Caine once again suspected she might be in shock. He could hardly blame her. In less than twenty-four hours she had seen more violence than most people did in their entire lives.

He handed her one of the boxes. 'Here. I wouldn't exactly call it food, but it's the best I could do.'

She took the box, but did not open it. Caine handed her a bottle of green tea. She unscrewed the cap and took a long sip, never taking her eyes off the window.

Alton grabbed one of the boxes and peeled off the clear wrapper. 'I like train food. Reminds me of vacation.' He broke apart the slim wooden chopsticks and began shoveling meat and rice into his mouth.

Caine handed a box to Sean. 'You should eat. I don't know when we'll get another chance.'

The young man opened the meal and picked at the scraps of food.

'Did you see anyone?' Jia asked.

Caine shook his head. 'No. The next stop is Zhengzhou East. That's a decent amount of distance between us and Beijing. If we don't see anyone there, I'd say we should be in the clear for a while.'

Caine opened one of the bottles and sipped some green tea. The cool liquid felt refreshing. For a brief moment he forgot the aches and pains radiating through his bruised body.

'And then what?' Jia asked.

Caine looked up at Jia. 'You can't go back to Beijing. Not for a while. Do you have someplace else you can go?'

She shook her head. 'I don't know, I'll have to think. I... I don't have any family. Some friends maybe, in Hong Kong.'

'Good. Don't call them until you get there. Don't call anyone. The fewer people who know where you're going, the better.'

A cloud of worry crossed Jia's face. 'Oh, my friend in Beijing! The one whose apartment I was staying at... I have to warn him, tell him to stay away!'

Caine nodded. 'We'll be in Hong Kong in eight hours. You can call then. Tell him to stay away from the apartment for as long as he can. When he gets back to China, he should report a break-in. I'm sure the authorities will have raided the place by then. Your friend should act like he has no idea what happened.'

Sean dropped his unfinished meal on the seat and looked up at Caine.

'I can't go to Hong Kong,' he said.

'I have some contacts there,' Caine said. 'It will be easier to get you out of China from Hong Kong.'

'I have to go back to Shanghai. I have friends there, people who—'

'No,' Caine said. 'We have to get out of the country as soon as possible.'

'Look, man, I appreciate what you did, but I don't know you.' Sean nodded towards Jia. 'I don't know her either.'

She gave him a nervous smile. 'I work with Human Rights Now, in Beijing. When we heard you were transferred to that place, we organized a protest. We thought since you were American, the government might release you as a gesture of good will.'

Sean nodded and looked back at Caine. 'Okay, what about you? How do you know my father? Where the hell is he? Why didn't he come to get me?'

Caine sighed. 'You can call me Tom. Look, I don't have time—'

'You just broke me out of a Chinese black jail,' Sean interrupted. 'You act like it's no big deal. Who the hell are you? Why should I listen to a word you say? Christ, now I'm an international fugitive. We all are!'

'Better than being a corpse,' Caine snarled. 'In case you forgot, someone in that jail wanted you dead.'

Alton swallowed a lump of food and nodded. 'That guy in the hallway, the albino. As soon as power go out, he come right to your cell. He knew where to find you.'

Caine lowered his voice. 'I can't explain everything, not now. Your father and I were friends, we worked together. I promised him I'd look out for you. You were in trouble, so I came to help. That's all I can say.'

'And where is he now? My father?'

Caine was no stranger to death. Sometimes he was the instrument of its execution. He delivered its cold embrace to his targets with swift, impersonal precision. Other times, more often than he cared to remember, he had borne witness to death's aftermath. Corpse-strewn battlefields, back-alley executions... forensic analysis, casualty reports, strategic calculations...

This was different. He had no experience in this. No statistics or tactical recommendations could blunt the cold hard truth.

Your father is dead, he thought. *I watched him die in a dark, dirty hole.*

He looked Sean in the eye. 'I'm sorry,' he said. His voice was flat, almost monotone. 'Jack is gone.'

Jia opened her mouth as if to speak, but the words seemed to die in her throat.

'Gone? What do you mean, gone?' Sean asked.

Caine's emerald eyes burned into the young man, cold and unyielding. 'You know what I mean.'

Sean stood up in the tiny cabin. 'This is crazy. I haven't seen my father since... I can't even remember. Now you show up in the middle of China and tell me he's dead? Oh, and someone wants to kill me as well?'

'I know it must be hard to hear, but it's true. All of it.'

Sean slid open the cabin door. As he made to leave, Caine grabbed the young man's arm.

'Where are you going?' he asked, his voice taut as steel cable.

Sean looked down at him. He no longer looked scared or nervous. He looked angry. Defiant.

'I just found out I'm an orphan,' Sean said. 'I need a drink. You mind?'

'Tom,' Jia said softly.

Caine let go of Sean's arm. The young man glared around the cabin one last time, then stormed out the door.

Alton shoveled another mound of food into his mouth and

stood up. 'He need to blow off steam. No worries, I go with him, make sure he okay.'

'Get him back here,' Caine growled. 'Our faces might be on the news. If someone recognizes him...'

'No problem.' Alton left the cabin and slid the door closed behind him.

Jia was silent for a moment, then she looked up into Caine's brooding face. 'Is it true? He has no family?'

'I didn't know about his mother. Until a few days ago, I didn't know anything about him, I guess.'

'But the father? He was your friend?'

'Yeah. But like I said, he's gone now.'

Jia rested her hand on his knee. 'Then you are like Sean... you have both lost someone. You have that in common, among other things.'

Caine tossed the empty green tea bottle into a small trash can in the corner of the cabin.

'What other things?'

'When you told him just now... the memories it brought back, they were painful, yes?'

Caine looked out the window. The misty green countryside streaked by. He said nothing.

'That's what I mean,' Jia said as she lay down on the bunk and closed her eyes. 'You both react to pain the same way. With anger.'

Her words faded to a whisper. Caine looked over at her and watched her breathe. Her chest rose and fell in a steady rhythm. It matched the cadence of the train's wheels jetting along the tracks.

Within minutes, she was fast asleep.

Caine's body ached, and his mind raced with memories and

doubts. The sound of Jia's breathing was relaxing, and he longed to lay down on the other bunk and rest across from her.

Instead, he continued to stare out the window. The speeding train painted the scenery outside in the window's frame. The blurred images felt like fragments from some hazy, long-forgotten dream.

The warm, welcome oblivion of sleep refused him.

18

The narrow room was dim, lit only by flickering candles. But to Rebecca, the light seemed blinding. Brick walls surrounded her, stretching into the shadows. She could hear muted words echoing around her, but they quickly faded. Beads of sweat dripped down her forehead. Her pulse beat faster and faster. She had to get out. She had to escape...

The man sitting across from her smiled. *He's going to ask me another question,* she thought. *There's nothing I can do about it...*

'So what exactly is it you do again?' he asked, after swallowing another sip of wine. 'I think your dating profile said, "civil servant"?'

Rebecca forced herself to smile. It was a common myth that officers of the CIA were not allowed to disclose their occupation. True, she was forbidden from discussing operational details and matters pertaining to national security. However, her position with the agency was a matter of public record.

The truth was, she preferred not to bring it up. She knew once she mentioned it, a barrage of questions would inevitably follow.

'I work in intelligence,' she said. She used her fork to break off a piece of the plump scallop sitting on her plate. 'And believe me, it's not as exciting as you might think.'

'Well, it sure beats being a lawyer,' the man chuckled. 'So wait, are you telling me you're a spy? Are you even allowed to say that?'

Rebecca wiped her mouth with her napkin. The flavors of butter, sage, and thyme exploded across her taste buds. The food at Nora's was spectacular, even if the company left something to be desired.

You're being a bitch, she thought. There was nothing wrong with the man sitting across from her... What was his name? Mitch? Matthew? A successful defense attorney, he seemed polite and friendly without being lecherous. Sharp dresser, too. Blue suit, black shoes, good skin. Too bad about the thinning hair. But he was in pretty good shape. Maybe spent a few hours each week at the gym. Probably some racquetball games at a sports club thrown into the mix.

He was perfectly normal.

Nothing wrong with him at all. So why are you mentally marking exit routes? She had no answer to her question. Just about every woman she knew was looking for someone exactly like him. But to her, he seemed like a mirage. She was looking through him, not seeing him. She was searching for something else.

She shook her head. 'No, I'm more like middle management. I mean, you're a lawyer, right? I'm sure people think that's more exciting than it really is, don't they? Like you must run around the city solving crimes, and all your cases settle in an hour or less?'

Her date laughed and took a bite of his steak. As she watched him eat, she recalled an article she had once read. It suggested that food should be chewed thirty times before swallowing for optimal digestion. She noticed he took his time, mashing the food between his teeth for several minutes.

He chewed it thirty times exactly. She counted.

'Well, have you ever been in a dangerous situation?'

She stabbed at a scallop with her fork but lacked the energy to take another bite. She pushed the plump white fragment around on her plate. It left trails of sauce across the white porcelain surface.

'There's an element of risk,' she said. 'It goes with the job.' She looked up and laughed. 'I mean, before, when I was in the field. Now, I work behind a desk, I'm not running around, out there...' She gestured with her free hand.

Not out there... not running around anywhere.

He reached out and set his hand on her wrist. 'You seem nervous. I'm having a great time. I hope you are too.'

She grabbed her glass of wine and took a long drink, letting the buttery, oaky taste relax her.

'Mmmm,' she said. 'The food is really good. Thank you for choosing this place.'

Her date looked down at the table for a moment. Then he looked up at her and smiled. 'Is that how you got hurt? Was it your job?'

Rebecca set down her fork. 'I can't talk about that.'

He nodded. 'Right, of course. Look, I hope... I'm just gonna come out and say it. I hope you're not worried about what I think.'

'What you think?' she repeated slowly.

'About the chair. I know it must be hard. But you strike me as a strong woman. I know—'

She grabbed the wheels of her chair. 'Would you please excuse me a minute? I have to go outside.'

'What?'

Her eyes spied a door to the rear of the narrow dining room they were seated in. It was between the kitchen and the restrooms.

'A cigarette. I need to smoke.'

A frown crossed her date's face. 'Your profile said you were a non-smoker.'

Your profile pic said you had hair, she thought. 'I'm sorry, Matt, I just need a minute. I'll be right back.'

She pushed herself away from the table.

Her date stood up and set his napkin on the table. 'Michael.'

'Huh?'

'My name is Michael, not Matt.'

'Right. Michael, sorry. I'll be right back, I promise.'

She headed towards the door at the rear of the restaurant. She fumbled with the door handle as the front of her chair banged into the door.

A waiter saw her struggling and stopped. 'Ma'am, please, let me help.'

'No!' She realized her voice sounded harsh, strident. She took a deep breath. 'I've got it. Thank you.' She backed up her chair and pulled the door open.

She was out. Free. The cool night air washed over her, driving the hot flush of panic from her face. Her hands were shaking. She gripped the wheels of her chair. A low brick wall sectioned off the rear patio of the restaurant. She could hear murmurs of conversation drifting up from the diners there. She wanted to be alone.

She pushed herself past the patio, into the darkness. The air became dank. She wheeled herself behind a dumpster. The metal container was packed with rotting food and bulging plastic trash bags. It stank of rot and mold.

She forced herself to breathe. *This must be some kind of panic attack*, she decided. She shook her head. She just had to breathe.

You knew what he was going to say, she thought. *You're strong. You're young. There's still hope. You can fight this.*

You can walk again.

She had said those same words to herself, over and over. Day in and day out since the injury had left her paralyzed. Not a moment went by that she did not repeat the mantra, remind herself mentally that she was strong. She could fight this. There was still hope.

But when she heard those words spoken from someone else's mouth... when she saw their sympathetic smiles, felt their pity...

Then those words of strength became trite and meaningless. They had no more weight or substance than the saccharine wishes of a greeting card. And all the doubts and fears they suppressed rushed to the surface at once.

Fighting back tears, she pulled her phone from her purse. She erased the dating app she had used to meet Michael. She couldn't do it anymore. The doctors had told her she had to adapt, had to re-learn to live a normal life. Do normal things, connect with people.

This is normal? she thought. *Hiding behind a dumpster, blubbering my eyes out over a random date?*

She wiped her eyes. *Enough. I decide what normal is. I decide when to adapt, and when to fight. And I'm not done fighting.*

She sighed and pushed herself out from behind the dumpster. The dark alley stretched away from her in either direction. As she moved closer to the restaurant, she saw a figure emerging from the door.

Probably my date, she thought. She had been outside for some time. He must have come to check on her. *Nice guy. Normal.*

Unfortunately, normal wasn't what she was looking for right now.

'Ma'am, are you all right?' the shadowy figure spoke as he walked closer to her. She realized it wasn't her date. It was the waiter, from inside, the one who had tried to help her with the door.

He stepped into the light. His jacket was open, revealing a clean, spotless white shirt underneath. No sweat stains.

That's wrong, she thought.

She had waited tables in college, and she knew the job was grueling. The heat from the kitchen, running back and forth carrying heavy trays of food. Even a half shift left her exhausted and drenched in perspiration.

The man walked closer. His face was lined and hard, and dark stubble covered his chin. He looked older than the other waiters she had seen in the dining room. Rebecca fumbled her phone back into her purse and snapped it closed.

'Ma'am?' he repeated. 'I heard noises out here.'

A distant voice screamed in the back of Rebecca's brain. It took her a second to realize it was instinct.

It was one second too late.

The man stepped behind her wheelchair and grabbed the handles. 'Please, let me help you.'

He began to push her back to the restaurant.

'No,' she said. 'I'm fine.'

'It's all right, ma'am. I've got you.'

He was pushing her faster now. She felt a cold pang of fear gnawing at her gut. She had been in danger before. She knew the signs, and she had ignored them.

He wheeled her past the restaurant door, farther down the alley. The wheels of the chair clattered against the pavement.

'Where are you taking me?' she shouted. 'Stop!'

She turned her head, trying to get a glimpse of his face. She heard the screech of brakes. A black van pulled to a stop ahead of them, and its tail lights filled the alley with a crimson glow. The rear door slid open with a loud thunk. The man pushed her towards the vehicle.

'Help! Someone help!'

He pressed a rag against over her mouth. She gagged as a dense, sickly-sweet smell overpowered her senses. A thick, translucent haze fell over her vision. The lights up ahead bloomed into beautiful red starbursts. They glowed in the darkness like neon poppy flowers.

CHCl3, she thought. *Chloroform.*

She had allowed self-pity and fear to cloud her judgment. She should have fought harder, should have trusted her instincts. Now it was too late.

The haze grew heavier. Her head tipped forward, but his hand did not release its relentless pressure. She couldn't breathe. The sweet, cloying smell was all she could perceive. Sweet like flowers...

No! It's not too late. You're strong! You can fight this! The old familiar words once again rang out in her mind, cutting through the haze of rotting flowers.

As her hands fell to her sides, they brushed against the wheel locks on either side of her chair. Her fingers were numb, tingling. She slapped her palm against the lock, but she couldn't quite grasp it. Her hand slipped off the lever and fell back to her side.

She heard the restaurant door crash open behind her. A voice called out.

'Stop! Don't move or I shoot!'

It was Josh! This was her chance...

The man pushed her faster, and her chair bounced over the

rough pavement. The dark maw of the open van doors loomed closer.

She reached for the wheel lock again. This time, her fingers hooked around the slim black handle on the left wheel. She pulled it with all her strength.

The wheel locked with a loud squeal. The man was rushing forward so fast, his momentum spun the chair sideways. The rag flew away from Rebecca's mouth. She had just enough time to gasp a fresh breath of air before she crashed to the ground.

Her head struck the pavement with a loud crack. Her purse tumbled forward, spilling its contents across the alley. The man pushing her lost his balance and fell to the ground as well.

Josh charged towards them, pistol drawn and ready. 'Rebecca, stay down!'

He fired twice. She covered her ears as the explosive gunfire echoed through the narrow passage.

Her kidnapper lurched to his feet and ran towards the van. He stopped and grabbed her purse, pausing just long enough to shove some of the scattered contents back into the expensive leather bag.

Josh fired again. The man jerked as a slug tore into his shoulder. He grunted in pain, but he didn't stop running. Clutching his shoulder, he leapt into the rear of the van. The doors slammed shut, and the vehicle's engine roared to life.

Josh sent a double tap of bullets into the van as it peeled away. The dark vehicle screeched around a corner and disappeared from sight. He rushed to the edge of the alley and scanned the sidewalk, looking left and right.

After he confirmed there were no more attackers, he knelt next to Rebecca.

'Hey, you okay?'

She realized she was sobbing. She turned her head away

from him and wiped away her smeared mascara. She used her arms to lift herself up to a sitting position.

'I'm fine. Only thing wounded is my pride.'

Josh examined the bruise on her forehead. 'Well, not the only thing. You took a bad tumble.'

'It's nothing. Could have been a lot worse.' She looked up at him. 'What are you doing here? I don't have a night detail.'

He gave her a sheepish grin. 'I was thinking about our conversation earlier, about Lapinski. I know how guys like that think. And I know you. I figured you pushed his buttons this morning.'

'So you followed me?'

'Um, well... yeah, I guess I did.'

She nodded. 'Good instincts.'

He slid his arms under her body. 'Come on, let's get you out of here. You ready?'

She nodded and wrapped her arms around his shoulders.

'Okay, one, two, three...'

He grunted as he lifted her up off the ground. Cords of muscle rippled beneath her fingers. She felt light-headed, flushed. A tingle ran through her body.

Butterflies? she thought. *No, it's just the chloroform wearing off.*

He set her down in her chair.

'You know, I gotta call this in,' he said, glancing around the alley once more.

She reached out and put a hand on his arm.

'Wait. Don't, not yet.'

'Rebecca, you're the D/NCS... an attempt was just made on your life. I can't just—'

'Ted said I needed to get some skin in the game. Well, now I do. And you're right, I must have pushed his buttons this morning. This attack, it has to be connected. I must have struck a nerve when I mentioned the intel from China.'

'So what's our next move?'

She looked Josh in the eye. 'The men on your team, do you trust them? I mean, 100 percent trust?'

He thought for a moment. 'There's one or two. Guys I knew in the service, fellow marines.'

She nodded. 'Call one of them and get a forensics kit over here. There's blood in the alley where you shot that asshole. Get a sample and bring it straight to my office. Don't check it in, don't log it with the agency.'

She headed back towards the restaurant.

'Hey, where are you going?' he called after her.

She rotated her chair and faced him. 'I have to ditch my date.'

'Too bad, I heard the food here is amazing. Any sparks?'

She smiled. 'Let's just say the attempted kidnapping was the highlight of the evening.'

He grinned back at her, then turned away and began dialing a number on his cell phone.

She flushed again, realizing that what she had said was true, in a way. Not the kidnapping, of course... but Josh.

Butterflies. Definitely butterflies.

She shook her head and entered the restaurant.

19

David Fang looked through the glass at the withered face below. He saw his reflection superimposed atop the old woman's sagging, jaundiced skin. He watched as she struggled to breathe. Her lungs drew oxygen into her body with a slow, stuttering rasp. Each exhale was a measured gasp of pain.

She was suffering. His mother was suffering.

Doctor Abigail Song, a petite woman wearing a white lab coat, stood by his side. She carried a slim tablet in her delicate hands. Her fingers danced across the screen, tapping on charts and notes.

'We've secured a donor organ,' she said. 'But I must remind you, this treatment course is experimental. So far, results have been... mixed, at best. It may not be advisable to put her through the strain of another operation.'

David turned from the glass tube. 'What about this machine? This, what did you call it? Hyperbaric oxygen treatment?'

Doctor Song looked up at him over the rims of her glasses. 'The atmospheric pressure in the chamber is one and a half times normal at this altitude. The increased pressure and oxygen levels should cause her body to stimulate production of new blood cells and stem cells. Those are both vital for healing.'

The tenor of her voice reminded Fang of his stock analyst. She sounded like she was noting fluctuations in an investment portfolio.

She swiped a graph across the tablet's screen, showing various test results. 'Studies have shown HBO treatment can have anti-angiogenic effects on cancer tissue.' She offered the tablet to him. 'Would you like to see the data on—'

Fang waved it away. The withered woman in the glass tube turned her head slightly. Her eyes were shut tight. They looked like two dry, old wounds, long since scabbed over. One of them cracked open, and a watery, bloodshot eye peered at Fang.

He smiled.

The eye rolled away from him and stared straight up. Then it closed once again.

He stepped away from the tube, and the doctor followed. He spoke to her in a firm but quiet voice. 'Doctor, I could care less about your data. All I want to know is, will it work?'

Song looked him in the eye. Her face was impassive. She did not frown or smile. 'We're confident she will survive the transplant. That being said, this is her third liver this year. To combat organ rejection, we've had to lower her medications. The strain on her body will be significant, and the cancer has spread to other areas. As a long-term strategy, this is not an effective course of treatment.'

'The Joyous Lake above The Gentle Wind,' a husky woman's voice called out. 'A preponderance of the great.'

Fang turned and saw Iris lying on the tufted carpet, her body draped in a green silk dress. A heavy gold necklace encircled her neck. The jewelry was inlaid with precious jade stones. She closed her eyes and brushed her fingers back and forth across rows of I-Ching sticks spread on the floor. Her nails made a soft clicking sound as they traveled over the slim rods.

The doctor stared at her for a moment, then looked at her watch.

'The lake rises above the trees, just as the superior man stands alone,' Iris continued. She looked up and focused her hypnotic gaze on Fang. 'In extraordinary times, extreme measures must be taken. Revolution must not be feared. Action promises success.'

'Do it,' Fang snapped. '*Shi xian ta*. I will transfer the money tonight.'

The doctor nodded and tapped the screen on her tablet. 'Of course, Mr. Fang. The Park East Clinic is grateful for your patronage.'

She turned to leave the room, but Fang grabbed her arm. She spun around and looked up at him with her unflappable stare.

'If she does not survive the operation,' Fang said, 'I assure you, you will no longer be grateful. Do you understand?'

Song tilted her head and regarded him with her icy stare. 'She will have the best care, Mr. Fang. *Wo fa shi*... You have my word.'

Fang let go of her arm and adjusted the cuffs of his cream-white dress shirt. 'For the money I am paying, I expect more than that. I expect a miracle.'

'This is a clinic, not a temple, Mr. Fang. She will survive the surgery. Beyond that, I cannot say.'

Fang nodded. 'Leave us.'

The doctor's heels clicked on the tile floor as she exited the room.

The Park East Clinic was one of the most exclusive medical facilities in China. The space looked more like a luxurious hotel suite than a hospital room. Recessed lights in the ceiling cast glowing pools over the sleek, modern furniture. The floors were polished concrete. Fang caught another distorted glimpse of his reflection in the glossy surface of the tile.

He sighed and stroked Iris's thick, dark hair. 'Where is Lucky Si?' he asked.

She nodded towards a wall of floor-to-ceiling windows. The vast expanse of glass looked out over a dark blue lake, hundreds of feet below them. The clinic was built into the side of an old rock quarry, just outside Shanghai. The pit's sheer granite walls arced below them.

Fang stepped out onto the room's balcony. Another man wearing a black trench coat was hunched over the edge of the balcony. Fang stood next to him. A glass barrier rose to waist height, allowing them to take in the spectacular view. To either side of them, more glass balconies sparkled in the morning light, like brilliant gems nestled in the dark rock walls of the quarry.

A light mist clung to the lake below. Fang could see a few small boats and canoes crisscrossing the surface. In the distance, rolling green hills blocked the skyscrapers of Shanghai from view.

'It's beautiful, isn't it?' Fang said, taking a deep breath of the crisp morning air.

The other man turned to face him. It was the albino, the man who had killed Wai in the restaurant. His coat fluttered behind him in the breeze.

'It's still a tomb, no matter how lovely the view,' he muttered. 'This family is cursed.'

Fang shook his head and laughed. 'Come now, Si. You and your brother are blessed. Four and six are auspicious numbers. Lucky Si and Lucky Liu.'

The albino gave him a sideways glance with his pink eyes. They were squinted, almost completely closed. He held up his right hand and peered at Fang between the three spread fingers and thumb. The missing finger had not been cut off or removed. It simply was not there, and the other digits had spread out to accommodate the gap. 'Easy for you to say,' he grunted.

'Your eyes... Is it too bright out here?' Fang asked.

The albino shook his head. 'Never mind that.' He rested his hands on the edge of the balcony. 'What do you want to do about Mother?'

'The doctors say there is an excellent—'

'The doctors here only care about the money you pay them. She is in pain. You, this place... You are bankrupting this family, and all you have achieved is to prolong her suffering.'

Fang gestured to the panoramic view of the lake and country-side. 'This clinic provides the finest medical care money can buy. The experimental treatments, the therapeutic environment... there's no other place like it. This is her best chance at beating her cancer.'

'Therapeutic environment? *Qin'ai de xiong di*, do you hear yourself speak? She lives in a glass tube.'

'That is part of her treatment, beloved younger brother,' Fang snapped. 'This family is on the cusp of achieving greatness. Soon, I will be Dragon Father of the *Lu Long*. The money I spend at this facility here will be as a drop of rain in that lake. Everything we have dreamed of is soon to be at hand. Do you think she would want to miss that? To miss seeing her sons rise to—'

A knock behind them interrupted him. He turned and saw Iris standing behind one of the giant glass panels, holding out his cell phone. She gave him an annoyed stare.

Looking at the screen, he could see Lewis was calling him. A frown marred his handsome features. '*Deng yi xia*. I have to take this.'

He paced back into the room and snatched the phone from

Iris's hand. She sighed and strutted back to the carpet. Once again she reclined on the floor and rolled her sticks back and forth.

Fang turned his back to her. 'Yes, what is it?' he said into the phone.

'The black jail, in Beijing... We went to get the American, as you ordered. Lucky Liu was in place, on the inside.'

'If you're calling, something obviously went wrong,' Fang replied. 'Can I trust you with nothing?'

'Sir, there was some kind of disturbance, a riot! The inmates broke free. And Sean Tyler, he...'

Fang clenched the phone tighter. 'Did he escape?'

'Yes, but he was not alone. Our informants in the Ministry gave us a copy of the surveillance footage from the jail. He had help... a Chinese man, another detainee at the jail, left with him. Also, a Chinese woman, we think she was a protester, a human rights worker of some kind.'

'Is that all?'

'No, there was another man. We don't have a clear picture of his face, but he appears to be Caucasian.'

'*Gai si*, if he was after the Tyler boy, he's probably another American.'

'Lucky Liu... We think he tried to stop them from escaping. They fought, and...'

Fang exhaled slowly. 'Say it, Lewis.'

'Your brother... He is dead. The guards at the prison say the white man killed him, threw him from—'

Fang roared into the microphone, then threw the phone at one of the enormous windows. The device shattered against the thick pane of glass. As the pieces of the phone cascaded to the floor, a spiderweb of cracks burst through the window.

Outside, Lucky Si turned back and looked through the

window at Fang. His image was splintered and refracted in the cracked, broken glass. Si stepped inside.

'Brother, I'm sorry we argued,' he said, bowing his head. 'I will respect your judgment in—'

Fang shook his head. 'It's not that. Sit down, Si. We must talk.'

Iris ceased the clacking of her sticks. 'Receptive Earth above Clinging Fire. The darkening of the light.'

'Iris, leave us,' Fang said.

She glared at him, then gathered her sticks and left the room. The silk of her dress made a swishing sound as it dragged across the floor, like wind caressing the grass in a field.

When she was gone, Fang turned back to Lucky Si. The albino leaned back in one of the room's comfortable chairs, his legs sprawled open.

'Si, I need you to do something for me. Something our brother failed to do.'

'Liu? I thought he was sent to—'

'Liu is gone.'

Lucky Si leaned forward in his chair. His strange pink eyes stared out from the pale white expanse of his face. 'What do you mean, *gone*?'

'Our brother is dead. He sacrificed himself for this family's destiny. Now, it is up to us to persevere. Find Sean Tyler. Bring him to me.'

Lucky Si leapt to his feet and cupped his fist in his palm, above his heart. 'Yes, brother. *Wu bo hui shi bai*. I will not fail you!'

He paced towards the exit of the room.

'Si, wait,' Fang called. The albino spun around. His black trench coat flared behind him.

'Tyler is with others. A Chinese man and woman. And a *lao wai*, a white man. Probably American.'

'Yes?'

Fang looked up at Si. 'Kill them all. For our brother.'

Lucky Si nodded and left the room.

Fang stood up and walked over to the glass tube. Inside, his mother's eyes were still closed. He heard a soft hiss come from the machinery of the hyperbaric chamber. It was the pumps, working to maintain the air pressure inside.

He rested his head on the glass, just above her face. 'We are so close, Mother. Our destiny... I can almost reach out and touch it. I will not fail. You will live to see your son rise. Then, all those who have wronged our family, all those who caused us pain... they shall finally pay.'

He heard a low groan escape his mother's withered lips. She turned away from him, leaving him staring at his reflection in the glass.

20

Zhengzhou East Station was one of the largest high-speed rail stations in the world. Its boarding platform was a vast, cavernous chamber of gleaming silver and white. A delicate latticework of metal beams crisscrossed high overhead beneath the domed ceiling. Caine knew those metal beams were studded with dozens of security cameras. As he meandered through the newsstands and food carts, he made sure to keep his face pointed down, out of view of the probing lenses above.

He kept a watchful eye on the sleek white train parked behind him. A crowd of new passengers boarded its various cars from the platform. Here, like the other stops along their route, no one attracted his attention.

He walked past a few police officers standing near the terminal exit. They stood ramrod straight. The creases of their olive-green uniforms were pressed to a razor-sharp edge. They paid him no mind as he ambled past. Either he had managed to avoid the cameras in the black jail, or news of the breakout had not reached Zhengzhou.

He walked past a tiny shop selling ornamental plates, chopsticks, and tea sets. Perched in the window was a dusty plastic sleeve that contained a set of three small paring knives with colorful plastic grips. Matching sheaths covered their steel blades.

Caine stepped inside the cramped booth and nodded to the wizened old man behind the counter. He grabbed the knives, along with a set of chopsticks and a tea cup. Placing them on the counter, he slid the man a stack of yuan notes. The old man smiled as he took the cash and bundled the items in a plastic bag.

Stepping outside, Caine made his way to the outer edge of the platform. He scanned the crowd to make sure no one was watching. Unobserved, he slid one of the paring knifes from the package and tucked it into his waistband. He covered the handle with his shirt and dumped the bag of trinkets in a trash can.

The knife's steel was cheap, and the tang of the blade wobbled in the handle. But it would serve as a makeshift, innocuous weapon. After his experiences in Beijing, he no longer felt comfortable traveling unarmed. A common kitchen knife would not attract undue attention if authorities searched his belongings. And in a train station, in the middle of China, it was the best option he was likely to find.

Next, he stopped to buy a burner phone at a small electronics store. The middle-aged woman working in the store waved her hand over a glass display case. It was filled with secondhand phones and iPods. Most of them were old, battered, and covered with stickers and sparkling charms. He selected a basic model. The woman hummed a tune to herself as she slipped in a SIM card and activated the phone.

Caine observed the train as he waited. The crowd of passengers slipping in and out of the long white cars looked perfectly normal. Businessmen in suits, women holding hands with toddling children, a few tourists... Nothing that scanned as out of place, or a threat.

She handed him the activated phone, cradling it like a precious gem in both her hands. Caine smiled and took the device, also using both hands. He gave her a slight bow. '*Xie xie*,' he said, thanking her.

He walked back to the train and dialed Rebecca's number. Her phone rang several times, then went to voicemail. He hung up without leaving a message.

He slipped the phone in his pocket. A series of chimes played over the station's PA system. '*Di er deng ji ti shi*,' a woman's voice announced. 'Second boarding call, all general passengers please board now.' Caine checked his watch. The train would be leaving in a few minutes. He took one last look at the crowd.

A group of five Chinese men wearing suits crossed the platform. They walked with an arrogant stride that made them stand out from the other passengers. It was as if they expected the rest of the crowd to part and let them pass.

Caine had crossed paths with numerous organized crime groups in his career. The Yakuza in Japan, the Russian mafia, the Chao Pho of Thailand. He knew a gangster when he saw one. The industrialist Sean had been investigating, David Fang... Jia said the man was rumored to have Triad affiliations. Caine had been expecting police, or agents of the Ministry of State Security to pursue them. But these men looked like neither. Did they work for Fang? Was he after Sean as well, or was it just coincidence?

He watched the group push their way closer to the front of the train. As their faces came into view, Caine clenched his jaw. The man leading them was slim, and of average height. His skin was stark white. He was wearing a long, black coat, and carrying a cane in his right hand.

Dark sunglasses covered his eyes, but there was no mistaking him. It was the albino, the man who had attacked them at the black jail. This was no coincidence. The ghost had returned to haunt them.

What the hell? Caine thought. *That's impossible!*

But he knew better than to doubt his own eyes. Somehow the albino man was here, alive and well. Caine didn't know if the man was Triad, Ministry, or Red Phoenix himself. But Sean was still in danger.

The men boarded the train near the front. The bells chimed again overhead. '*Zui hou deng ji de dian hua.*' Final boarding call. The train was leaving the station.

Caine hopped through the doors of the car next to him just as they began to slide shut.

With a hiss of rushing air, the wheels gripped the track and began to crawl forward. The hum grew to an electric wail as the train picked up speed, streaking out of the station like a gleaming white rocket.

* * *

Sean slammed the empty Tsing Dao can on the counter of the restaurant car. '*Ling wai, qing,*' he drawled, as he ordered another beer.

'Hey, I didn't know you spoke Chinese,' Alton said. He gestured to the girl working behind the counter and held up a finger. She slid two more cans and two plastic cups over the counter. Alton popped open his can and filled his cup with the golden beer.

'I don't speak Chinese,' Sean said. He popped the tab on his can, guzzled a long sip of beer, and sighed. 'I can order a beer, ask for the bathroom, and tell a girl she's pretty. That's about it.'

'That's more than most white dudes. How long have you been in China?'

'To tell you the truth, I lost track. Six months, maybe a little more.'

Alton nodded. 'And you came here to write a story? About David Fang?'

Sean stared down into the mouth of his beer can. 'After my mom passed away I... I guess I needed something to keep my mind off things. So I joined Human Rights Now. They sent me to this little town, out in the countryside. Xingtai. I just started writing what I saw. The stuff about Fang, and the cancer villages... I guess you could say the story found me.'

Sean took another drink and wiped his mouth with the back of his hand. 'After Xingtai, I traveled from town to town, writing and taking pictures. Always found the same deal. Bad soil, chemicals in the water. Sick kids. And David Fang. His name kept popping up, everywhere I went.'

Alton nodded. 'Same in my village. The children... That's why I do it. I knew petitioning in Beijing would be dangerous. But I had to go. I could not look at their faces anymore and do nothing.'

Sean clapped him on the back. 'You're a good guy, Alton.'

Alton pulled a small, battered cell phone from his pocket. 'That reminds me, I should text my family, tell them I come home soon. They must be worried.'

'Where the hell did you get a cell phone?'

'I bought it in the station, after I get my ticket. Prepaid phone.'

'A burner phone? Look at you, man, all gangster up in here!' Sean laughed. 'Let me borrow it when you're done, I've had internet withdrawal since I got arrested.'

Alton began tapping on the keyboard. 'Sure, sure, just let me text first.' He finished his typing and handed the phone to Sean. 'Here you go.'

Alton sipped his beer as Sean checked his email. 'That's weird,' the young man muttered as he stared at the screen.

'What is it?' Alton asked.

'My friend, the one I was working with in Shanghai. He sent me an email right after I got arrested. But it's just an audio file.'

Sean tapped the screen and the slow, pulsing beat of a Chinese pop song emitted from the phone's tinny speaker. The female singer's light, chirping voice was a strange contrast to the soulful, electronic ballad.

Alton nodded his head to the beat. 'Hey, I know this song. That's Wushi Wu. She's hot, man. Number one C-pop star.'

Sean squinted at the screen. 'Chinese pop music? Why would he send me this? He hates that stuff.'

Alton sang along, his voice cracking as he struggled to match the high notes of the song. '*Wo dui ni de ai zai ran shao*, my love for you it burns!'

Sean winced and downed the rest of his beer. 'Don't quit your day job, bud.'

The door at the front end of the car slid open and Caine stepped through. Sean could tell from the intense look on his face that something was wrong. Caine stalked over to them at a rapid pace.

'What now?' Sean asked. 'You gonna tell me I'm secretly adopted?'

'Shut up and listen,' Caine snapped. 'The man who tried to kill you in Beijing, the albino, who is he? Does he work for the government?'

Sean shrugged. 'I have no idea. I never saw him before.'

Alton looked up from his phone. 'That guy had to be Triad. Why?'

Caine shot a wary glance towards the door he had just passed through. 'Because he's on this train.'

Sean's face went pale, and his voice lost its angry bravado. 'What? No way, that's impossible.'

'Move,' Caine ordered, his voice low and steady. 'This way. Now.'

Caine herded Sean and Alton toward the rear of the dining car.

The door at the front of the car slid open. Sean looked back and saw the pale, sinister face of the albino glaring at him from the doorway.

A waitress rolled a cart filled with trays of food down the aisle, between the men and the rear of the car. One of the men grabbed her shoulder and shoved her to the side. The cart toppled over, spilling platters of noodles and sandwiches to the floor.

'*Ta men zai na li*,' he shouted. 'There they are!'

Sean saw the man draw a pistol, then the door slid closed behind him.

21

The clattering noise of the train roared through the tiny connecting passageway.

'Keep going,' Caine shouted to Sean and Alton. They stepped into the next car. Alton looked back, a grimace of fear clouding his timid face.

'They coming, right behind us.'

'Move!' Caine ordered.

A heavyset man opened the tiny bathroom door and made his way towards them down the center aisle. He looked up at them with an indignant glare as Alton squirmed between him and the row of seats.

'*Hei ni,*' he shouted. '*Xiao xin!*'

Sean pushed past him, following Alton. 'Sorry, man.'

Caine put his hand on the man's shoulder and pushed him down into an empty seat.

'Sir, get down, stay in your seat!' He hoped the man spoke enough English to understand him.

Caine looked over his shoulder. The door at the front of the car slid open and the group of Chinese men filed into the narrow corridor. The albino was no longer in front; he had dropped to the rear of the pack. Their new point-man was taller than the others. He wore a gray suit and a pale pink shirt with matching tie. A thin scar ran along the left side of the man's harsh face.

He aimed his pistol at Caine.

The passengers in the front of the car spotted the gun. A chorus of screams and shouts filled the air. The noise of the panicked crowd drowned out the roar of the train as it raced down the tracks.

Caine followed Alton and Sean through the rear door as it slid closed. The man with the gun pushed through the frantic passengers and opened fire.

Bullets smashed through the door's glass window and ricocheted down the adjoining corridor. Sean and Alton ducked down as they charged into the next car. Caine followed behind them.

Another attendant was pushing a food cart toward them. The passengers were mumbling in hushed tones. Outside, the countryside continued to streak by. The train charged forward at a relentless pace, racing down the tracks at hundreds of kilometers per hour.

'Keep moving!' Caine snapped. 'Get to Jia, head towards the back of the train!'

'Aren't we gonna run out of train?' Sean called over his shoulder.

'Let me worry about that,' Caine replied.

The attendant gasped as Sean and Alton leapt over a row of empty seats next to her. She turned to Caine. 'What's going on? I hear noises!'

'Get these people out of here,' Caine replied. 'Move them back.'

Caine grabbed her cart and pushed it out of the aisle. He drew his kitchen knife from its plastic sheath and brandished the blade in a forward grip.

The attendant looked like a deer in headlights. 'I don't understand—'

More gunshots rang out. The tiny window in the cabin door shattered, and screams erupted through the car.

'Go!' Caine made a stabbing gesture with the knife, pointing towards the back of the train. 'Now!'

As the attendant tried to control the stampede of passengers, Caine crouched low. He crept down the corridor and took up a position next to the doorway. A split-second later, the door slid open.

A gray-sleeved arm wielding a gun slid into view. Caine grabbed the arm and yanked forward. The lead man stumbled into the car. As he flew forward, Caine grabbed the man's necktie and spun him around. Using the strip of fabric to pull his target close, he stabbed down with the paring knife, jabbing the blade into his man's trachea.

Hot blood sloshed across his hand as he twisted the knife. He pivoted, keeping his hostage between himself and the door. The man uttered a gurgling scream. He flailed his arms, desperate to escape from the death grip Caine had trapped him in.

The men in the forward car opened fire. Caine felt the impact of the bullets as they thudded into his hostage's body. The man ceased his struggling. His hands dropped to his side, and the gun tumbled from his grip.

Caine pushed the man forward and tossed him through the door. A splatter of crimson painted the pristine white interior of the train car as he jerked his blade free. He reached up and slammed his fist on the door button. The panel slid shut, blocking the other men from view as they fought their way towards him.

Caine knelt down. Using the bloody knife, he sliced through the rubber mat covering the floor in front of the door. He tore off a chunk of the flimsy covering, revealing a small metal panel underneath. Using the blade of the knife, he pried the metal plate open, exposing the wiring of the door mechanism.

Another barrage of bullets thudded into the door. One shot burst through the thin barrier and struck the floor next to Caine's knee. He flinched but remained in position. Grabbing a bundle of the colorful cables in his fist, he tore them up from the floor. The LED speed display on the wall flickered and went dark. Sparks exploded from the door's track as the locking mechanism shorted.

That should slow them down, he thought.

He reached across the floor and grabbed the thug's discarded pistol. It was a Chinese-made CF-98 chambered in 9mm. His fingers wrapped around the polymer grip.

He leaned in front of the door and fired two shots through the broken window. Blood exploded from a thug's chest, and the man collapsed. The rest of the gang, including the albino, stepped over him, and began to kick and pound on the jammed door.

The door buckled. Caine knew it wouldn't hold for long.

He moved back to the next car and closed the door behind him. He heard muted screams and cries from farther down the train. The passengers must have hit a bottleneck. As Sean had said, sooner or later they would run out of train.

Once again, he slashed through the floor and tore at the wires. All he could do was slow them down. The fact that the train had not stopped meant one of two things. Either their attackers had a man in the engine room, or the conductor was unaware of what was happening.

He looked out the window. If anything, the train seemed to be speeding up. The landscape outside rushed by faster and faster.

He heard more crashing and screaming on the other side of the door. A hail of bullets shattered the window. Then the door buckled and bent as they forced their way through again.

Caine crouched behind a row of seats. The door gave one last metallic groan, then crumpled and tore loose from its track. The men charged into the car. Caine popped up from his cover and opened fire.

Muzzle flashes burst from the barrel of Caine's pistol as he fired at the lead thug. The man squeezed off a shot of his own, then stumbled back, falling into his comrades.

Bullets struck the seat next to Caine. He ducked back down as the albino barked orders to his men. Then he dove sideways, firing as he flew through the air.

Blood spurted from the remaining thug's shoulder as one of his wild shots tore through the man's clothes. The albino tracked Caine's movement with his pistol and opened fire.

As Caine crashed to the floor on the opposite side of the car, a barrage of gunfire tore through the seats above him. Shredded fabric and tufts of cotton stuffing floated in the smoky haze, like heavy snow drifting down onto his face.

Caine waited until there was a lull in the deafening storm of gunfire. He popped up and aimed his pistol at the albino. He had the man dead in his sights.

Before he could pull the trigger, the albino grabbed the thug in front of him, the one whose shoulder Caine had nicked. He charged forward, pushing the man ahead like a battering ram.

Caine stepped into the aisle and fired. His gun roared as he pumped round after round into the twitching, bloodied body.

Caine readjusted his aim and fired a final double tap through the crook of the thug's arm, trying to hit the man behind him. But the ghostly figure twisted out of the way. Safe behind a shield of human flesh, the albino continued to push forward.

The pistol's slide locked back, and Caine felt the trigger go flat.

Empty.

He hurled the useless gun towards the advancing albino. It bounced off the thug's lifeless head and clattered to the floor. The albino dropped the body and leapt towards Caine. As the pale man ran screaming towards him, Caine saw him raise his cane and tug at the handle.

A long, thin blade slid out. The albino tossed the empty sheath aside, slashing the sword in a wide arc in front of him. Caine leapt backwards. The razor-sharp edge of the weapon passed inches from his chest.

Caine took a cautious step back. He kept his eyes on his opponent's blade as it danced through the air.

The albino eyed him and smiled. *'Ni sha le wo de di di,'* he hissed. *'Xian zai, nin jiang jia ru ta zai di yu!'*

Caine shrugged. 'Whatever you say, pal.'

His enemy snarled and lunged forward with his blade. Caine darted back and grabbed a service cart parked behind a row of seats. He rolled the cart into the aisle. It slammed between them, blocking the albino's progress.

As the pale, leering man tried to kick the cart out of the way, Caine took another step back. He grabbed the rails of the luggage racks that lined the roof on either side of the train car. Pulling against the bars, he lifted his legs up and kicked forward. He felt the ledges buckle as the strips of metal just barely supported his weight. His feet struck the albino in the chest full force, knocking the man backwards.

The man cursed as he tumbled back and struck the ground. The sword fell from his grip and rolled under the seats. His dark glasses tumbled from his face. He snapped his head around, staring at Caine through squinted, demonic eyes. Caine leapt over the cart and charged towards him. Suddenly, the train car went pitch-black.

A roaring echo filled Caine's ears. He realized they were passing through a tunnel. He paused for a moment. A second later, he squinted as bright sunlight once again flooded through the windows. The train screamed out of the tunnel.

He looked down. The albino was crouched on the floor, rummaging through the bloody jacket of the thug Caine had riddled with bullets. Bright beams of sunlight struck the man's pale face. He shielded his eyes with a free hand as he continued to frisk the body.

Caine snarled and lashed out with a kick. His foot slammed into the albino's ribs with a loud thud. The man rolled backwards onto the floor of the car. As he rolled over, he whipped up his arm. He was holding the dead thug's gun.

Screaming darkness filled the car again as the train plunged into another section of tunnel. A burst of orange muzzle flash cut through the blackness as the albino fired the pistol. The bullet missed, striking the window on Caine's right.

Caine heard glass shatter. The roar of rushing wind drowned out all other sounds as they charged out of the tunnel. Papers and debris whipped around them. The albino stood up, again shielding his squinting eyes with his free hand. He aimed the pistol again. His arm shook as the three-hundred-kilometer wind buffeted them both from the broken window. Caine lunged towards him and swung out with his left arm. The blow knocked the man's aim wide.

The gun fired again. Another window shattered behind

Caine. The wind in the car intensified. It gusted through the two broken windows like the concentrated exhaust of a jet engine. A few purses and small pieces of luggage whirled around them as if grasped by a miniature tornado.

Caine turned sideways and rammed his shoulder into his opponent's chest. He pushed forward and they slammed down into a row of seats. Caine gripped the man's throat in one hand and the wrist of his shooting arm in the other. He slammed the man's hand into the next row of seats, but the albino displayed the same uncanny strength as before. Caine could not make him release the gun.

The slender man drove a knee into Caine's abdomen. Caine winced and loosened his grip on his opponent's neck for a split second. He felt the man's weight shift beneath him. They tumbled forward into the crevice between the seats. The albino was on top of him now, forcing the barrel of the gun towards his face.

Caine squeezed the man's throat harder. His attacker coughed and spat. The man continued fighting against Caine's grip. The gun moved closer and closer to Caine. The albino's pink eyes bulged, but his thin lips curled into a smile.

Caine stared at the man's hand as he struggled to push the weapon back. In the prison attack, he had counted six fingers on the man's hands. Now, he counted four... Three fingers and a thumb.

'Who are you?' he gasped over the wind. 'Who do you work for?'

The man's voice came out in a harsh croak as Caine's fingers dug into his neck. 'You kill my brother,' he snarled. 'Now I kill you. Then I make your friends bleed!'

Brother? That was it, Caine realized. *This man wasn't the albino from the prison... They were twins!*

The man grunted as he struggled to aim the gun at Caine's head. Like his twin, his strength seemed uncanny compared to his slim frame. The gun moved another inch closer.

Caine's arm trembled. He was exhausted, and he knew it was only a matter of time before his strength gave out. He heard a rattling noise above them. He looked up and saw the luggage rack vibrating in the high-speed wind.

The muscles in his back and legs screamed in protest as he forced both their bodies up off the floor. He let go of the albino's neck. Reaching up, his fingers grasped at the thin metal rail. He grabbed the edge and yanked down with all his strength.

The shelf buckled and tore loose. An avalanche of suitcases and bags tumbled down, striking the albino in the face. The gun dropped away, and the man leaned back to avoid the barrage of luggage. Caine kicked his attacker off him and leapt to his feet. His fingers wrapped around the handle of a suitcase as he charged forward.

A shadow descended over them. Caine glanced right. Through the destroyed car doors, he could see down the length of the train ahead of them. A wall of darkness streaked towards them.

They were entering another tunnel.

He has sensitive eyes, Caine thought. *This is my chance.*

The albino swung his pistol towards Caine just as the roaring darkness engulfed them. In the blackness, Caine ducked down and charged forward. The gun roared, but the shot went wide, filling the car with a brief burst of light. Caine drove his opponent back towards the shattered window.

Sunlight flooded the car as the train streaked out of the tunnel. The albino paused for a split second and again brought his hand up to shade his eyes. Caine was right in front of him, already moving to attack. He swung the suitcase up with both hands.

The heavy bag slammed into the albino's chest. The man fell back into the shattered window. Behind him, Caine saw blue sky and brown, brush-covered hills. A river snaked lazily below them. The tunnel had emerged onto a narrow bridge. The train streaked across the elevated track. They were hundreds of feet above the plunging crevasse of a river valley.

Caine swung the bag again, this time in a sideways arc. The suitcase slammed into his opponent's chest. The man grunted from the impact as the powerful blow shoved him back into the shattered window. His pink eyes opened wide with fear as he realized he was wedged into the window frame. He dropped the gun and grasped the edges of the window, struggling to pull himself free.

Caine dropped the suitcase and grabbed a red emergency handle mounted next to the window. He pulled the lever down. The entire window assembly fell from the train, taking the albino with it. The man's scream rose above the howling wind as he flew away from the car. His body plummeted down toward the tiny river below.

His cry faded to an echo as he disappeared from view. The train sped away, leaving the bridge behind.

Emergency brakes screeched to life. Caine's body lurched forward as the train slowed down. *We're finally stopping,* Caine thought. Maybe the window release had triggered the emergency brakes. Or maybe whoever was guarding the controls realized the albino wasn't coming back.

Either way, they had to get off the train.

The rear door of the car slid open and Jia ran towards him. Sean and Alton followed her as the car came to a stop on a curved section of track. Several passengers peered at them from behind their seats as the trio entered Caine's car. Caine couldn't understand the crowd's panicked mumbling. The look of fear in their eyes, however, was clear enough.

Jia turned and shut the door, blocking them from view. 'What happened? Did the police find us?'

Caine shook his head. 'Definitely not the police. They'll be here soon enough, though. We have to put some distance between us and this train.'

He looked out the shattered window to his left. Outside he saw a steep, sloping hillside, covered with dry brush and scrub. Wrapping a discarded jacket around his arm, he cleared the remaining fragments of glass from the frame.

'Everybody out. Let's go.'

He hopped out the window and felt his legs groan in protest as his feet struck the hard ground. He reached up and helped Jia down. Sean and Alton jumped out after her. The scrawny lawyer fell to his side and rolled a few feet down the hill.

He coughed and wheezed as he stood up and brushed the dusty earth from his clothes. He pointed down the hill. A few rusted cargo containers lay in a clearing.

'I know this place. There's a service road about a mile down the hill, past those containers. Warehouse nearby, lots of trucks. Maybe we catch ride?'

Caine eyed the small man and thought for a second. Sean seemed to trust him. But even if Alton was what he appeared to be, a sympathetic stranger, he could still be a liability. Jia too, for that matter. The more time he spent with these people, the more danger they were all in.

But at the moment, he didn't see an alternative. He was a fugitive in a foreign country. He didn't speak the language. He was unfamiliar with the terrain, and he didn't have any friends here. For now, these two were his only allies.

He nodded. 'Down the hill it is. Let's move.'

They made their way down the steep slope, sending small trails of rocks and dirt tumbling down the hill. They soon disappeared into the countryside, leaving the long, sleek train behind them.

22

Rebecca lifted herself up on her hands and crawled back to her chair. Her hair was damp and plastered across her flushed face. Her workout clothes clung to her skin. The foam mats on the floor stank of sweat and disinfectant. No matter how many times the facility wiped them down, they could never remove the lingering odor of human exertion.

It was late, and the gym, a tiny brick building on Kalorama Road, was empty. She was friends with the owner, a Brazilian martial arts instructor named Yasmin. Due to Rebecca's erratic schedule, they had worked out a special arrangement. Yasmin lent her a key, and she was free to work out after hours. She had not visited the sweat-infused dojo since her injury in Thailand. But when Josh had suggested some specialized training, she remembered that she still had the key.

Rebecca had worked out at this gym many times in the past, and the smell didn't bother her anymore. It reminded her of sparring, and her physical training classes at Camp Peary, Virginia – known by CIA recruits as 'The Farm.' The nine-thousand-acre Army Experimental Training Activity site served as a boot camp of sorts for those inducted into the CIA's Directorate of Operations.

To begin basic hand-to-hand combat training at The Farm, new recruits had to pass the APFT: the Army Physical Fitness Test. For Rebecca, a political science major fresh out of Princeton, it had been the greatest physical challenge of her life. It had also been the first test she had ever failed.

Now, as she struggled across the mats towards her wheelchair, she remembered picking herself up back then. In the middle of her test, she had lost her grip. She'd fallen from the chin up bar to the mats below. She remembered being thankful for the deluge of sweat dripping from her face and hair. The sweat had hidden her tears from the instructor and her classmates.

That incident alone was not enough to fail her; the rest of her scores were subpar as well. But she had not given up. She pushed through the pain and humiliation. She trained more, trained harder. She took up running in the early mornings.

Day by day, mile by mile, she built up her endurance, increased her strength. Her body grew lean and – more importantly – her mind grew stronger, sharper. With each passing mile, she grew more confident and challenged herself to do more. She pushed herself further, both in her physical training as well as her other areas of study at The Farm.

She took the test again. She passed. She kept running and never looked back.

'Earth to Rebecca,' Josh said. His eyes twinkled, and a mischievous smile played across his lips. 'You still with us? Got to keep your head in the game.'

He reached out a hand to help her up, but she ignored it. Grunting with exertion, she pulled herself up into the chair and released the wheel locks.

'You know, I think you take way too much satisfaction in beating up on a girl in a wheelchair,' she gasped.

Josh laughed. He brushed a hand over his buzz-cut, dislodging his own fine mist of sweat into the air.

'That's nothing compared to how satisfied you'll feel when you knock me on my ass,' he replied. 'You came close that time, I know you can do it. Remember, being in the chair gives you some advantages. You've got a lower center of gravity. You can pivot faster than I can, and the extra weight gives you more momentum. Ready to try again?'

She nodded. 'Absolutely. I have to do this. I can't... I don't want...'

The words choked in her throat as she thought back to the night before. The dark alley, how easily her attacker had controlled her. When she closed her eyes she could still smell the stench of rotting flowers. She could see the open maw of the van, its gaping darkness threatening to swallow her whole. If her attacker had succeeded, if he had managed to trap her in that black abyss...

'Hey, I get it,' Josh said softly. His voice pulled her up from her mental well of fear and self-doubt. 'Look, plenty of guys I served with in Iraq got hurt. They found themselves in the same position as you. Fighting was all those guys knew, and all of a sudden it was taken away from them. I trained them, taught them special techniques, showed them how they could use the chair as a weapon. But the most important thing I did was I showed them that they weren't helpless.'

'Well in case you didn't notice, I'm not exactly a two-hundred-pound marine,' she said.

Josh shook his head. 'Strength and size are factors, sure. But intelligence, awareness, and willpower are much more important. And as much as I loved those jarheads in my class, I'll tell you right now, you are way smarter than any of them. Hell of lot more stubborn too.'

She couldn't resist cracking a smile. 'Okay, fine. Any pointers, Mr. Miyagi?'

Josh crouched low and cupped his hands around his head. 'Remember to control the head. You control the head, the body will follow.'

She nodded. 'Okay, I'm ready.'

Josh sprang into action. He charged towards her and darted behind the chair. Rebecca felt him grab her shoulder and pull her backwards. Her arm shot up, and her nails raked across Josh's ear and neck. She clamped her hand on the back of his neck and flexed her elbow, knocking his hand loose from her shirt.

As her body tilted back, she snaked her other arm up and grabbed the side of his head. As the chair toppled over, she used her grip on his head to rotate his body away from her. The chair crashed to the ground, and she fell on top of him. He was face down on the floor, with her right arm looped under his neck.

Panting with exertion, she squeezed up with her arm and pushed down on the back of his head, forcing him into a tight chokehold.

Josh tapped the mat, and she released her hold. She lay on the mat, exhausted. He rolled onto his back and lay next to her. She could feel his warm breath on her ear as he looked over at her.

'You did it! That was awesome!'

'Yeah, it was,' she said, exhaling. She turned to face him. Her skin was glowing, eyes bright and wide. She smiled. 'I want to do it again.'

Josh paused for a moment, then blinked. 'Uh, yeah, sure.' He stood up and held out his hand. This time she took it. He pulled her up, slung an arm under her legs, and lifted her into the chair.

'Okay, let's try a frontal assault.'

'Music to my ears.'

Josh scratched the back of his neck. 'Right. So, same deal, control the head, and—'

An electronic chirp rang out.

'Hold that thought,' she said. She rolled to the edge of the mats, grabbed her purse, and fished through the voluminous leather bag. Police had found the bag a few hundred yards from the restaurant; the attackers had ditched it in their haste to escape. All of which confirmed Rebecca's suspicions. Her attackers had acted more like security contractors than muggers. They were not there to rob her.

The drugs, the van... She had planned similar operations herself. They were performing a kidnapping. An 'extraordinary rendition' as it was known in her trade. They had tried to take her alive. Which meant someone wanted to talk to her.

Someone wanted to know what she knew.

She fished her phone out of the bag and answered the call. 'Freeling... I'm fine, thanks. Just trying to lay low for a while. Do you have anything?'

Josh walked over to her. He offered her a bottle of water, and she nodded her thanks. He wiped his face with a towel.

'Got it,' she said into the phone. 'Thank you, Michael, I owe you one. And again, sorry about last night.'

She hung up.

'Your date?' Josh asked. His voice had a sullen tone, and she gave him a sideways glance.

'Yeah, it was. He's a defense attorney, and he put me in touch with a forensics lab he works with. Not affiliated with the agency. They did a DNA check on the blood sample you pulled from the alley.'

She held up the phone for him to see. 'Meet waiter imposter and Hermès purse enthusiast Mr. Wallace Ganda.'

Josh took the phone and scrolled through the email. 'Ex-military. Dishonorable discharge, August 12 2013, United States Army. Court martial, records sealed, no civil charges filed.'

'What does that mean?'

'It means he committed a crime, and the army swept it under the rug. They got him off duty and shipped his ass back on the next flight out of Afghanistan.' He consulted the information on the screen. 'He was serving in Kandahar with the 1st Cavalry Division. They dumped him back here, and that was the end of it. No one followed up with local law enforcement or pressed charges. Might be something like rape or sexual assault. Something people don't want to talk about.' Josh stared at the man's picture, and his eyes narrowed. His mouth twisted into a snarl of contempt. 'Whatever it was, this Ganda guy is the one I shot in the alley. I'm positive.'

Rebecca checked her messages, then slid the phone back in her purse. 'Lapinski must have sent him. If there was any doubt before, this settles it. No way was that just a mugging.'

'Guy like this, even money says he's working for a private military contractor. Blackwater, XE Services, whatever they call themselves now. Or Delta Blue, ACS Defense, Vinnel Corporation. Hell, there's so damn many of them these days, I can't keep track.'

Rebecca gritted her teeth. 'Bernatto liked to use contractors to do his dirty work. Looks like Lapinski learned from the best.' She moved back to the center of the mats. Josh followed a few steps behind her.

'Yeah, but a snatch and grab on a high-level CIA officer? That's pretty ballsy. I know a guy, kind of like a recruiter. If the word got out that Ganda was working this job, I bet he'll know something about it.'

'Will he talk to you?'

Josh looked down at her and smiled, but there was a smoldering, intense glare in his eyes. 'I'll ask real nice.'

Rebecca matched his stare. 'Good. But first, I believe we were discussing a frontal assault?'

'Remember, if you control the head, the body will follow. Ready?'

She nodded. Josh charged towards her. He reached out with both hands, pushing her shoulders back in the chair.

She ignored her instinct to try and block his hands. Instead, she reached up and looped her left arm around the back of his neck. As he pulled away, she allowed him to drag her out of the chair. Her right forearm shot up and jammed into his neck as they tumbled to the ground.

Josh pulled back, but the harder he fought, the tighter her hold became. He tapped the matt; she released the hold. She draped her arm across his back. He looked down at her, panting for breath.

'That was good,' he said. 'Better than good. You're a natural.'

'Maybe now you won't have to follow me around after hours.'

Josh looked into her eyes. 'Look, if I was out of line, I'm sorry, I just—'

'I'm glad you were there,' she said. 'I'm just giving you a hard time. I'm known to do that when I'm nervous.'

He paused for a moment. 'Aw, the hell with it,' he muttered. He bent his head down and kissed her.

A shock ran through her body. She knew she wanted this, just as much as Josh did. But it had been so long. As their lips touched, a jumble of images rushed through her mind. The gunfight in Thailand, the explosion that scarred her legs. Endless hours spent in a sterile white operating room.

And Caine... His emerald-green eyes, the orange and yellow leaves outside her window. That autumn morning so many years ago. The last time she had seen him before he had disappeared. Before everything changed. Then, when she found him at Bwang Kang prison, in Thailand... those mesmerizing eyes burning behind metal bars, staring back at her like a tiger in a cage.

She gently pushed Josh away.

'Josh, wait. I'm sorry, I...'

Josh began to get up. 'Damn, I'm sorry,' he said. 'I thought—'

She looked into his eyes, and the flood of jumbled memories and anxiety seemed to rush from her mind. They were replaced by a feeling of warm clarity, a pleasant tingling at the edge of her senses. It was a sensation she knew well. It felt like running. Like freedom.

She just had to push through.

She grabbed his shirt collar and pulled him back to her. Their lips met, and they devoured one another as her hands raked up to his neck.

They parted for breath. She gasped as she realized how strong her attraction was. How much she had denied her feelings over the past few months. Her injuries had stolen her ability to walk, but not her capacity for pleasure. At least there was that. She felt a wave of phantom heat pulsing up and down her body, growing in intensity.

But did she want him? Or did she just want someone, anyone, to make her feel something again? Someone who made her feel whole, and desired. Not broken. Not helpless.

His teeth bit down on her lip and she felt another flash of pleasure mixed with a sweet hint of pain. She knew one thing for certain... she wanted this. She didn't care why.

She tore his damp shirt off over his head and tossed it aside. It landed on her wheelchair and hung from one of the handles like a faded flag.

'Rebecca, you sure about this?' he asked in between gasps. 'Do you know what you're doing?'

'Yeah,' she exhaled into his ear. 'I'm getting some skin in the game.'

She pulled his mouth back to her lips. There were no more words.

23

A sudden lurch of the truck shook Caine awake. He heard the rattling of the vehicle as it bounced over broken, uneven pavement. Wooden shipping pallets towered around them, creaking under the weight of hundreds of bags of rice. They shook and vibrated as the vehicle continued on its way.

Jia had flagged the truck drivers over to the side of the road. Some yuan notes convinced them to transport the group to Huagu, Alton Lung's hometown. The fact that it was closer to Shanghai earned Sean's approval. The group had wedged themselves among the pallets. The drivers sealed them into the darkness, and they were on their way.

Caine was ambivalent. On the negative side, it kept him in the company of Jia and Alton longer. It also took them farther away from Hong Kong, his planned point of egress from the country. But he had to admit, it was the fastest way to put some distance between them and the bodies on the train. And after that incident, Chinese authorities would no doubt determine that Hong Kong was their destination anyway. Changing the plan was safer. So why was he still hesitating?

He knew the answer, although it bothered him to admit it.

Sean Tyler. His promise to Jack, and his failure to keep it. This time, if his plans fell apart, if the package was not delivered safely...

Stop! The voice in his head slammed down like a wall of ice, exiling those dark thoughts to the outer recesses of his mind. *You're in the field now. This mission is no different than any other.*

The truck lurched again, and the wall of the trailer vibrated behind him. Jia was asleep next to him, and her body slumped into his. Her head rested on his shoulder. She uttered a soft moan and exhaled. Her breath was a warm caress against the skin of his neck.

There was something about her. He could not put his finger on it, but her presence calmed him. He doubted she truly understood all the risks she was taking right now, on his behalf. But her serene determination was somehow reassuring.

He thought back to their walk through the beautiful *hutong* in Beijing. Her wide, luminous eyes staring at him through the flickering candlelight over dinner. She seemed to glow with her own inner warmth and beauty.

A part of him would regret leaving her behind. In his life, there had only been a handful of women he had allowed himself to grow close with. When he had been operational, it was the demands of the job that kept him detached. But after Afghanistan, after Bernatto's betrayal... a life spent hiding in the shadows had surrounded him with a wall of cold mistrust and suspicion. It had kept him alive. But it also kept him isolated. Alone.

Only a few people had ever penetrated that icy barrier. *People like Rebecca*, he thought. *And look what happened to her.*

The longer Jia was with him, the more likely she was to be swept up in his curse...

After his betrayal, Caine's thoughts often turned to the work he had done with Bernatto, Jack, and others. The violence he had witnessed... the lives he had snuffed out. Now he had to live with that blood on his hands. Some of it was justified, perhaps. But some was the blood of innocents. Pawns on a board, pieces Bernatto sought to remove from play. All to preserve his power, or wealth, or whatever other agendas he pursued in secret.

Caine was not a superstitious man. But the stain left by all that blood, he knew, was a curse. And more often than not, it inflicted itself on those he cared about most.

He sighed and leaned his head against the rattling wall of the cargo trailer. Cursed or not, he had lived with the specter of violence and death for most of his life. He knew the secret to surviving its cold hand of vengeance, and how to protect his loved ones as well.

Brick by brick, he rebuilt the wall of ice in his mind. The secret, he had learned, was to let no warmth inside.

Next to him, Jia sighed and shifted, turning her body away from him as if to escape a chilling draft.

* * *

The truck dropped them off at a gas station on the outskirts of Huagu. Caine watched it pull away, leaving them standing in a cloud of diesel fumes and dust. A cold wind blew through the station. Jia shivered, rubbing her arms for warmth.

In the distance, Caine saw factories and smokestacks towering above the barren, empty brown hills. Beyond that, the sloped concrete walls of a dam rose up, blocking the rest of the valley from view.

A muddy brown river cut through the skeletal industrial buildings and wound its way towards them. It passed behind the gas station, a sliver of slow-moving water in the distance. A thick, pinkish film of floating chemicals clung to the water's surface. The soil of the river bank was ashen gray. It turned black as it dipped down to meet the sludge-covered water.

'Where are we?' Jia asked. Her mouth twisted into a frown as she surveyed the dismal terrain surrounding them.

'It not always like this,' Alton said as the wind spun more dust around them. 'Huagu means "valley of flowers." When I was a boy, these hills were covered with yellow flowers. Rapeseed.'

'What happened?' Jia asked.

'Beijing pass stricter environmental laws. They want tourist dollars, and tourists don't want to see dirty factories and red water in river. So factories move here, and other small towns outside the capital. Different laws here, different rules. We try to fight them, try to petition the capital to do something. But...'

Caine nodded. 'Right. I saw how that worked out.'

Sean eyed their surroundings with a quick, jaded glance. 'I've seen dozens of towns like this throughout the countryside,' he said. 'This is what you get when people like David Fang call the shots. It's no different here than anywhere else. Golden rule in action.'

'He who has the most gold, rules,' Caine replied.

A horn honked three times from down the road. Caine turned and saw a battered old pickup truck driving toward them. Jia coughed as the vehicle's headlights cut through the dusty haze in the air.

Alton smiled. 'That's my brother-in-law, Tiao. I texted him from train. He give us ride.'

The truck groaned to a stop. A tall, middle-aged man with a shaved head stepped out and nodded to Caine and the others. His skin was dark and ruddy, and Caine noticed a few dark red splotches on the man's neck.

The man hugged Alton and slapped his back, causing the slim, younger man to break out in a fit of coughing. He released Alton from his bear hug and regarded Caine and the others with a solemn glance. He grunted some words in Chinese, then got back in the car.

Alton turned to them. 'He said pretty lady gets shotgun.'

Jia blushed. 'No, it's fine, I...'

Sean opened the door for her. 'Go ahead... This wind is stirring up a lot of dust, and it's only going to get worse.'

The truck's suspension groaned as Caine and Alton climbed into the pickup bed. The vehicle dipped lower to the ground as Sean scrambled in after them. Alton opened a rusted tool box and fished around. He pulled out a few old, sweat-stained bandanas.

He passed them out to Sean and Caine, then tied one around his face, covering his mouth and nose.

They tied their bandanas in the same manner and sat in silence as the truck chugged down the road. The service station diminished in the distance behind them. Soon it disappeared from view, lost in the hazy air.

Thirty minutes later, they drove through the center of Huagu. The town was a cluster of small concrete buildings running along the river banks. The chemical foam on the river was thicker here. Slow-moving ribbons of crimson and black stained the water's surface. A few patches of green grass sprouted up randomly along the banks. Weeping elm trees bent down to kiss the toxic sludge with white, decayed branches.

On the opposite side of the river, the ground sloped up. Acres of barbed-wire fence surrounded a sprawling industrial complex perched above the town. Its metal sheds, and the maze of pipes and valves surrounding them, were spotted with rust and corrosion. An array of exhaust pipes spat thick plumes of gray smoke into the air.

Alton pointed at the warning signs on the fence. 'That Fang's factory. One of many. Our government say he make medicine and chemicals for the military. They say his work save many lives. But here, he kills everything. He is like a *jiang si*.'

'A what?' Caine said, eying the plumes of toxic smoke.

'Like, how do you say? A vampire. He poison the earth, spreads death, and he becomes stronger. It's as if he feed off *qi*, the life energy of the people he kills.'

Caine shook his head. 'Men like that feed off money and power, not life energy.'

Alton said nothing. He remained silent as they drove past the gated road that led up to the factory. He held his breath, as one would crossing the entrance of a graveyard.

24

It was early evening when they reached the low, single-story house of Tiao and Alton's sister. The sun had just dipped below the horizon. Thick, noxious clouds hovered over the tiny shops and homes. An explosion of orange and purple tinted the sky above... particles and debris in the air, reflecting the last dying beams of daylight.

Tiao did not look back at the stunning sky as he shuffled from the truck towards his front door.

Alton's sister, Guan-yin, an attractive but tired-looking woman in her thirties, opened the door. She greeted Tiao with a hug and kiss on his cheek. He grunted a few words to her, then stepped into the house. Guan-yin wiped some sweat from her brow. She beamed a radiant smile at Alton and the others and greeted each of them as they walked through the door. *'Huan-ying, huan-ying,'* she said, giving Alton a hug as he walked past.

She followed them inside and gently guided Caine by the shoulder to the kitchen. *'Xie xie ni bang wo de xiong di,'* she said, offering him a slight bow. *'Bai tuo ni bi xu chi.'*

Alton sat down at a large, simple wooden table that dominated the room. 'She thanked you for bringing me home. Said we have to eat.'

A large cast iron pot was bubbling on the stove. The hearty scent of braised beef and ginger filled the air. It had been hours since any of them had eaten a proper meal, and Caine's stomach growled with hunger.

'Thank you, we're star—'

Jia rested a hand on his knee and squeezed, cutting off his words. 'We're so grateful for your hospitality,' she said. 'But we couldn't possibly impose. You and your husband must eat first.' She and Guan-yin spoke back and forth in rapid Chinese, and finally Jia nodded. '*Xie xie*, we are in your debt.'

She turned to Caine and whispered in his ear. 'You must refuse at least once. It is rude to be so eager.'

Caine's stomach emitted another low rumble. 'Tell that to my stomach,' he muttered. 'It doesn't speak Chinese.'

The group watched as Guan-yin rolled a large block of dough onto a wooden cutting board. When the dough formed a thin square sheet, she held the cutting board above a pot of boiling water. Using a small, square-shaped knife, she made a series of quick slicing motions over the dough.

With each stroke, the knife shaved a long thin strip of dough off the board. The knife-cut noodles, known as *Dao Xiao Mian*, fell into the bubbling water to cook. Caine watched as Guan-yin shaved the last of the dough into the water. Then she used a wire strainer to sift out the cooked noodles, dropping them into large white bowls. She ladled a generous portion of beef broth over the noodles and set them down on the table.

Caine used a pair of chopsticks to shovel the noodles into his mouth. They were thick, chewy, and satisfying. The amount of meat in the bowl was small, but each chunk of beef had been boiled to exquisite tenderness. It fell apart in his mouth, mixing with the ginger, onion, and other flavors in the hearty broth.

As they ate, Tiao sat in a rocking chair, facing away from them. He watched the local news playing on a small TV in the corner, slurping soup from his bowl with a white plastic spoon.

'Alton,' Sean mumbled, as he stuffed his mouth full of noodles. 'You gotta tell your sister, this is amazing.'

Alton addressed his sister in Chinese. She smiled, took Sean's bowl from the table, and refilled it. 'Yeah, she good cook,' Alton said. 'She use bottled water for the soup, so no worries. We used to purify the river water with aluminum powder, but now it get so bad, we can't drink it. Only use for bath and shower.'

'*Niang*,' a small voice called out. A young girl wandered into the kitchen. Her skin was pale and had a sallow look to it. Her short, dark hair was braided into twin pigtails that hung from the sides of her head at odd angles. Caine guessed her to be about eight years old. She walked toward them with small, weak steps. '*Wo xiang he yi xie tang le.*'

Alton dropped his chopsticks and grinned ear to ear. 'Baozhai, you're awake? You mother says you supposed to be sleeping.'

Guan-yin gave the girl a concerned look, but she did not intervene as Alton lifted her onto the bench next to him. She coughed, then looked up at him and smiled.

'This is my niece, Baozhai,' Alton said. 'Her name means "stockade of treasure".'

Jia leaned over the table and adjusted one of the girl's pigtails. 'What a pretty name for such a pretty girl.'

'She said she wants some soup,' Alton said. He brought a spoon of broth to the girl's mouth. She sipped it, and her face lit up with a wide grin. He gave her some more but stopped when she began to cough. Her tiny, frail body shook as the spasm of coughing grew worse.

Guan-yin dropped her dishrag into the sink and hurried over. She wrapped the shaking girl in her arms and carried her from the table. 'That's enough, little one,' she said. '*Ni bi xu xiu xi*, you must rest.'

Jia looked at the table. Her eyes squinted at a small spray of red flecks where the child had been sitting. 'Oh my God, is that blood?'

Alton sighed. 'She is sick. She is the reason I go to Beijing. I petition the capital. Try to make them close down Fang's factory, make him and others like him pay for what they have done to us. What they have done to our children.'

He paused. Guan-yin had taken his niece to the back of the house. They could still hear her faint coughing in the distance.

'Lung cancer,' Alton said. He pushed the bowl of soup away and stood up from the table. 'Eight years old, and she has lung cancer. Whoever heard of such a thing?'

He glared at Caine. 'You still think Fang is no monster? That he is just a man, like any other? What kind of man could do this to innocent children?'

Caine's emerald eyes met Alton's angry gaze. 'I said he was no vampire,' Caine replied. 'Trust me, I've known plenty of monsters. They were all just men. That's all it takes.'

'He is *jiang si*.'

Everyone turned and looked at Tiao. The large man had stood up from the rocking chair. His face held a blank, emotionless stare. His eyes looked towards the back of the house. In the distance, Baozhai continued to cough.

'He is a demon,' Tiao said in a low, scratchy voice. 'He feeds off the living. And I am no better.'

Tiao did not look at them as he walked towards the bedroom. He slammed the door closed behind him.

Alton looked at the others. 'He works at the Fang factory. Everyone here does, or at one of other factories in the area. There is an aluminum plant, and a natural gas mine as well. Those are the only jobs left. Everything else is gone.'

Jia stood up. She put an arm on Alton's shoulder. 'You are a good brother. And a good uncle.'

She looked up at Caine. 'I'll see if I can help Guan-yin.'

Jia and Alton left the room and headed to the back of the house. Sean stood up to follow them, but Caine grabbed his arm.

'Sean... sit down.'

Sean gave him a strange look, but he sat back down at the table.

Caine looked him in the eye. 'We need to talk.'

25

Josh struggled to focus on the farmhouse in distance. The two-story building was in good shape and looked like it had been recently painted. The wood planks that made up its outer walls were brick-red. The crimson paint had not yet faded from exposure to the sun and elements. Someone was taking good care of the place.

Josh tried to catalog these and other specifics, to focus his mind on noticing the tiny details. Tiny details, he knew, could mean the difference between life and death.

But instead, his thoughts continued to drift to the events of the previous night. Like a boat moored by a short length of rope, he found himself dragged again and again into the swift currents of memory. Had he done the right thing? Had he overstepped his bounds? Had he taken advantage of her? Or was it the other way around?

He shook his head and forced himself to return his attention to the farmhouse. Two men crossed the dew-covered grass, heading toward the red building. Josh twisted the focus knob of the binoculars he held in his hands. Their twin lenses magnified the figures. As the image resolved, more details came into view.

One of the men had tan skin, salt and pepper hair, and dark, furtive eyes. He turned left and right, scanning the perimeter as he approached the door of the farmhouse.

Wallace Ganda.

Josh's contact, a man called Tiny, had come through.

Tiny ran a biker bar in Leesburg. The beefy, rotund man had put on weight since the last time Josh had seen him. But back in the day, Tiny had been a bona fide ass kicker. He was a former marine, Force Recon, just like Josh. After his discharge, Tiny had done some time as an independent contractor... a polite way of saying 'gun for hire.' Now, he was a recruiter of sorts. He had ties to private security, mercenaries, and other soldiers of fortune.

A rendition attempt on the Director of the National Clandestine Service was out of Tiny's league. But if the men involved were in town, Tiny would know about it.

It took Josh a few broken bottles and the business end of a pool cue to make his point. In the end, he had convinced Tiny that protecting a washed-out piece of shit like Wallace Ganda was not in his best interests.

Ganda had made a mistake. He had attacked Rebecca.

Josh respected the director. She was like him. A fighter. A warrior. And it was his duty to protect her. She was his people. And one thing Josh had learned in his years of combat was that when the enemy struck your people, you hit back twice as hard.

Now, after last night, things had become even more personal.

Josh returned his attention to Ganda. He and another man approached the door. Both wore jeans, casual shirts, and windbreakers. Ganda was carrying bags from a local grocery store.

The other man hefted cases of bottled water and soda on his shoulder. He was tall and well-built. Wraparound sunglasses covered his eyes, and his head was shaved. A thick mustache and goatee covered his chin. Like Ganda, his movements were smooth and precise. *Ex-military*, Josh thought. *Just like the others.*

So far Josh had counted at least four people entering and leaving the house at various points. Judging by the items they were carrying, it appeared Ganda and his partner had gone on a food run. But why were these men camped out in this remote farmhouse in the first place?

Even if they believed the police report and thought there was no evidence left behind in the alley, they had still bungled a high-profile snatch. The safest course of action would have been to leave town. Unless there was some other priority here. Something special at this location that Josh hadn't seen yet. Or a mission parameter that had yet to be completed.

Josh heard footsteps crunching across dead leaves. Someone was approaching his position. With slow, silent movements, he tucked the binoculars into a pocket on his 5.11 Response jacket. His hand reached for the Glock 19 pistol he carried in a shoulder rig.

He stopped himself. The sound of a gunshot would carry. If Ganda and his men heard it, they would pack up and leave. And if that happened, he and Rebecca might never find out exactly what they were doing here.

The footsteps moved closer... beneath him.

Josh stretched out his body, trying to blend in with the foliage. He was perched fifteen feet off the ground, nestled in the branches of a Carolina Poplar. Hundreds of identical trees lined the acreage around the farmhouse.

The morning sun was low. Pinpoints of light reflected off the droplets of moisture that dotted the ground. The orange and red leaves surrounding him were still shrouded in shadow. It was a decent hide, but if the man moving beneath him looked up, Josh doubted he would escape notice.

The man stopped beneath Josh's tree. Peering down, Josh spotted the black stock and barrel of a Bushmaster M4 carbine.

Okay, he thought. *Things are getting serious up here.*

Civilian M4 models were semi-automatic only. They fired a single 5.56 x45 NATO round each time the trigger was depressed. But simple aftermarket kits could convert the rifle to burst and full-auto fire. Josh had no doubt these men would have installed such modifications on their weapons.

A pair of mourning doves burst into the air, to the man's right. He spun around. The barrel of his M4 tracked the explosion of fluttering wings and feathers as the birds took flight.

Josh caught a glimpse of the man's features. He was new – Josh had not seen him entering the house earlier. That brought the total count to at least six hostiles.

The odds were getting worse.

The guard swept the area one more time with his rifle, then moved on. The crunching of his footsteps grew fainter. He descended the hill and headed across the field towards the big red house.

Once he was out of sight, Josh took a deep breath and shimmied down the tree. He ducked into the forest at the perimeter of the property, then made his way back to the winding dirt road where he had parked his car. As he walked, he scanned the tree line, searching for any signs of movement. But the dense forest of trees was still, unmoving.

He slipped his phone out of his pocket and dialed Rebecca's number.

She picked up on the first ring. 'Josh, I was worried. You were supposed to report in an hour ago.'

'Sorry. Almost got spotted. Had to lay low for a while.'

'Did your contact come through?' she asked.

'Yeah. It took some convincing, but he talked. Said he heard a rumor Ganda was holed up in a farmhouse in Roanoke Valley. One of Tiny's guys spotted him in town, making food runs, buying beer. That kind of stuff.'

Josh emerged from the forest and paced over to a green rental Jeep parked on the side of a winding dirt road.

'And?' The concern in Rebecca's voice was replaced with a hint of impatience.

'And I have good news and bad news. Good news first, our man is definitely up here. I followed Ganda back to the farmhouse. It's pretty remote. Not too far from the mountains. Middle of nowhere.'

'Well, that makes sense, I guess. So what's the bad news?'

Josh started up the engine and drove the Jeep down the winding trail. The tall, dark trees receded in his rearview mirror.

'The bad news is he's not alone. He's got a small army camped out with him.'

26

The house was quiet. Alton and Guan-yin took turns tending to Baozhai. The little girl was resting, and her coughing had finally subsided. Earlier, Caine had watched from the doorway as her mother lay a thin, moist towel over her mouth. The damp rag helped filter the air the child breathed as she slept.

He and Sean were alone in the kitchen. Jia had retired for the evening, and Tiao had not left his self-imposed exile in the bedroom.

'We can't stay here,' Caine said in a low voice. 'It's not safe for you, and it's not safe for them.'

Sean nodded. 'You're right. Besides, I have to get to Shanghai.'

'Why? What's so important in Shanghai?'

Sean leaned closer, an uneasy look on his face. 'Before I say anything, I want to know exactly who the hell you are. How did you know my father?'

Caine stared at the young man for a moment, then sighed. He stood up, went to the fridge, and grabbed two cans of beer. Then he sat back down, popped one open, and slid the can to Sean. He opened his own and took a long sip.

'Like I said, my name is Tom. I worked with your father.'

'What kind of work?' Sean asked.

Caine thought for a moment. 'Government work.'

Sean slapped the table. 'I knew it. You guys were spies, right? Or some kind of commandoes, something military.'

Caine nodded. 'Something like that, yes.'

Sean ran a hand through his hair and exhaled. 'He... Dad... would never tell me what he did for a living. Always changed the subject or made a joke out of it. Whenever I saw him, it was like a day here, a day there... He was always traveling. Every now and then I'd get postcards with no signature, no return address. Something random, like "happy birthday"... three months past my birthday. Never a phone call, or an email. Nothing like that.'

Caine leaned back in his chair. 'Sean, you have to understand, what your father did, what I did... it made it hard to have people in our lives. It was dangerous. For us, but also for them. He may have seemed distant, but he did it to keep you safe.'

'So what happened to him?'

Caine fumbled for words. He struggled not to sound like he was delivering a debriefing... struggled to sound human.

'Your father and I were on a mission together. We were betrayed. He didn't make it out. I barely survived myself.'

Sean narrowed his eyes. His voice took on an edge of anger. 'Betrayed? Betrayed by whom?'

'Doesn't matter,' Caine said, his voice taking on an icy tone. 'They'll get what's coming to them. I can promise you that.'

'Oh, you promise?' Sean laughed. 'You know how many promises my dad made to me? He promised to see me again soon, or to be home for Christmas. He promised to drive me to my first day of school. He never kept any of those promises. Not a one. Why should I think you're any different?'

'Maybe you're right,' Caine said. 'I promised Jack I would look out for you. And I failed.'

Sean took a swig of beer. 'Yeah, well, don't sweat it. I'm used to it.'

'I'm here now. I'm sorry I wasn't there for you before; things got complicated. But you're in danger here, and not just from Fang.'

'What are you talking about?'

'There's more at stake than you think. The National Security Agency has a Chinese hacker in custody. China wants him back, and they were planning to exchange you for him. It's all tied to the president's new trade deal.'

Sean's eyes narrowed in thought. 'This guy from the ministry came to see me. He said they had to keep me safe, that's why they moved me to the black jail, in Beijing. He said I'd be home soon, and this would all be over.'

Caine nodded. 'Yeah, well, unfortunately, the NSA has different plans. This hacker accessed some sensitive information. They don't want to give him up until they find it. They're willing to kill you to stop the exchange from happening.'

'Wait, this trade agreement... Do you mean the Global Environmental Accords? China actually signed the protocols, they're onboard?'

Caine shrugged. 'You seem to know more about it than I do.'

'If they kill me, and the exchange doesn't happen, couldn't that ruin the whole deal?'

'I think the NSA is more concerned with covering up their dirty work than clean air and water for China.'

'So that albino, he was some kind of government assassin?'

Caine shook his head. 'I don't think so. I think he worked for Fang. But either way, it's too dangerous to stay here. You have too many enemies, on both sides of this. You have to get out of China as soon as possible.'

Sean stood up. 'Look around you, man. Sure I can leave, but what about Alton? What about Jia, and Guan-yin? Or that little girl coughing up blood in the back room? Fang, and others like him, are poisoning these people. You could just leave them behind, like nothing is happening?'

'You getting killed won't help these people.'

'Neither will running away. You want to be there for me, help me? Then help me for real. I have friends in Shanghai, a hacker group called the Jade Enclave. They work with Human Rights Now.'

Caine nodded. 'Jia told me about them. They got us the plans to the black jail where you were being held.'

'We found something. Something that could stop Fang.'

'That's why Fang is after you?'

Sean looked down at the table. 'I guess. We broke into Fang's offices. HRN got a tip that Fang kept secret records. Documents that would prove he was breaking what little regulations there were at his factory in Huagu. He kept them in an isolated computer, something off the network. We could only access it from his new building in Shanghai, the one he's building downtown. Fang Plaza.'

'Well, did you find them?'

Sean shook his head. 'No, but my friend said he found something bigger. Something that could destroy Fang, put him away for good. But before he could explain what he meant, we triggered an alarm. He did something, messed with the file somehow. We ran out of the building and split up. I laid low for a while, then I went back to his apartment to try and find him. The cops had the place staked out; they arrested me outside.'

'And your friend?' Caine asked. 'What happened to him?'

'I don't know... I tried calling him before I was arrested. I couldn't reach him. If Fang was after him too... it might be too late.'

'All the more reason why you should leave,' Caine said.

Sean leaned back in his chair. 'Is that what my dad would do? You knew him better than I did.'

Caine stared at Sean in silence.

Sean stood and looked away. 'I get it. You made a promise to my dad. You feel bad. But Jack... He's gone. And I'm here now. Maybe that sounds cold to you, but you're talking about a man I saw, what? Maybe forty-eight hours my whole life? I've spent as much time with you as I did with him. So if you want to help me, then help me. But if you've just got a guilty conscience or something... Sorry, man, I got no time for that.'

He turned and began to leave the room.

'Sean, wait.'

Sean turned around and rested his hand on the doorframe. 'Yeah, what?'

'The last time I saw your father, we were in Afghanistan. That mission I told you about, the one where we were betrayed? Jack was watching me from a sniper hide, feeding me intel. He had high ground, he saw the threat before I did. He could have bailed and ran out on me. He could have saved himself. That would have been the smart play.'

'But he didn't?' Sean asked in a hesitant voice.

'No. He fought his way down to my position. He saved my life. Got himself killed in the process. I was there with him when he passed. I heard his dying words. He talked about you.'

'What did he say?'

'He said the things he did, the work we did together... He wanted you to know he did it to make the world a better place for you.'

Sean's eyes squinted, and his lips turned up in a cross between a smile and a frown. 'Well, I guess my father and I had something in common, after all. We don't run out on our friends.'

Caine finished his beer and stood up. 'That's not all you have in common. You're also two of the most stubborn men I've ever met.'

Sean's smile grew wider. 'So... Shanghai?'

Caine sighed. 'Fine. But just you and me, we leave the others here. We check on your partner, see what we can find, and that's it. After that, we leave the country.'

'And what if he does have something big? Something that can take down Fang?'

'Then we get the info to the proper hands, someone who can use it. We can't get involved in a personal crusade against Fang, no matter how much of a monster he is.'

Sean nodded. 'Okay, I can live with that.'

Caine slipped his burner phone from his pocket. 'We leave before sunrise. Get some sleep, it's going to be a long day.'

He wondered if he was making a mistake. He had broken his promise once to Jack. If something went wrong now, if Sean was hurt, or worse...

'Who are you calling?' Sean asked, interrupting his thoughts.

'Someone who can help. An old friend.'

As the phone rang, Caine watched the young man slip back into the shadows of the dark house.

27

'Have you lost your mind?' Rebecca snapped into the phone. 'I told you to give me some time!'

As she talked, she watched a small bank of monitor screens in the back of the dark unmarked van. The van was parked about a mile from the farmhouse Josh had reconnoitered earlier in the morning. Something was keeping Ganda at this location. There was either something of value inside, or they were awaiting further orders. Either way, she intended to find out.

'And I told you I couldn't wait,' Caine said, his voice crackling in her ear. 'Someone was already there, in the prison. In the middle of a riot, they were trying to break down the door to his cell. They were targeting him, just like I told you.'

'A riot? You mean the disturbance you created? Christ, Tom, you do realize you attacked a government facility on foreign soil?'

'It's not an official government facility. It's off-books, the Chinese government won't even admit the place exists.'

'That makes me feel so much better,' she said. 'And what am I supposed to do when my Chinese counterpart calls? He may have a few questions about an agent of mine who broke into a black jail and released a prisoner of the People's Republic.'

'You tell him the truth. You didn't authorize any such operation. You have no operatives working for you in China. You haven't debriefed me yet, remember? I'm still on the outside.'

Rebecca was only half-listening. Her attention was focused on one of the screens. It displayed an aerial shot of the farmhouse. Two men were switching places for guard duty on the perimeter of the property. From the high vantage point of the camera, the men looked like tiny black dots pacing across the field.

She sighed and turned away from the monitors. 'Tom, you can't keep working like this. And I can't keep covering for you. I know I was upset before, about Bernatto, about letting him go. But this... this isn't the life I want for you.'

'You didn't choose this life for me. I made my own choices. My own mistakes. Now, what about Lapinski? Do you have any intel on his assassin?'

'I thought you said you stopped them, in the prison?'

Caine paused for a moment. 'I don't know. I don't think so. Things are a little more complicated than I thought.'

'They usually are,' Rebecca said.

'The human rights group Sean was working with... they were investigating an industrialist named David Fang. Can you check if you have anything on him? According to a source here, he may be Triad-connected.'

'Triads? You think they're after Sean as well?'

'I don't know. The guy in the prison was... well, he was a little distinctive for a government assassin. Albino. White skin, pink eyes. Oh, and six fingers on each hand.'

Rebecca arched an eyebrow. 'You've got to be kidding me.'

'I'm not finished. Apparently he has a twin brother.'

Rebecca chuckled. 'You do meet the most interesting people in the field, huh?'

'Tell me about it. Anyway, these guys felt like gangsters to me. My guess is they were working for Fang.'

'Were?' she asked. 'As in, past tense?'

Caine was silent.

'Forget it,' she said, 'I don't want to know. Anyway, I came at Lapinski hard, and he took the bait. Sent a contractor to jump me in the middle of a date.'

'What?' The note of anger in Caine's voice cut through the static and distortion of the phone line. 'Why didn't you tell me?'

'I didn't know how to reach you. You said you'd call me, remember?'

'Are you all right?'

She took a deep breath. 'Little shaken up, but no permanent damage. You were right, I wasn't taking Ted seriously enough. Somehow he was able to track me, he knew where I would be. Anyway, I'm fine. One of my bodyguards was monitoring me.'

'On a date?'

'Long story. The point is, I pushed Ted, and he pushed back. We were able to identify the contractor he used, an ex-military piece of shit named Ganda. He's holed up in a farmhouse in Virginia. My men are getting ready to move on him now.'

'Copy that. Look, I was planning to get Sean out of the country through Hong Kong. I have some old contacts there, but things...'

'Got complicated?' Rebecca said.

'Yeah. We'll be in Shanghai tomorrow. I could use an extraction team.'

'I might be able to set something up. But there's one condition.'

'Condition?'

'After this, you come in. It's getting too dangerous on the outside.'

'But Bernatto is still—'

'Killing Bernatto isn't... Look, we both know it's not going to undo the past. What he did, to both of us... It's going to take time to fix. Let someone else chase after him. You deserve some peace. At least for a while.'

The static crackled and popped on the line. She wished she could see his face, look into his eyes.

'I'll think about it,' he replied.

'Tom, you have to—'

'Director,' a voice called from the front of the van. It was one of Josh's handpicked men, a thirty-two-year-old former marine named Clayton DuBose. 'We have another vehicle,' he said. 'Monitor three.'

Rebecca turned her attention back to the monitors. She watched as a BMW SUV pulled up in front of the farmhouse. A tiny black figure stepped out of the car and made their way towards the front door.

'Magnify,' she said. 'Give me a face!'

The aerial camera zoomed in and froze on the blurry image of a man's face. 'Running enhancement,' Clayton said. A scan line ran down the image. The surveillance system's software processed the digital signal, reducing noise, enhancing light, pulling detail from the shadows.

Rebecca stared at the image in shock. 'Oh my God, he's here. It's Lapinski. That stupid son of a bitch is on-site! What the hell is he doing here?'

'Bernatto said Lapinski had leverage on Red Phoenix,' Caine said. 'Something he used to turn them, force them to do his dirty work.'

'That must be what's in the house,' she said in an excited

voice. 'That's why they didn't leave town. Tom, I have to go. I'll text you a secure web address. I'll leave extraction details for you there.'

'Thank you. Be careful, all right?'

'You too,' she said.

'And Rebecca... good hunting.'

There was a click and he was gone.

Rebecca leaned over a mic mounted next to the monitors. 'Magpie One, this is Mobile. Do you read me?'

'Go for Magpie One,' Josh's voice came back in her earpiece.

'Lapinski is on-site. Repeat, Lapinski is on-site. Move in, now!'

* * *

Ted Lapinski paced back and forth across the uneven wood floor of the old farmhouse. The location was remote, isolated, and far from prying eyes. But it was also dark, cold, and stank of mildew. The boarded windows and secondhand furniture made the place feel like a claustrophobic prison.

He took a swig of water from a plastic bottle. Then he eyed the bank of surveillance monitors stacked on a folding table in the corner of the living room. They were taking too long. He didn't want to stay here a minute longer than necessary.

'We need to get moving. Where the hell is Ganda?' he asked, raising his voice to be heard over the football game playing on the widescreen TV.

Royce, one of the contractors he had hired, sighed and crumpled a beer can in his hands. He stood up. The old, frayed sofa he had been sitting on creaked as his weight lifted from the springs.

'What's so important about Ganda?' Royce asked. 'The guy's a screw-up. Bungled a simple snatch and grab.'

Ted gave Royce a knowing look. 'After we find him, I'd like to talk to you about that. We need to discuss his retirement plans.'

Royce raised his eyebrows. 'Damn. Okay. Usual bonus?'

Ted nodded. 'Of course.'

'Music to my ears. Let's take a look. This game sucks anyway.'

He shut off the TV. He tossed the remote on the sofa and ambled over to the monitors.

Royce wasn't exactly in his prime. His hair was sparse and his face was pale and sagging. But his piercing blue eyes held an alert gleam. Ted knew the man's résumé. Royce had seen plenty of combat in his time. Plenty of death. Kamdesh, Fallujah, Ganjgal... His service record was a checklist of bloody, merciless hotspots across the Middle East. The fact that he was still walking around was a testament to his skills.

'All right, I've got Swanson and Duval out front,' Royce said. He pressed some buttons on a small video switcher. Images from security cameras mounted all around the property played on multiple screens. 'So where the hell is Ganda?'

The men turned as they heard footsteps coming from the rickety wood staircase on the other side of the room. Matheson, the youngest of the team, teetered down the stairs balancing two enormous duffel bags across his wide shoulders.

He set the bags down and stretched his back. 'That's all our gear from upstairs,' he said. 'All that's left is the stuff in the girl's room, and—'

'Matheson,' Royce interrupted. 'Have you seen Ganda in the last hour?'

'Not since I relieved him on the perimeter,' the young, clean-cut operative said. 'I think he's in the barn, with the Cougar. He's got a hard-on for that truck.'

'Yup,' Royce muttered as he punched more buttons. 'There he is with Daniels in the barn, cam three.' The image switched from the front of the farmhouse to a high-angle view inside a barn. Two men were leaning over the open hood of a large truck.

Ted squinted his eyes and peered at the screen as the cameras switched angles. 'Wait, go back.'

'Huh?' Royce looked up from the switcher.

'Go back to the front of the house, whatever camera that was.'

'Cam two,' Royce said as he switched one of the monitors back to a wide-angle view looking down at the front porch. A gentle breeze blew a few stray leaves past the front door.

'There's no one there. I thought you said Duval and Swanson were out front?'

Royce switched through all cameras. They watched as various angles of the house flashed in front of them.

'The cameras, how mobile are they?' Ted asked.

'Three hundred and sixty degrees,' Royce answered, as he continued switching angles.

'Up! Point them up! All of them!'

Royce grabbed a small joystick mounted next to the switcher and began panning the cameras up. A few angles were blocked by the trees, the roof, or other obstacles. But one panned all the way up, offering a clear view of the blue skies above the farmhouse.

Ted pointed to a small black dot on the screen. 'Zoom in.'

'Motherfucker! You've got some good eyes, man,' Matheson said, as he looked over Ted's shoulder. 'What is it?'

The dot grew larger and more detailed. Ted knew what it was before the camera stopped zooming.

'It's a drone,' Ted snapped. 'We're under surveillance.'

Matheson gave Royce a puzzled look. 'By who?'

Royce stood up and drew a Glock 19 pistol from a holster at his belt. 'Doesn't matter. Get the package down here, we're leaving now.' He picked up a walkie from the table and thumbed the talk button. 'We are blown, repeat, we are blown. Everyone drop your shit and get to the barn, before—'

CRASH!

The front door splintered and flew open. Royce spun around and raised his weapon. Before he could fire, a tiny metal cylinder rolled across the floor.

Ted dove under the table and covered his ears. The cylinder exploded. A brilliant white flash filled the room. Even with his eyes closed, the light was blinding. A split second later, the explosive shockwave assaulted his ear drums. As the ringing grew louder, he opened his eyes. Dark shapes swept through the smoke-filled room.

He saw the muzzle flash of automatic weapons pierce the smoke-filled air. The gunfire was silent to his ears. The only sound he could hear was a high-pitched ringing, growing louder and louder.

He stumbled out from under the table, dropped to his knees, and clasped his hands over his head. He prayed that it was Rebecca and her Special Operations Group who had tracked him here. If that was the case, he might survive.

And if it was option number two?

Well, in that case, welcome to Vegas, buddy. Because you've just been cashed out.

28

It was dark when Caine woke. He could tell by Sean's rhythmic, loud breathing that the younger man was still asleep. Caine stood up and dressed. The two of them had slept in the living room, in the front of the house. Jia had shared the child's room, and Alton was in Tiao and Guan-yin's bedroom.

Caine's muscles ached from spending the night on the hard wood floor. Still, he had to admit, it was far from the most uncomfortable place he had ever slept. He took a few minutes to stretch and listened for any signs of movement in the house. He heard nothing. Everyone else was still asleep.

Sean was sleeping on a threadbare sofa that ran along the front wall of the house. Caine reached over and shook him. The younger man awoke with a start. He gasped, and Caine covered his mouth to prevent him from crying out. Sean's eyes adjusted to the dim light, and he relaxed when he saw Caine's face staring down at him. Caine removed his hand.

'Jesus, you scared the hell out of me, man,' Sean whispered. 'I think I was having a nightmare or something.'

'I'm not surprised. Keep your voice down.'

Sean sat up on the sofa and fished around for his T-shirt. He sniffed the filthy, worn garment and grunted. 'Damn, this smells like roadkill. We need new clothes.'

'We'll have to worry about that later. Maybe we can pick something up in Shanghai. Get dressed and meet me outside. Be quiet, I don't want to wake anyone.'

Caine walked into the kitchen as Sean gathered the rest of his clothes in the living room. He heard the door open, and a gentle breeze drifted through the house. It carried the acidic, bitter taste of the air outside. Then the door closed as Sean slid outside.

Caine stood still for a few seconds, letting his eyes continue to adjust to the light. He remembered seeing Tiao hang the keys to the pickup truck on a hook near the stove. He felt along the walls until the keychain jingled beneath his fingers. He paused and thought for a moment. Stealing a car from Alton's family hadn't exactly been his original plan.

Plans change. Don't make it personal. Keep moving.

He snatched the keys up in his hand and left the kitchen.

Outside, the wind was beginning to pick up again. A sliver of orange light rose above the horizon. It peered out between the towering smokestacks and black clouds of the Fang factory. The industrial pipes and buildings of the complex stood silhouetted against the rising sun. Their black, twisted shapes looked like the skeletal remains of some ancient beast.

Sean stood next to the car, surveying the small, silent town. He turned and looked at Caine. 'So now we're car thieves?'

'If you've got a better way to get to Shanghai, I'm all ears.'

Sean shook his head.

Caine walked over to the car. 'That's what I thought.'

He heard the door to the house open. He spun around, his hand instinctively dropping to his waist.

It was Jia. She stood in the doorway, dressed in a long T-shirt that fell just below her knees. Her hair was pulled back in a thick ponytail. It trailed behind her in the wind as she stepped off the porch.

Her liquid brown eyes searched Caine's face. 'You are leaving, aren't you?' she asked. Her voice was almost lost in the wind.

'Sean, get in the car,' Caine said.

'Sorry, Jia,' Sean mumbled as he opened the passenger door and slid into the seat. He closed the door with a soft thunk.

Caine took a step towards her. 'Look, Jia, I'm sorry, but it's too dangerous. We can't stay here.'

'I understand. I just thought...'

She moved closer to him and put a hand on his chest. The wind whipped through her T-shirt, plastering the thin fabric to her body.

'I thought that night, in Beijing, there was something there. I thought you would at least say goodbye.'

'It's safer this way,' Caine said. 'The more time you spend with us, with me... the more danger you'll be in. Please, trust me. The less you know about all this, the better.'

She nodded. 'I understand. The work I do, the things I fight for... here, in China, it can be dangerous. I take risks as well. That night at dinner, you called me brave. But sometimes, it's the ones we care about most who pay the price for our bravery.'

A shiver ran through her body. Caine fought the urge to embrace her, to wrap his arms around her. 'You're right,' he said. 'I've seen it firsthand. Too many times to count.'

Jia lifted her chin and stared up at him. One of her hands moved up to his face. Her fingers traced the hard line of his jaw, then pressed into his stubble-covered cheek.

'It makes it hard to live a normal life,' she said. 'Hard to get close to anyone.'

Her eyes were so close, he felt like the twin pools of brown and black filled his vision; they were all he could see. Then her eyes closed, and her lips touched his.

He was surprised to find himself kissing her back. It was brief, but he felt her lingering touch after he broke away tingling across his lips and flushed skin.

'*Zhu weishou de sha gua,*' she whispered into his ear as her face drifted away from his.

Caine smiled. 'You never told me what that means.'

She laughed. Then she turned and walked towards the house. As she opened the door, she looked back at him over her shoulder. 'I'll tell you later.'

Then the door closed and she was gone. Caine stood still for a minute, letting the wind carry the scent of her away, along with the memory of her touch. The electric shock of her lips faded.

Time to go.

Caine opened the door and slid into the driver's seat. Sean struggled to wipe the grin off his face.

'Hey man, you need a few minutes? If you want to go back in there, no worries,' he said.

Caine gave him a sideways glance as he started up the truck and shifted into drive. 'What about this super important thing you have to do in Shanghai?'

'Man's got to have his priorities, know what I mean?'

'Kid, you're an international fugitive. Plus, you're marked for death by the Triads and the NSA. Maybe you should re-examine your priorities.'

Sean laughed. 'That's cold, man. Cold.'

They pulled away from the house. As they drove down the long, empty road, the crumbling buildings and polluted waters of Huagu disappeared in their rearview mirror, lost in the dust and the hazy glow of the rising sun.

29

Fang paced down the sterile corridor at a rapid clip. Doctor Song walked beside him, her heels clicking on the glossy white floor. Her attention was focused on the tablet in her hands. Medical charts and data flashed across the glowing screen.

'These are excellent results, Mr. Fang. Hormone and blood cell counts are far better than we could have hoped for a woman of her age, and in her condition.'

'She doesn't look good,' Fang snapped. 'When I look at her, do you know what I see?'

'I don't understand what you mean.'

'I see a corpse. She is dying.'

'Yes, she is,' Doctor Song said in her flat, matter-of-fact voice. 'As I told you, transplanting the cancerous organ is a delaying tactic at best. It is not a long-term strategy.'

'And I told you, Doctor, I want results! What exactly is your strategy then?'

'Assuming her recovery continues at this pace, we can accelerate the next phase of treatment. The clinic recently installed a Mevion Proton Therapy system. It's the most advanced form of radiation therapy available. Only a select few hospitals have access to such a device.'

'She's undergone radiation before; what makes this any different?' Fang asked.

Song tapped the tablet, bringing up a presentation video for the device. She held the tablet up for him to see as they walked.

'The machine uses a miniaturized particle accelerator to increase the energy level of protons. The beam of radiation is much more controlled. We can direct it to a specific depth in the patient's body. This allows us to target her tumors, while minimizing damage to healthy tissue.'

Fang pushed the tablet away. They reached the door to his mother's room and stopped. 'How soon can you begin the treatment?' he asked, lowering his voice.

Song consulted her charts, then looked up at him. 'She must have time to heal from her surgery. Normal recovery for a transplant such as this would be three weeks. However, due to the successful HBO treatment, I believe we can shorten that to two.'

'Two weeks? What if her condition worsens before then?' Fang grabbed the doctor's arm. His eyes were two black dots of concentrated anger, and his lips curled into a snarl. 'I tell you, she does not look better. She looks worse. I warned you what would happen if she does not survive this treatment.'

A look of fear shimmered across Dr. Song's porcelain features. An instant later, it was replaced by her usual calm stare.

'Your mother is elderly. Her body is being ravaged by two different forms of cancer. And she has survived more surgical procedures than most women half her age. Thanks to you, this clinic is the most advanced cancer treatment facility in the world. If she were anywhere else, she would be dead by now.'

The rage in Fang's face intensified. He gripped her arm tighter, twisting his fingers into the fabric of her white lab coat.

Then he exhaled. The fury seemed to drain from his handsome features. They were replaced by a look of bewilderment and confusion. He looked away from the doctor, staring at the door next to them. More medical charts flashed across the screens mounted to its polished metal surface.

'You're right of course. I just... I wanted to—'

Song pulled her arm from his grip. 'What do you think is going to happen here, Mr. Fang? What do you want for your mother? Because as a doctor, I must tell you... no matter what we do, her time is limited.'

Fang looked at the doctor and gave her a sheepish grin. 'What do I want for her? Immortality, of course.' He uttered a quiet, bitter laugh. 'What else?'

The doctor lowered her chin and looked at him over the rim of her glasses. Her dark, almond-shaped eyes scrutinized him, trying to see if he was joking. '*Dui bu qi*,' she said, her voice still calm, but somehow softer. 'I am sorry. I cannot give her that. No doctor can.'

Fang nodded. His face hardened, and his eyes once again burned with intensity. 'Very well. For now, she must live. Do whatever you have to.'

'*Wo hui jin wo suo neng*,' she said. 'I will do my best.'

She strode off down the hall, the clicking of her heels growing fainter as she left him. He opened the door and walked into his mother's suite.

He forced a cheery smile onto his face and waved. '*Mu qin!* Good morning... How are you feeling today?'

He walked over to his mother's bed. The old woman had been removed from the hyperbaric tube. Her withered body lay beneath the crisp white sheets of her adjustable bed. A small bank of electronics surrounded her. The equipment monitored her vital signs. Computers adjusted her medication drips, as pumps forced oxygen into her lungs through a tube in her throat.

Fang's smile beamed down on the old woman, but his eyes darted over the tubes with concern. They seemed to be everywhere... sprouting from her arms, her chest, and running beneath the sheets to God knew where. Each time he saw her, it seemed more ghastly devices clung to her body.

Fang's mother turned her head. Her eyes parted a fraction of an inch. The two dark slits stared at him.

'*Wo de erzi*,' she rasped, her voice a hoarse whisper. 'My son... Where are your brothers?'

Fang sighed. 'They are not here, *mu qin*. They are busy, working for me. Preparing for our day of triumph.'

The old woman stared at him through her slit eyes. 'Do not lie to me, my son. I know your heart as well as I know my own.'

Fang looked down at the floor, then back up at her. His smile faded, and his eyes filled with concern. 'Forgive me, I did not want to disturb you.'

'They are dead, aren't they?' she croaked.

He nodded. 'Yes. They sacrificed themselves for me. For this family. Very soon now, I will ascend. I will become Dragon Father of the *Lu Long*. Our family will have power, money, and influence beyond our wildest dreams. We will get you the best treatment, the most advanced medicine. Nothing will—'

'David, I have already had all the treatment I can stand. This life... It has become a curse.'

She struggled to reach out to him. Fang grabbed her hand and cradled it in his own.

'My boys... my beautiful boys. Gone.' A tear slipped from the thin sliver of her open eye.

'My brothers were born... different,' Fang whispered. 'They were symbols of the pain and injustice that was inflicted upon you, and Father. But they proved their worth in the end. They gave their lives, so that we may prosper.'

'Your brothers were a blessing,' the woman hissed. 'Their hearts were pure, they were kind, gentle spirits. *You* introduced them to the gangs. *You* turned them into *da shou*... thugs and killers.'

Fang felt her hand tug away from him. He let go and it slipped back down onto the bed. His mother turned and looked away from him.

'Mother, please. You don't understand, everything I have done has been for—'

'You were the eldest,' she croaked. 'It was your duty to look after your younger brothers. Their shame is yours. It is you who has cursed this family.'

Fang's voice rose in volume. 'Shame? You mean the gangs? The Triad was the only thing that kept us alive, Mother. After Father died in his foolish display, what was I to do? Nothing? Watch as you struggled to raise two *zou shi er tong*, lost children who were not allowed to work, or go to school? Watch while your sickness grew stronger each day?'

'You are the one who is lost, David. Si and Liu... The poisons we drank and breathed marked them on the outside, on their skin. But you... you carry that poison still. You carry it inside, in your heart. It has deformed your spirit.'

Fang stood up. 'Enough. You do not know what you are saying. Your mind has grown feeble, but I will still care for you. You will live to see me take my place at the head of the most powerful Triad the world has ever known.'

'Let me go, David.' Her voice was weak, faint. 'I wish for no part in this. And I am so tired. Please, I have suffered enough. Let me go.'

'You wish to join your husband? Be with my father, and my brothers?'

She nodded. 'This place, what they are doing to me... This is not life. This is eternal death.'

Fang looked into her old, tired eyes. 'Always, you favor them over me. My wishes, my sacrifices mean nothing to you.'

His face twisted in rage and pain and he grabbed her hand again. She struggled to pull it back, but her weak, aged flesh could not escape Fang's white-knuckled grip. He squeezed her hand tighter.

'You think you are the only one who suffers?' he shouted. 'I fought, bled, and killed for this family. I have watched governments betray us, punish us, try to grind us under their heels. But I fought back. I became strong. And I made my brothers strong. I have kept you alive, kept this family alive. And I promise you this. You will live to see me grasp the dragon rod in my hands. You will not die until I allow it, you understand? I have given you this time, I will decide when it ends. And you will see me rise!'

'David, please. You'll give the poor woman a heart attack.' Iris slinked into the room. She wore a dress of red beaded silk. The dress ended just above her knees, but a long silk fan trailed from the back and down to the floor. It swept behind her clicking heels like the plumage of an elegant bird.

'Sir,' a man's voice called out. It was Lewis. He followed Iris into the room. He was sweating and his face was red with exertion. 'A man in Huagu, an employee at our factory there... He says he has some information about the Americans we are seeking.'

He held out a cell phone towards Fang.

Fang dropped his mother's hand and stepped away from the bed. He snatched the phone from Lewis's hand.

'This is Mr. Fang.' He listened for a moment. 'Yes, yes, your daughter will receive the finest care,' he said. 'I will arrange for her to receive whatever treatment she needs. Assuming, of course, you tell me what I want to know.'

Fang listened and nodded. He could hear Iris rolling her sticks on the glass table behind him. She laughed, a light titter, as if she were privy to a joke he could not perceive.

'Very well,' he said into the phone. 'Lewis will call you to make the arrangements. Well done, Mr. Lung, you will be rewarded.'

He hung up the phone and turned to Iris.

'That was the brother-in-law of the lawyer, the one who escaped the black jail with Sean Tyler. He says Tyler and the American are coming here, to Shanghai.'

'Shall I alert the Red Poles?' Lewis asked.

Iris brushed her long, lacquered nails over the grooves and dots of her sticks. She closed her eyes.

'Joyous Lake over Still Mountain,' she intoned in her husky voice. 'A man who searches for game where there is none, shall soon starve. Persistence is not enough. If one does not look in the right way, one will not find what they seek.'

Fang nodded. 'This Sean Tyler... He was working with Huang Ju, the Jade Enclave hacker who broke into my offices. He must be seeking what we also seek. Why else would he come here? Let them enter the city. Follow them, but do not interfere. With any luck, he will lead us straight to the key.'

Lewis nodded. '*Shi pei le.*'

'Iris, watch over Mother,' David said as he and Lewis left the room.

'Of course, darling.' Iris shot a sideways glance at the elderly woman, and her nose wrinkled with distaste.

She rolled the bamboo sticks again. A new pattern emerged.

Fang's mother moaned and rolled over on her bed. 'What is that noise?' she croaked. 'Who is there?'

'Do not fear,' Iris called out. 'Soon your son will bring honor to your family, old woman. It has been foretold.'

She looked down at the sticks and frowned. The hexagram was different than earlier. She had seen this pattern before, last night, after Fang had his way with her.

She had assumed it was a mistake then. Perhaps her mind was unfocused, her energy weak. She'd rolled the sticks again, read Fang a different fortune.

But here was the same pattern as before, repeated.

She collected the sticks and dropped them into her clutch.

Her heart skipped a beat.

She could hear the faint call of fate. The pattern of the sticks... Joyous Lake above Arousing Thunder. A new destiny. A darker destiny.

An ill omen.

30

Rebecca surveyed the carnage inside the farmhouse. She approached one of the bodies, a heavyset man wearing jeans and a camouflage T-shirt.

'This one... You looked up his record?' she asked.

Josh looked up from the bank of monitors in the corner. 'Yeah, Adrian Royce. Same background as Ganda. Ex-military, spotty record, discharge. Did a few tours with the usual security contractors, then dropped off the grid. Lapinski's assembled himself a nice little private army here. Keyes even found a Force Protection Cougar out in the barn. It's a stripped-down civilian model, but still pretty heavy-duty.'

The air inside the farmhouse was heavy with the odor of gunpowder, smoke, and blood. Lapinski, Ganda, and a young man named Matheson had been taken alive. They awaited interrogation, secured in various rooms of the house. The rest of Ted's group were killed in the initial raid. Their bodies were sprawled across the floor. DuBose snapped pictures and fingerprinted each corpse, as he prepared their action report.

Rebecca looked at the staircase that led to the second floor of the farmhouse. 'Josh, the girl you found... I have to see to her. And we sure as hell can't bring her down here.'

Josh eyed the bodies spread out on the floor and nodded. 'Right. Keyes is up there with her now. She seems to have taken a liking to him.'

He walked over to her and smiled. 'Josh Galloway, reporting for escalator duty.' He slid his arms under her, lifted her up, and began to carry her up the stairs.

'Clayton,' he called over his shoulder. 'Little help, please?'

Clayton snapped another picture. 'Sorry, sir... just trying to get the exposure right.'

'It's an action report, not a coffee table book. Wheelchair, now.'

DuBose set down the camera, folded up Rebecca's chair, and hauled it up the stairs after them.

Once again, her body tingled as she felt Josh's muscular arms coil around her. She found herself remembering the other night. His hands, touching her, moving across her body... She shook her head and blinked.

You've got three dead bodies downstairs, and you still have to interrogate Lapinski. Get your head in the game!

She resisted the urge to nuzzle his neck.

They reached the upstairs landing. DuBose hurried in front of them and set up her chair. Josh set her down in it, and she headed down the narrow hall to an old, warped wood door.

She knocked.

'One sec...' It was Keyes's voice. A moment later the door creaked open. Keyes stood in the doorway, his short, muscular frame blocking her view of the room.

'She's pretty scared, Director,' he said. 'She heard the gunfire and explosions when we came in. I don't know how long she's been here, but there's a bunch of food wrappers and empty water bottles in the trash.'

Rebecca nodded. 'I understand, but I need to talk to her.'

He stood aside, and Rebecca rolled into the small, dark bedroom. As her eyes adjusted to the light, she saw a single bed pushed against the far wall. The sheets were white, and a dusty, crocheted pink blanket lay rumpled in the corner.

Sitting in the center of the bed was a small Chinese girl.

She looked about six years old. Her knees were drawn up to her chin, and her tiny hands were clasped tight in front of her shins. She peered up at Rebecca with wide, frightened eyes as she rocked back and forth. Her cheeks were bright red, and her eyes glistened with tears. A few plastic toy horses lay scattered on the bed in front of her.

'We were playing horses, Director,' Keyes said. 'I was telling her my family has some horses just like her toys, back in Pennsylvania.'

Rebecca smiled at the girl. She stopped rocking, but did not smile back.

'What's your name, honey?'

The girl was silent. Rebecca moved closer.

'My name is Rebecca. These men are my friends. Who brought you here?'

'*Huai nan ren*,' the child said in a soft, quiet voice.

'Do you speak any English?' Rebecca asked. 'Ah, *ying yu ma*?'

The little girl nodded. 'A little,' she said. 'Mama sent me to special school.'

'Very good,' Rebecca said, trying to sound comforting and encouraging. 'Where is your mama? Is she here?'

The girl shook her head. 'No. I don't know where she is.'

'Is she in China?'

'I don't know. The bad men don't let me see her. Only sometimes.'

'Sometimes?'

'Only when she does what they want.'

'What's your name, sweetie? Can you tell me your name?'

She looked at Rebecca for a moment, then nodded. 'Lian.'

Rebecca fished her phone from her purse and held it up. 'Lian, I'd like to take your picture, okay?'

The girl looked worried. 'Is Mama in trouble?'

Rebecca reached out and let her hand glide through the girl's shoulder-length dark hair. 'I don't know, honey. But I'm going to try to find out, okay? I'm going to make the bad men tell me.'

Lian bit her lip, thought for a second, then nodded. 'Okay. *Xie xie*. Thank you, ma'am.'

Rebecca snapped the picture on her phone. 'Call me Rebecca.' She showed the girl the picture. 'See? Look how pretty you are.' She rested her hand on the girl's shoulder. 'Very pretty, and very brave.'

She texted Caine the picture and typed the word 'LEVERAGE?' underneath. Then she dropped the phone back in her purse. 'Lian, I'm going to go for a little bit, but I'll be back soon, okay?'

The girl nodded. 'I want to go home. I want to see Mama. *Qing!*'

'I know, honey. I'm going to try to help. I promise.'

She pulled her fiery hair into a ponytail and turned to Josh. Her eyes flashed with anger. 'I want to speak to Ted. Now.'

* * *

Lapinski stared across the table at Rebecca and shifted in his chair. His eyes darted around the room.

'Focus, Ted,' Rebecca snapped. 'I'm right here. And I'm going to ask you nicely one more time. Who is the girl?'

'Rebecca, you don't know what you're dealing with here.' Ted leaned across the table and lowered his voice. 'Trust me, I'm on your side, and you're in over your head!'

'My side? That's your angle? You sent your hired thugs to take me out!'

Ted shrugged. 'I don't know what you're talking about.'

'Really? So Wallace Ganda isn't on your payroll? We're holding him in another room. I have a feeling his story is going to be a little different. You know, once we start throwing around words like "treason" and "enemy combatant."'

'Enemy combatant?' Ted laughed. 'That's a reach. He's an American citizen on US soil.'

'He tried to drug me and stuff me in a van, Ted. I'm the Director of the National Clandestine Service. If I say he's an enemy combatant, then he is. That's the way this works.'

A look of doubt flashed across Ted's face. He licked his lips and looked down at the table.

It's starting to sink in, she thought. *He's screwed and he knows it.*

'Ted, you're going to go down for this. You have one, and only one shot at seeing the light of day. Work with me. Who is that little girl? Who is your asset in China? Who is Red Phoenix?'

Ted looked away.

'You don't want to talk to me? Fine. I've already alerted the DNI. You're fucking with the president's Global Environmental Accords. If China pulls out over what you've done, John Blayne will throw you in a hole for the rest of your life.'

Ted's head shot up and he looked her in the eye. 'Wait, Blayne? You talked to Blayne?'

Rebecca leaned forward. 'Of course, he's the president's intelligence advisor. Why?'

Ted appeared lost in thought. 'Blayne has connections to every intelligence service. He could be talking to anyone. There's no way to contain things anymore.'

'Talk to me, Ted. Is Blayne pulling your strings? Is he behind this?'

Ted refocused on her. His eyes were wide with panic. 'No... I mean, I don't think so. Blayne is in the loop, he knew about Red Phoenix. Not the particulars, but he knew I had an asset in China. But he's not the one giving me orders. I... I don't know who it is, but they're high up. Higher than you and me.'

'Who is it, Ted? Why do they want Sean dead? What information are they so afraid of this hacker releasing?'

'You have to protect me. We can't stay here. Whoever it is, they know about this place. They set this all up, do you understand?'

Rebecca glared at him. 'The sooner you talk, the sooner we leave, Ted. What files did this hacker access?'

'It's not the files. I mean, they're bad, but nothing that hasn't been leaked before. The files were just a smokescreen, to get Blayne on board, for deniability purposes.'

'So what is this really about?'

Ted took a deep breath. 'TANGENT. It's about TANGENT.'

'And what the hell is TANGENT?'

Ted eyed Josh, then turned his attention back to Rebecca. 'TANGENT is an NSA cyber-weapon. Something we developed based on the FBI's Cybercrimes Research Unit. The hacker we have in custody, Sun Wai Tong... He did hack sensitive files, but more importantly, he downloaded TANGENT from our servers. We've been trying to figure out who he gave it to, but so far he's been... uncooperative. We can't release him until we know who has it.'

'I'll ask again. What the hell is TANGENT? Why is it so important?'

Ted shook his head. 'You really don't get it, do you? Your whole world? Field ops, HUMINT, "Boots on the ground"... You're the past. TANGENT is the future. The next battleground isn't going to be Iraq, or Syria, or China. The weapons of the next war aren't guns or bombs. It's all going to be ones and zeroes, in cyberspace. TANGENT is a weapon for the digital battlefield.'

Josh rested his hand on the pistol at his hip. 'Director, this guy is just running his mouth.'

'Ted,' Rebecca said, slowing her words as if speaking to a child. 'You've got about ten seconds of my patience left. Start making sense.'

'We have to get out of here, there's no time—'

'Then talk faster,' Rebecca snapped.

'Okay, look... The NSA spent billions of dollars and years of research weakening internet security. BULLRUN, QUANTUM, PRISM... Those programs and systems are like our nukes. Using them, we can hack into just about any system on the planet, anywhere, anytime.'

'Your data is our data,' Rebecca said.

'Exactly. But every hacker, no matter how skilled, no matter what tools they use, leaves traces behind. Things like favored malware, keyboard language settings, server location. The FBI assembled a database that analyzes these traces. Their goal was to profile and identify specific hackers and groups based on these digital fingerprints. And you can bet our enemies do the same.

'TANGENT is the next step. We built on that database and improved it. Perfected it. We built a series of algorithms that can *plant* those traces after we hack a network. We can decide who the enemy will profile for the hack, with a 95 percent success rate.'

Rebecca bit her lip. 'In other words, you could hack a Chinese military contractor and make them think the Russians did it?'

Ted nodded. 'Exactly.'

'And you're telling me no other country has anything like this? That killing an innocent man, and derailing a presidential initiative, is necessary to prevent this program from leaking?'

Ted sagged his shoulders. 'No. TANGENT is advanced, but other countries will soon have similar capabilities. Within three to five years, we estimate.'

'So why is your Chinese asset hunting down Sean Tyler?'

'We can't release Sun Wai Tong, not until we get TANGENT back. It's not just the program... it's the log.'

'Come again?'

'Within the TANGENT program is a log... a database of every time it's been used. TANGENT has never been activated against a foreign power. We felt that even at 95 percent effectiveness, the risks were too great if it was detected.'

'So where was it used?'

'Domestically.'

Rebecca blinked. 'Wait, what?'

'Programs like PRISM and QUANTUM depend on coopera-tion from corporations. Telecom giants, internet providers, equipment manufacturers. You think Google or Apple couldn't figure out a way to block us from their networks if they wanted to? We offer them enhanced security, special privileges, and billions of dollars. That's the carrot. TANGENT is the stick. Remember that movie studio hack a couple years ago?'

Rebecca nodded. 'The FBI Cybercrimes unit blamed the North Koreans.'

Ted smiled proudly. 'TANGENT in action. That studio was owned by a cellular communications conglomerate. They were going to implement end-to-end encryption on their entire network. They refused to give the NSA the key. After we hit them with TANGENT, they were willing to play ball.'

Rebecca stared at him and shook her head. 'Jesus, Ted. This is insane. You've committed cyber-terrorism against American interests.'

Ted stared back at her and laughed. 'American interests? Are you fucking kidding me? These are multi-national corporations we're talking about. They don't give a shit about America. They move their factories to China, they set up corporate tax shelters in Ireland. They make billions in profits, and they pay less taxes than the average middle-class family. They only act in "America's interests" when people like me force them to. And we need programs like TANGENT to make that happen.'

'So what does David Fang have to do with all of this? Why is he after Sean?'

Ted's features twisted into a confused glare. 'Who the hell is David Fang?'

Rebecca pulled out her phone and flipped to one of the pictures Caine had sent her. She held it up for Ted to see. 'This man. Fang owned the building that Sean and the Human Rights Now group infiltrated. What did Sean find there? Why does Fang want Sean dead? Are you working with him?'

Ted squinted as he stared at the picture. 'I don't know, I... Wait. I recognize him. He's older, but I recognize him.' He looked at Rebecca. 'But his name's not David Fang.'

Suddenly the door to the room burst open. DuBose stood in the doorway, panting. 'Sir, we have a chopper inbound, three o'clock. About two clicks out.'

Josh glared at Ted and drew his pistol. 'Is this your mysterious boss? Are they coming for you, Lapinski?'

Ted's face went white. He shook his head. 'I told you, you're in over your head. They're not just coming for me. Now they're coming for us all.'

31

Shanghai... After endless hours of travel, the city was like a shimmering starburst of concrete and metal rising up in the distance.

Caine and Sean had abandoned Tiao's truck a few towns past Huagu. Caine didn't want to take the chance of police pulling over the stolen vehicle. Instead, they caught a bus in another small, nameless town a couple hours down the road.

They were the only Westerners on the vehicle. The passengers that boarded in the other towns along the way gave them curious looks. But after a few hours, they hit a long stretch of open road, and no new passengers came onboard. They kept to themselves during the long trip. Caine stared out the window, and Sean slept in short, restless bouts.

Finally, the dust and empty roads had given way to busy freeways. Towering apartment buildings surrounded the outskirts of the massive city. Then the futuristic Lujiazui skyline of the Pudong district came into view. The gleaming buildings formed a dense cluster across the rippling water of the Huangpu River.

The late afternoon sun glinted off the spheres of the Oriental

Pearl Tower. The sleek, angular slab of the World Financial Center pierced the hazy sky like a blade. Both buildings were dwarfed by the elegant lines of Shanghai Tower. Its mirrored form twisted in a Möbius-like curve as it rose over two thousand feet into the air.

Caine couldn't help but marvel at the city. The bus drove along the Bund, a riverside route that curved around the scenic view. Sean began to stir. He rubbed his eyes, looked out the window for a moment, then turned towards Caine.

'Pretty wild, huh? Biggest city in the world; over twenty million people live here.'

As they drove closer, Caine noticed dozens of yellow and red construction cranes scattered through the city, perched between the massive buildings like birds pecking for scraps. The towering structures that surrounded them made the cranes look tiny by comparison.

'The buildings are impressive, all right,' he said. 'Looks like they're just getting started. There's even more construction here than Beijing.'

Sean nodded. 'Yeah, some people call this place Construction City. I read an article that said over 70 percent of the world's construction cranes are in China. And half of those are here, in Shanghai.'

The bus pulled to a stop in front of a low, sprawling mirrored building. Massive red Chinese characters hung from the roof. An English sign read 'Shanghai Long Distance Bus Station.' They disembarked and made their way to the taxi line. Caine instructed Sean to keep his head down to avoid any security cameras.

Twenty minutes later, they entered a rickety old apartment building and took the elevator to the sixth floor. As the doors opened, Caine stopped Sean from exiting. He leaned his head out, glancing left and right. The hallway was empty. Faint echoes of clanking pots and television broadcasts pierced the thin walls.

Caine lowered his arm and the two of them walked down the corridor, towards the eastern corner of the building. Caine glanced at the frayed carpet and peeling wallpaper.

'You sure this is the place?' he asked. 'I would think a hacker could afford better housing.'

Sean nodded. 'Yeah, this is it. The Monkey King and I, we hung out here a few times.'

Caine raised an eyebrow. 'Monkey King?'

'That's his hacker name. His real name was Huang Ju... I think. I just called him Monk. Anyway, the state-sponsored hackers have money, sure. Those guys get bounties for breaching American and European tech firms. They steal patents and state secrets. Or they work directly for the government, in one of the Cyber-Warfare units. But Monk and the rest of the Jade Enclave, they're not just in it for themselves.'

Caine glanced over his shoulder. 'Jia told me about them. She said they help human rights groups. Warn them about government crackdowns, that kind of thing.'

'Yeah. They're trying to make a difference.'

The reached the end of the corridor. A dusty, cracked window looked out over a fire escape. Beyond that lay a massive construction project next door. A vast field of tiny houses spread out beyond the building's eastern perimeter. The minuscule, sagging dwellings were little more than shacks and hovels. The houses closest to the building had been razed to the ground, leaving behind a barren patch of dirt.

A cavernous foundation pit had been cut into the earth only a few feet away from the apartment building. Construction was already underway on a new structure. Steel girders and scaffolding sprang up above the foundation. Large dump trucks roared out of the pit, clearing out loads of rocky earth and debris. The sounds of jackhammers and truck engines vibrated the pane of glass and echoed down the hall.

Caine watched the other apartments as Sean slipped the key into the unit's deadbolt lock. No one looked out from the identical green doors that lined both sides of the musty hallway. Sean turned the key and the lock clicked. The door creaked as it swung open.

Sean whistled. 'Jesus... this place is a disaster!'

'Wait here.' Caine stepped past him into the apartment, keeping close to the wall. His eyes darted across the corners of the dim living room. He continued moving sideways along the wall. Sean was right, the room was a mess. Overturned furniture, shattered glass, scattered clothes... Someone had searched the apartment thoroughly, leaving the place a shambles in the process.

Moving to the nearest doorway, he ducked through and listened. He heard no sounds other than the construction work outside.

'Sean,' he called as quietly as possible. 'Come in, close the door.'

Sean entered the apartment. Caine repeated his quick series of movements through each room.

Finally, he emerged back into the living room. 'Place is clear,' he said, looking around at the mess. Sean stood in the center of the room, staring at the clutter that spread across the scratched and pitted floor.

'What the hell happened in here?' he asked.

'What do you think happened? Someone searched the place. Looking for the same thing we are, most likely.'

'I was hoping Monk... Huang... would be here.'

'Sean, if Fang really is Triad, and he got to your friend...'

Sean nodded. 'I know, I know. It doesn't look good. I was just hoping.' His foot crunched over some broken glass. He bent down and picked up a shattered picture frame lying on the floor. The torn photo inside showed a young Chinese couple. The man was rail-thin, with a short, spiked haircut. The girl was pale and tall. Large pink glasses obscured her face.

Sean smiled. 'That's Monk.'

'Who's the girl?' Caine asked.

'It's his girlfriend, I think. She was a hacker too, but I never met her. They were fighting. Monk was kind of a player, liked the ladies a little too much, you know?' He dropped the frame back on the floor.

Caine looked around the room and took a deep breath. 'Well, if Fang is after you, then that tells us something. Either he didn't find what he was looking for here, or you know something he doesn't want to get out. What did Huang tell you about this information he found?'

'Nothing. He just said to lie low for a while, and that he'd explain everything later. Then I got arrested. Oh, I checked my email on the train. He sent me a file, but it made no sense.'

Caine turned his attention from the scattered debris to Sean. 'What kind of file?'

Sean walked over to a toppled desk in the corner of the room. A pile of smashed electronics surrounded the battered furniture. 'It was just a song. C-pop, Chinese top 40 stuff. Weird, because Monk hated that kind of music.'

'It might be some kind of code, or signal,' Caine said. 'Can you play it?'

Sean kicked at the cracked screen of a computer monitor. 'Not on this... They destroyed all his computer stuff.'

Caine followed Sean into the bedroom. The mattress hung off the bed at an odd angle. It had been slit open from top to bottom, and scraps of foam littered the floor like a thin layer of snow. The rest of the bedroom furniture was smashed to pieces, the same as outside.

The walls were bare, save for a framed poster. It was pushed aside, as if someone had looked behind it. The image on the poster was a pretty Chinese girl in her twenties, dressed in tight, colorful clothes. She was winking at the camera, and a sly smile stretched across her young, flawless face. Rainbow-colored Chinese characters filled the bottom of the poster.

Sean pointed at the picture and shook his head. 'No way. No way did Monk put that up. That's Wushi Wu. She's the singer on the song he sent me. He hated C-pop music, said it was all state-approved propaganda for tweens.'

'Then he knew you'd recognize it as wrong. He was trying to send you a message,' Caine said. 'It's called steganography. Hiding something in plain sight. The audio file, and this poster, were clues for you.'

Caine tapped on the wall. His knuckles struck the surface with a loud, solid thunk. Then he tapped on the blank space behind the poster. A hollow, empty knock rang out.

'There's a space behind this wall,' he said as he glanced around the room. He picked up the splintered leg of a chair. 'Stand back.'

Sean took a step backwards as Caine slammed the piece of wood into the wall. The smooth drywall tore open like paper and a confetti of dust and plaster fragments rained down. Caine smashed the wall a few more times, then used his hands to clear out a large hole.

A frame of wooden beams was sunken behind the plaster, leaving a six-inch gap between it and the wall. Resting on one of the beams was a small, rectangular package wrapped in plastic. Caine grasped it and pulled it out of the jagged hole. He swept a light covering of plaster dust off the bundle with the back of his hand. 'Your friend was pretty resourceful,' he said.

'He was the Monkey King,' Sean said with a sigh. 'Master of mischief.'

Caine tore the plastic away, revealing a sleek silver laptop, power cord, and a USB thumb drive. He set the device on the ground, plugged it in, and flipped open the top. A black screen and some glowing white Chinese characters greeted him. A cursor blinked in silence, waiting for the correct input.

Caine slid the machine over to Sean. 'I assume you know the password?'

'No password,' Sean said. He looked into the webcam and placed his thumb on the trackpad. 'Biometric security. Iris scan and thumbprint. Monk said he added me to the white list, so this should do it... Bingo!' Sean smiled as the black security screen disappeared and the machine began to boot up. After a few seconds, they found themselves staring at a blank Linux desktop.

'That's weird. He wiped this machine... There're no apps or files left at all. Wait, hold on. Here's a folder.'

Sean moved the cursor to the lone folder and clicked it open. 'Okay, we got a browser, and some kind of audio app called Deep Echo.' He tapped the keys again, navigating the browser to his email account. Within a few seconds, he downloaded the audio file to the desktop.

'You're pretty good with a computer,' Caine remarked. He peered out the window at the street below.

'Lots of alone time and lots of video games,' Sean said as he dragged the audio file into the Deep Echo app. A waveform scrolled across the screen as the song played. The bright, electronic ballad filled the room as the singer wailed a mournful refrain. '*Wo dui ni de ai zai ran shao*, my love for you burns!'

Sean winced. 'God, this song sucks.'

The song played to the end and stopped. The only sound in the room was the distant clanking of jackhammers outside.

'That's it... There's nothing else in the file.'

Caine peered over his shoulder. 'If he left this computer here for you to find, there must be something useful in this app.' His eyes ran over the various menus and functions of the programs. 'Good thing this is in English. There...' He pointed to one of the menus on the screen. 'LSB decoding. Try that.'

'What the hell is LSB?' Sean asked as he ran the file through the processing filter.

'Least significant bit. It's another form of steganography. This song is a digital file, made of bits, tiny pieces of digital information. Some audio bits are more significant than others. LSB encoding replaces the least significant bits of the song with bits of a coded message. Your ear can barely hear the difference when you play the song. The message is hidden throughout the file. It's just spread out, so you can't put it together without software like this.'

The computer finished the decoding process and beeped. The image of the waveform faded from view.

'Hey, you're right! It worked!'

A dense mass of computer code filled the screen. Row after row of numbers and letter scrolled in front of Sean's confused face.

'Well?' Caine asked. 'What is it?'

Sean bit his lip. 'I have no idea. Some kind of file, but it looks like gibberish to me.'

Caine glanced at the laptop for a moment. 'He must have left you the USB stick for a reason as well. Copy the file, then pack it up. We're leaving.'

'Wait, where are we going?'

'There's nothing more left to find here. We can't stay any

longer. Fang and his men obviously know about his place. They may have it under surveillance.'

Sean slammed the laptop shut and pulled out the USB drive. He followed Caine as they stepped back into the living room.

'We'll lie low until I hear from my contact, and then we get the hell out of this country. Maybe they can help decode this file. Got it?'

Sean took a long look around the disheveled apartment. He handed the memory stick to Caine. 'Yeah,' he said in a quiet voice. 'I got it.'

Caine eyed Sean and sighed as he slid the drive into his pocket. 'I'm sorry about your friend. But we have to keep moving. It's the only way we'll get out of this.'

Sean nodded glumly and they stepped out the door. 'Is that more of your life experience talking?'

Caine looked down the hall and confirmed it was clear as they made their way towards the elevator. 'Yeah,' he muttered.

Sean shook his head. 'Some kind of life.'

32

As soon as they stepped into the building's lobby, Caine knew something was wrong.

The room had been empty on their way in. But now he spotted three men dressed in casual clothes: jeans, dress shirts, leather jackets. Two of them sat on the sofas, flipping through the old, tattered magazines. The third was leaning against the front desk as if he was waiting for something.

They felt wrong.

The front desk was empty and dark, no sign of a manager. The horizontal bars of a steel security gate ran along a track above the desk. The gate was half-closed.

Caine felt the old familiar tingle on the back of his neck. A sixth sense of impending violence attuned by spending years in its company. The hazy afternoon sunlight beamed through the front doors of the building.

Those doors are a choke point, Caine thought. *That's where they want us to go.*

Caine nudged Sean and stepped left, towards the desk. Sean gave him a knowing look and followed behind him in silence.

Kid feels it too, Caine thought. *Good instincts.*

Caine's hand dropped to his front pocket. His fingers wrapped around a loose handful of coins, change left over from their dim sum lunch. The man standing in front of the desk looked up. A flicker of surprise flashed over his stony features, and Caine smiled.

'Hey, where's the front desk guy?' Caine asked. 'Our cable's out.'

The man's right hand drifted towards the waistband of his jeans. It was a slow, casual movement, but to Caine it was as obvious as a neon sign. The Chinese man shook his head.

'*Mei you ying wen*. No English.'

'Bullshit,' Caine snarled. 'Catch!'

Caine yanked his hand from his pocket as the Chinese man's pistol cleared his waistband. Before the man could aim his gun, Caine flung the handful of coins towards him. The man instinctively raised his free hand to block his face. The barrage of shiny metal coins pelted his open palm. They were a distraction, nothing more.

That brief window of time was all Caine needed.

He stepped towards the man and pivoted right. The Chinese man struggled to turn with him, but he was too slow. As he raised the gun, Caine's left arm shot out and grabbed his wrist. He pushed the gun away from him, pointing the muzzle behind the empty desk.

His right hand formed a stiff L shape and slid up under the barrel of the pistol. The man struggled to re-orient the weapon towards Caine, but he was trapped. Caine yanked his wrist back with his left hand. A quick twist wrenched the gun from the man's grasp. As Caine's fingers wrapped around the butt of the pistol, he threw a left hook into the man's face.

The man staggered backwards. Caine's right arm swung

toward him. The butt of the pistol slammed into his nose with a loud crack. He fell back onto the front desk, clutching his broken nose. A crimson spatter of blood sprayed from his nostrils.

Caine didn't stop moving. He leapt up into the air and grabbed the lower bars of the security gate. His weight drove the gate down, and it slid along its track with a loud, metallic clatter. The heavy metal bar slammed into the Chinese man's chest. He gasped in pain as it struck him with a dull, fleshy thud and bounced off his ribs. Then he rolled off the desk and fell to the floor, groaning.

From the corner of his eye, Caine saw the other two men moving towards them. More men streamed in through the front doors, led by a tall, slim man wearing a tailored suit. His skin had a pale, waxy look, and dark tortoiseshell sunglasses concealed his eyes.

Caine grabbed Sean. 'Move!' he shouted. 'Behind the desk!'

They leapt over the desk, sliding under the half-open gate as the other men opened fire. A hail of bullets screamed above them, punching holes in the wall behind them. Caine heard a man shout.

'*Bu yao sha si ta men,* do not kill them! I want Sean Tyler alive!'

'Back the way we came, upstairs,' Caine whispered. 'Go!'

They crept behind the desk and out into the hallway that led to the apartments. The frosted glass doors exploded behind them. Shards of white powdered glass flew into the air.

Sean pounded the elevator button. Caine grabbed his arm and dragged him towards the stairwell.

'Elevator's no good, they can shut it down.'

Sean panted as they raced up the stairs. 'That guy in the suit... he's from the Ministry of State Security. He visited me at the black jail.'

'We can't let him take you in. The assassin, Red Phoenix... It could be anyone in the Ministry, including him. Keep going up. If we can make it to the roof, maybe we can jump to the next building.'

'Wait, what? Did you say jump?'

They ascended to the third-floor landing. Caine heard more shouting, this time from above them. He grabbed Sean and pulled him backwards. A hail of automatic weapon fire tore into the floor in front of them. Bullets screamed and whined as they ricocheted through the stairwell. A stray shot thudded into a door to their right.

Caine muttered a silent curse. 'They must have had men on the roof. This way!' He kicked open the door, and they charged down another hallway. Rows of apartment doors flanked them on either side.

An elderly man in a bathrobe opened his door and bent down to grab a newspaper off his door mat. He looked up and saw Caine and Sean sprinting down the hall. Caine raised his pistol. The elderly man's sunken eyes opened wide with fear.

'*Shen me gui dong shi!*' he screamed, slamming the door shut as they rushed past.

Caine aimed the gun at the dusty, cracked window at the end of the hall. He fired three shots. The glass shattered, revealing a fire escape perched on the side of the building. Beyond the rickety metal platform, the steel beams and girders of the construction site rose up into the air.

'Through the window!' Caine shouted.

The stairwell door crashed open behind them. Caine looked over his shoulder. Men dressed in SWAT tactical gear flooded into the hallway. They were wearing body armor and carrying QCW-05 submachine guns. Caine recognized the bullpup design of the stocks. He knew the weapons were capable of firing subsonic armor-piercing rounds. Quiet and lethal, they were able to punch through armor plating at a hundred meters or less.

He fired a few more wild shots behind him. The SWAT team dropped to their knees as they took up defensive positions along the walls.

Whipping off his jacket, he tossed it to Sean. 'Here, wrap your hands in this.'

He vaulted through the broken window, wincing as shards of glass bit into his flesh. The rusty metal fire escape shook as his weight slammed into it, but it held.

Caine planted his foot on the railing of the fire escape and leapt off. He flew across the gap between the buildings and landed on the other side with a grunt. He rolled across several sheets of plywood, a temporary floor that covered the metal beams. A skeleton of steel and concrete columns rose around him. He sprang to his feet and took cover behind one of the columns.

Sean ran to the edge of the fire escape, then stopped. Caine peered around the column. In the darkness beyond the window, he could see shadowy figures stalking towards Sean. They were closing in on the frightened young man.

'Sean, jump!' he shouted. 'Don't think, just do it!'

Caine heard muted shouting from inside the apartment building. Sean looked over his shoulder, then back at Caine. He took a deep breath and jumped.

Bad take-off, Caine thought. *He's not gonna make it.*

Sure enough, Sean screamed in panic as his torso slammed into the side of the other building. His hands clawed at the metal beam as his legs flailed in the air beneath him.

Caine charged forward, firing into the shattered window of the building. The SWAT team inside took cover behind an open apartment door.

Caine knelt down and grabbed Sean's hand. 'I got you. Stop kicking!'

Bracing his feet against the beam, he used one hand to pull Sean up. Gunfire roared through the air as he sent another double tap towards the men in the opposite building.

One of the SWAT team broke cover and charged for the window. Caine pulled Sean towards one of the support columns as the man opened fire with his QCW-05 submachine gun. The subsonic shots sounded like popping fireworks rather than the explosive boom of Caine's pistol. The wood flooring rattled and shook as bullets slammed into it, nipping at their heels.

They ducked behind the concrete column just as a trail of sparking gunfire ran up its length. The armor-piercing rounds gouged deep holes into the concrete. White dust exploded into the air. Sean winced as a sliver of shrapnel cut across his cheek.

'Holy shit!' he exclaimed as he brought his hand up and felt blood.

Caine glanced at the cut and squinted. 'It's just a scratch.'

Sean's face was pale and his bloodied hand was trembling. 'They're shooting at us! I thought they wanted to take me in alive?'

'That's their primary objective.'

'Primary? What's their secondary objective?'

Caine didn't answer. Several heavy thuds shook the plywood flooring. The SWAT team had jumped over.

'We have to keep moving,' he shouted. 'Get behind me, go!'

Caine stepped out from behind the column. He fired as they backpedaled towards the other side of the skeletal building. Three members of the SWAT team had followed them across the gap. The men positioned themselves behind the columns, taking turns covering each other as they advanced forward.

On the other side of the partially constructed building, a

long, orange cage clung to the side of the structure. Caine saw the platform of a hydraulic air lift resting in the metal framework. He pointed forward.

'There! We can use the lift, get down to street level.'

Sean sprinted towards the lift. Caine ducked behind another column and looked left and right. The SWAT team was moving down the center of the structure. They crisscrossed left and right, continuing to take cover behind the columns. He waited until the closest man ducked behind cover. Then he darted back the way he came and threw himself behind the next column.

Their attention is focused on Sean, he thought. *With any luck, they didn't see me double back.*

He heard the footsteps of the men tramping closer. They were wearing heavy combat gear, and the wood flooring vibrated with every footfall. Caine was motionless, taking in soft, shallow breaths. These men were well-trained. They would be difficult to surprise.

The footsteps thudded closer. One of the men approached the column.

Now!

Caine darted out from hiding just before the SWAT officer moved past. Keeping his body turned sideways to make it a smaller target, he wrapped his left hand around the barrel of the man's QCW-05. He jerked forward and pivoted, keeping the SWAT officer's body between him and the rest of the team. As he moved, he wrapped his right hand around the butt of the rifle and drove his knee upwards.

The blow connected with the man's groin. He was wearing a cup, but he instinctively stepped back. He dropped one of his hands to protect his vitals. Caine tore the submachine gun free from his grip. He saw the other men closing in behind the officer he had just disarmed. There were three more of them. The flooring trembled under their combined weight.

He aimed the submachine gun at the men charging towards him.

Caine had killed many men in battle, more than he could ever count. He didn't enjoy it, but in matters of life or death he had no qualms about doing what was necessary. But now, years of experience told him he would not be able to drop all four men before they were able to take out him, or Sean.

In a fraction of a second, he made a decision. He lowered his aim and kicked the man he had just disarmed backwards. The other men charged closer. Caine took a step back and felt his foot make contact with a metal beam. He pulled the trigger on the submachine gun.

Gunfire crackled through the air. He swept a line of automatic weapon fire across the plywood sheet just in front of the SWAT team.

The weakened panel snapped in half and collapsed. The SWAT team tumbled down to the floor below. As they fell, they fired their weapons, but their shots went wild. Bullets ricocheted off the metal girders, and Caine ducked as a stray shot whistled past his ear.

Caine turned and saw Sean leap onto the air lift. The metal platform buckled a bit, and Caine could see the air tanks and hoses shake underneath the lift.

'Come on, man, let's go!' Sean called. As Caine jogged over, he heard more footsteps echoing through the structure. These were lighter, farther away. He looked up and saw the plywood sheets above him buckling. There was a gap in the flooring ahead, between him and Sean. Someone was running toward it on the floor above.

The footsteps paused. A beam of green light pierced through

the plaster dust that filled the air. It swung towards Sean, aiming straight down through the gap in the floor. Caine recognized it immediately. Green laser sights were brighter, and easier to see in daylight. The figure above them was a sniper.

'Sean, get down *now!*' Caine shouted.

Sean crouched down next to the lift controls. A high-pitched whine sliced through the air and a bullet sparked off the orange frame of the lift.

'What the—' Sean yelled in surprise. Caine continued running towards him. He aimed the submachine gun at the floor above and opened fire. Bullets tore into the sheets of wood.

Through the gaps in the flooring, he could just make out a dark figure leaping and dodging above him.

Not SWAT. The assassin... It must be Red Phoenix! he thought. *Bernatto wasn't lying after all.*

Sean squeezed himself between the controls and the edge of the lift. Another shot streaked toward him, slamming into the lift controls. The panel exploded in a shower of sparks. Sean cried out, covering his head with his hands.

Caine cursed and turned his gun towards the lift. He aimed at the air hoses underneath the platform and pulled the trigger. After a brief crackle of gunfire, the gun's magazine was empty. He heard a loud hissing sound. The hoses underneath the lift whipped and snaked through the air. His bullets had torn them to shreds, releasing the compressed air in the tanks.

The lift platform dropped. Its descent was slow at first, but an instant later it picked up speed. One more high-powered shot rang out from above, but it struck the empty lift cage as the platform fell out of view.

The shadowy figure above him leapt through the gap and landed in a crouch on the floor, next to the empty lift. The assassin was dressed head to toe in black tactical gear. A hood covered their face, and a variety of knifes, pistols, and other weapons hung from a harness. A DT SRS A1 Covert, a compact short-range sniper rifle, was slung around the assassin's shoulder on a strap.

Caine charged, swinging his empty gun like a club. The figure sprang up and sidestepped the blow. Whoever it was under the hood, they were small, nimble, and fast. Without missing a beat, the assassin closed in, pummeling Caine's chin and shoulder with a series of rapid elbow strikes.

A leg swung up in a sideways kick, aiming towards Caine's knee. He twisted his body, blocking the kick with the empty gun. Then he released the gun and slammed an elbow into the assassin's face. He heard a gasp of pain as the blow connected. The dark figure took a step back.

Caine hunched down into a boxer's position... Head down, shoulders up, hands loose in front of his face. He feinted with a left jab. The assassin bobbed and ducked, weaving back and forth like a cobra. Caine caught a glimpse of brown eyes beneath the hood.

Something about those eyes... he thought. They were familiar.

He pivoted and his right arm exploded out in a powerful hook. The assassin blocked with an open left hand, then clutched Caine's shoulder as the punch went wide. The nimble attacker ducked underneath his outstretched arm and grabbed his knee with both hands.

The movements were like lightning... Rapid, precise, and devastating.

Caine struggled to maintain his balance, but the assassin's momentum was working against him. The compact, muscular body spun around, and Caine felt his leg rise up into the air.

As he slammed down to the ground, his legs sprawled open.

The dark figure raised a foot into the air. Caine rolled right, barely avoiding the boot as it stomped into empty space.

He heard a deafening roar beneath him. The flooring rattled and vibrated. Through the cracks below, he could see some kind of massive vehicle moving beneath them. It was driving towards the edge of the foundation pit.

A leg shot at Caine in another kick attack. He hooked the descending leg with his left arm and pushed his up, using his right arm as a lever across his opponent's knees.

The assassin tipped backwards and dangled over the edge of the building. Caine rolled on top of them and pulled his fist back for a punch attack.

As he swung, the dark figure went limp, letting their upper body drop lower over the edge. Caine's punch sliced through thin air. He felt legs wrap around him, the powerful muscles crushing his torso.

Gunfire screamed overhead and ricocheted off the metal bars of the lift cage. Caine turned his head and saw more SWAT team members charging towards them. He knew that, unlike Sean, they had no need to take him in alive.

The rumble of the construction vehicle was deafening. Caine looked down and saw it moving directly beneath them as it exited the pit.

The assassin shifted, struggling to reach for a knife strapped to the harness. Caine grabbed the black-clad arm at the wrist and gave one last look back at the armed men storming towards his position. They were aiming their weapons, preparing to unleash another barrage.

There was only one avenue of escape left. Caine moved without hesitation. He rolled towards the edge of the building. The assassin gasped. As the SWAT team opened fire, the two

entwined figures tumbled over the edge and plummeted towards
the foundation pit below.

33

Sean grasped the metal railing in a white-knuckled grip. The plummeting lift wasn't quite in free fall, but it wasn't what he would call a controlled descent either. With a loud crash, the platform slammed into the bottom of the lift cage. A shockwave ran through his body from the impact.

He tumbled out of the cage, stood up, and looked back up at the building. He heard gunfire and saw sparks fly through the air as bullets ricocheted off metal girders. A massive rumbling filled the air. Something was moving towards him.

He turned and saw a massive dark shape rise up from the sunken pit below the construction site... A towering yellow construction vehicle bore down on him.

Sean darted to the side as the monstrous truck roared towards him. As he moved, he caught a glimpse of two bodies tumbling over the edge the building. They fell towards the truck. Then the mammoth vehicle was upon him, and he could see nothing else. It seemed to go on forever. The ground shook beneath his feet. Eight pairs of heavy-duty wheels, each one taller than him, thundered past.

More gunfire crackled above him. A man in SWAT gear looked down from the edge of the building and pointed his way.

'Time to bounce,' Sean muttered as he ran from the construction site. He headed towards the street.

Reaching the sidewalk, he waved his hands, struggling to flag down a taxi in the mass of traffic whizzing by. Instead, a sleek white limousine cut through the rows of cars and cruised to a stop in front of him.

Sean squinted his eyes in surprise. The dark, tinted window hummed down, revealing the face of a beautiful Chinese woman. Something about her amused stare was hypnotic. He could not bring himself to look away. She leaned towards him. The creamy tan skin of her neck and chest was accentuated by droplets of jade... A dangling necklace splayed across her exposed skin.

'*Ni hao*, Sean. My name is Iris. Would you like a ride?'

'You know my name?' he asked hesitantly.

He heard shouting behind him. He turned and saw the man in the expensive suit burst out the front door of the apartment building. The man jogged towards him, flanked on either side by SWAT team members.

'Your destiny is in your hands,' Iris said in a husky voice. 'You can stay here, with them. Or you can come with me.' She smiled. Sean felt the hypnotic pull of her uncanny stare.

'Well, when you put it like that,' he muttered. He opened the door and slid into the back seat of the limo. Iris moved over to make room and arranged her flowing dress to cover her shapely legs.

The limo pulled away from the curb. 'You see,' she said, as she looked out her window. 'I told you he would come. No one can escape their destiny.'

Sean turned and saw another figure sitting in the front of the limo. Dark shadows covered the man's face, but Sean could see he was dressed in a pristine white suit.

The man leaned forward. A cold smile flickered across his chiseled, handsome face.

It was David Fang.

'Welcome, Mr. Tyler. Please, don't worry about your friend... My men will take care of him.'

Sean tried to force a note of confidence into his voice. 'Wouldn't count on that if I were you.'

Iris tilted her head and gave him a sultry stare. She laughed. 'I like this one. He has *yong qi*... courage.'

'We shall see,' Fang snapped.

The man reached into his ivory blazer and removed a short, fat knife. Chinese characters adorned its worn blade. The handle was smooth, polished wood.

'This is a *ling chi* knife, Mr. Tyler. It was used in ancient China to execute prisoners. *Ling chi* is known as "the death by a thousand cuts." Small knives like this cut tiny strips of flesh from a man's body, one at a time, over a period of days. Starting with the eyes, then the ears, then genitals. As you can imagine, death did not come quickly. Such mutilations were said to carry over into the afterlife. The victim was condemned to an eternity of pain and suffering.'

Sean eyed the knife but said nothing.

Fang placed the tip of the blade on his index finger. He twirled the knife until a tiny drop of blood appeared and ran down the length of his finger.

'Now, Mr. Tyler, I am quite interested to hear everything you know about something called... TANGENT.'

* * *

Caine and the assassin struck the mound of earth and debris that filled the massive truck's rear. They split and rolled in opposite directions towards the edges of the enormous vehicle.

Caine grunted in pain as his head struck the metal sidewall. Every bone and muscle in his body ached, but he forced himself to stand. He struggled to maintain his balance as the vehicle shook and vibrated.

Looking around, he realized he was standing in the rear bin of a WTW220E, one of the largest dump trucks in the world. The incredible vehicle was almost fifty feet long and twenty-five feet wide. At over twenty feet tall, the goliath towered above the other traffic in the street.

Caine felt the vehicle lurch as it left the construction site and picked up speed. The roar of the engine was deafening, and wind blew dust from the vehicle's payload into his eyes. The size of the truck was mind-boggling. It felt as if a small city block had been torn up and placed on wheels.

Caine squinted, looking left and right, searching for the assassin. In front of him, the slanted wall of a demolished house jutted out from the hill of earth and rocks. It had been sheared off and deposited in the dump bin with the rest of the debris. Jagged shards of broken glass still clung to the window frame. Scraps of wood siding stuck out from the wreckage like broken bones.

As he trudged forward through the loose earth and rock, he heard footsteps pounding across the dirt. The assassin vaulted over the jagged wall and leapt through the air towards him.

The flying kick knocked Caine towards the front of the truck. His head slammed into the metal wall of the bin. He threw up his hands just in time to block a rapid series of pummeling strikes. Caine pivoted his body left and right, bearing the brunt of each blow on his shoulders and forearms.

Ducking down, he scooped up a handful of dirt and flung it into the masked face. As the assassin coughed and stepped back, Caine charged forward, slamming into his attacker's solar plexus.

He heard the assassin gasp for breath as he lifted their body into the air. He continued to push forward, launching them into the remains of the house. His opponent smashed through the broken window and tumbled to the ground on the other side of the wall.

Grabbing the upper sill of the window, Caine swung through the opening. He dropped down next to the prone, gasping figure in black. Dirt and rocks shifted as they struggled to get up. The assassin rolled away from him, tumbling down the side of the dirt mound.

Caine slid down the dirt in pursuit. They were both moving towards something sticking out of the debris. Caine squinted as his feet skidded down the mound. He realized it was the short-range rifle... It had fallen from the assassin's shoulder when they struck the vehicle!

The dark figure rolled to a stop and reached for the rifle's polymer stock. Caine charged, shifting his body to adjust for the vehicle's motion. As he closed in, he dipped down and felt his hands wrap around a shattered metal pipe.

Dirt flew through the air as the black-garbed figure yanked the rifle from the debris. The bolt action clicked, and Caine saw the green laser flash towards him.

He swung the pipe, striking the rifle barrel. The gun fired and a bullet whined past his ear. He had thrown off their aim just in time.

The assassin leapt up and aimed the rifle at Caine once more, but the vehicle lurched into a right turn. The killer wobbled on the loose dirt and rocks, struggling to balance.

Caine lunged forward, slamming the pipe into his opponent's

gut. The dark figure dropped the rifle and gasped for breath. Caine kicked the weapon away and it clattered across the rocky debris.

He darted behind the assassin and wrapped his forearm around their throat. With his other hand, he yanked off the black hood and threw it into the wind.

A wave of long, dark hair flew across his face.

'You!' he gasped. 'You're Red Phoenix!'

Finish it! the voice inside his head screamed. He tightened the grip on her neck. He felt her struggling, felt her nails clawing at his arms. He heard her gasp for breath.

She lied to you! She tried to kill you, tried to kill Sean!

He clenched his teeth. He knew the voice was right. She was dangerous. She had made him lower his guard, blinded him to her true intentions.

She's an enemy, he thought. *A foreign assassin. She's a killer.*

She's just like you.

Suddenly, his body rebelled against his own cold, emotionless logic. He pushed her away. The woman fell to the ground. She rolled into a sitting position, her back against the shattered wall.

'Enough,' he said. 'It's over.'

Jia Zhao looked up at him, her face twisted in a combination of rage and sorrow. Her hand moved towards the knife on her harness as her chest heaved up and down, sucking in lungfuls of air.

Caine shook his head, 'Don't. Just don't.'

She dropped her arms to her side.

He glared at her, panting for breath. 'The prison riot... I didn't save you, did I? You were trying to get arrested. You wanted them to bring you inside. So you could get to Sean.'

She returned his glare with equal intensity. 'I had no choice. I was doing what I had to do.'

'A man named Ted Lapinski has leverage on you. He's turned you, made you work for him.'

Her eyes narrowed. 'How do you know that?'

He looked down at her, still unsure if he had made the right choice. 'What does he have on you? What made you turn? Money?'

'*Qu ta ma de zi ji!*' She spat the words out, like venom. 'You think I would betray China for *money*? Do you know the things he made me do? Can you even imagine?'

'I can imagine.'

The truck swung around a corner. Caine felt his body sway with the motion of the massive vehicle. To his right, above the edge of the metal dump bed, he could see row after row of tiny shacks. Abandoned homes, silent and empty, soon to be demolished for future construction.

Jia's cold anger seemed to thaw slightly, and she gave him a curious look. 'Perhaps you can. Why didn't you kill me? What stopped you?'

Before Caine could answer, a pair of gray Audi sedans shrieked around the turn. They accelerated towards the massive vehicle.

Caine ducked down next to Jia as a hail of gunfire sprayed the rear of the truck. Chunks of wood exploded from the crumbling wall. Without hesitation, his hand darted towards her chest. She gasped as his fingers wrapped around the barrel of a small pistol hanging from her harness.

'Hey, *dui bu qi*!' she snapped.

Caine yanked the pistol from the holster and opened fire on one of the cars. The gun was a tiny Glock 42, chambered for .380.

It was not a powerful weapon, but in Caine's hands it was accurate and effective.

The gun roared three times. A spiderweb of cracks spread across the lead Audi's windshield. The car screeched across the pavement, veering away from the truck. Caine grinned and fired again, sending a double tap towards the other Audi. A Chinese man leaned out the rear passenger window of the sleek sedan. He was wielding a submachine gun.

Caine ducked back behind the mound of dirt as more bullets thudded around them.

'Are they from the Ministry?' Caine asked, shouting to be heard over the noise of the truck.

She shook her head. 'Those vehicles and weapons aren't standard issue. They must be Triad.'

'David Fang,' Caine snarled. 'If he was watching the construction site, he may have captured Sean.'

Jia was silent. Caine glanced over at her. 'I know your orders. Lapinski wants Sean dead.'

'Who are you? How do you know all this?'

'There are people in the US working to expose him. This whole operation, what he's done to you... It's about to blow up in his face. When that happens, he's going to have to clean up loose ends.'

Jia's face went pale. '*Wo zhi dao...* I know. I've seen how he operates. He's used me to clean up loose ends before.'

'This time you're the loose end. You have to trust me. Jia, please...' Caine grasped her face in both hands. His emerald-green stare met her wide, fearful brown eyes. She looked confused... lost. Something he had said had struck a nerve. 'Trust me. Help me. And whatever he has on you, I'll help you get out of it.'

Finally, she nodded. Her eyes hardened into a determined

glare. 'All right. I will help you. But if you betray me, I swear I will kill you.'

More gunfire pelted the dirt around them.

'Join the club,' he muttered.

Caine heard bullets ricochet off the front of the truck. The lead Audi was firing at the driver.

The truck made a violent turn, lurching to the right. Caine and Jia fell to the ground as the wheels of the massive vehicle trampled over a row of parked cars. Their metal frames crumpled under the weight of the 220-ton vehicle. Windows shattered and shards of glass exploded across the street like glittering snow.

The Audis followed the massive truck. They charged over the curb, weaving through the maze of demolished cars. Clearing the sidewalk, all three vehicles tore across the dirt field.

They were on a collision course, heading straight for the rows of abandoned houses.

34

'This thing is out of control!' Caine shouted.

'They must have hit the driver,' Jia shouted back. 'If I can get to the controls, I can stop it.' She slid a spare magazine for the Glock from her harness and handed it to Caine. 'Cover me.'

Caine nodded as he checked the load remaining in the small pistol.

Jia charged up the side of the dirt mound and ran to the front of the box bed. She leapt up, grabbed the edge, and pulled herself onto the front upper lip of the dump bin.

The rear Audi opened fire. Bullets traced her movements across the dirt, sending puffs of dust and debris flying. A few stray shots ricocheted off the metal edges of the truck.

Caine sent another double tap towards the rear sedan. Glass fragments exploded from the windshield as his bullets slammed into the car. The slide on the tiny pistol flew back and locked in the open position. The weapon was empty.

The car swerved back and forth across the street as Jia climbed over the lip. She dropped down to a metal deck mounted a few feet above the truck's cabin.

Caine reloaded the pistol. As he racked the slide, he felt his stomach lurch. The truck heaved up into the air, and he heard an explosive crash from the front of the vehicle. The truck slammed back down to the ground. He spun around and saw smashed beams of wood and debris flying through the air.

The truck was plowing through the abandoned houses as if they were made of matchsticks. The vehicle towered over the tiny dwellings, its giant, heavy-duty wheels grinding the crumbling shacks to dust as it lumbered forward.

Caine heard the snarl of the Audi's high-performance engine. One of the sedans closed in, bumper to bumper with the truck's rear. Ladders ran down both sides of the massive truck's rear deck. The Audi's front end hovered below the bottom rung on the right side.

Caine fired three times. The driver jerked behind the shattered windshield as bullets tore into his body. The gray sedan veered off. It vaulted over a mound of dirt and launched into the air. Caine watched as it flew through the wall of one of the abandoned houses and crashed to a halt.

The truck lurched into the air again and Caine tumbled to the ground. He heard a splintering crash as another shack was pulverized beneath the surging vehicle. Then he felt the truck shift to the left. They were moving back towards the street. Up ahead, an intersection ran underneath the concrete bridge of a freeway overpass.

Had Jia regained control of the vehicle? If so, why weren't they stopping?

As he picked himself up from the dirt, he sensed movement behind him. He spun around and saw a blur of motion, someone charging towards him. The rear ladders... Someone must have climbed up from the sedan! The truck was so high off the ground, he hadn't been able to see them beneath the edge of the dump bin.

The pistol roared in his hand, but he was too late... the Chinese man was upon him. Caine saw a bright red gash open on his attacker's shoulder, but the bullet had only grazed him.

The man grabbed Caine's gun hand, pushing it off to the right side. He swung a right hook towards Caine's face. Caine ducked and his left arm shot up, diverting the force of the blow. Caine's left hand wrapped around the back of his attacker's neck. As soon as he felt his fingers make contact, he dropped his weight, keeping his body as close to the man as possible. Rounding his back, he fell to the ground and kicked up. His attacker flew over him, crashing into the wall fragment behind them.

As the man picked himself up, Caine aimed his pistol. Before he could pull the trigger, the howl of automatic gunfire assaulted his ears. Dropping to the ground, he saw puffs of dirt and rocks fly through the air. Bullets sprayed across the back of the truck. The remaining Audi had fallen behind them, and the driver was firing through the shattered windshield.

Suddenly, the car slammed on its brakes and fell back. Rocks and debris began to spill from the rear of the truck. Caine felt his weight shift. His view of the houses and buildings around them began to tilt at a strange angle.

His attacker picked himself up and looked around in shock. He began to slide towards Caine.

A hydraulic whine filled the air, and Caine realized what was happening. The enormous bed of the dump truck was tilting up, spilling its contents onto the road... with Caine and the Triad gangster still inside!

The mountain of dirt and rocks began to shift. The partially demolished house splintered and cracked as it tore loose from the pile of dirt.

Caine rolled to the side of the dump bed, scrambling to find a handhold as the avalanche of debris slid towards him.

* * *

Jia crouched down on the upper deck of the massive truck. A low metal railing stood between her and the edge of the deck. Beyond the railing, she could see the rows of tiny houses standing in the truck's path.

She gripped the railing and held on as the truck drove over one of the shacks. The front end of the huge vehicle lifted up into the air, then slammed back down as it crashed through the tiny dwelling.

The truck leveled out and Jia leapt over the edge of the railing. She fell ten feet through the air and landed in a crouch on the lower deck. To her right was the passenger side of the vehicle's control cabin. Although it was the size of the semi-truck cab, it looked comically small in the center of the monstrous industrial vehicle.

The body of the driver slouched over the controls and blood spattered the bullet-ridden front windshield. She yanked open the door and slid into the cabin. As the enormous vehicle plowed through another shack, Jia unbuckled the dead driver. She kicked him out the driver's side door.

'*Bao qian*, sorry about that,' she muttered as the corpse fell to the deck on the other side of cabin.

Another shack loomed ahead of her. Jia spun the wheel to the left, sending the truck careening back towards the street.

She heard footsteps clanging across metal. Looking to her right, she saw another one of Fang's men charging towards the open door on the passenger side of the cabin. His jacket and hair whipped in the wind as he ran across the deck.

She accelerated, throwing him off balance. He stumbled forward and grabbed the edge of the doorframe. Swinging into the cabin, he launched a kick that slammed her head into the driver's side window.

As he scrambled across the seat, she threw a quick jab into the soft flesh of his neck. She heard a metallic click. Looking down, she saw him flip open a balisong knife. She ducked as he swung the blade towards her face. The knife grazed her hair and plunged into the cushioned driver's seat.

The truck drifted into traffic as she let go of the wheel and slammed both fists into her attacker's kidneys. The other cars honked their horns as they swerved out of the lumbering truck's path.

Her attacker grunted in pain and released his grip on the knife. She reached back and grasped for it with her left hand. She used her right arm to block another kick, pinning his leg against the back of the seat.

Her fingers wrapped around the hilt of the knife. She tore it lose from the seat and stabbed it into the man's inner thigh. He screamed and his hands dropped to his groin.

Before he could remove the knife, Jia grabbed the hair on the back of his head and slammed his face into the cracked windshield. Glittering shards exploded onto the outer deck as his head smashed through the weakened glass.

The thug screamed in pain as the glass tore bloody gashes across his face. He clawed at the dashboard, struggling to pull himself back inside. Jia turned her attention back to the road. She gritted her teeth as she saw a rickety double-decker bus growing closer through the windshield. A few excited tourists pointed out the rear window. The passengers on the top level screamed as the truck loomed over them.

The wheel shuddered beneath her clenched fists. It took all her strength to steer the vehicle. The monster truck swerved left, missing the bus by a matter of inches.

As she drove around the screaming tourists, her attacker grabbed a lever on the dashboard. Grunting in pain, he pulled himself back into the cab. Weak from blood loss, he threw a half-hearted punch towards her face. She blocked the blow, but he grabbed her hand, trapping her right arm in a lock. He yanked the knife from his leg and blood sprayed across the controls.

A droning alarm sounded in the cab, and a yellow warning light flashed on the dashboard. Jia saw something moving in the rearview mirror. The rear dump bed began to tilt up. She struggled to maintain control of the truck as she dropped her eyes to the bloodstained dashboard. Which lever had he pulled?

The Triad gangster lunged towards her, wielding the bloody knife in a shaking, pale hand. With her other arm pinned, she had to let go of the wheel again to block the attack.

As the two combatants struggled, Jia glanced out the shattered windshield. The truck drifted towards a freeway overpass. Behind the cabin, the dump bin tilted higher and higher. The front lip was now several meters taller than the rest of the vehicle.

Her eyes opened wide, and she muttered a half-whispered curse. With the dump bin open, there was not enough clearance... the massive vehicle would not fit beneath the overpass!

35

Caine tucked his pistol in his waistband and scrambled to the edge of the dump bed. His fingers curled around a protruding metal ridge and he hung on for dear life as the bed tilted farther and farther back. His attacker struggled to maintain his balance on the shifting mass of dirt and rocks beneath his feet.

He took several lurching steps towards Caine, his lips curled in an angry snarl. Before he could close the distance, the tumbling wall of debris rolled into him, smashing him to the ground. Caine watched the man's glare turn to a look of stark horror. He clawed at the mass of earth that was carrying him towards the rear of the truck.

Behind them, Caine heard a splintering crash. The house's remains slid out the back of the truck and struck the pavement. The Audi's brakes squealed in protest as the sedan darted around the debris. The angle of the tilting bed continued to grow steeper. Falling dirt and rocks pelted the sedan as it drifted back into position behind them.

The Triad gangster uttered a final shriek before the falling mass of earth swept him out the back of the truck. He struck the pavement and tumbled like a rag doll. The pursuing sedan careened over the man's limp body with a loud thud.

Caine was hanging almost vertically from the side of the dump bed. Using the metal ridges that ran along the side, he pulled himself up as if climbing a ladder.

Behind him, the Audi swerved again as the last chunks of rock emptied from the truck. It darted back into position, and the driver opened fire again with his submachine gun. Bullets sparked and whined across the truck. Hanging from the side of the now empty dump bed, Caine had no more cover. He had to climb over to the other side of the dump bed, put it between him and his attacker's bullets. Grunting with exertion, he pulled himself further up the ladder of metal ridges.

Caine reached the last ridge and balanced his feet on the thin strip of metal. He reached out, but the front lip of the dump bin was still just beyond his grasp. He would have to bridge the gap somehow before he could climb to safety.

Grabbing the side of the bed to steady himself, he prepared to jump. Another barrage of gunfire ricocheted off the metal around him. Caine felt an arrow of hot air streak past his ear. The man's aim was improving.

Suddenly, the truck lurched across the road. Caine felt his feet slip on the tiny ledge of metal. Pushing off, he leapt for the front lip, but the clumsy jump fell a few inches short. His left arm flailed, unable to find a grip. He swung out into the middle of the vertical bed, hanging by one arm.

More gunfire sliced beneath his dangling legs. He lifted his feet as the bullets sparked and whined beneath him. The muscles in his shoulder and arm screamed in pain as he pulled himself up. Finally, his left hand grasped the top edge of the dump bin and he hauled his body up.

As his head cleared the edge, he looked up and saw a gray

wall of concrete looming in front of him. It was the side of the freeway overpass... They were charging towards it at full speed! The top of the dump bed was now least fifteen feet higher than the rest of the truck. There wasn't enough clearance... It was going to hit the side of the overpass and crush him to a pulp in the process.

Move your ass, his mind screamed. *Now!*

Using his last of strength, Caine pulled himself up and over the edge. More bullets ricocheted nearby, but he paid them no mind. The concrete wall of the overpass seemed to speed towards him, growing larger and larger. It was just a few feet away...

Caine cleared the ledge and dropped to the deck above the truck's cab. He struck the metal surface and rolled forward, stopping when he slammed into the front railing.

He heard a tremendous crash, followed by the shriek of scraping metal. The front wheels of the giant truck rose up into the air. Caine grabbed the railing in front of him to stop himself from flying off the deck. Behind him, hydraulic lines hissed and popped as they tore loose from their moorings.

Looking back, he saw concrete chunks raining onto the truck as the edge of the dump bed struck the overpass. The twin metal prongs of the lifting mechanism wrenched free. The massive yellow slab of metal tore loose from the truck. Caine braced himself as the vehicle dropped back to the ground.

As the truck roared out from under the overpass, the eighty-ton dump bed toppled over. It fell to the ground, crashing onto the Audi sedan. The edge of the metal truck bed bisected the pursing vehicle like a giant razor blade, slashing the car in two. Caine watched as the rear half of the sedan flipped up, spinning through the air. The driver's body was obliterated by the impact.

The rest of the truck cleared the overpass and groaned to a stop. Caine heard the sound of shattering glass. Looking down, he saw another of the gangsters launch out the front windshield of the cabin. He rolled off the front of the truck and tumbled to the pavement. He did not get up.

Caine leapt down to the lower deck. Jia opened the passenger door and slid out of the cabin. She limped over to him as he surveyed the path of devastation the truck had caused.

She glanced over at him. 'That didn't go as well as I planned. Are you hurt?'

He stared at her for a moment, then shook his head. 'A few minutes ago we were trying to kill each other. Now you're worried about me?'

She shrugged. 'Things change.'

The shriek of police sirens rose above the traffic noise. Caine made his way to the side ladder. 'Yeah,' he said. 'But sometimes they change for the worse.'

A crowd of spectators began to gather around the smoking fragments of the wrecked vehicles. Caine did his best to hide his face as the crowd snapped pictures with their cell phones. The wailing sirens grew closer. 'We have to get off the street,' Caine said.

Jia ignored the shocked pedestrians and pushed her way through the crowd. 'I have a safe house nearby. Follow me.'

Caine paused for a moment. Jia, if that was even her real name, was a wild card. She was smart, driven, and well-trained. She had played him before. Was she doing so now? Was she using him to get close to Sean, to complete her mission?

She's an unacceptable risk. Take her off the board.

That was the smart play, he knew. But he could have killed her before... Something had held him back.

Something happened to her, he thought. *She's been used. Manipulated. Betrayed...*

Caine had survived a life of violence and bloodshed by

trusting his instincts. Why was he so unsure now? What was it about this woman that thawed the unbreachable ice of his defenses?

He made his decision. He followed her, pushing forward through the crowd, ignoring their strange looks and chatter. He did not look back at the devastation left behind them.

36

The whoosh of the rotors outside was deafening as Rebecca entered the main room of the house. Behind her, Josh and DuBose led Lapinski out of the makeshift interrogation room.

Keyes was already outside, behind one of the stone columns in the room. A dark shadow moved across the windows as the helicopter made another pass. Ganda and Matheson lay face down on the floor, their wrists zip-tied behind their backs.

'Lapinski, on the floor!' Josh barked. Lapinski fell to the ground next to his men. DuBose grabbed a pair of H&K UMP submachine guns from a table in the corner. He tossed one to Josh, who caught it and slung it around his shoulder.

'Sit-rep?' Josh shouted. He grabbed Rebecca's chair and pushed her behind a stone kitchen island. Old dishes and pots covered the counter. A wood block filled with kitchen knives stood next to a half-eaten plate of salami.

'Didn't get a good look at them, sir,' Keyes replied, 'but this is their third pass. Probably trying to confirm their target is on-site.'

Lian was already hiding in the kitchen, hugging her knees to her face. 'The bad men are coming back, aren't they?' she chirped.

Rebecca shook her head. 'Honey, we're not going to let anything happen to you. Stay close to me, okay?'

Josh ducked behind another stone column. 'What are they packing?'

Keyes shot him a nervous glance. 'Based on the rotor noise, I'd say it's a light chopper. Maybe an AH-6. Could be carrying anything from twin 50 cals to Stinger missiles.' He hugged his UMP to his chest and peered around the edge of the column.

The whoosh of the aircraft's rotors roared once again.

'They're coming around,' Keyes shouted.

A burst of gunfire tore through the interior of the house. The front windows exploded into showers of sparkling glass and wood fragments. Stone chips and other debris whizzed through the air. The rattle of heavy machine gun fire drowned out Lian's scream of terror. Rebecca grabbed her, pivoting her chair to shield the crying child with her body. She clutched the girl to her chest as the dishes on top of the counter burst into ceramic fragments.

The gunfire ceased, and the roar of the aircraft receded into the distance.

'Twin 50s, for sure!' Keyes shouted as the dust of the first barrage settled through the room.

'DuBose,' Josh called out. 'The truck in the barn, the Cougar... You said it was a civilian model. I assume that means no weapons?'

'Negative, but it looked like its armor was intact. Keys are in the visor.'

The helicopter swooped over the house again, even lower this time. The wood beams in the ceiling shook and rattled as it buzzed overhead.

'Then that's our play.' Josh looked back at Rebecca. 'Director, they're making another run on us. Stay down!'

Gunfire ripped through the house again, tearing the furniture to shreds. Sparks ricocheted off the heavy stone columns. Rebecca hugged Lian tighter as the child burst into another fit of screaming.

The gunfire stopped. Once again, the sound of the rotors diminished as the helicopter veered off.

'It's okay,' Rebecca whispered. 'It's going to be okay.' She wasn't sure who she was trying to sooth – the child or herself.

Josh gestured to DuBose. 'You, me, one of the prisoners, we make a run for the barn. We get in the Cougar, drive it around back, and get the others. Then we haul ass out of here.'

DuBose nodded. 'Sounds like a plan.'

Josh turned to Keyes. 'Keep eyes on these two shit bags,' he said. He nodded towards Ganda and Lapinski. 'And watch out for the director and the kid, got it?'

'I can handle it,' Keyes replied.

The helicopter swooped back around. The sound of its engine grew louder and louder.

DuBose grabbed Matheson and hefted him up from the floor. 'That chopper's here for you assholes. You slow me down, I drop you in the dirt, understand?'

The young man nodded, his face pale.

Josh positioned himself next to the front door. 'Okay, let's do this. On my mark. Three... two... one... Mark!'

He kicked open the door and charged out into the front yard, DuBose following close behind.

Rebecca heard the muted bursts of the men's UMP submachine guns firing in the distance. The noise of the helicopter suddenly changed. It was veering off again, changing course.

It's following Josh, Rebecca realized. She felt a cold, empty feeling in the pit of her stomach. She couldn't just sit hiding, doing nothing.

She set the girl down on the ground. 'Lian, I want you to stay here for a minute. Can you do that for me?'

The child burst into tears. 'Please, don't leave me!'

'I'll be right back, and then we're going to get you out of here. We're going to help you find your mother, okay?'

The child nodded, but tears continued to stream down her face. Rebecca hugged her one more time. Then she wheeled behind one of the stone columns, next to where Lapinski and Ganda lay on the ground.

Keyes gave her a sharp look. 'Ma'am, you should really—'

'Didn't Josh tell you I hate being called ma'am?' Rebecca shot back.

Outside, the chopper's machine guns roared.

'It's strafing the barn,' Keyes shouted. 'They're going after Galloway and DuBose.'

Rebecca turned towards the prisoners. They were squirming, struggling to get a look out the front windows.

'Ted,' she hissed. 'This is your last chance. Help me or I swear I will leave you here to die. Who is David Fang? Who is he really?'

The helicopter changed course again, swooping back towards the farmhouse. The rotors grew louder and louder, and the few intact windows in the house rattled in their frames.

'I don't know David Fang,' Ted whimpered. He turned and looked back towards her with fear in his eyes. 'But the man you showed me, the man in the pictures... He was in the files Sun Wai Tong accessed. They're old CIA case files. He was younger then, but I swear it's the same man!'

'Who is he?' Rebecca shouted.

'His name is Dan-zu Huang! Operation Canary... Look up Operation Canary!'

Gunfire tore through the room as the helicopter made another attack run. Ted screamed and rolled toward the wall.

A stray shot struck the microwave in the kitchen. The appliance exploded, sending a shower of bright sparks raining down on Lian. The little girl screamed and leapt to her feet. She ran into the living room as fast as her tiny legs could carry her.

'Lian, get down!' Rebecca shouted.

The girl ducked behind the sofa. Rebecca could see the chopper outside, flying low across the field. It spun around and moved back towards the farmhouse, making a horizontal attack run.

'Keyes!' Rebecca called out.

'I got her,' the man shouted. He darted from his position behind the column and charged towards Lian. Grabbing her in his arms, he stood up and raced towards another column on the other side of the room.

The chopper opened fire. Keyes' body jerked and flew through the air. He fell forward, dropping Lian to the ground. The little girl bawled as she hit the ground. She stood up, shaking, her eyes wide and terrified.

'Lian, no!'

Rebecca flicked the switch on her chair. The motorized wheels hummed as she sped across the floor towards the girl. She scooped her up in her arms and rolled behind the column as the chopper once again opened fire.

Bullets ricocheted off the stone pillar. The chopper swooped away again.

Suddenly, she felt an arm loop across her throat. It pulled tight, yanking her backwards. She clawed at the thick cord of muscle cutting into her windpipe, but she couldn't pry it back.

'You fucking bitch!' a man's voice hissed in her ear. 'You're going to get us all killed!'

That voice... She felt dizzy. She remembered the attack in the alley. The dark maw of the van doors, the sickly-sweet smell of flowers...

Ganda!

He pulled her away from the crying Lian, back towards the kitchen.

'You couldn't leave well enough alone, could you?' he muttered. He dragged her past Keyes' body. Her chair left tracks through the slick pool of blood on the ground. Ganda's arms were still tied together, but he had managed to slip his hands in front of him. He tightened his chokehold on her neck.

There was no one to help her. She was alone. This time, Josh could not come to her rescue.

'Maybe,' he whispered into her ear, 'maybe if I kill you now, they let me live. Worth a shot, right?' Ganda pulled harder. His arm dug into her throat as he dragged her towards the kitchen.

She looked down and saw light glint off steel blades. The kitchen knives... The gunfire had knocked them off the island. They lay scattered across the floor, among the shattered glass and broken crockery.

She coughed and spat as she gasped for breath. 'You're going to die here today,' she wheezed.

'You don't know that,' he shouted. 'You don't know anything!'

Her grasping fingers found the controls for her chair. She flicked one of the switches, and the motor whined to life.

'I know one thing, asshole,' she rasped.

'Yeah,' he shouted, digging his forearm deeper into her throat. 'What's that?'

'Control the head, and the body will follow.'

'What the—'

The motor on her chair screamed in reverse, cutting him off. She flew backwards and the momentum lifted Ganda up off his feet. His back slammed into the kitchen island, knocking the wind out of him.

As he slumped forward. Rebecca thought back to the gym, and her night with Josh. She moved without thought, acting on instinct and muscle memory. Her arm shot up, raking her nails across Ganda's ears and face.

As he screamed, she clamped her hand on the back of his neck and pulled her head free of his hold. She let her chair topple backwards, using her grip on his head to spin his body away from her. The chair clattered to the ground and she fell on top of him.

Ganda struggled to turn over, but with his hands still tied in front of him, it was difficult to get leverage. Rebecca's grasping fingers wrapped around the wooden hilt of a kitchen knife that had fallen to the floor. She raised the blade over her head.

Ganda bucked his hips, and his body spun around beneath her. His eyes opened wide, and he screamed as the blade plunged towards him.

Then it was over. A red stain spread across his shirt. The handle of the knife protruded from his chest. A wet, gurgling sigh escaped his lips as his head lolled to the side.

Rebecca thought back to the alley. To the fear and helplessness she had felt that night. She wanted to stab him again. She longed to plunge the blade into his heart, over and over.

But she looked up and saw Lian staring at her. The child was standing in the center of the room, in front of the shattered windows.

She was shaking.

'Lian, I'm sorry you had to see that. Are you okay?'

'You killed the bad man,' the little girl said, her voice quaking.

'Yeah. I guess I did.'

Before she could say anything else, a rush of wind filled the room. The torn, shredded curtains whipped through the air, and a cloud of dust and debris filled the room.

The helicopter lowered into view, only a few feet from the front of the house. She could see the pilot behind the domed canopy. The aircraft hovered just above the ground. The long, black barrels of the twin machine guns pointed straight at them.

Lian turned around and stared at the helicopter. Her hair and clothes billowed in the prop wash.

'Lian, get down!' Rebecca screamed. The terrified child froze like a statue.

Rebecca heard another sound rising above the roar of the chopper's rotors... Splintering wood, and the rumble of a high-powered engine.

The pilot's hands seemed to move in slow motion as he reached for the switch that triggered the guns.

Rebecca dragged herself across the floor, struggling to reach the child.

'Lian, no!'

The roar of the other engine grew louder. A large, armored SUV tore across the field, bouncing over the rough ground. It was racing to intercept the low-hovering chopper.

It was Josh, she realized. He had made it to the Cougar.

The SUV charged past the farmhouse windows. It was only a few feet away and picking up speed. The engine roared even louder.

The Cougar slammed into the chopper's fuselage at full speed. The impact knocked the aircraft sideways before the pilot could trigger the guns. The screech of crumpling metal filled the house, as the helicopter crashed to the ground, and the Cougar flipped up into the air.

Rebecca made it to Lian and threw her body over the girl. Fragments of the downed helicopter's rotors sliced through the room. The flying metal sheared a huge chunk of stone loose from one of the columns. It crashed to the floor, missing Rebecca's head by inches.

Silence descended over them.

She ran a hand through Lian's hair. 'You okay, honey?' The girl nodded and looked up at her.

'Are you okay, ma'am?' she said.

Rebecca laughed. 'I am now. But please don't call me ma'am.'

The girl nodded. 'Okay.'

Rebecca tried to look over her shoulder. The muscles in her neck screamed in agony from Ganda's chokehold. 'Ted?' she called out. 'Still with us?'

There was no response.

She turned and scanned the patch of floor where Lapinski had been lying.

He was gone.

37

Jia's Shanghai safe house was a small, barren apartment. No art decorated the white walls, no pictures of family or friends sat on her nightstand. Caine had lived in many places like this himself. Empty, sterile rooms that could be abandoned in a heartbeat. A temporary dwelling for a temporary life.

The faint patter of running water came from the bathroom down the hall. Jia had stood watch while Caine had taken the first shower. The thin drizzle of hot water was barely able to wash the dust and filth from his skin, but it was better than nothing. Now it was Jia's turn.

Caine parted the curtains and peered out the tiny window. The apartment was on the second floor of a crumbling building and looked out over a narrow alley. Known as a *longtang*, the labyrinth of narrow streets below was Shanghai's version of a *hutong*. The narrow stretch of pavement passed through the ground floor of a nearby residential building. The cramped tunnel was decorated at either end by intricate stone carvings that depicted creatures from Chinese mythology... Celestial dragons, guardian lions, and the ever-present vermillion bird.

The Red Phoenix, he thought.

Caine closed the curtain and sat down on the futon mattress in the center of the tiny room. He pulled out the USB drive. As he turned it over in his fingers, his mind raced. What was so important? What had Sean and his friend uncovered?

The appearance of Fang's men near the apartment couldn't be a coincidence. They had been waiting. Which meant they needed something. Was it this memory stick? Regardless, Sean was in Fang's hands now. Caine was certain of it.

He closed his eyes. Once again, he had failed. He should never have listened to Sean. They should have left China immediately instead of going on this fool's errand.

He felt a quiet buzz in his pocket. His phone. He pulled it out and checked the screen.

Rebecca.

He answered the call. 'It's me.'

'Tom, thank God! I've been trying to reach you for hours.' There was a rushed hint of adrenaline in her voice mixed with impatience. He glanced at the phone's screen and saw several missed calls and texts.

'Sorry. I was in the middle of nowhere for a while. Once I got to Shanghai, things...'

'Got complicated?' she asked, finishing his sentence.

He smiled. 'Yeah. Occupational hazard.'

'Tom, we linked the man who attacked me to Lapinski. We caught him on-site with a team of private security contractors. They were hiding out in Virginia, up in the mountains. Six-man team, all ex-military. As far as I can tell, they were here to watch over a six-year-old girl. I texted you a picture.'

'One sec...'

He opened the text and saw the picture. A round-faced

Chinese girl with a pensive look of fear in her wide, dark eyes. She was just a child.

And underneath, a single, brutally efficient word. LEVERAGE?

He remembered Jia's concern over Alton's niece, Baozhai. And her last words to him before he left for Shanghai.

It's the ones we care about most who pay the price...

'It's her daughter,' he said in a quiet voice.

'Whose daughter?'

Caine gritted his teeth. He felt a wave of doubt, uncertainty.

'Red Phoenix. Her real name is Jia Zhao.'

'You've made contact with the assassin? When were you planning on telling me this?'

'She's not my biggest problem right now. The Triad gangster I told you about, David Fang... He has Sean. And I have something he wants.'

'I have more intel for you there. You're not gonna believe who he really is.'

'Try me.'

'David Fang's real name is Dan-zu Huang. He was a part of the student movement in China, back in 1989. He was a member of a group called Voice of Freedom. China considered them to be dangerous radicals. They staged protests, harassed police, threw firebombs at tanks, that kind of thing. They also ran a pirate radio station. It broadcast pro-democracy messages twenty-four hours a day.'

'Sounds pretty elaborate. And these were just students?' Caine grunted.

'Most were. Some members were suspected to be professional agitators, trained by a CIA program known as Operation Canary. And the Voice of Freedom received almost all its funding from a private company. Something called the International

Student Endowment Organization. I'm sure you won't be surprised to learn the ISEO was a CIA front company.'

'This is all way before our time. Where are you getting your intel?' Caine asked.

'Lapinski. When I showed him Fang's picture, he cracked. Said the Operation Canary report was one of the files Sun Wai Tong stole in the hack. Not only did he steal it, he tried to erase all copies of it he could find. He must have been in a rush though, because the Tailored Ops guys were able to reconstruct a partial copy.'

Caine squinted. 'Wait a minute... We still don't know who hired Sun Wai, right? The fact that he specifically tried to erase this file... Maybe that's the missing link. Maybe whoever his contact is didn't want that file to ever be released. Did Lapinski give you any more intel?'

'No, he escaped custody during—Never mind, I'll fill you in later. But if Tong was specifically trying to erase David Fang's file, that could mean...' her voice trailed off. 'Oh my God.'

'David Fang, or Dan-zu Huang, whatever you want to call him,' Caine said. 'He could be Sun Wai Fong's contact.'

'Tom, there's more. The files, the black ops stuff... Ted says that was just a smokescreen. The real thing they're after is something called TANGENT.'

'Never heard of it.'

Rebecca's voice was terse. 'In a nutshell, it's an NSA cyber-weapon. It can be used to implicate anyone they want for hacking attacks. It also contains a database that proves the NSA has used it on American corporations. A list of cyber-attacks they blamed on other state-sponsored hackers.'

Caine shook his head. 'And you wonder why I want to stay on the outside?'

'Tom, if Fang is somehow involved in this... You can't let a

Triad gangster control something like TANGENT. It's too dangerous.'

Caine looked down at the USB stick in his hands. 'That's not my priority right now. I'll do what I can, but no promises.'

'Tom, please—'

'Are you okay? What the hell happened over there?' Even as he cut her off, a note of concern crept into his voice.

Rebecca paused. She took a breath. 'It's a long story… But yes, I'm fine. And so is the girl. Her name is Lian.'

'Good.' The water shut off. Caine heard Jia rustling in the bathroom. 'Rebecca, I have to go. Is the extraction arranged?'

'I sent you the info. It's a boat, at Yangshan Harbor. They'll take you to the US airbase in Osaka.'

'Thank you. Bring the girl.'

'What?'

'You're meeting the plane when it lands, right?'

'Of course, but—'

'Rebecca, please. Just bring the girl.'

He hung up, cutting her off her protests.

Jia stepped out of the bathroom, rubbing her damp hair with a towel. She was wearing a cotton robe belted at her waist.

'Jia…' He paused, not sure how to continue.

She looked up at him, her dark eyes peering out from behind long, thin strands of wet hair. 'What is it?'

'I know what Lapinski has on you.' He handed her the phone.

Jia stared at the picture of the little girl on the screen. The towel fell from her hands and dropped to the floor with a wet slap. Caine couldn't tell if the dampness in her eyes was from the shower, or if she was tearing up.

'*Wo ke lian de tian shi*… my angel,' she whispered.

She turned her gaze back to Caine. The luminous, warm look

her eyes usually held was replaced by cold, bitter rage. 'You have her now?'

'It's not like that. She's with friends of mine. She's safe.'

'Take me to her. Now!' Jia snapped.

'I will. But first I must get Sean.'

Her mouth twisted into a snarl. '*Ni zhe ge hun dan!* Bring me my daughter now!'

She charged him. Caine stepped back, surprised by her sudden ferocity. He saw a glint of steel in her right hand... Somehow, she had concealed a knife in the thin robe. Caine reached out with both hands and grabbed her wrist. As he pushed the knife out to his left, Jia drove her forearm into his chest and shoved him back. The tiny apartment shook as his back slammed into the plaster walls.

'Jia, stop it! That's enough!'

Her pupils flared with anger and hate. Her body pressed up against him, lean, sinewy muscles stretched taut beneath the thin fabric of the robe.

'I don't care who you are,' she hissed. 'I don't care what you are doing here. I want my daughter!'

Using his right shoulder, Caine knocked her backwards. As she moved away from him, he used both his hands to pull her knife arm through the gap between them. He spun her body around and looped around her throat. Using his right hand, he savagely twisted her wrist. The knife clattered to the floor, and he kicked it across the room.

'Jia, please! She's all right, I promise!'

All at once, Jia stopped fighting. Her body stiffened. Then, as if the release of all her toxic anger left her empty and deflated, she sank to the floor.

Caine slid down the wall with her, loosening the grip of the arm that circled around her. What started as a hold became an embrace.

He felt her body tremble. After a brief moment, droplets of moisture ran down his arm.

She was sobbing.

He repeated his words, softer. 'She's okay. I swear, Jia, she's fine. As soon as I get Sean, I'll take you to her, I promise.'

Her head leaned back and rested against his cheek. Her damp hair smelled of shampoo and chlorine.

'It's my fault. It's all my fault,' she cried, her words quavering as spasms of grief wracked her body. 'Lian... She has paid the price for the blood on my hands.'

Caine shifted his body so he could look her in the eye. 'No,' he said in a firm voice. 'That's not going to happen.'

'Her father...' Her words were a breathy whisper. 'The Ministry did not approve of him. I thought she would be safer abroad. I sent her to a school in Europe, I wanted her to learn English, learn about the world. I thought, when she was older, when I was out of this life, I could bring her home, show her China. But somehow, this man, this Lapinski...' She hissed the name as if it was a foul curse. 'He found her. He took her. He knew who I was. He knew what she meant to me.'

'Lapinski was looking for an asset in China,' Caine said. 'He works for the NSA, and China is big into cyber-espionage. A man named Bernatto arranged for some contractors to rendition your daughter. Lapinski's been holding her in Virginia.'

She wiped her eyes and looked up at him. 'How do you know all this?' she asked.

Caine grunted. 'Bernatto was already on my list. Now Lapinski is too.'

'Your list?'

'They've hurt me. And they've tried to hurt people I care about.'

She pushed the curtain of dark, dripping hair from her face. 'So what will you do?'

Caine stood and offered Jia his hand. When she took it, he pulled her to her feet.

'What do you think?'

She nodded. 'Sean is important to you. His father... He was more than just your friend, wasn't he?'

Caine nodded. 'He was my partner. The other man I told you about, Bernatto? He had him killed.'

She bit her lip and looked at him. Her eyes were clear now, thoughtful.

'I will help you get Sean back. And you will bring me to Lian,' she said in a firm voice.

'Yes,' he said.

'One more thing. I don't approve of everything China does. But I will not betray my country. Never again.'

'You won't have to. I'm not working for the NSA, or the CIA, or anyone else. I'm here on my own. I just want to keep my promise. To keep Sean safe.'

'First we must find him,' Jia said.

Caine looked down and saw the USB drive on the floor. He had dropped it in the fight. He bent down, picked it up, and stared at it for a second.

'Do you still have access to those hacker contacts?' he asked. 'Could you arrange a meeting?'

'The Jade Enclave? Yes, I think so. Why, what is that?'

Caine handed her the towel from the floor. She took it and began to wrap up her hair.

'I don't know. But it's something Fang wants. I need to find out what it is.'

He sat down on the futon. His muscles burned with pain as the adrenaline of the day's battles began to ebb and wear off.

'Tom,' Jia said quietly. 'I'm sorry, about before. I...'

Caine shook his head as he slipped the USB drive back in his pocket. 'Forget it. I understand.'

He fell back onto the bed and closed his eyes. He could still smell the shampoo from Jia's hair, feel the humidity left in the air from her shower. He listened to her soft rustling as she slipped into her clothes.

She tossed something on the bed. 'Here. These are clean. They should fit you.'

Caine opened his eyes. He sat up and slipped into the T-shirt and jeans she had thrown next to him. The fit was snug, but close enough. He thought about asking who they belonged to but decided not to.

Turning, he saw she had slid open a hidden rear panel in the closet. He followed her into the tiny, secret storeroom. The walls were lined with weapons and equipment. Racks of pistols, rifles, and knives surrounded him.

Jia looked over at him, nodding in approval. 'We must resupply ourselves. Then we will meet with my contact from the Enclave. She calls herself Betty. Betty Binary. She is... unusual.'

'I can hardly wait.' Caine exhaled as he scanned the racks of weapons. 'The way you fight, what style is that? Kung fu?'

Jia grabbed a rifle from the wall and set it down on a narrow work bench. 'It is called *sanshou*,' she answered. 'It combines elements of multiple fighting styles. Kung fu, kickboxing, wrestling.'

Caine turned towards her. 'I've heard of it. Military training, special forces, right? Are you with the SL Commando Unit?'

Jia shook her head. 'No, my unit designation is classified. We report directly to the Ministry of State Security.' She did not look back at Caine as she continued gathering equipment. 'When I was a young girl... I had no one. I was like Sean. An orphan. My unit was my family. But now, I am a traitor. Alone.'

Caine picked up a Beretta PX4 Storm Compact pistol from one of the racks. He pulled back the slide and checked the weapon. Like all her equipment, it was clean and well-maintained.

'I know the feeling,' he muttered. Jia glanced at him. The faint hint of a bitter smile touched her lips. She slipped a magazine into a Glock 42.

Caine moved over to a medical shelf. It was filled with tranquilizers, painkillers, and other drugs used in their trade. He picked up one of the vials and held it up to the light.

As he scanned the label of the tiny glass bottle, a plan began to form in his mind.

38

Caine and Jia faced the window of the tram car as it sped through a tunnel beneath the Huangpu River. Outside, the tram was surrounded by brilliant, shifting panels of light. They dove deeper, plunging through concentric rings of pulsing blue neon. Brilliant orange orbs that resembled hot lava flowed past the windows. Electronic music played through the tram car, giving the glowing scenery outside a surreal accompaniment.

A cluster of other passengers stood in the car, but Caine and Jia stood alone in the rear corner of the tram. The colorful lights outside reflected off the glass, lighting Jia's face with an intense pink glow.

'We're traveling under the river, right?' Caine asked.

She nodded, staring at the light show outside as the tram descended. 'Yes, this is the Bund Sightseeing Tunnel. The original plan was to build a glass tunnel that showcased the river, but the water was too polluted. Nothing lives in it, so there was nothing to see.'

Caine uttered a dark laugh. 'So instead we get some kind of Las Vegas light show.'

Jia was silent for a moment. She seemed mesmerized by the tunnel of light surrounding them. 'There was a man,' she finally said. 'At the apartment building. Expensive suit. His skin is... strange.'

'I saw him,' Caine said. 'Sean had met him before, said he worked for the Ministry of State Security.'

She looked up at Caine. 'Yes, his name is Yong Jin. He was my handler at the Ministry. He was burned once, in the field. Plastic surgery was required to repair his face. That's why his skin looks...'

She paused. After a short breath, she continued. 'I worked with him on several missions before I was assigned to infiltrate Human Rights Now. He knows me well. Lapinski made me... made me kill for him. I believe Yong already suspects I am compromised. He is hunting me.'

Caine put a hand on her shoulder. 'Then it's even more important that you leave China as soon as possible.'

She looked back out the window. 'I know. I feel like part of my heart is being ripped from my body. But at the same time, it's almost a relief. Have you ever worked deep cover?'

Caine stood next to her, both of them staring out the window, but oblivious to the lights outside. 'Yes,' he replied.

'The people at HRN, I have stood with them in demonstrations. Fought alongside them, protested injustice with them. The things I once believed, the things I was told to believe... I am not the same person I was then. Things are different now. I am different.'

Caine continued watching the lights move by. He had worked undercover many times, including a long assignment in Japan. After his betrayal, he had lived off the grid, survived as a two-bit smuggler in Thailand. He thought back to his time there, in Pattaya and Tokyo. Faces flickered across the hazy screen of his memory. People he had helped. People he had hurt. People who had died.

He cleared his throat. 'This job, this life... It changes you. Your cover is a lie. A pack of lies, and you have to live with them day in and day out. One day you wake up, and you realize those lies are more real for you than the truth ever was. The person you're pretending to be... That's who you become, for better or worse.'

She leaned her head against him. 'I knew you would understand. It has happened to you as well, hasn't it?'

He said nothing and continued to stare out the window. The brilliant tunnel of light flashed by.

* * *

After exiting the tram, Jia led them to the Oriental Pearl Tower complex. It was late in the afternoon, and the sun hung low in the sky, casting a shimmering glow. Its light bounced off the enormous mirrored sphere at the base of the tower.

The bulbous lower sphere was over a hundred feet in diameter. A smaller sphere hung above them, fifteen hundred feet in the air. Suspended near the top of the tower, it reflected the burning glow in the air like a second sun.

They purchased their tickets and moved through the line of people that led to the base of the tower. An elevator took them up to the first sphere. They walked past row after row of skill cranes, video games, and other amusements. The smell of sweat and rancid popcorn infused the stale air. Here and there, a teenager smashed buttons on a video game. A girl jumped up and down with excitement as one of the cranes dumped a prize at her feet. But most of the machines were empty and the area uncrowded.

The blinking lights and electronic squawks seemed lonely and muted without an audience to enjoy them.

Caine glanced around as Jia led them down a dim service corridor, but he saw no sign that they had been followed. At the end of the corridor, a security door blocked their path. Jia pulled out her cell phone and tapped on the screen.

They heard a series of clicks. The door swung open. A Chinese girl in her early twenties peered through the half-open door. Her narrow, dark brown eyes shifted from Jia to Caine. She was tall, almost able to look him in the eye. Her hair was long and straight and looked unwashed; her skin had a pale, translucent quality. The fluorescent lights reflected in the lenses of her cat's eye glasses. The frames were chunky pink plastic, and tiny glitter-covered bows decorated each temple.

She was wearing a black and white polka dot dress. The fabric was faded, and the garment looked old and worn, as if purchased from a thrift store. Something about her was familiar, but Caine couldn't quite put his finger on it.

'Who's this *ben dan*?' she asked.

'Beg your pardon?' Caine drawled, an amused smile on his face.

Jia smiled. 'She called you a stupid egg. In Chinese, to call someone an egg is a mild insult. It implies your lineage is of animalistic origin.'

'If you're just gonna stand outside gawking, we might as well hang up a sign,' the girl snapped. '*Zhi shi wo shuo ni shi lai pi gou.*'

Jia stared at the girl for a moment, then burst into laughter. She covered her mouth as she snorted in amusement. The girl stepped aside, allowing Caine and Jia to enter the room.

'Do I even want to know what she said?' he asked.

Jia managed to stifle her giggling for a few minutes and

waved her hand at him. 'She called you a... Never mind, I'll tell you later.'

Inside, the room was dim and looked like a storage area. Old arcade game cabinets, their electronic guts removed, stood beneath the sparse overhead lights. The bright, garish designs painted on their empty frames were covered with a layer of dust. They looked like they had not been moved in years.

A young Chinese man sitting at a desk glanced up in alarm as Caine and Jia entered the room. Unlike the girl, there was nothing unusual about his looks at all. He wore a short-sleeved button-down shirt, slim khaki pants, and simple glasses. He looked a few years older than the girl, Caine thought.

'*Wo bu xi huan zhe yang.* You shouldn't bring people here,' he said.

'Chill out, she's with me.' She sat down and threw her feet up on the desk. Her neon-green combat boots rested on a filthy, battered computer keyboard. Every inch of the desk's surface was covered with USB hubs, tangled cables, and computer equipment.

'Don't mind Edgar,' she said. 'My brother's kind of paranoid, with good reason.'

'And you must be Betty?' Jia asked.

'My name's Shirley Chen. Betty Binary is just my online name.' Her eyes shifted from Jia to Caine. 'So are you two an item, or what? I was sure you were gonna start making out on that tram car.'

'You were watching us?' Jia asked, looking around the room.

Shirley shrugged. 'Hacking the cameras in the tram was no big deal.'

Jia blushed and muttered something in Chinese. Caine gave the teenage girl a thin smile. 'Actually, a couple hours ago, she tried to kill me.'

The girl blinked and pushed her glasses up the bridge of her nose. 'So? That doesn't mean anything. I wanted to kill Monk all the time.'

'Monk? You mean the hacker, The Monkey King?' Jia asked.

'I thought you looked familiar,' Caine said. 'I saw your picture in his apartment. You're his girlfriend.'

Shirley looked away and ran her hands through her long, dark hair. 'I was. Nobody's seen Monk in weeks. I mean, he must be... I'm sure Fang had him...'

She lowered her voice. 'He was a pretty shitty boyfriend. Lately, he spent more time with his *gui lao* friend than he did with me.'

Caine narrowed his eyes. '*Gui lao*... You mean Sean?'

Shirley nodded. 'He cheated on me with all these skanks he met online. And he always smelled like warm soda and dirty socks. But yeah, Monk was my boyfriend. And now he's gone. So let's just shut up about it.'

She reached down and flipped some switches on one of the monitors. It sprang to life. A colorful graphic of a cartoon monkey rolled around the screen, making a noise each time it bounced off one of the corners. '*Ooh ooh ooh... eee eee eee...*'

'So this is it? You two are the Jade Enclave?' Caine asked. 'A couple of kids working out of an old arcade?'

Shirley glared at him. 'No. But we're the only ones willing to risk meeting a pair of strangers. Now, do you have Monk's data or not?'

Caine paused for a moment, staring at Shirley and her brother. It seemed ludicrous that this unlikely pair held the key to saving Sean. But what other option did he have? He reached into his pocket and pulled out the USB drive. She took it and plugged it into a tangled mass of cables.

'Monk encoded the data in an audio file that he emailed to

Sean,' Caine said. 'I think it might explain why Fang was after him. Fang may be in possession of a cyber-weapon that allows him to—'

'TANGENT,' Shirley said, her eyes locked on the screen. Line after line of code filled the monitor. The numbers and symbols scrolled across the screen so quickly, Caine could barely make them out.

'Yes. How did you know that?'

'Monk left information about it here.' Her eyes darted, drinking in the data. She spoke as if she were in a trance. 'TANGENT. NSA cyber-weapon. Capable of perfectly mimicking techniques and patterns of all known hackers profiled in US cybercrimes database.'

Edgar paced back and forth behind them, running his hands through his short black hair. 'Something like that, in the hands of a Triad? He could start a war!'

Jia stared at the monitor. 'But why did Fang kidnap Sean?' she asked. 'If he already... If Monk is dead, and Fang wants to keep this a secret, why didn't he just kill Sean too?'

Shirley continued tapping on the keys. 'There's more. When Monk found TANGENT on Fang's mainframe, he put a lock on it. Fang needs the key on this drive to unlock it again.'

'That's why Fang needs Sean alive,' Caine said. 'He thinks he has the key to unlock the program.'

'*Deng yi xia*... Wait a minute,' Shirley said, tapping on the keys. 'The data on this USB drive is meant to look like the key. Fang thinks he can use it to unlock TANGENT. But Monk was working on something else... A trap.'

She moved the cursor to another section of code. It flashed red on the screen. 'There's another program hidden in the decryption code. Or at least part of one. It looks like Monk wasn't able to finish it before...'

Jia crouched next to her and rested her hand on the girl's shoulder. Shirley flinched but did not move away. She continued staring at the screen, the blinking red light reflecting in her glasses.

'Shirley, can you finish the program? Can you finish the code he was writing?'

Shirley nodded. 'Yeah. I was a way better hacker than he ever was, anyway.' She looked up at Caine and blinked. Her pale cheeks were flushed a light pink. Her eyes narrowed.

'What are you, a cop? Or a gangster?'

Caine shook his head. 'Neither. But I need what's on that drive to save Sean.'

Shirley bit her lip. 'That smell I told you about... Warm soda, dirty socks?'

'Yes?' Jia said softly.

'I miss that stupid smell. If I finish this code, you're going to use it against Fang? You're going to hurt him. Maybe kill him. Right?'

Caine clenched his jaw. 'I'm going to get Sean back. If Fang tries to stop me...' Shirley stared into his emerald-green eyes. They were hard, cold, and unyielding.

She nodded and focused her attention back on the computer screen. 'Okay. Then shut up and let me work.'

Jia stood up and moved next to Caine. He felt a tingle run through his body as her arm brushed against his. They glanced at each other but said nothing. Edgar muttered to himself and stormed off into the depths of the storeroom.

The only sound in the dark chamber was the clicking of Shirley's fingers as they darted across the keyboard.

39

David Fang's mouth twisted into a snarl. Beads of sweat dripped down his chiseled face. His slick hair was mussed and disheveled. Behind him stood Lewis and two of their Red Pole enforcers.

Across the room, Iris chanted to herself. She rolled her sticks across the surface of a small table, oblivious to the violent tableau playing out before her.

'Boss, please,' Lewis murmured, staring at Sean with hate-filled eyes. 'Dealing with *gou shi* like this... I should not allow you to dirty yourself by touching him.'

Fang took a deep breath, then smiled. 'The great man is hard on himself. The small man is hard on others.' He panted, then looked down at his bloody, bruised knuckles. 'Perhaps right now, I am a bit of both, eh?'

Sean's head lolled forward, hiding his battered face. His arms and legs were strapped to the chair. His filthy T-shirt had been torn from his body.

A light breeze rustled the sheets of plastic covering the unfinished structure of The Fang Plaza Building's upper levels. Fang tipped his head back and let the wind cool his face.

Then he lunged forward, powering another blow into Sean's abdomen. The young man coughed and gasped for breath as he struggled against the bonds holding him in the chair.

'Where is it? Where is the key?' Fang shouted.

Sean continued coughing, glaring at Fang with a defiant stare.

'I can admit,' Fang said, panting for breath, 'I was hasty. Impatient.' Reaching forward, he grabbed a handful of Sean's hair and jerked his head up. He stared into the young man's puffy, bruised eyes. They were bloodshot, wild with pain and disorientation. But they focused and held Fang's gaze with steely determination.

'I should have made sure,' Fang hissed. 'I should have checked the server you two accessed before I took care of your *yi kuai gou shi* partner. What was his ridiculous name again? Sunwukong?'

Sean spit blood on the concrete floor. 'His name was The Monkey King. He really screwed things up for you, huh?' The young man chuckled. 'Monk was always good at pissing off assholes like you.'

Fang glared at him then grabbed the back of Sean's chair and dragged the young man across the concrete floor, towards the edge of the building. As they reached the ledge, he tore away a curtain of plastic, revealing the blood-red setting sun. The jagged skyline of Shanghai was silhouetted in the distance.

He set the chair down at the edge of the skeletal structure. Sean looked back, eyes wide with fear. The shadowed buildings and streets loomed below. The wind picked up, rustling through the plastic sheets with a crackling whisper.

With an angry snarl, Fang kicked Sean in the chest. The young man screamed as the chair tipped backwards over the abyss. Fang quickly dropped his leg and braced his foot on the bottom rung of the chair. He leaned forward and smiled. His weight was the only thing keeping Sean from toppling over the edge of the building and falling to his death.

'Your friend, the American who freed you in Beijing...' He said. 'This is how he killed my brothers. Lucky Si and Lucky Liu. They fell to their deaths, squashed like common vermin.'

'Guess they weren't so lucky.' Sean spat out the words, despite the obvious look of fear on his battered face.

'You think destiny will favor you over them?' Fang asked. 'Shall we find out?'

Sean looked back at Fang. He closed his eyes and took a deep breath. Then he opened them. A look of calm descended across his face.

'You'll find out about destiny soon enough. Trust me.'

Fang began to speak but stopped. An electronic chirp echoed through the unfinished room.

Lewis pulled his cell phone from his pocket. He stared at it, a look of uneasy surprise on his face. Then he answered.

'*Wei?*' he said. He was silent for a moment, then held the phone out towards Fang. 'It's for you.'

Fang cursed and pushed down with his foot, steadying the chair. 'Get him back in here,' he snapped as he strode towards Lewis. The two enforcers scrambled over to Sean and pulled the chair back from the ledge.

Fang snatched the phone from Lewis's outstretched hand.

'Who is this?' he asked. 'How did you get this number?'

'You know who I am.' The voice was cool, confident, and cold as ice.

'You,' Fang muttered. 'The American. The one who broke Sean out of prison.'

'My name is Thomas Caine. I'm sure a man like you has friends in the Ministry. Ask them about me. I want you to know who I am. And what I'll do to you if you hurt Sean.'

'A man who makes threats betrays his own weakness,' Fang answered. 'You think you can frighten me with words? You think I would cower at the mere mention of your name? Do you have any idea who you are dealing with?'

'I've crossed paths with plenty of men like you,' Caine said. 'Most of them are in the ground now. And I'm sure I'll bury plenty more. But that's not why I'm calling. I have something you want. I have the key to TANGENT.'

Fang sucked in his breath. 'You are but one man, Mr. Caine. I am *Lu Long*. We are the Triad behind all Triads. As soon as my men find you, what is yours will be mine.'

'Some of your men found me a few hours ago. You can scrape what's left of them off the pavement.'

'And what of the woman, from the prison? I assume she is with you as well?'

'I had to cut her loose. Turns out she was working for the Ministry. Those who betray me... Well, let's just say I've got trust issues. Things didn't end well.'

'So what do you propose, Mr. Caine? A trade? The key for this *ke bei* friend of yours?'

'See? It's not so complicated. We both get what we want, and Sean and I leave China for good.'

Fang looked at his watch. 'Very well. Lewis will text details to this number. We make the exchange tonight. Here in Shanghai, my building, Fang Plaza. Come alone, Mr. Caine. Or both you and Sean will join my brothers.'

'That's not a problem. I prefer to work alone. But know this. If you betray me or hurt Sean... There is nothing on this earth that will stop me from choking the life out of you.'

Fang laughed. 'Again with the impotent threats.'

'That's not a threat,' Caine said, his voice still perfectly calm. 'That's professional courtesy. From one killer to another.'

There was a click and the line went dead.

Fang turned to Iris. 'This man, Caine... Does he have what I seek?'

Iris ran her fingernail across the groves and markings in her I-Ching sticks. She looked up at Fang with her wide, uncanny eyes and smiled. 'Joyous Lake above Clinging Fire. Supreme success shall be furthered by perseverance. Remorse shall disappear.'

Fang handed the phone back to Lewis. 'Summon Tan Sying. Operation Dynasty commences tonight.'

'*Shi de, long dei fu qin*,' Lewis said as he began dialing numbers on the phone. 'It shall be done, Dragon Father.'

'Tonight my destiny shall be fulfilled. We must let nothing stand in our way,' Fang said. He narrowed his eyes as he watched Iris slip her bamboo sticks into her purse. She marched towards the elevators. 'Where are you going?' he asked.

'I just want to freshen up, darling,' she said. Her voice dripped with a sultry tone. 'I must prepare for the evening's entertainment.'

Fang nodded and waved his hand in dismissal. When her back was turned to him and his men, her face went pale. She remembered the sensation of her fingers traveling across the grooves of her sticks. She had neglected to mention the tiny dot she felt between the two hexagrams... The change line. The marking that shifted the pattern to Joyous Lake above Arousing Thunder.

Once again, the pattern of a new, dark destiny had revealed itself.

She stepped into the elevator and forced herself to smile as she turned around to face Fang. She could not tell him now. She was afraid, afraid of what he would do to her when he learned she had hidden this omen from him. The doors slid shut, blocking his handsome face from her view.

As the elevator descended, she turned and looked into the mirrored wall of the car. She reached out and touched her reflection.

'Joyous Lake above Arousing Thunder...' she whispered. 'Starting brings misfortune. Perseverance brings danger. Haste and ruthlessness shall bring disaster.'

40

It was dark when Caine's taxi pulled up outside Fang Plaza. The Pudong skyline sparkled in the distance, bathing the city in a dim, electric glow. Coronas of light reflected in the mirrored sides of the Shanghai World Financial Center. To the east, pinpoints of glowing purple danced up and down the Pearl Tower, circling the massive spheres like a curtain of amethyst jewels.

Inside the lobby, five men stood waiting. Even from across the street, Caine could detect the bulge of weapons beneath their rumpled jackets.

Caine looked up at the building. The lower half of the skyscraper was a stark, angular design. Its sleek, modern architecture was similar to the other structures in the area. Long, crimson banners flowed down its sweeping polished metal sides. Yellow Chinese characters on the banners proclaimed the opening date for the plaza.

The upper stories of the tall building were incomplete. Steel beams and glass panels stretched up into the dark night sky, like a skeletal claw grasping at the heavens.

Caine reached into his jacket and slipped out a small silver case. He held it up in his hand and marched across the street towards the building. The men in the lobby leapt to attention, and their hands darted inside their jackets. Caine grinned as they drew a variety of pistols and weapons.

He stopped a few feet in front of the building. The men opened the door and fanned out around him. One of the men patted him down for weapons. A short but muscular man with buzzed salt and pepper hair stood silent, watching. The man frisking him turned to the shorter man and barked a few words.

The shorter man stared at Caine. He nodded towards the slim silver case Caine held in his hand.

'Is that the key?' he asked in English.

'It is. I'll give it to Mr. Fang when he gives me what I want.'

The man leveled his pistol at Caine and held out his free hand. 'My name is Lewis. I work for Mr. Fang. Give it to me, now.'

Caine shook his head. 'Not until I see Sean. And Lewis, you should know this case contains a processor and a file-shredding program. All I need to do is press the button on the side, and the key gets deleted. So if you're going to pull that trigger, you better be sure you can drop me with one shot.'

Lewis stared at him for a second, then lowered his gun. He gestured to the other men. '*Dai shang tai*. Bring him.'

Caine felt the barrel of a gun press into his back. A strong hand clamped down on his shoulder. 'Move,' a deep voice commanded. 'Now.'

They led him into the building's lobby. The doors slid open with a chime. Caine, Lewis, and one other man stepped in. 'The rest of you take the next car,' Lewis said as the doors closed. Caine clenched the silver case in his hand as the glass elevator ascended.

His eyes darted to a towering yellow construction crane perched next to the building. Its mechanical claw hung motionless in the air, a short distance from the unfinished structure. The claw grasped a massive section of metal industrial piping in a vise-like grip.

The claw hung from a heavy-duty steel cable. Caine's eyes followed the cable up. It attached to the long jib arm of the crane, parked parallel to the upper floors of the building. A narrow walkway ran down the two-hundred-foot length of the jib arm. A small control booth sat above the slewing motors that controlled the crane.

In the harsh glow of the halogen lights, the motionless crane seemed like a stark, lonely sentinel, standing watch over the unfinished building.

The elevator stopped and the doors slid open. Lewis led Caine into a partially finished lobby, one of the upper levels still under construction. Plastic tarps whipped and rustled in the cool night wind. He could see the night sky through the beams and girders above.

A pair of huge gold doors were set into a finished section of wall. Lewis pushed him forward. The other man stepped in front of him and pulled open the doors. The man grunted with exertion as the massive slabs creaked open.

Caine stepped through the doors and found himself in a large, oval-shaped chamber. A line of green columns ran along either side of the room. Between the columns, terracotta statues of armored Chinese warriors stood at attention. Glass cases displayed jewels, artifacts, and scrolls from the Chinese Dynastic periods. At the far end of the room, in front of a vast panel of windows, a shimmering golden throne sat upon a raised platform. A handsome man in a white suit lounged on the throne, an embroidered robe of crimson silk draped across his shoulders. His hard, dark eyes followed Caine as he stepped into the room.

David Fang.

Lewis shoved Caine forward again. 'Move!' he snapped. 'Do not keep him waiting!'

Caine walked towards the throne. Halogen lights illuminated the statues along his path. The eerie glow gave their features a grim, demonic cast. More lights surrounded the raised throne. Caine counted ten men standing around the base of the platform, armed with a variety of pistols, submachine guns, and swords. A large object, hidden under a black tarp, stood to the right of the platform.

On the left side of the platform, a young man with spiked hair sat at a circular desk, surrounded by computer equipment, monitors, and cables. It looked similar to Shirley and Edgar's computer setup.

A figure emerged from behind one of the columns at the far end of the room. To Caine's surprise, a tall, attractive woman sauntered towards him. She wore a long red silk gown, with ruffled shoulders and a plunging V-neck. Ruby earrings dangled from her ears, and a collection of orchids were pinned in her hair. Feathers of black and red mascara highlighted her intense, wide-eyed stare.

She met him in the center of the room and stopped. The guards fanned out around them.

'Welcome,' she said in a deep, husky voice. 'My name is Iris. Mr. Fang and I are honored by your presence on this auspicious evening.'

Caine smiled and looked around the ornate hall. 'All this just for me? You really shouldn't have.'

Fang shrugged off his robe and descended the stairs of the throne platform. The pale ivory fabric of his suit reflected the glow of the halogen bulbs. He was almost blinding to look at.

He clapped his hands together and chuckled as he approached Caine and Iris. 'Don't be modest, Mr. Caine,' Fang replied. 'And please, forgive my theatrics. I couldn't resist.' He gestured with his hands and looked up at the jade-inlaid ceiling of the vast chamber. 'This room is my favorite in Fang Plaza. I made sure it was finished first. It's my one concession to the past, in a building dedicated to the future. Dedicated to *my* future, I should say. My destiny.'

'That's a lot of significance to put on a bunch of steel and concrete,' Caine said. 'After all, buildings, and destinies, fall every day.'

Fang's dark stare met Caine's emerald gaze. His lips curled into a thin smile. 'I'll give you the benefit of the doubt, Mr. Caine, and assume that is not a threat. And as you said, I do have friends in the Ministry. I made some inquiries. You are quite an interesting man.'

Caine shrugged. 'Oh, I'm nothing special.'

Iris smiled at him. There was something about her eyes, something that made him uncomfortable in her presence.

'The superior man, if he must stand alone, remains unconcerned,' she intoned. 'If he must renounce the world, he is undaunted. That is the wisdom of the I-Ching.'

'I think I read that in a fortune cookie once,' Caine said.

Fang laughed. 'Please, let us drop this silly posturing. We are both extraordinary men. We both have a role to play in tonight's events. But while I am here to fulfill a great destiny, I'm curious... What caused you to cross my path?'

Caine held up the slim silver case. He placed his finger above the button on the side. 'I'm just keeping a promise to an old friend.'

'You have come all this way, risked your life, killed my men... all to keep a promise?'

Caine smiled. 'It's that simple. But if you'd like to chitchat, we can reminisce about our past, Mr. Fang. Or should I say, Dan-zu Huang?'

Caine saw Fang stiffen at the mention of his other name, and the woman's eyes opened wide. Two of Fang's men stepped forward, raising their guns towards Caine. Fang shook his head and waved them off, then flashed Caine a wide smile.

'You've done your homework. I haven't gone by that name in a long time.'

'I can imagine,' Caine said. 'Might upset those friends of yours at the Ministry.'

Fang shook his head. 'Since you seem so interested, allow me to fill in the gaps in your knowledge. You see, I too am here to fulfill a promise. One I made long ago.'

He approached one of the display cases. 'Come, come, you'll enjoy this.' Iris followed behind him, her red gown spilling across the floor like a puddle of blood.

Caine looked at the guards to his left and right, then stepped forward, following Fang and the woman. They stopped next to a glass display case. Inside stood a detailed model of the Chinese countryside. A wide blue river cut through the model, held back by a towering dam. A tiny hydroelectric power plant overlooked the reservoir.

'As you say, I was born with the name Dan-zu. I was from a tiny *pi shi* village. The name does not matter. It no longer exists. It lies buried under hundreds of feet of water... The Baishan Reservoir, as this model here shows. There was a dam constructed across the river, not too far from my home. China needed more power. Needed to modernize, to join the technological world, as quickly as possible.'

'The price of progress,' Caine said.

Fang glanced over at him. 'Progress, Mr. Caine, is relentless. It is a boon for some, a curse for others. But either way, no one can stand against it. You can't fight destiny. I learned that the hard way.' He sighed. 'And so did my father. Or rather, he failed to heed that lesson. When construction on the dam began, our village was scheduled for relocation. Families were ordered to leave their homes, bringing only what they could carry.'

'Forced relocation,' Caine said. 'Like the Three Gorges Dam Project?'

Fang nodded. 'Nothing on that scale, I assure you. But yes, forced relocation was once common. These days the PRC government is a bit more restrained. More eyes are upon them. Negative news coverage can upset markets, derail their precious trade agreements. Still, they usually find a way to get what they want.

'But back then, the party's word was law. Our house was just a shack. There was no toilet or shower. Just a hose and a concrete stall in the back. But my father had built it with his own two hands. He had lived in the village his whole life, it was all he knew. And his mother, my grandmother, was too elderly and sick to travel. He refused to leave. He and some of the other villagers organized a protest, to fight the relocation.'

'He sounds like a brave man.'

Fang glared at him and shook his head. '*Fei hua!* He was a fool. On the final day of relocation, the National Police swept through the town. Anyone who remained was beaten. They burned houses, forced people out at gunpoint. I was six years old, and I remember standing in the muddy street. My mother covered my ears with her hands. Her skin was warm, and I thought she did it because it was cold outside. Later I realized it was because she didn't want me to hear. There were gunshots inside the house. Two of them. One for my father, and one for my grandmother. I heard them, despite my mother's efforts.'

Caine was silent. Fang looked down at the model. He ran a

hand across the glass of the display case, as if trying to touch the plastic miniatures inside.

'As we were led away from the village, I looked back. I saw the police drag the bodies from our house. My grandmother... I watched as they burned her. Then they hung my father from the roof of his pathetic shack. A warning to other protestors. For years, whenever I saw pictures of the Baishan Reservoir in books, I imagined his corpse, floating in the water. Just beneath the surface, just out of sight. Still tied to that old, rotting shack.'

Caine tapped the silver case against the glass display case. 'I didn't come here for a history lesson.'

Fang tore his attention away from the model. 'Of course. Let us look to the future, then.'

Caine followed Fang and Iris as they walked towards the young man sitting at the computer screens. The entourage of guards stayed nearby but maintained a respectful distance from Fang.

Caine's eyes darted across the screens. He saw a series of maps, all regions of China. Blinking red dots marked four towns, one on each map. He recognized one of the dots as Huagu, the home of Alton Lung and his family. Caine remembered the sight of the little girl, Baozhai, coughing blood at the table... Fang's chemical plant, looming over the town, the clouds of poisonous smoke in the air.

'This is Tan Sying,' Fang said. The young man looked up at Caine with a sullen stare, his eyes peering out beneath a fringe of black hair. 'In the realm of computers and the internet, he is a true warrior. Not an amateur like Sean's friend, the foolish "Monkey King." Tan is a soldier, a member of PLA Unit 61398. Have you heard of them?'

Caine nodded. 'The Advanced Persistent Threat Unit. The Chinese government admitted their existence in 2015. US Intelligence has been tracking their activities since at least 2002. Cyber-warfare group. Hackers. They steal trade secrets from defense contractors around the world.'

Tan smiled. 'You cannot steal what seeks to be free,' he said in a sing-song voice.

Caine eyed the screens. He noticed that the towns marked by the blinking dots were all located along rivers or waterways.

'I think Boeing and Lockheed might disagree,' he said, keeping his eyes on the maps.

Fang laughed. 'It seems Tan here suffered quite a losing streak at the casinos in Macau.' Fang sucked in his breath. 'A silly addiction for such an intelligent young man.'

'Triad-owned casinos, I assume?' Caine asked.

Fang nodded. 'Of course. Now, Tan works for me, to pay off his debt. And I assure you, my sights are set on bigger game than corporate trade secrets.'

'I don't care if you're after all the gold in Fort Knox,' Caine growled. 'We had a deal. I came here for Sean.'

Fang clapped his hands, and two of his men grasped the bulky object hidden beneath the tarp. They rolled it over towards Fang, stopping a few feet away.

'Patience seems to be a virtue you lack, Mr. Caine,' Fang snapped. 'Please, let me keep you no longer.'

One of the men grabbed the tarp and pulled it away, revealing the object underneath.

It was a cylinder mounted to a rolling frame. About seven feet tall, a curved glass window covered the top of the metal tube. Sean pounded on the glass, trapped inside. The heavy-duty construction of the device muffled his screams. An array of tubes and compressors were mounted beneath the strange cylinder.

Fang pulled a small remote from his pocket. 'Do you like my new toy? This is a Hyperbaric Oxygen Treatment Device. I don't just work in chemicals and poisons, you know. I've also invested in cutting-edge medical technology. Did you know that changing the concentration of oxygen in the air we breathe can have a dramatic effect on the body's ability to heal itself?'

Fang pressed a button on the remote. The machine made a hissing sound. Sean began to gasp for breath. His fists pummeled the glass, but his blows became slow, weak. His eyes began to roll back into his head.

'Of course, if the concentration of oxygen becomes too low, it can lead to severe consequences,' Fang said. 'Increased heart rate, loss of motor skills. Unconsciousness, followed by—'

'Let him out,' Caine snarled. 'Now!'

Fang turned and glared at Caine, an arrogant sneer marring his handsome features. 'I'll consider it,' he said. 'After you give me the key to TANGENT.'

41

The city lights surrounded Jia like glittering jewels cascading across the dark curtain of night. Twinkling neon from nearby buildings bathed her face in a crimson glow. She paid no attention to the lights, or the cool breeze blowing through her hair. Instead, she focused her gaze on a small circle of glass. A set of crosshairs hung over the blurry image on the other side.

She shifted her body in the tower crane's cab. Then she adjusted the focus ring of the scope mounted above the AS VAL silenced assault rifle. The image became sharp and clear.

David Fang was in her sights.

She rested a finger just behind the laser sight mounted beneath the integrated silencer of the Russian-made rifle. Rather than the green daytime unit, this weapon was equipped with a crimson beam. Once she activated it, she knew her position would be compromised. For now, she kept the beam switched off. She would wait until the perfect moment. Then she would strike.

The crane's jib arm was only a few stories higher than Fang's mock throne room. It provided a perfect vantage point. Through her scope, she watched as Fang lifted himself from his golden throne. He descended to greet Caine, leading him through his collection of artifacts like a smug, spoiled child.

She pictured Lian, somewhere dark, unfamiliar. Her daughter, scared, alone... Her body tensed, and her finger began to tighten around the rifle's trigger.

She took a deep breath and forced herself to relax. *No,* she thought. *Wait till Caine has Sean. He gets Sean, you leave China, you go to Lian.* That was her mission now.

She watched through the tiny scope as Fang and Caine talked. A woman joined them. Tall, dark-skinned, attractive. The Ministry kept detailed files on the various Triad factions. Jia recognized her as Iris Yip, Fang's girlfriend and advisor. According to the reports, Fang had murdered Iris's husband, Sam Yip, in the midst of a turf war during Fang's rise to power as a *Lu Long* Red Pole. Iris seemed to have taken up with Fang in the bloody aftermath of that power struggle. The two had been lovers ever since.

Strange woman, Jia thought. *Then again...* She looked back at the things she had done, both in the line of duty and more recently, while compromised by Lapinski. She knew she was in no position to judge.

She shifted the rifle slightly. The guards inside wheeled a large platform towards Fang and Caine. The men yanked back the tarp, revealing a metal cylinder and a mass of medical equipment, hoses, and air tanks.

Through the tiny circle of magnification she could see Caine. His jaw clenched, and his eyes glowered with rage. Whatever was in the strange-looking device, it had clearly had an effect on him.

She adjusted the scope again and zoomed in on the glass window mounted to the front of the metal tube. The image came into focus. She could see Sean's face, gasping for breath.

Gai si! Bloody hell... This was not part of the plan.

She felt a tremor vibrate through the towering metal structure of the crane. Looking out the window, she saw flashing red and blue lights, gathering at the base of the narrow metal structure. A pair of spotlights beamed up at the crane.

The Ministry. Yong Jin had found her.

The vibrations intensified. A mechanical hum emitted from the long, narrow tower behind the booth. It was the elevator. Men were ascending towards her position. The humming grew louder. The elevator was nearing the top of the tower.

There was no time for a fight. She had to move her position, she had to help Caine before these men reached her.

She had to get to Lian.

Her eyes hardened. She pressed a large red button on the control panel of the cab. It lit up, and a buzzing siren echoed through the air. Orange warning lights flooded the booth with a warm glow as they spun to life.

She threw a series of levers on the panel. An alarm bell rang out, cutting through the droning buzz of the siren. The crane's slewing unit groaned to life. She felt the floor of the cab shudder as it began to move.

Jia grabbed her rifle and darted out of the tiny control room. Her feet clanged across the metal catwalk as she charged towards the far end of the crane.

As she ran, the long jib arm lurched through the air, swinging closer and closer towards the delicate glass and metal skeleton of the Fang Plaza building.

* * *

Caine looked Fang in the eye. Behind them, Sean pounded on the glass of his cylindrical prison. As each second ticked by, more oxygen was sucked from the tube.

Caine held the case out to Fang. 'Fine,' he said. 'Take it.'

The handsome man stared at the slim silver box for a second, but he did not reach for it. Iris slinked over to Caine and wrapped her long, delicate fingers around the case. She slid it from his grip.

'*Xie xie*,' she said, giving him a slight bow. Fang pressed a button on the tiny remote and the compressors stopped. There was a hiss as oxygen began to flow back into the hyperbaric tube. Sean gasped air into his lungs.

'Pray this works, Mr. Caine. If it does not, I will make you watch as your friend dies, gasping for breath. Like a fish out of water.'

'I held up my end of the bargain,' Caine snarled. 'Now let Sean go.'

Iris walked over to the bank of computers and handed the case to Tan. Fang gave Caine a lingering stare, then turned to Tan. 'You have what you need? Be certain. We can afford no more mistakes.'

Tan opened the case and disconnected the tiny USB stick from the microprocessor inside. He inserted it into one of the computers. Caine watched as the familiar stream of code flashed across the monitors.

Tan nodded. 'Looks good. Booting up TANGENT now.'

He connected a rugged blue hard drive to a cable and checked a series of settings on another monitor.

'What is this all about, Fang?' Caine asked. 'What's your connection to Sun Wai Tong?'

Fang kept his eyes on the monitors. 'Who?' He turned and flashed Caine an innocent grin. 'Oh, you mean that pitiful hacker in NSA custody? I've never even met the man.'

Tan continued tapping on his keyboard. '*Bu yao rang wo fa xiao*,' he barked. 'Don't make me laugh. Sun Wai is an amateur.

His skills are nothing compared to mine. Why the Ministry would work with a *bai chi* like that, I have no idea.'

Caine thought for a moment. The pieces of the puzzle swirled in his mind. Lapinski, Sean, Fang... and now this man, Tan. A disgruntled cyber-warrior, in deep to Fang's *Lu Long* Triad. They all orbited around this mysterious program, an enigma that drew them together... TANGENT.

Then it clicked. The missing piece, the corrupted bit of data. An assumption that had been wrong from the start.

'Sun Wai didn't hack the NSA server, did he?' Caine said. 'Tan did. And to cover his tracks, he ran TANGENT from inside the system. He used it to implicate Sun Wai Tong. Sun was a known state-sponsored hacker. The FBI already had his profile in their cybercrime database.'

Fang clapped. 'Very good, Mr. Caine. You're several steps ahead of your own government's intelligence agencies.'

'This whole time, they've been interrogating the wrong man,' Caine continued. 'They're looking for a connection that doesn't exist.'

Fang gestured to the array of computer equipment. 'Tan discovered the existence of TANGENT during one of Unit 61398's probes into NSA servers. He brought it to me, along with other information he thought I might find... valuable.'

Caine turned away from Fang and wandered over to another display case. The glass box was filled with a circular array of sharp daggers arranged on a cushion of red silk. 'Other information? You mean the file that shows you were a CIA plant at Tiananmen?'

Fang stood on the other side of the case. He ignored Caine's question and looked down at the slim, ancient weapons. 'These are Fei Dao... flying knives.' He pointed to a weapon with an elegant, curved blade, and a thick, polished wood handle. 'This one was favored by Chinese soldiers during the Ming and Qing Dynasties. It was known as the willow-leaf knife due to the shape of its blade.'

He looked up at Caine. 'China took my father from me and destroyed my home. They struck the first blow against me and my family. But it was the United States CIA that twisted the knife in my back.'

'Yeah, welcome to the party,' Caine replied, glancing at the chipped metal blades.

Fang waved a dismissive hand towards Caine. 'Yes, I know you were betrayed as well. You know what they are capable of. After the tragedy, my mother and I moved to Beijing. She got a job at a fabric mill, tried to put the past behind us. But I was bitter. Angry. I was perfect fodder for the Beijing Spring movement. Revolution was in the air. To be honest, I cared little about democracy or reform. All I wanted to do was hurt those in power and strike back at the men who had hurt my family.'

'Didn't work out that way, did it?' Caine asked.

'Of course not. I spouted their propaganda. I marched with my allies across campus and studied the pamphlets passed out by the CIA-backed Student Organization. And on 3 June, I threw firebombs at Type 59 Battle Tanks when the CCP declared martial law in the city. I helped set fire to buses parked across the bridge at Muzidi, to slow the army's march towards the square. And I fled as the soldiers opened fire. They inflicted heavy casualties, and the civilians on-site became enraged. They fought back with rocks, sticks, anything they could get their hands on. The massacre had begun.'

Caine looked over Fang's shoulder. Outside the bank of windows at the end of the room, he saw something moving. A black shape, barely visible in the darkness, swung towards the building. Fang and his men didn't see it. They were facing Caine, looking away from the windows.

He gave the case of knives a nonchalant glance, then turned his attention back to Fang. 'You're talking about Operation Canary, right?'

'Yes. Ridiculous name. I don't know if the goal was to promote democracy or force the PRC into an embarrassing act of bloodshed. But either way, the fuse was lit. I fled the scene and met my mother at the rendezvous point my CIA contact had provided. The final phase of the operation involved smuggling dissidents like myself out of the country, through Hong Kong.'

Iris walked over to them and spread her bamboo sticks across the surface of the glass case. She began to murmur and chant.

'So what happened?' Caine said. He risked a quick glance at the window. Fang's attention seemed focused on Iris's long, jade-tipped fingers. She raked her nails across the rows of I-Ching sticks.

'I have no idea,' Fang said, his voice low and gravelly. 'We stood waiting outside an abandoned cafe. It was a meeting place other students and I had used to distribute propaganda pamphlets. We huddled in the darkness for hours, like jilted brides at a rotting altar. No one came for us. History says the CIA smuggled over 400 dissidents out of Beijing that night. But they left me and my family there alone, helpless. They left us there to die.'

'Sounds like you're taking things a little personally,' Caine said. *Got to keep him talking,* he thought.

'How would you suggest I take it?' Fang snapped. 'My mother and I fled to the countryside, to another *ke lian* town. A pathetic hole, surrounded by factories and waste dumps. The water was poison, the earth was toxic ash. But my mother did her best to start over yet again. She married one of the disgusting villagers. I took his last name, and she christened me David. We hid from the shame of my failed little rebellion. And she gave him two sons. But they were born... *wai ren*. Different.'

'The twins. The albinos,' Caine said.

'Lucky Si and Lucky Liu. My brothers,' Fang replied. 'I joined one of the gangs in the village. Out there, the Triads were the only law we had. They protected their own. So I became one of them.

'One night, her new husband got drunk. Angry. He kicked open the door, stormed into our little shack. He looked down at my brothers, cowering in the corner. Their appearance shamed him. He blamed my mother, said she had cursed him with demon children. Then he grabbed a knife off the kitchen table. He did not know I was in the house. Or that an elder Triad brother had given me my first gun, to protect myself.'

'You killed him,' Caine said. His voice was flat, monotone, as if he were describing a simple errand rather than an act of bloodshed.

Fang nodded. 'Yes. I put one bullet in his head. He fell to the floor, and I stood over him. I looked into his eyes, and I emptied the gun into his heart. When it was finished, my hands were covered with blood. They were dripping red. And it was then I made my promise.'

'Promise to who?'

'To my mother. To my brothers. To myself. All that had happened to us... misfortune, betrayal, death... it was not for nothing. Each horrific event was a milestone on my path to destiny. I would rise in the Triads. I would become strong. And I would use my strength to protect my family. I would become leader of the most powerful Triad in China. Dragon Father of the *Lu Long*. All who have stood in my way have fallen before me, Mr. Caine.'

Iris looked up at Caine. Her dark eyes scrutinized his features. Her mouth hung half-open, and formless whispers drifted out. Then she blinked.

'What is your role here tonight, Mr. Caine?' she said, her voice slow and languorous. 'What is your destiny?'

Caine looked down at her fingers as they danced over the sticks.

'I didn't come here to play pick-up sticks,' he said.

Fang's voice was hard as iron. 'The I-Ching revealed my destiny to me, Mr. Caine. It showed me the path. I have devoted my life to following its guidance. It led me to Iris, then it showed me TANGENT. Now it will show you your path.'

'Ask a question, Mr. Caine,' Iris said. Her strange, piercing eyes seeming to gaze right through him, as if he were a ghost. 'For one who knows his true desire, knowledge shall be granted.'

Caine brushed his hand over the sticks. 'There's only one thing I want to know,' he said, turning to look at Fang. 'Why do you need TANGENT to take over your little Mickey Mouse club? Those dots on the map... they're locations of your factories, right?'

'Not quite,' Fang answered. He turned to the bank of screens. 'They are the locations of dams, built next to my factories. Three Gorges, Huangdeng, your friend's town, Huagu, and up there in the top... the Baishan Reservoir. My father's watery grave. Each dam holds back an unthinkable volume of liquid. Combined, they control billions of cubic feet of water.'

'And your factories are downstream from each... Insurance?' Caine asked.

Fang nodded. 'To rise to the rank of Dragon Father, I must win the council vote. I have eliminated my main rivals, and I am confident the other families will fall in line. But I must also pay a tithe to the departing Dragon Father. The amount is... considerable.'

'I wouldn't think that would be a problem for a big shot like you.'

'After spending years in that piece of shit town, my mother developed liver and stomach cancer. I have used my fortune to prolong her life, but it has been a great burden. China's economy has slipped. And now, I am forced to adapt my factories to comply with the new GEA guidelines. Part of your president's trade deal with my country. I am wealthy, yes, but liquidity has been a problem. Tonight, that changes. Tonight, I lay the final stones in the road that leads to my destiny.'

'TANGENT is ready,' Tan called out. New streams of code filled the screen as Tan typed on his keyboard.

'And this is your big plan?' Caine asked. 'You're going to hack into a dam, flood one of your factories? Collect some insurance money?' He shook his head. 'Sounds kind of small-time to me.'

Fang stepped away from the glass case, moving closer to the bank of computer screens. He stared at them with a feverish intensity. 'No, Mr. Caine. I am going to hack all four dams. And obliterate my four highest-performing factories. Each one generates millions in annual profit. And each one is insured for billions of dollars.'

'Each one of those dams has the potential to kill thousands of people,' Caine growled. 'Innocent men, women, and children. People who suffered just like you.'

Cords of muscle burst from Fang's neck as his mouth curled into a snarl. 'Like me? They are nothing like me! They are weak, pathetic. They lack the will to seize their destiny. But I will rise above them. I will achieve greatness. And in doing so, I will strike back at those who sought to destroy me and my family. China took my father, but it was your country, Mr. Caine, that abandoned us. Your country that forced us to flee to that poisonous hellhole. Your country that has stolen my mother's life, one piece at a time. Tonight, both China and America shall learn the price of betraying me.'

He spun around and marched over to Tan. 'Load the NSA database Tailored Access Operations profiles.'

Tan looked up at the screen. 'Initiating hack. Loading database... now!' Profiles of American NSA officers began to fill one of the computer screens.

Fang looked back over his shoulder. 'Tomorrow, the Ministry of State Security will have to confront a cyber-attack that has killed tens of thousands of Chinese citizens. Their investigation will implicate the American NSA. Trade talks with the United States will cease. The president's Global Environmental Accord will be torn to shreds. Freed from those restrictions, the productivity of my remaining factories will double, making up for the loss of these four. And my mother will live to see me become the Dragon Father of the *Lu Long*. I will have kept my promise, Mr. Caine.'

Iris set her hand on top of Caine's. He looked at her in surprise, but allowed her to move his hand, pushing three of the sticks aside. She lifted his hand and looked down at the hexagram they formed.

Again the dreaded pattern stared back at her.

'Joyous Lake above Arousing Thunder...'

She looked up and gazed upon Caine's face with a strange combination of hunger and fear.

Her voice lowered to a whisper. 'It is *you*! You have changed the pattern of fate! The shadow of death follows you into this house!'

Caine ignored her rambling. Through the panoramic windows behind Fang's throne, he saw the object outside move closer. As it grew larger, he could just make out a black, gaping circle. He knew what it must be.

The massive industrial pipe, hanging from the claw... The crane's jib arm was rotating through the air, and the pipe was moving with it. Jia had been positioned in the crane... Something must have gone wrong. The crane was spinning towards the unfinished structure of the upper floors. And the swinging pipe was about to collide with Fang Plaza!

42

Tan's brow furrowed in concern as he hunched over his keyboard. One of his screens was blinking red. A beeping alert sounded from the speakers on the cluttered desk. 'Something is wrong,' he said. 'The TANGENT database, it's being accessed from outside the building.'

Fang shot Tan an angry glare. 'Accessed by who?'

'Give me a minute!' The young man's fingers danced across the keys.

Fang's voice dropped to a low hiss. 'That database contains a record of every TANGENT hack, including this one. If that information goes public, we will be identified. All of this will have been for nothing!'

'It's the key,' Tan exclaimed. He yanked the USB stick from the computer, but the screens still flashed red. 'It's too late, the code is already uploaded. It's auto-executing malware... The database is being hacked!'

Fang turned and glared at Caine, then looked back at the screens. He grabbed Tan's shoulder in a talon-like grip. 'As you are so fond of informing me, you are the most skilled member of your unit. Fix this! Now!'

Tan blinked, then glared at the empty silver case sitting next to him on the desk. It was the case Caine had used to deliver the TANGENT key.

He snatched the slim silver object off the desk and pried it open with shaking hands. The case clicked open, and Tan clawed at the tiny circuit board inside.

'This,' he gasped. 'This is not a microprocessor. It's a decoy!' He tore the tiny circuit board free. The blinking screen of a cell phone was hidden underneath. He grabbed the phone and held it up for Fang to see. The screen of the phone indicated a file transfer had taken place. 'This phone acted as an internet connection. When the key was used, it triggered a remote download of the malware program into TANGENT.'

The screens of streaming code suddenly blinked pure white. An image faded into view, replacing the white glow. It was a cartoon monkey, rolling back and forth across the screen. '*Ooh ooh ooh... eee eee eee...*'

Fang grabbed the phone from Tan's hand and dashed it to the floor, stamping on the remains. Tan's fingers raced across the keyboard. 'That won't help,' he said in a calm voice. 'The malware has taken over my system; it's using our internet now. But if I can isolate it, I can remove it before it finishes downloading the file.'

On the screens, the image of the rolling monkey disappeared. White text on a black background faded up in its place.

UPLOAD PAUSED AT 95 PERCENT. RESUME Y/N?

The white characters blinked on and off as Tan leaned back in his chair. 'Got you, Monkey King, or whoever you are.'

Caine gritted his teeth. *Have to stop him... Shirley's program needs more time...*

Outside, the huge pipe swung closer to the panel of windows.

'Fang,' Caine shouted. 'You want to know my role in your destiny? I'll tell you why I'm here.'

Iris took a step back from the case. Her mouth hung open, and she took a deep breath.

'It doesn't matter,' Fang snapped. 'You will not stop me. My victory is inevitable.'

Caine's arm dropped to his side. A slim wooden object slid from his sleeve into his cupped hand. One of Iris's bamboo sticks... He had palmed it from the table earlier.

Fang gestured to the guards flanking Caine. 'Take him to the roof. Throw him off. Let him join my bothers in the underworld. But first...'

Fang pulled the tiny remote from his pocket, pointed it at the hyperbaric tube, and pressed a button. The compressors hissed to life, pumping oxygen out of the tube.

'Enjoy watching your friend take his last breath,' Fang taunted.

Caine felt strong hands grab his shoulder.

Just a few more seconds, he thought.

'Like I said, Fang,' Caine shouted. 'Buildings and destinies fall every day. I should know.'

Fang lifted his eyebrows in mock surprise. 'Oh? And why is that?'

Caine focused his intense, emerald-green stare on Fang. 'Because I'm the one who tears them down.'

The wall of glass behind Fang exploded, sending a rain of sparkling shrapnel flying into the room. The enormous length of pipe swung into the chamber like a battering ram. Fang's guards scattered as the pipe smashed through rows of statues and display cases. Fang spun around and threw himself out of the makeshift wrecking ball's path.

The taut cable that anchored the pipe to the crane sliced through the ceiling as if it was tissue paper. Caine heard the scream of metal tearing through metal as the jib arm slammed into the girders above them.

The two men holding Caine craned their necks, following the motion of the pipe as it tore through the room. They appeared stunned by the sudden destruction surrounding them. Tan paused his typing and stared in shock as the metal object careened past him.

Now! Caine thought.

With a loud crack, Caine snapped the slim bamboo stick in half. Exploding into motion, he jabbed a sharp fragment into the neck of the guard standing next to him.

Iris screamed as a plume of crimson blood jetted from the wound, striking her in the face.

The guard to his left pivoted towards him. Caine drove the second shard of wood into the man's inner thigh. The guard dropped his weapon and clutched the wound, desperate to stop the hemorrhage of blood.

Caine grabbed the screaming man to his right by the back of his head. He drove a knee up into his abdomen, then moved behind him as the guard bent over in pain. Using all his strength, Caine slammed the man's head down, smashing it into the display case.

The impact of the man's skull scattered Iris's sticks. The top of the glass case splintered into a spiderweb of cracks. Blood gushed from the guard's crushed nose.

Shoving the stunned guard aside, Caine punched the weakened case. His fist smashed through the glass with ease. His fingers wrapped around the hilt of the willow-leaf knife. With a single fluid motion, he wound his arm back and threw the knife. It made a whistling sound as it cut through the air. The blade seemed to spin in slow motion, slicing past Fang, missing the man by inches.

But Fang was not Caine's target...

With a loud thud, the blade buried itself in Tan's back. The hacker's eyes opened wide, and his fingers stopped dancing across the keys. With a wet gurgle, he slumped forward in his chair.

Caine ducked under the case and rolled forward as the stunned guards behind him opened fire.

The glass case exploded into glittering shards. The guards sprayed bullets as they struggled to dodge the towering metal pipe swinging through the room.

Iris darted away from the case, glancing over her shoulder as she ran. Her gaze caught Fang's eye as he picked himself up off the floor.

'Iris!' he shouted. He reached a hand towards her. Her face hardened and she turned away. She sprinted towards the golden doors at the rear of the room.

'Iris, look out!' Fang called behind her.

She felt a breeze lift her hair. She spun around, her crimson gown billowing behind her like liquid flames.

The pipe swooped towards her as the cable cut a trail through the ceiling overhead. She could not outrun it.

She closed her eyes.

The heavy pipe slammed into her. The impact tossed her into the air like a rag doll. Her body flew across the room and crashed through a row of display cases. She rolled to a stop, her body sprawled across the floor. Glass shards sparkled in her hair like diamonds, and a thin trickle of blood dripped from her mouth. A crimson streak followed her path across the marble tiles, matching the color of her long, flowing dress.

'Fate calls...' she whispered. Her pale face settled to the floor, motionless.

Fang stood on shaky legs. His face was a distorted mask of hate and rage. The shriek of scraping metal vibrated through the building. He looked up as the ceiling overhead collapsed. The metal girders above him tore loose and came crashing to the floor. The anger in Fang's eyes was replaced by shock and fear. He struggled to dodge out of the way as a huge segment of torn metal plummeted straight towards him.

The massive girder fell amidst a shower of concrete chunks. Caine lost sight of Fang in the haze of dust. A rumbling filled the room, and cracks ran through the intricate marble designs laid into the floor. With a final, thunderous crack, a giant hole opened up in the center of the chamber. More debris plummeted into the dark, skeletal depths of the unfinished building.

Fang was gone, lost in the cascade of wreckage.

Caine sprinted towards the computer console. Across the room, two guards broke away from the disorganized pack and raced after him.

Caine reached the console and shoved Tan's body out of the way. The text continued blinking on the screen.

UPLOAD PAUSED AT 95 PERCENT. RESUME Y/N?

Caine jabbed his finger down on the Y key and hit enter. The message blinked again then changed.

UPLOAD COMPLETE. ERASING TANGENT HARD DRIVE. BETTY BINARY WAS HERE.

The image of the rolling monkey returned to the screen. This time it was joined by a second cartoon monkey wearing chunky pink glasses.

'Next time, skip the fancy graphics, Betty,' Caine muttered to himself.

The screen exploded in a shower of sparks and glass shards. Caine dropped to the floor and rolled. The two guards skidded to a stop as they sprayed the computers with automatic weapon fire.

Caine rolled up against the throne's platform. He huddled behind the steps as another barrage of gunfire flew towards him. Streaks of hot air whizzed past his forehead.

Behind the guards, the metal pipe spun around and swung back. One of the guards heard the creak of the metal cable and looked over his shoulder. He threw himself to the floor. His partner continued firing at Caine, oblivious to the danger swooping towards him.

The pipe swung over the prone guard and struck the other man square in the back. He screamed as the impact launched him into the air. His cries echoed through the building as his body plunged into the gaping hole in the floor.

More debris fell, striking the edge of the crater. Another section of marble flooring crumbled and fell. The slab of concrete formed a sloping ramp leading to the dark construction site below. The tube that held Sean rolled towards the opening, gaining speed as it struck the ramp.

Caine leapt from his cover and charged towards the falling cylinder.

A hail of bullets tore across the floor near his feet. The second guard, the one who had ducked under the swinging pipe, picked himself up from the ground. Caine tried to pivot in another direction, but he knew he was too late. The Triad had him in his sights.

A bright red dot appeared on the man's forehead. A muffled crack rang out, and a plume of blood exploded from the man's skull. He crumpled to the ground. Caine turned and looked up. His lips curled in a grim smile.

Jia slid down the taut steel cable on a rappelling harness, her AS VAL rifle held at the ready. She landed on top of the pipe and dropped into a crouch.

'Here!' she cried. She tossed something to him as the heavy metal weight swung around the room in a lazy circle, smashing through everything in its path.

Caine reached out and grabbed the object... It was his Beretta PX4 Storm pistol. His fingers wrapped around the grip and he spun around. One of Fang's men was charging towards him. It was Lewis, the one who had brought him to Fang. The short, stocky thug raised his machine gun to fire.

Caine's pistol barked twice. A cloud of red mist burst from the man's face. His body dropped to the floor and tumbled over into the gaping hole.

Jia balanced atop her spinning perch. She pivoted left and right, lining up shots. With every burst of her rifle, another guard crumpled to the ground.

The pipe swung towards Tan's bank of computer equipment. The stacked monitors and CPUs exploded into fragments as the massive pipe collided with the delicate equipment. The impact sent the pipe spinning back towards Caine. He ran forward, trying to dodge its path of destruction. As he sprinted across the room, more falling debris pummeled the crater in the floor. The gaping hole crumbled into a chasm that divided the room, cutting him off... There was nowhere to run.

Looking down, he could see the cylinder that held Sean. It had torn from its cart and rolled down the collapsed floor. It now lay on its side, balanced against the girders in the corner of the building. Below him was endless darkness... A long fall through the unfinished floors of the towering building.

Caine turned and faced the spinning pipe as it tore through the room towards him. If the pipe struck him, he would be knocked into that black, endless abyss. He watched as a pair of statues were pulverized, reduced to clouds of red dust by the impact of the massive object.

Caine balanced on the balls of his feet. The pipe spun toward him, moving closer and closer. He saw Jia, hanging from the steel cable. Her long hair trailed behind her like a ribbon of black silk. She gasped as she looked down at him, standing in the path of the immovable object.

Got to time this just right, he thought. He glanced down once more at the yawning pit of death beneath him.

He felt the rush of air as the pipe swung just a few feet away from him. The black opening gaped before him.

Caine made his move. He dove forward, rolling into the pipe. His body tumbled across the slick metal surface, and he felt himself slam into the curved sidewall. He grunted in pain, then shook his head. Looking out the hole at the other end of the pipe, he caught a brief glimpse of destruction and chaos spinning before him.

He was inside it now, careening around the room. He could feel his stomach lurch as the heavy metal tube swung out over the gaping chasm in the floor. A trio of fleeing guards dodged the pipe's onslaught, opening fire as they ran across the room. Their bullets ricocheted off the thick metal walls of the pipe as it continued to demolish the chamber.

Suddenly, the pipe's motion jerked to a stop. Caine felt his stomach lurch as he dropped downwards. He heard a metallic scream, then a grinding noise. The crane's motor was giving out. The momentum of the spinning pipe, the impact as it tore through the building... The gears of the winch couldn't take the strain!

Caine hear a loud twang, followed by a snap. The view to his right tilted downward. He peered down into the cavernous interior of the building's lower levels. One of the support cables that kept the pipe level had broken. The heavy pipe listed to the right. Caine felt his body slide down the curved wall towards the dark abyss below.

He dug his feet into the pipe's smooth, metal walls, pressing his hands outward. It took all his strength to stop his descent as the pipe tipped to a vertical position. It swung to a halt, pointing straight down like the barrel of a giant gun. Beads of sweat dripped down his face. Looking down, he saw Sean's tube balanced near the edge of the building.

Above them, the winch's gears continued to scream in protest. The pipe plummeted through the hole in the floor. It jerked to a stop just above the patchwork of girders and support beams. Caine's hands and feet scraped against the curved metal walls. His stomach heaved as his body slid a few feet closer to the end, closer to oblivion. His arms and legs trembled from exertion. He could not hold himself in place much longer.

'Tom, are you in there?' Jia called out.

'I'm here,' Caine grunted, struggling for breath. 'For now.'

'Hang on, I'll throw you a line.'

He heard the click of a carabiner attaching to the steel cable. A black cord unfurled down the interior of the pipe, brushing against his sweat-soaked hair.

Caine grabbed the rope, then gasped in relief. He let his feet dangle for a moment, then braced them against the wall of the pipe. Inch by inch, he pulled himself up to the top opening.

As his hand grasped the edge, the winch screamed again and

the pipe dropped several more feet. Jia screamed as they tore through the unfinished floor beneath them.

Again, they jerked to a stop. Caine pulled his head up out of the pipe. A few feet away, he could see Sean's cylinder. It rattled slightly as vibrations ran through the building's structure. Sean's screaming face was pressed up to the glass, and he pounded his fists against the window.

Jia hung from a harness attached to the support cable. She helped Caine pull his arms up and over the edge, and he managed to balance in a sitting position on the edge of the pipe.

'Jia, it's Sean! Do you have another line?'

She shook her head. 'That's the last one. But here...' She handed him her rifle. She unbuckled her harness from the cable and pulled it taut. 'This is ballistic webbing, it should support both our weight.'

'Alright.' Caine nodded towards the hyperbaric cylinder. The winch groaned again, and the pipe shuddered slightly. 'Let's see if we can get him out of there. We don't have much time.'

Before he could move, the pipe dropped down another foot. Jia screamed as she flew off the edge. Caine grabbed for her, but he was too late.

'Jia!' he screamed.

The winch's groaning grew louder. Debris from above sprinkled down, a rain of dust and concrete particles.

'Jia, answer me!' he shouted again, struggling to look down over the edge of the swaying pipe.

'It's okay,' she gasped. 'I'm still here.'

He caught sight of her gloved hands hanging from one of the girders. She had managed to stop her plunge into the depths of the building.

Grunting with exertion, she began to pull herself up onto the beam.

Before she could lift herself to safety, muzzle flash lit the dark interior of the building. Gunfire ricocheted off the girders around them. Someone below was firing at them.

Caine looked down the length of the pipe. He saw Fang bathed in the glow of a halogen work light. The man perched on the edge of an orange safety net strung across the gaping interior of the building. Below him, in the harsh glow of the light, Caine could make out a lattice of more nets. They descended the length of the building.

Fang wielded the machine gun of a fallen guard. He pulled the trigger again, and more bullets ricocheted off the spinning metal pipe.

Jia pulled herself onto the girder. She ran towards Sean's cylinder, gunfire sparking at her heels.

Caine aimed the rifle at Fang. He fired, but the swaying motion of the pipe threw off his aim. The bullets ricocheted off a nearby girder.

Fang crawled farther out onto the net. He fired again, and this time his stream of bullets found their way into the hole at the end of the pipe. Gunshots echoed through the length of the metal tube. Sparks and ricochets lit up the interior of the pipe. Caine winced as a fragment of shrapnel tore across his shoulder.

Looking through the collapsed floor above them, Caine saw the crane's jib arm, buried in the upper structure of the building. A thick cloud of smoke billowed from the winch mechanism. Its damaged gears were struggling to support the weight of the massive metal pipe.

Jia pried open the lid of the hyperbaric chamber. Caine heard Sean coughing and gasping for air. 'Tom, I have him!' she called out.

'Get back here and strap in,' he shouted.

More bullets streaked towards them from below. Jia and Sean

sprinted towards the pipe. Caine pointed the rifle down and fired blind.

As Fang dodged the gunfire, Jia looped her harness through both her and Sean's belts. Then she clipped the other end to the taut steel cable.

'Into the pipe!' she hissed. 'Move!'

Sean scrambled into the metal tube. Another blast of gunfire lit the dark interior.

'I warned you, Mr. Caine!' Fang shouted, his voice echoing through the cavernous building. 'You cannot stand in my way! You cannot stop my destiny!'

Jia slid next to Caine. 'We're in,' she said.

'And I warned you,' Caine shouted back to Fang. 'Destinies fall every day.'

He aimed the rifle at the crane. Holding his breath, he settled the crosshairs over the smoking gears. 'Today is your day, asshole!'

He squeezed the trigger.

Sparks flew from the winch mechanism as the bullets tore into the overloaded gears. Steel cable rushed out of the spool at rapid speed.

Caine looked down and caught a brief glimpse of Fang's face. Fang screamed as the massive metal pipe came crashing towards him. Then he disappeared as the pipe tore through the net. His scream descended into the darkness until it was just a faint echo. It was soon drowned out by the deafening roar of metal smashing against metal.

Caine felt the pipe shudder and bounce as they crashed through the structure of the building. All they could do now was hold on for dear life as they plunged deeper and deeper into the blackness.

43

Caine and the others stepped out of the entrance to Fang Plaza and stumbled into the street. They were coughing and covered in a thin sheen of dust and sweat.

Sean looked up at the building. The crane's jib arm was still wedged in the demolished upper floors. The top half of the structure bent around it at a precarious angle. Plumes of smoke billowed from the winch and slewing motor.

'That was, without a doubt, the most bat-shit crazy thing I ever saw,' Sean said, shaking his head. He turned to Jia. 'So was taking out half the building part of your plan? Or was that just improvising?'

Jia's eyes darted across the shadows that surrounded the building. 'There's no time to talk. We have to get out of here. The Ministry has tracked us here. They will—'

A spotlight glared to life, casting a white-hot circle around the three of them.

'Too late,' Caine growled. 'They're here.'

His eyes darted left and right as heavily armed SWAT officers flanked them. He stepped in front of Sean. 'Whatever happens,' he whispered, 'follow my lead.'

Jia clenched her teeth. 'I will not let them take me,' she hissed. 'I will not lose Lian, not after all this!'

Footsteps echoed towards them. A figure emerged from the shadows.

It was Yong Jin. The man with the pale, wax-like skin. He stopped a couple meters from the group and looked up at the smoking building. Then he uttered an exasperated sigh.

'An American assassin. A Chinese double agent. And a Triad gangster. Mr. Tyler, you still seem to have difficulty with the concept of "staying out of trouble."'

'Story of my life,' Sean replied.

Jia stepped forward. 'Jin, please. They have my daughter, I had no choice. I—'

'I'm sorry, Jia,' Yong interrupted. 'You must come with me. All of you are under arrest for endangering state security.'

'Tom,' Sean said under his breath. 'This time, you follow my lead.'

Before he knew what was happening, Caine felt Sean's hands tug his pistol from his waistband.

'Sean, what the hell—'

'Stop! Nobody move!' Sean stepped out from behind Caine.

He pointed the gun at his own head.

The SWAT officers pivoted their weapons, training them on Sean as he stepped away from Caine and Jia.

Yong waved them off with his hand. '*Ting zhi!* Everyone, just relax!'

He narrowed his eyes at Sean as the young man stepped towards him.

'What on earth do you think you are doing, Mr. Tyler?'

'I'm the one you want, Yong. You need me alive for this prisoner exchange, right? You want your hacker back. That's why you transferred me to the black jail, that's why you've been hunting Jia. That's what this has been about from the beginning.'

'I was instructed to keep you alive, Mr. Tyler. I was following orders.'

'Okay, well, I have another deal for you. Let my friends go, and take *me* in. The exchange goes through, and everyone is happy.'

'Sean, what the hell are you doing?' Caine snarled.

Yong chuckled. 'Our last deal didn't go so well, did it, Mr. Tyler? We have you surrounded. And I don't believe for a second that you have any intention of taking your life.'

Sean smiled. 'Yeah, well, did you believe an American assassin and a Chinese double agent would break me out of that shithole you hid me in? Or that David Fang would try to kill thousands of people with a stolen cyber weapon? Did you believe any of this would happen?'

Yong shook his head. 'This is insanity. Put down the gun. I assure you, you will all be treated fairly.'

Sean cocked the pistol. The SWAT team members readied their weapons.

Yong raised his hands in a calming gesture. '*Mei you huo zai!* Nobody fires!'

'Things are looking pretty tense here,' Sean continued. 'Lots could go wrong. Maybe my finger slips. Maybe one of your men gets nervous and takes a shot. And if anything happens to me, then no more Sun Wai Tong. No more exchange. Think of all the juicy intel he has hidden away. Losing that won't make your bosses too happy.'

Yong peered into Sean's unblinking blue eyes.

'You're bluffing,' the Chinese man said.

'Is it worth taking the chance?' Sean replied.

Yong shook his head. '*Wei she me shi wo?* What did I do to deserve you? Fine. The others are inconsequential.'

Sean smiled. 'Give me five minutes?'

Yong nodded. 'Say your goodbyes. Then they leave, and you come with me. Agreed?'

Sean turned and faced Caine. 'Not much time. You two should go.'

'What the hell are you doing?' Caine hissed. 'We know you're not safe with him. What if the NSA tries—'

'There was a speaker in the tube. I heard everything,' Sean interrupted. 'Sun Wai Tong didn't hack the NSA. Fang and his boy did. When the TANGENT database gets released over the internet, everyone will know it. There won't be any more reason to stop the exchange.'

Caine eyed the Chinese man with the expensive suit. The man stared back at him, then shook his head and began pacing back and forth. 'Jia, what do you know about this guy? Can we trust him?'

Jia stepped forward and spoke in a low, soft voice. 'He is like us. Relentless. Uncompromising. A dangerous enemy. But if he has been tasked with protecting Sean, he will give his life to do so.'

Sean nodded. 'Look, I came to China for personal reasons. But working with Monk, taking on Fang... I did that to help people. This Global Environmental Accord could make a real difference to people like Alton and his family. And thousands of others. You were in Huagu, you saw what it was like. There are dozens of other villages like that. The GEA must pass. And if this prisoner exchange makes that happen, I can't just run away. I have to go through with this.'

Jia put a hand on his shoulder. 'You are very brave. I am honored to have met you.'

Sean wrapped his arms around her in a hug. 'Get out of here. And keep an eye on this guy for me.'

He turned to Caine and held out his hand. 'Thank you. For keeping your promise.'

Caine stared at his outstretched hand for a moment, then shook it. 'Sean, your father... He wasn't perfect. But he loved you. And he would have been proud of you. Trust me on that.'

Sean smiled. 'Maybe once I get back to the States, I can look you up? I'd like to hear more about him.'

Caine hesitated for a moment, then nodded. 'I'd like that too.'

Sean took a deep breath. 'Well, here goes nothing. Take care.'

He turned and walked towards Yong. He held out his hands, and the older man gestured to two of the SWAT officers. They handcuffed Sean as Yong turned his stare on Jia.

'You are sure this is what you want?' he called out. 'Once you leave, there will be no coming back.'

'My heart left China when my daughter was taken,' she said. 'Now, the things I've done, the things I've seen... There was never any chance of going back. I am already gone. You will not see me again.'

Yong looked up at the plumes of smoke billowing from the mangled building, then turned his inscrutable gaze on Caine. 'You were correct, Mr. Caine. Fang did have friends in the Ministry. Luckily for you, I was never one of them. For what it's worth, you've done my country a great service today.' He checked his watch. 'You have four hours to leave China. After that... our bargain is ended. Understood?'

'I got it, Yong. But there's something you should understand as well.'

The older man raised his eyebrows. 'Go on?'

Caine nodded towards Sean. 'Anything happens to him... you will see me again.'

'Is that a threat?'

Caine's lips curled into a grim smile. 'No. That's a promise. And I keep my promises.'

He and Jia turned and stalked off into the darkness between the buildings. Within seconds, they had disappeared into the shadows.

Yong turned to Sean. 'Well, Mr. Tyler, let's see if you can go another twenty-four hours without causing me any more trouble.'

As he led Sean towards a waiting SWAT van, the younger man smiled. 'You know, you were right, back in the prison. My father did teach me something else besides how to fight.'

'Oh, what was that?'

'He taught me that when it comes to protecting your friends, sometimes you have to get a little crazy.'

'Then for both our sakes, I hope you don't make any new friends in China.'

Yong helped him up into the back of the van and shut the door. He thumped it twice and watched as the van drove off into traffic. The vehicle's spinning lights were soon lost in the endless neon haze of the Shanghai night.

* * *

Forty-eight hours later, Caine and Jia stood at the rear of a Lockheed C-130 transport plane. They watched in silence as the aircraft's ramp descended to the ground. A slice of light from outside filled the dark interior of the plane.

Caine stood motionless, exhausted. After a long and uncomfortable journey by cargo vessel, they had been met in Japan by a pair of nameless men. The duo identified them-selves as 'liaisons' sent by Rebecca. Their features and mannerisms were as bland as the matching gray suits they wore.

Rebecca had arranged their passage on the massive transport plane. They departed the US Kadena Air Base in Okinawa and settled in for the long flight back to the States. Caine had slept for a good deal of the flight, but Jia was restless, nervous. Several times he had cracked open his eyes and noticed her pacing back and forth. Her cat-like balance had seemed unaffected by turbulence as the plane had pitched and rolled through the rough air.

Now, she stood next to him and brushed a hand through her hair. She looked tired, but alert. She gave him a nervous glance.

'Jia, relax. It's over. Everything is going to be okay.' He tried to force a note of reassurance into his voice.

She nodded, but they both knew he was lying.

It wasn't over. Not yet. There was still one thing left to do...

The ramp touched the black cracked pavement of the airstrip with a metallic thud. Caine slung a duffel bag over his shoulder, and they descended to the ground. He squinted as they stepped out into the light. Behind them, the afternoon sun cast dappled patches of gold across the brackish waters of the York River.

'Welcome home,' a woman's voice called out.

It was Rebecca. She rolled her wheelchair towards him. A group of five men followed behind her. They were dressed in casual sportswear, but Caine spotted the telltale bulges of weapons under their clothes. He clocked them as a CIA Special Operations Group unit. Rebecca's security detail.

Standing behind Rebecca was a tall, lanky man with muscular shoulders. His right arm was in a sling. Aviator sunglasses hid his eyes, but he watched Caine and Jia's movements like a hawk. Caine assumed he was the leader of the detail.

He eyed the man's sling and frowned. An injury like that should have removed him from duty.

Caine looked around the long airstrip. A few unmarked planes were the only other aircraft in the area. Red brick buildings with green roofs dotted the sides of the airfield. A few SUVs were parked out front. Behind the buildings, acres of dense forest stretched as far as the eye could see.

He knew the area well. The buildings, the trees, the earthy brine smell of the river. Memories came flooding back to him. His recruitment, the training... Bernatto.

'Camp Peary,' he said. 'The Farm. Haven't been here in years. Quite a homecoming.'

'That's not what I meant,' Rebecca said. She followed his gaze across the sweeping woodland. 'But it sure does bring me back.'

She turned to Jia and held out her hand. 'Ms. Zhao, welcome to—'

'Where is my daughter?' Jia said, flashing Caine a sideways glance.

Rebecca stared at her for a second, then turned as a jeep motored towards them. 'Here she is. I'm sorry for the delay; we wanted to make sure the area was secure before we brought her to you.'

The jeep pulled to a stop. An MP in a green army uniform stepped out. Lian Zhao sat in the passenger seat of the jeep. When she saw Jia, her face lit up.

The MP lifted Lian from the seat and set her down on the ground. Laughing, she ran in short, hopping steps towards Jia.

'Mama!' she called out. 'You came back!'

Jia swept the child up in her arms. Tears streamed down her face as she kissed her girl's cheeks.

'*Dang ran.* Of course I came.' She smoothed back the girl's short, dark hair and looked into her shining eyes. 'I will never leave you again, *qin ai de.*'

Rebecca smiled. 'Ms. Zhao, on behalf of the CIA, I would like to apologize for what happened to you and your daughter. And on a personal note, I want you to know I will not stop until those responsible are brought to justice.'

Jia stood up, holding Lian in her arms. 'Thank you. Is there somewhere I can clean up and talk to my daughter for a few minutes?'

Rebecca nodded towards one of the small brick buildings. 'There are restrooms in there. One of my men will escort you. After that, I'm afraid we are going to need some debriefing time at Langley. There's a lot we have to sort out.'

'I understand,' Jia said, her voice cold and flat. The MP followed her as she walked towards the small building.

Caine looked down at Rebecca. 'Debriefing?'

Rebecca glared back at him. 'What did you expect? Milk and cookies?'

He shook his head. 'Never mind. What about you, are you okay?'

Rebecca sighed, then looked back at the man in the sling. 'Josh, could you give us a minute?'

Josh lifted the sunglasses off his eyes and shot Caine a wary look. 'Director, I—'

'Josh, please.' Her voice was soft. It was a request, not a command.

That was when Caine knew.

They're together.

Josh gave him one last glare, then stepped away towards his other men. He barked an order, and the SUV's engine started up.

'Well,' Rebecca said. 'Looks like you're finally back on the inside.'

'I... Rebecca, look,' Caine stumbled over the words. 'Whatever happened to us, I want... I want to be more than just a voice on the phone. I hope you know that.'

She blinked and was silent for a moment. 'Tom, I don't know what to say.'

Caine shook his head. 'I'm not asking you for anything, I just wanted you to know. Is there any news on Sean?'

She stared at him for a moment, still processing his words. Then she brushed a strand of copper hair from her face. 'The exchange is scheduled to take place tomorrow. Sun Wai Tong was transferred to a facility in Egypt. He'll be released from there, to minimize US involvement. And there's more good news... The GEA was signed by all parties. David Fang's factories will be closed for non-compliance. The Chinese government has declared Huagu an environmental emergency site. They'll be providing medical and clean-up assistance to the inhabitants there.'

Caine nodded. 'Sounds like a good start.'

'I understand Sean chose to stay behind to make sure the agreement passed?'

'Yeah. He takes after his father. TANGENT was erased, and the database was uploaded to the internet. It proves Sun Wai Tong didn't hack the NSA. He never had any intel to recover. There's no reason for anyone to block the exchange now.'

Rebecca smiled. 'Brave guy. So the database is public? Not exactly how I would have handed it.'

'I told you, protecting the NSA's dirty laundry wasn't my priority,' Caine said. 'Before, on the phone, you said you were attacked. Lapinski escaped?'

Rebecca lowered her voice. 'The man who attacked us was another private security contractor, a military vet. Then we dug a little deeper.'

'Let me guess,' Caine said. 'Scorpion Unit.'

'Got it in one. How did you know?'

'Scorpion Unit is NSA's Special Forces team. If Lapinski had to clean up a mess, it makes sense that's who he would call.'

Rebecca shook her head. 'Lapinski didn't call them, or at least I don't think he did. When I mentioned that I'd spoken to John Blayne, he was terrified. He said there was someone else behind this. Someone above him in the intelligence community. I think Scorpion Unit was there to eliminate him. He was the mess they were sent to clean up.'

'Could Blayne be behind all this?' Caine asked. He turned his gaze to the small building where Jia had taken her daughter.

'Lapinski didn't know. But Blayne is the Director of National Intelligence. He's connected to high-ranking members of every intelligence service in the country.'

'Which means if he knew you were about to expose Ted, and he leaked the info...'

'It could be almost anyone. Blayne, or anyone he's connected to.'

'We have to find Lapinski!' Caine snarled.

She nodded. 'I've got people on it, but the NSA isn't exactly eager to help—'

A woman's shriek echoed from inside the tiny building. Josh sprinted towards Rebecca, drawing his pistol with his left hand. The other men fanned out around her in a circle as Caine charged towards the building.

The MP threw open the door and Jia stumbled out, carrying Lian in her arms. The child's face was pale. Her eyes were closed.

She wasn't moving.

'What happened?' Caine shouted.

'She just passed out. She's not breathing!' Jia screamed. She placed a hand on the girl's cheeks. 'Her face, it's cold. Oh my God, they must have given her something, they drugged her, or...'

She glared at Rebecca. 'If anything happens to my daughter, I swear I will—'

'Someone call an ambulance,' Rebecca shouted, cutting her off.

'Already on the way,' Josh replied. 'We should get you out of here. Now!'

A loud siren rose in the distance. Caine turned and saw a military ambulance rushing towards them.

'Rebecca, he's right Go. I'll ride with Jia; you can send your detail to follow us.'

The ambulance pulled to a stop and its rear doors swung open. Caine leapt into the back with the paramedics. The MP helped Jia in after him. She cradled the unconscious Lian in her arms, refusing to let go.

Rebecca turned her head and met Caine's eyes. He bit his lip and looked away. He could not meet her gaze. Then Josh blocked her view as he grabbed her chair and pushed her towards her SUV.

The ambulance's lights and siren screamed to life as it drove away from the building.

* * *

An hour later, Rebecca sat outside the base's military police station. A light breeze blew through her hair. The sun hung low on the horizon, bathing the trees and buildings in a deep orange glow.

An SUV pulled up and Josh got out. He walked up to her, a troubled look in his eyes. 'You shouldn't be out here alone. Where's the rest of your detail?'

She sighed. 'They're inside. I slipped out the side door.

Needed some fresh air. It smells like old coffee and motor oil in there.'

Josh struggled to keep an angry look plastered on his face, but he couldn't help smiling. 'Well, it's about to smell worse, 'cause someone is gonna get their ass chewed out big time over this.'

'No sign of them?' Rebecca asked.

Josh shook his head. 'Oh, there's plenty of signs. They found the ambulance on the outskirts of the base. The MP assigned to them was inside, unconscious. The paramedics were tied up and blindfolded. They think the woman, this "Red Phoenix," administered a sedative to the girl in the bathroom. The whole thing was planned. There's no record of them leaving the base, cameras didn't see anything, but...'

'Forget it. He's long gone.' Rebecca looked up at him and bit her lip. Her crimson hair reflected the orange glow of the setting sun. 'It's my fault. I should have known better.'

'We'll find him. I'll call it in, get a surveillance order on—'

'Don't bother,' she cut in. 'Just find Lapinski.'

'What about Caine?'

'If you find Lapinski, I guarantee you'll find Caine. He's going after him.'

'Why would he do that?'

Rebecca looked up at the sky. The setting sun had turned the rolling clouds into a mosaic of fiery orange and pink.

'I told him about the attack, at the farmhouse. He thinks he's protecting me.'

Josh looked her in the eye. 'Is there something I should know? What's the story with you two, anyway?'

Rebecca rolled over to the SUV and waited as the lift for her chair lowered itself to the ground.

'There is no story. Not anymore.'

44

Ted Lapinski fumbled with his keys as he opened the tiny motel room door. He had always known he might have to flee. He had lived with the threat of exposure, the fear of discovery, for years. In some ways, this was a relief. He was finally out. It was ironic, but as a fugitive in hiding, he could finally stop worrying that someone would discover his greatest secret.

And his family... Teddy Junior. Julie, his wife. She had never known, never really understood him. They were better off without him now. Safer.

He pulled his cell phone from his pocket. There were no messages.

Ted glanced around the parking lot. The motel sat alongside the 110W freeway in Baltimore, Maryland. It was late, but the traffic on the busy highway roared by. Car after car whizzed past, each on their way to an infinite number of destinations in the night.

The parking lot was empty save for a few nondescript sedans and a pair of Harley Davidson motorcycles. Lights beamed down on the vehicles, casting long, dark shadows over the rest of the lot.

Ted had paid cash for the motel room. The car he had used in his flight was registered to a fake identity, one he had created for just such a purpose. Sooner or later, he knew, he would be spotted, traced. It was impossible to disappear in this day and age. He knew that better than anyone. But the more distance he could put between himself and his pursuers, the more time he had.

There was something he needed. Something he had been promised. He typed a message on his phone.

> I want the videos.

The phone was silent. There was no response.

'Son of a bitch!' Ted hissed as he opened the door and stepped into the dark room.

> I did as you asked. You promised to release them to me.

He closed the door behind him. The glow of the tiny cell phone screen was the only light in the pitch-black darkness of the room. From the corner of his eye he saw his unmade bed, the sheets a rumpled, tangled mess. Lime green curtains covered the front windows, which faced out towards the parking lot. The muted roar of the freeway traffic echoed through the small room.

He stared at the phone. There was still no response.

'Motherfucker,' he grunted through clenched teeth. He tossed the phone on the bed.

As the small screen of light flew through the room, he glimpsed movement to his left. He reached for the pistol tucked into his waistband. His fingers wrapped around the butt of his tiny Smith & Wesson Bodyguard .380.

Before he could aim, he felt an arm wrap around his neck and pull backwards. He stumbled back as another hand grabbed his shooting hand. His attacker twisted his wrist and he screamed as he felt the bones snap. The pistol tumbled to the floor.

His attacker spun him around. Ted ducked his head low and threw a punch towards the shadowy figure standing before him.

Instead of falling back, the figure darted in close and blocked Ted's punch. An elbow cracked into his jaw, and his head snapped back.

Ted felt a powerful kick slam into his gut. He stumbled away from his attacker, gasping for air. He tripped and fell, collapsing into a small, worn chair in front of the room's tiny desk. The springs in the chair creaked in protest as they compressed under his weight.

Before he could stand, he heard a familiar metallic click. It was the slide on his pistol, racking back. A bright red dot pierced the darkness and crawled up his shirt. The laser sight flared across his eyes, then landed on his forehead.

'I wouldn't do that, Ted.' It was a man's voice.

The room's light clicked on. Ted found himself staring into a pair of cold, emerald-green eyes perched above the chiseled lines of a clenched jaw.

'Do you know who I am?' the man asked.

Ted nodded. 'Rebecca's asset in China. Caine. I thought you were dead.'

Caine's lips curled into a cold, humorless smirk. 'Do I look dead to you, Lapinski?'

Ted's eyes darted towards the door, then back to Caine. 'How did you find me?'

'I had a little help from a friend. Her name is Betty Binary. You should get her résumé. I think she might be better at facial recognition than some of your TAO boys.' Caine sat down on the bed, never taking his eyes off the terrified NSA operative.

'Okay, okay,' Ted babbled. 'I get it, you want to kill me, but—'

'No, you're wrong about that.'

Ted slumped in the chair and breathed a sigh of relief. 'That's good. Smart. Look, I can help you. I know things, I—'

Caine's eyes blazed above the pistol, silencing Ted with the power of their intense stare. '*I* don't want to kill you, Ted. I can't speak for her, though.'

Ted heard footsteps behind him. Before he could turn his head, a black silken cord looped around his neck. With a soft hiss, it pulled tight.

His hands shot up to his throat. He clawed at the cord, but he couldn't loosen it. He gasped for breath as his face turned pale blue.

The cord pulled tighter. He felt the chair tipping back. He tumbled over and collapsed to the ground. The cord bit deeper into his neck. His bulging eyes stared up into a woman's face. Her mouth was a hard slash, and her eyes were two black pools of rage. She was dressed in her usual tactical gear, minus the hood and goggles.

It was her...

'Red Phoenix reporting,' she hissed.

'Please!' he gurgled.

'*Na nuo ruo de gou!*' she said, twisting the cord tighter. 'My daughter is only six years old. Do you know how scared she must have been? How does it feel, you piece of shit? Will you piss yourself before you take your last breath?'

Caine stepped into view. 'You went after her kid, asshole. I wouldn't expect any mercy there. Your best bet is to make yourself useful.' He nodded towards Jia. 'You were running her, but someone else was running you. You were texting them just now, weren't you? Who's pulling your strings?'

The strangling cord turned his reply into a meaningless series of croaks and squeals.

'Jia, let him talk,' Caine said. She glared at him but then loosened her grip. Color rushed into Ted's cheeks. He sucked in a lungful of air with a rattling wheeze.

'Last chance, Lapinski. Who was running you?'

'I don't know, I swear!'

Caine's eyes narrowed as he held up the pistol and aimed it again at Ted's face. 'Bullshit,' he said.

'I swear it's true, I don't know who they are. They had video of me. Doing things. A bar, in DC. Men... go there. They threatened to show my boss, my wife... I would have been compromised. I would have lost everything.'

'You're going to have to do better than that,' Caine growled.

'It had to be someone in the intelligence community. Someone high up. They knew about Rebecca, about you. And...' He looked up at Caine. 'Bernatto... They must have been close to Bernatto.'

'Why do you say that?' Caine snapped. His voice was cold and sharp, like a blade of ice.

'They knew about Red Phoenix... I mean, her.' Ted looked up at Jia. 'The kid. They knew everything. Only Bernatto had those details.'

Jia's lips curled into a snarl. She slid a knife from a sheath on her combat harness. The metal gleamed in the dim light of the motel room. She pressed the blade against the skin of Ted's cheek. A drop of crimson blood sprouted from his flesh and flowed down the knife's razor-sharp edge.

'Give us something we can use, or I will skin you alive, *yi kuai gou shi*!'

'I have records... I erased all our texts, but I kept an encrypted backup. I'll turn them over, I can help you find them!'

Jia looked up at Caine. An unspoken question softened the rage in her wide, dark eyes.

Caine thought for a moment, then nodded. Jia released the cord from Ted's neck. Again, the NSA operative sucked in lungfuls of air as Caine held up a cell phone. He knelt down, bringing the phone close to Ted's face.

He tapped the phone, and a picture of Rebecca filled the screen. 'Rebecca Freeling,' he said. He swiped again, and the image was replaced by a picture. Jia's daughter.

'Lian Zhao,' Jia said in a solemn voice.

Caine swiped again, and the picture was replaced by an image of Sean.

'Sean Tyler. These people are under our protection. And you'd better hope that from this point on, they lead charmed lives. Because if anything, and I mean *anything* happens to them...'

Caine pressed the barrel of the gun into Ted's temple.

'If my daughter so much as catches a cold, I will hunt you,' Jia hissed. She dragged the knife down the length of his body, skimming his clothes. The point of the blade stopped between his legs.

'I will find you,' she whispered into his ear. 'And I will make you beg me for death. I will take my time with you.' She tilted her head and blinked. 'Do you understand?'

'I get it! I get it!' Ted looked from her to Caine with pleading eyes. 'Please, don't let her—'

'You're going to turn yourself over to Rebecca at the CIA,' Caine said. 'You're going to hand over your computers, all your records. Whatever info you have on these people. But most importantly, you're going to remember something. Something you can't ever forget.'

'What, what are you talking about?' Ted stuttered.

'Who's running you?' Caine demanded.

'I told you, I don't know, I—'

Caine slammed the butt of the pistol down on Ted's nose. There was a loud crack as the delicate cartilage inside snapped and cracked. The man moaned in pain as blood sprayed across his shredded shirt.

'Wrong answer. Now think carefully. Who is running you?'

Caine's green eyes glowered down at him, like jewels lit by the fires of the sun. Ted nodded his head. He understood.

'You are,' he whimpered. 'You're running me.'

Jia stood and looked down at him, a snarl of contempt marring her beautiful features. 'Do not ever forget this,' she said.

'We'll be in touch,' Caine added. 'And Ted, if you're thinking of running again? You should know I tracked Allan Bernatto across three countries. I can find you across a few state lines in my sleep.'

Ted nodded, panting for breath. He heard the door open. The light switched off, and the door closed. They were gone.

He was left gasping in the darkness.

* * *

The tiny runway at Frederick Municipal Airport was dark, save for a few lights spaced along the 3,600-foot strip of concrete. The airfield cut through a rural, tree-lined field about an hour away from Baltimore. Frederick County was a sleepy, quiet town. There was no sign of activity in the collection of hangers and buildings that surrounded the runway.

A cool, light mist filled the night air. Caine peered through the windshield of his rental sedan, scanning the trees and buildings for any sign of movement.

'We're clear,' he said.

He opened the door and got out, clutching Ted's small pistol in his hand. Jia opened the rear passenger door and lifted Lian from the seat. The child was sleepy, still groggy from the sedative Jia had slipped her at Camp Peary.

She mumbled in a quiet, chirping voice, rubbing at her eyes, '*Wo men xian zai yao hui jia?*'

Jia looked over at Caine as she carried the child across the runway. Caine moved next to her, his eyes alert and his gun at the ready.

'She asked if we are going home,' Jia said.

'Are you?' Caine asked.

Jia shook her head. 'There is nothing left for me there. I could not go back if I wanted to. You heard Yong. The Ministry will never forget my betrayal. And the memories... I can't forget what I did either.'

'I know what you mean,' Caine replied. 'Look, she's a tough kid. Wherever you go, she'll be fine. You'll make a new home.'

Jia kissed the child on the cheek. '*Ni shi wo de jia,*' she whispered to the sleepy girl. 'You are my home.'

They hurried towards a small private jet parked at the end of the strip. As they approached, the aircraft's taillights lit up and a low hum emitted from its engines. The side door slid open. A Japanese man stepped out and waved to them. He was wearing a headset and a black windbreaker.

'Koichi Ogawa sends his regards,' the man said. 'I am Hondo, your pilot. I understand certain, uh... arrangements have been made. We should leave soon. Before questions come.'

Jia eyed the pilot with a wary gaze and set Lian on the

ground. 'This man who sent the plane, you are sure he is reliable?' she asked Caine.

Caine laughed. 'That depends on your definition of reliable. Koichi is yakuza.' He placed a reassuring hand on her back. 'But I've worked with him before. I contacted him while we were in Okinawa. If Koichi sent this guy, you can trust him.'

Hondo smiled at Lian, and the skin around his eyes wrinkled like tanned leather. 'I can get the little one seated, if you like.'

The girl looked up at her mother with wide, pensive eyes. Jia knelt down next to her. 'Go on, Lian, *mei guan xi*. I'll be right there.'

The child stepped forward and took the pilot's hand. He led her up the stairs to the jet's small cabin.

Jia stood and faced Caine. 'You understand what I mean, don't you? About the memories? The betrayal... So much death.'

'I do,' he said.

'How do you move past it? How do you make the nightmares go away?'

He was silent for a moment.

'You don't,' he finally said. 'Sometimes they go away for a while, but sooner or later they always come back. Some of the memories might fade with time. Others never do. Maybe they're not supposed to.'

She brushed a strand of long, dark hair from her face. She looked into his eyes, as if searching for some small sliver of hope in his gaze.

'You should come with us,' she said.

'I can't, Jia. There are things I have to finish here. And trust me, you'll be safer without me. You have Lian to worry about now.'

'I have you to thank for that. But maybe you're right... maybe you can find your peace here. Sean... He is all right?'

'Rebecca said the exchange happens tomorrow. There's some political bullshit involved, but at least he's safe now.'

She smiled. 'I'm glad. He's going to need someone in his life, you know. Someone he can look to for guidance.'

'I'm not exactly a role model.'

'You don't have be. You just have to be there for him when he needs you.'

'Parenting advice?'

She wrapped her arms around him in an embrace. His heart beat faster as he felt the warmth of her body pressing against him. 'Human nature,' she whispered. 'I've spent years undercover. I'm a good listener.'

She pulled back and looked up at him. 'Thank you for everything. Take care of yourself, Tom.'

'Wait. Before you go, I have to ask you something.'

'Yes?'

'Back in Huagu, that morning... when you kissed me...'

She smiled. 'I remember.'

'You said you felt something between us. Did you mean that? Or were you just working your cover?'

Her pale skin flushed pink and her eyes glinted in the darkness. Her lips parted. She leaned towards him and kissed him. Again, he felt the electric shock run through his skin as her lips touched his. He closed his eyes and returned the kiss, drinking in the taste and smell of her.

Then she pulled away. Her eyes held the mischievous gleam he had seen that night at dinner, in the beautiful *hutong* by the lake.

'I think we both know the answer to that,' she said. 'But right now, your heart is in the past. If you ever change your mind, come find me.'

He nodded. 'Fair enough.'

She stepped away from him. He felt a sudden shiver of cold as their bodies parted. Then she turned and climbed the steps into the plane. When she reached the top, she looked back at him.

'*Zhu weishou de sha gua*,' she called to him, shaking her head.

'You never told me what that means,' he shouted back, already knowing what her answer would be.

She flashed him one last luminous smile. 'I'll tell you later.'

The door closed.

He walked back to the car as the plane began to taxi down the dark runway.

Later, he sat in the car, parked beneath a flickering pool of light cast by a streetlamp. The street was dark and empty; his was the only car in sight. The buildings surrounding him were empty, abandoned husks. They cast long shadows across the deserted street. Their inky black tendrils reached out to him like grasping claws.

After so many years abroad, being back in his home country felt strange, unsettling. The landscape around him was a vast, dark forest of unfamiliar shadows.

Caine picked up his cell phone and dialed her number.

Rebecca.

She picked up. 'Tom.'

'Yeah.'

She sighed. 'I thought you were ready to be more than a voice on the phone.'

'I'm sorry.'

'Sorry you lied to me? Or sorry you let a Chinese agent run free on US soil.'

'You know what she's been through. And we both know what a "debriefing" would mean for someone like her. She deserves better than a CIA cage. She's out of the country now; you won't see her again.'

'Where are you?' Rebecca asked.

'I texted you an address. You'll find Lapinski there. He has information that might help. You were right, this thing goes higher than we thought.'

'You didn't answer my question.'

Caine looked around the empty, dark buildings surrounding him. He wasn't sure what to say.

'I can't come in, Rebecca. I can't protect you, or Sean, or anyone else... not from inside. Bernatto is still out there. He's involved in this, somehow. Him, and others like him.'

'I don't need you to protect me.'

'That agent, the head of your detail...' he began.

'Galloway? What about him?'

'There's something between you two, isn't there?'

He heard her breathing speed up on the other end of the line. 'How is that any of your business?' she snapped.

'It's not. I'm happy for you.' His voice softened. 'Honestly, I am. But you should take him off your detail. He can't do his job anymore. He let things get personal. That's dangerous. Believe me, I know.'

'Tom, listen to me. I want you to come in. I want you to have a life, outside of all this.'

He was silent for a moment. 'Maybe someday,' he said. 'Right now, I have work to do.'

'Where are you? Will you please tell me where you are?' He could hear the concern, the fear in her voice. That, more than anything, made him feel even worse about what he had to do.

'I'm where I need to be, Rebecca. I'm on the outside. I have to go now.'

'Tom, wait—'

He hung up.

He felt a surge of emotions flood through his body. Anger,

pain, frustration... His breathing quickened, his hands were shaking. He was falling again, falling into darkness. He was alone; there was no one left to pull him out. The shadows had him in their grasp. There was no escape.

You don't have to escape, the voice in his head said. *This is where you belong.*

For once, the cold, flat logic comforted him. He took a deep breath. The tremors passed. His nerves calmed. His breathing slowly returned to normal.

As he drove away, he recalled Jack's last words to him. The dark, dusty well was just a hazy memory now, but he could remember Jack's question as clear as day.

Why do you do it, Tom?

The pool of light receded in the rearview mirror, and the night surrounded him in its cold embrace. His restless mind thought for hours as he drove through the shadowed landscape. No answer came to him. He only knew that for now, he was compelled. He had to keep moving. Keep hunting.

You're operational, he thought. *No more questions. No fears. No doubts.*

You just have to let go.

* * *

MORE FROM ANDREW WARREN

Another book from Andrew Warren, *Fire and Forget*, is available to order now here:

https://mybook.to/FireAndForgetBackAd